Stella Rose

Stella Rose

A NOVEL

TAMMY FLANDERS HETRICK

SHE WRITES PRESS

Published 2015
Printed in the United States of America
ISBN: 978-1-63152-921-4
Library of Congress Control Number: 2014957846

For information, address:
She Writes Press
1563 Solano Ave #546
Berkeley, CA 94707

She Writes Press is a division of SparkPoint Studio, LLC.

Dedicated to The Girls

Part One
Summer

Time present and time past
Are both perhaps present in time future,
And time future contained in time past.
If all time is eternally present
All time is unredeemable.
What might have been is an abstraction
Remaining a perpetual possibility
Only in a world of speculation.
What might have been and what has been
Point to one end, which is always present.
Footfalls echo in the memory
Down the passage which we did not take
Towards the door we never opened
Into the rose-garden. My words echo
Thus, in your mind.
But to what purpose
Disturbing the dust on a bowl of rose-leaves
I do not know.
Other echoes
Inhabit the garden. Shall we follow?

"Burnt Norton," Verse I
Four Quartets, by T. S. Eliot

June

*F*inally. The pain, the anguish, and the struggle are over.

Well, *your* pain, anguish, and struggle are over. Me? I'm looking over a cliff, and pain, anguish, and struggle roil below amid jagged rocks of grief.

And you know how I hate heights.

This used to be my favorite month, as you also well know. For Vermonters knocking on the Canadian border, June promises winter is over, sunshine after months of slate skies, shivery mornings, and dark, snow-squalled commutes. Instead, this June brings frost warnings. Are undertakers able to break the still-frozen earth, let alone dig the requisite six feet to bury the dead? This is not my problem, because you chose cremation, but I wonder about this anyway. It's easier than wondering about life without you.

Across my rumpled bed lies a black sheath dress; black lace-up boots wait by the door, next to piles of taped boxes ready for the movers. I finger the scarves—seventy-two in all, now mine—wondering which to wear. The one best to shock funeral-goers in Stella's honor, the one

Rob will take back in memory when the guilt he pushes away during the day attacks him at night, the one that will bring a faint smile to Olivia's face—a shadow of the smile that left us nine months ago.

"AbbySol."

I smile, not bothering to turn around. It's just my best friend's voice in my head. Sometimes she says Abby, sometimes Abby Solace, but mostly AbbySol, her favorite.

My hand rests on hot pink, tangerine, and indigo orchids dyed into blood-red silk. The last scarf Stella wore, even after her hair grew back, a downy halo.

I dress quickly, knot the scarf at my neck. The tiny black dress, tailor-made compliments of Stella, hangs perfectly on my slender, five-seven frame. "Abby Solace St. Claire, you must attend my funeral in style."

But in the mirror I see the dark dress and brilliant scarf only highlight my pallor. With my blond hair pulled back in a tight bun, my pale blue eyes loom large, the circles below dark and deep. I look more dead than Stella did three days ago, lying in her bed, her hand resting in Olivia's, her empty gaze on me.

Christ, how am I going to get through this day without you, Stella?

After brushing color on my cheeks, balm to chapped lips, I grab my bag and run for the ancient Saab, late as usual.

The parking lot of St. Mary's Nativity Church overflows, of course. For all her claims of being an introvert, Stella was no such thing. "You are how you act," she would say. Of course, as with many Stella-isms, she claimed this did not actually apply to her.

I tug hard on the cold iron ring, and the church door springs open with an alarming squeal. All eyes are on me as I stumble, blinking, into the gloomy interior. Soft organ music emanates from the back of the church. I pause to get my bearings, nearly overcome by the perfume of orchids, gardenias, and, of course, roses. So many roses, as though every person spilling out of the pews ignored Stella's demand to direct all remembrances to the American Cancer Society, the Nature Conservancy, the Vermont Food Bank, and the

Humane Society. Stella's love for flowers was too compelling to forgo.

God, she would have loved this.

I scan the crowded front pews for Olivia. To my left, Paula and Cecile cast puffy eyes toward me. Paula reaches out, squeezes my hand. "She's up there." I glance toward the front again and realize the thin teenager with dark hair pulled back under a black lace kerchief, pinched between Rob and Wife #2, is Olivia—so like her mom. And so not.

Olivia's head turns as she, too, surveys the church. Her wide-eyed gaze finds me. I lift my hand in a wave at the exact moment she does. The organ music swells, signaling the official start of the service. I watch Olivia struggle to stand. Rob reaches for her, pulls her down. She wrestles away, climbs over him and out of the pew.

We meet halfway up the aisle, crush each other close.

The organ drones on. The congregation is silent. I feel hands on my shoulders, look up into Rob's somber face. His eyes are sorrowful, and I realize this brings no satisfaction. He grieves Stella despite the last decade, which dismantled their life together.

I nod, and together we help Olivia down the aisle. Her hands remain clasped around my arm. Clearly, we will endure the next hour side by side. Wife #2 moves down to make room as the service begins.

A parade of people eulogizes my best friend, talking about her kindness, generosity, sense of humor. All true, but no one mentions the annoying way she picks up a Canadian accent two minutes after crossing the border, or how fear creeps into her eyes when she says she's excited about Olivia's going to college. And that bossiness? Stella knows everything but says she doesn't—and means it, in that maddening way of hers.

Then you realize that, actually, she does know everything after all.

But rather than share any of this myself, I criticize each heartfelt oration as being off the mark and deficient because this is easier than admitting I should be up there, telling all these people who Stella Rose really is.

Was.

But no one asked me to speak. Everyone assumed that upon losing Stella—who was, in many ways, my voice—I would be incapable. So Paula offered to represent The Girls, collecting material from us in preparation. Now she stands at the podium with tear-streaked poise.

"The following is brought to you by the Stella Rose Fan Club." Paula nods to Cecile, seated to her left. Behind the altar, images appear on an improvised screen—a montage chronicling our collective preteens, adolescence, and womanhood. Slumber parties, bonfires, graduations, annual girls' weekends in Maine, New Hampshire, New York, and then the last one, in Vermont, in Stella's house. The slide show stops at a picture of us gathered around Stella's bed, smiling for the camera, no one's smile wider than our Stella's, her tiny fingers clasped around a margarita glass.

"Laura and Jo aren't here today because they were with us last month at Stella's insistence," Paula says quietly. "Stella said, 'What good are you to me at my funeral? Come now so I can take your lovely faces with me to the next destination.' She made them promise not to make the trip again for the funeral. It's been the hardest promise they've ever kept, based on the weepy calls I got this morning."

My heart contracts at the thought of Laura in Colorado and Jo in New Hampshire. I have not called them yet. I'm glad they reached out to Paula.

"We all miss Stella like crazy," Paula says as Cecile brings up the final picture. It's from our girls' weekend two years ago, at Hampton Beach. We stayed at a fleabag billed as four-star, a total dump we bitched about for three days. But we had the best time playing in the icy Atlantic, eating too much lobster and steamers, and dancing at every local dive until we all had blisters.

Before departing, we lined up in front of the wilted hotel for the requisite trip photo. The proprietor grudgingly took Jo's camera in his nicotine hands, snapped the picture. And there we are, the six of us one happy knot of women, arm in arm in arm, smiling broadly, Stella in the middle.

"But," Paula resumes, "I'll bet Stella misses us even more. Rest in peace? I doubt it. Stella, our loudmouthed, opinionated, workaholic, bleeding-heart, generous, lioness-loyal friend, may you launch another posse as amazing as ours wherever you are, with room for us as we make our way to you."

I blow Paula a kiss, which she returns. We both look over at Cecile; more kisses blown around. The congregation applauds softly as the picture fades.

I feel a squeeze on my arm, look down at Olivia's head resting on my shoulder. I belong here, holding Olivia close, holding the subtleties of her mother's complicated life close. These people don't need to know everything.

I tilt my head back, examine the massive wooden beams arching high above, cocooning us in sorrow. Closing my eyes, I hear, quite clearly, Stella's voice: "Thank you." I mouth the words "You're welcome" and give Olivia a return squeeze.

～

After the service, I tell Olivia I need to remove my illegally parked Saab from the church lawn before Father Scully sees it. Olivia turns to Rob, says she'll ride with me. He objects, but relents under his daughter's steady stare. Suppressing a smile, I assure him I will get her home in one piece.

Stella's ashes rest in a small russet ceramic urn in Olivia's lap as we make our way to her house, which will be my house for the next year. The Moo-ve It Movers will arrive tomorrow morning with my stuff. Though this has been the plan for a while, I have deftly avoided the reality until this moment. I find it hard to breathe as I navigate the hills and turns of Vermont's Route 36, stretching between the civility of St. Albans City and the wilds of Fairleigh, where Stella Rose lived for nearly twenty years.

"Are you okay?" Olivia gives me the hard-eyed stare she inflicted on Rob.

It's not so cute now.

I pull onto the grassy shoulder of the road, inches from an electric fence ostensibly keeping twenty-some lounging Holsteins from running amok. As I roll down the driver's side window, I inhale deeply. Sweet, grassy air rushes into my lungs. Exhaling, I say, "What was the question?"

"Are. You. Okay."

"No, Liv, I'm not. You?"

"Nope," she says quickly. "I'm so not okay. I'm glad I'm not the only one." She settles back in her seat, her gaze now on the road ahead.

"Feels weird having you in the passenger seat and not driving," I say.

"I was thinking the same thing," Olivia says, smiling just a little. Nearly two years ago, I taught Olivia how to drive because Stella simply couldn't let go of the wheel.

Slowly I merge onto Route 36 and into the procession heading for Stella's house.

~

Rob arranged the catered reception, which is well under way as we enter. Classical music drifts from stereo speakers nested in various spots throughout the living room, accenting muted conversations that will surely grow louder as the wine flows.

Olivia, standing on tiptoe, whispers in my ear, "Can you come with me?"

I follow her up the stairs.

She shuts her bedroom door behind me, then stands there, clutching the urn. "Where should I put this?" she asks, her voice thin like it was when she was twelve, before puberty, before high school, before leukemia. "It's just so crowded downstairs, and there are lots of bad memories in her room, and she'd be . . ." Olivia stops; her face reddens.

"What?" I ask. "What were you going to say?"

"Lonely," she whispers, eyes filling. "I was going to say she'd be lonely."

Taking her in my arms, I feel the cold stone urn between us. "She shouldn't be in her bedroom all by herself," I hear myself say. "She should be here with you."

Stepping away, Olivia blinks back tears. "Okay. She will stay here until . . ."

"Until July."

Olivia walks to the round, tapestry-covered table before her large, multipaned window. She removes an unwieldy grape ivy, puts it next to her computer. Then she gently places the urn on the center of the table and stands back to gauge the effect.

I place my arm across her shoulders. "Perfect."

Olivia nods. "We should go back downstairs."

"Ready when you are."

"Just a minute," she says, walking over to her vanity. Pulling the black scarf off her head, she shakes loose the folds of her long onyx hair. Carefully, she places the scarf on a hook over her closet door. She grabs an elastic hair tie off her vanity, bends at the torso, gathers thick waves of hair into her hands. Hinging back up, she wraps the elastic around the wad of hair twice, executing a perfect messy bun, loose hairs framing her heart-shaped face. "Okay, let's go."

"Right behind you," I say, marveling at her ability to perform this maneuver without a mirror. Such a teenager move for one who has lived an entire lifetime in sixteen years.

Downstairs the swelling mass of mourners overflows into the den and kitchen areas. Rob emerges from behind the makeshift bar and takes Olivia to his side.

Spotting Paula in the kitchen doorway, I wave. She calls to Cecile somewhere behind her. They descend and drag me out onto the back deck, where we all light up in Stella's memory. Normally nonsmokers, we smoke as a ritual when we get together. Today Paula lights a Salem just for Stella, places it on the edge of the rusty coffee/butt can. We watch it burn, and cry.

~

Back inside, I watch Olivia wander the room, pale as the ghost her mother is, a courteous smile fixed on her face. Stella would be so proud of her.

Stella's heart would break for her.

On Olivia's first day of kindergarten, Stella called me at 8:35 a.m. "Liv's just getting to school. She's probably scared. All those kids, lots of bullies, ya know."

"Stella Rose, she's fine. She was excited about school. She's—"

"I remember my first day . . ." And she was off, recounting the horror of her own kindergarten days, convinced history was repeating itself with Olivia.

At 11:10 she called again. "They're heading for lunch in five minutes. I hope she doesn't end up eating by herself. It's so lonely." I heard tears in her voice.

"If she's having a hard time, the school will call. If it'll make you feel better . . ."

"I just called them, actually."

Of course she had. "And?"

"They said she's fine. Great, actually. But that was before lunch."

"I enjoyed lunch."

"Well, you were Miss Popular."

I let this go. "Stell, you're paranoid and you love your daughter. Knowing that will help Olivia through days much tougher than this. Stop worrying."

"AbbySol . . ."

"You're welcome. Now, get back to work, or you'll be paranoid *and* unemployed."

∿

"Are you sure about this?"

I start at the voice behind me.

It's Rob, pale like his daughter and looking uncharacteristically lost. Handsome in his mid-forties, Rob is tall and fit; the gray in his black, shellacked hair touches only the temple area. He looks at me anxiously. "I should be there for my daughter. She can come back to California with me, enjoy a change of scenery. This house has seen awful days."

True—but not awful enough to erase Olivia's entire childhood of wonderful memories with Stella. "Olivia wants to spend her senior year in her own high school. She knows what she wants."

"How can she? She's sixteen! What did you know at sixteen?"

Rob has a point, but it's moot. Olivia is stubborn like Stella. She will stay here until she leaves for college, and so will I. That's the promise I made to my best friend—one of those stupidly rash promises I am prone to making, a fact Stella knew well.

"Rob, we'll figure all this out. It'll be okay."

He looks unconvinced. "I'll come see her once a month. I'll stay at the Hilton."

"You can stay here if you want."

"Let's see how it goes." He squeezes my shoulder before heading back to the bar.

Scanning the room, I spy Richard Rothschild standing danger-ously close to the swinging door that separates the living room from the kitchen. I smile as I make my way over. I take his elbow and lead him two steps to the right just as Johnson Keller, Stella's moose of a law partner, barrels through the swinging door holding a bucket of ice over his head, announcing, "Coming through" a tad too late. I give him a slant-eyed glare. He winces, mouths "Sorry" as he is swallowed by the crowd.

"He's a nice young man," Rothschild says, unperturbed.

"I suppose," I say, my heart still thumping. All I need is my boss seriously injured at my best friend's post-funeral extravaganza. "I want to show you these pieces I got in Greece," I say, pointing to two solid bronze statues—a mother giraffe standing nearly three feet tall, and a child giraffe, slighter and ten inches shorter.

After fumbling in various pockets, Rothschild finds his silver wire-rimmed glasses perched on his head and pulls them down. He blinks twice, as though focusing a camera lens. His practiced gaze travels the contours of the mother, then the child. I know he appreciates fine details missed by most, who see only hunks of bronze shaped like zoo animals.

"This is something one would expect to see in . . ." He gropes for the place.

"Nearly anywhere but Greece," I say, my gaze lingering on the lines of the mother giraffe's neck, which is curved subtly, protectively, toward her child.

"I knew I sent the right person," Rothschild says.

I am surprised, as Rothschild is a man of few words. He has run the Harmony Museum of Culture and Art for over twenty years, promoted—many say pushed—into the position of curator when Dr. Dean Chaplin died at his desk from a heart attack. Because the museum is small, the role of curator comprises nearly everything—except curating. Much of that actually falls to me. But Rothschild is happiest poring over old manuscripts and digging artifacts out of the ground and insists on three months each year in the field, during which time I take over his wide-ranging administrative duties.

I watch him survey the pieces, and I'm gratified by the appreciation in his eyes.

"Stella loved giraffes," I say. "If you look around, you'll find them in the strangest places—wooden ones, brass ones, stuffed ones, tiny ones, tall ones. And they all have names. These are Jezebel—the mom—and Lucy. When I saw them in the Lambropoulos's home, I knew Stella would love them."

"Indigenous?"

"In a strange way. Luka's great-great-great-grandmother visited Kenya as a girl and was fascinated by the giraffes. When she returned to Greece, she fashioned hundreds of them from bronze. These were her favorites, so they stayed with the family."

"Until now."

He does not ask how I got the man of the house to part with a family heirloom of such importance, or at what price.

~

At last, all the guests leave, and Rob kisses Olivia good-bye before departing with Wife #2. I help Olivia into bed. An old friend of Rob's, a physician, has given her a sedative. Hearing her snore softly as I pause at the door, I feel my own body relax.

Drifting room to room, I see Stella's home for the first time through her eyes: a simple three-bedroom saltbox with a large front porch and sunny back deck. Stella kept the house neat—austere, even. She joked she had no time to decorate, but clutter made her nervous. She preferred blank spaces to objects that demanded attention, needed dusting, distracted the eye. Her life was a maelstrom, her home a sanctuary, located far from the craziness of the city that claimed too many hours of her days and years.

In Stella's home office, her computer sits blank and expectant, papers stacked neatly to one side. I look out the window into the gloaming.

I pull up the sash. Let some of the grief out.

In the glass I see my reflection superimposed on the darkening outdoors. Tears track down my face. Stella's face no longer there, assuring me I'm okay, I am loved.

My phone buzzes from the living room. It's late, so I know who it is.

"Hi, Mom."

"Hello, Abby! How are you?"

Oh, where to begin with my mother? "I'm fine, Mom, and you?"

"Fine, fine, hon. What time is it there?"

"Nine thirty," I say, adding for emphasis, "*p.m.*"

"It's seven thirty here in Phoenix."

This I know.

"I'm calling to see . . . to ask how the funeral went."

I am surprised my mother remembered the funeral was today.

"It was great, Mom," I say brightly as I pace the length of the living room.

"You don't need to take that tone. I was just calling to see if you were okay."

"I'm sorry, Mom. It's been a rough day." It feels good to admit this.

"I'm sure it has," she says, and I swear I detect true sympathy in her voice. I experience a rare rush of feeling for this woman who is distant in more than geography. Before I can say anything, she adds, "But now you can move on to the next phase."

The feeling fizzles. "Sure, Mom." *I'll get right on that.*

"Have you moved into the house yet? It's best, despite what people say—"

"What are people saying?" I stop pacing.

"Folks think you aren't equipped for this. But you are. That's all I called to say."

"Well, Mom . . . thanks," I say, more like a question.

"Howard sends his love."

"Mine to him."

"And mine to you," my mother says, and hangs up before I can send mine to her.

~

I climb the stairs, stand outside Olivia's room. Her rhythmic breathing soothes me. I wonder, for the thousandth time: Is she angry with me? Does she think I abandoned her mother by throwing myself headlong into the biggest project of my career? That I hired full-time nursing care only to spare myself the horror of Stella's decline?

Or is it just me?

Slipping quietly around the corner to Stella's room, I see, per Stella's instructions, the room restored to its pre-cancer state. My shadow, cast by the dim hall light, slides gray against the soft peach wall as I climb onto the window seat she insisted on having and never sat in. I gaze at the moon, wreathed in wispy clouds. Branches from a hundred-year-old maple strain toward me, lush green leaves waving from the gathering darkness.

Here I am, miles from my tiny High Street apartment and my dusty, saggy bookshelves; cupboards filled with granola, dried fruit, whole-grain pasta, and protein bars; the ratty futon against the wall with my favorite crocheted afghan balled up as a pillow at one end; two anemic philodendrons too stubborn to die from neglect.

Restless, I slip back onto the floor and pad softly across the room, the silver carpet cushiony under my bare feet. Lying on the perfectly made bed, I rest my head on Stella's pillow and stare at Stella's ceiling, white and smooth as marble. What thoughts entered her head at the end of every day, all these years?

Tears come again, hot and stinging. Does anyone ever truly know another person? Does it even matter? I am starting to believe friendship has nothing to do with intellectual or even emotional connection, that my friendship with Stella was more . . . visceral. What else explains the achiness in my heart, the nonstop tears, the fact that I sense her presence everywhere, like the phantom leg of an amputee?

Do you remember that crisp and colorful day last September, Stella, when you arrived at my apartment earlier than expected? I had returned the night before from my trip to Greece. You'd harangued me for weeks to get my ass home; you needed to talk about something you didn't want to get into over the phone. My antennae should have been up. You never, ever arrived anywhere on time, let alone early. But I was too happy to see you, to really see you, Stella, or to see what was coming.

As your car pulled in, I flung open the door, braced myself for your shrieks of delight. Then watched you pick your way too carefully down my driveway. When finally you looked up, your face portentous as rain clouds, my hands began to shake. Could you feel me trembling when we hugged at the door?

"Stell?" I asked, holding your shoulders, my heart hammering your name short.

You smiled crookedly. "Chamomile," you said, as you toed off your shoes in the foyer and headed for your spot on the futon, pulled close to the woodstove.

I drew the basket of tea from the cupboard, turned on the gas burner for the kettle. Glancing over, I noted your wild honey hair was pulled back into a large barrette and appeared unwashed, that you were still in sweatpants. Not my Stella.

Retreating to my rocking chair, I waited.

You shivered, hugging your knees to your chest. "I'm glad you have the fire going," you said, holding your hands out toward the heat.

"Stell, what's going on? What couldn't you tell me over the phone?"

You looked confused for a moment. "Oh, that . . . that will have to wait."

What, Stell, what had to wait? We never did get to that. So many things we never got to. So many things rendered meaningless in a moment.

"Okay . . ." I said, watching your face intently.

"They don't like what they see. The doctors. Oncologists."

My blood chilled instantly, a freezing wave from my scalp to my toes. "What do you mean, 'They don't like what they see'?"

"They think . . . it could be . . ."

"What?" *Christ, Stella, just say it!*

"Leukemia."

I saw in my mind a scythe laying low the lives we knew.

You stared into the fire.

"Leukemia?" I said. There was no space to breathe with that one word filling every recess in the room, bloating every cell in my body, squeezing everything out. The room tilted. I excused myself, went to the bathroom, threw up. Swished mouthwash, avoiding in the mirror the eyes of someone I had not been just five minutes earlier.

But this was not about me.

It took a moment to realize the shrieking in my head was an echo of the teakettle whistling violently on the stove. I returned to the kitchen, turned off the burner.

You never heard the kettle, I could tell. Keeping one eye on you, the other on our teacups, I managed to fill them without spilling. You didn't hear the rattling of the cups in their saucers as I made my way over to you, placed your tea on one wooden arm of the futon frame and mine on the other, then took my place by your side.

Taking your tiny, smooth hand in mine, I said, "What exactly did they say?"

They said it was leukemia. Over the next nine months, rare hopeful moments were crushed by a relentless, remorseless reality—weeks of remission followed mercilessly by a relapse of apocalyptic proportions. A slow, delicate, dreadful death.

~

Before heading to the guest bedroom, I check on Olivia once more. She favors her father in looks, but I've always been able to see Stella in Olivia's face when she's sleeping, even when she was a baby, and all the times she slept over when Stella traveled. I catch my breath at the sight of my best friend's daughter—alive, Stella's blood coursing through her.

I walk over, reach for the quilt to pull across Olivia's shoulder, and notice something dark wrapped tightly in her arms. The urn.

I step back, surprised. A floorboard creaks underfoot. Olivia stirs; her eyes open slowly. Patting her shoulder, I sit on the edge of the bed. "Is it okay?" she mumbles.

"Of course. Good night, sweetie." I softly kiss the top of her head and start to get up. She grips my hand.

"Can you . . . ?"

I squeeze her hand. "Sure I can. Shove over, kiddo."

After clicking off the hall light, I climb under the covers. With my hand on her shoulder, Olivia soon falls asleep. I'm not far behind.

~

I'm up at dawn and ease out of bed quietly. I stretch the kinks out of my neck and spine, then dig my yoga mat out of the cardboard box marked EXERCISE/OUTDOOR. Instead of heading down into the basement, where Stella set up a home gym–cum–torture chamber, I clear a small spot in front of the window. I roll out my mat, place my palms together at my heart, and begin my first sun salute in my new home.

$$\sim$$

Breakfast is an awkward affair. First off, I don't know where anything is, even after years of drinking tea in here. Soon I am irritated by the total lack of culinary logistics in this oversized and underutilized kitchen. Miles of empty, orange-speckled cream Corian counters top bright yellow cabinets and drawers of various sizes, all containing the wrong stuff. Why would utensils be mixed with Rubbermaid lids ten yards from the stove? Pots and pans stacked—more accurately, tossed—to the back of a cabinet behind juice pitchers and a waffle maker?

In exasperation, I call Olivia down to the kitchen and ask, for the love of Pete, where the bread would be. She points to a drawer next to the refrigerator. I yank the drawer open, and there is the bread, one loaf of whole-grain white and a half loaf of rye.

"She didn't like stuff on the countertops," Olivia says, her voice small.

"I know," I say, instantly contrite for being short with Olivia on our first morning. "I just can't seem to find anything."

"I did the best I could, but . . ."

Of course she did the best she could. I wasn't around much to help Olivia manage the house before Stella died. I wasn't around much to get acquainted with the kitchen before Stella died. I wasn't around much before Stella died.

"Olivia," I whisper, "I just need to get my bearings. I'm sorry I snapped at you."

Eventually I locate two serviceable pans, a spatula, bacon, and eggs to go with the bread. Once the bacon is frying, I find the coffee mugs in the canary-yellow cupboard above the counter, near the sink— right where they should be. Using a wide-mouthed mug with the logo

Virginia Is for Lovers, I cut circles out of two slices of bread. I pop the circles in the toaster, then turn my attention to the remains, delicate now with their centers missing. I butter them, put them in a small, heated pan, crack an egg into each empty circle, and cook the eggs over easy. Olivia watches intently.

When we're ready, Olivia pours juice and places a vitamin next to each glass. I smile. Stella believed utterly that a vitamin a day makes up for lousy dietary habits.

Olivia picks up her fork and pierces her yolk.

"What's on your agenda today?" I ask.

Olivia looks at me blankly.

"Not that there *is* an agenda," I say quickly. "We can make it up as we go."

Olivia looks relieved and uneasy all at once. "Are there more . . . arrangements?"

I wrack my brain. "Not today. We meet with the lawyer tomorrow." We already know what's in the will, as I am the executor. But it's another ritual. Yes, we get it. Stella's gone, though her scent remains in the drapes, in the shampoo bottle, in the towels. Her sunny face, surrounded by teased and sprayed chestnut hair, smiles at us from various tiny picture frames, her presence shrunk to glassed rectangles of memory.

"I keep . . ." Olivia's voice falters. "I keep hearing . . . expecting to hear . . ."

"Her voice?"

"Yeah, telling me to get my butt out of bed." Olivia laughs, a strangled noise.

I smile. "I'm still waiting for feedback on my scarf choice yesterday."

Olivia smiles, her eyes full and shiny. "I keep expecting her to walk right in . . ."

The doorbell rings, startling us. Our gazes meet, and we laugh nervously. I glance at the clock: 8:30 a.m. "It's the Moo-vers. I'll be right back, Liv."

It takes forty-five minutes to unload and stack the boxes in their appropriate places. After signing the paperwork and waving the movers off, I realize I haven't seen Olivia since breakfast. Stepping inside, I call out to her—no answer. In the kitchen, the table is clear, dishes gone, counters clutter-free.

Upstairs, her door stands ajar. I knock softly—no answer. Knock louder—nothing. I poke my head in, see Olivia lying on her bed, staring at the ceiling, mouthing words to a song only she can hear through tiny earbuds tucked into multipierced ears.

I wave my hand slowly, trying to get her attention without scaring the crap out of her. Catching my movement, she sits up quickly, pulls the buds out. "What?"

"Just wondering where you were." Should I have tracked her down like this? She is probably used to having alone time, something all sixteen-year-old girls surely crave.

We blink at each other.

"Okay, I'm going to unpack some boxes," I say. An indecipherable look crosses Olivia's face, gone in an instant, but it makes me uneasy. "If you need me, I'll be in the guest room." I turn to go.

"It's your room now," Olivia says.

I look back, but she has already reinserted the earbuds.

$\sim$

I take out only the essentials, reticent to unpack everything. What if it doesn't work out?

Stella drafted me on a particularly bad cancer day, when her voice was the thinnest thread, her eyes sunken and dark like tiny buttons. She asked if I would take care of Olivia. Please. Just until she left for college. Could I do that for her?

Like I could look into those twin pools of darkness and pain and say no. "Of course. I'll take good care of her, I promise."

Stella smiled, her eyes closed, the creases in her forehead smoothing away, and she extended her frail pinky toward me. My pinky, of its own accord from years of practice, encircled hers, and the deal was sealed.

~

I'm relieved when Rob arrives at noon to take Olivia to lunch. I hadn't realized how I've been tiptoeing around Olivia. Carrying her grief with mine is crushing me.

I fix some tea, then sit and scan the paper. I get sucked into a story about Lyric Theater's performance of *Macbeth* later in the season. Stella would love to see it again. I pull out my cell phone, punch 1. Within seconds, the phone on the wall rings. Sobbing, I let it ring. Stella's voice soon reminds me she can't come to the phone right now.

~

We gather in the office of Johnson Keller, Stella's former colleague and the man who nearly killed my boss with a swinging door. Rob, Savannah—aka Wife #2—Olivia, and I try to make ourselves comfortable. Johnson walks in, hair slightly mussed, suit hanging off just a bit; he's the junior version of his father, John, the first Keller of Keller, Keller, Beech, and Rose.

Johnson pulls out a three-inch-thick folder containing documents I reviewed with them—just four weeks ago? Rob takes Olivia's hand in his. She is pale, her lips a hard, colorless line, her gaze on her lap. I extend my arm across the back of her chair.

"Let's begin with assets." Johnson proceeds with a long list of savings accounts, insurance payments, and retirement investments. Everything will go to Olivia, most at twenty-one. College funds are set aside, enough to cover one-fourth of anticipated expenses. Stella points out that Rob will also kick in one-fourth, and the rest is up to Olivia. Johnson recites, "Kids must be at least as invested as their parents in order to own their education experience." Olivia nods, having already heard this numerous times.

Stella paid off all debt before her death, with the exception of the mortgage, which has now been paid in full by the insurance company.

"I will execrute the next part" says Johnson, looking straight at me. "With regard to the house, title shall pass to Abigail Solace St. Claire."

A collective gasp fills the office.

Rob shoots me a glance. I shrug, as clueless as he is.

"Quoting Stella—Ms. Rose: 'Abby, under considerable duress, agrees to help Rob raise Olivia until the age of eighteen. I would like our home to remain available to Olivia for a lifetime. To that end, I am prevailing once again on my best friend to indulge me by taking possession of our home. Abby, if you find the boonies too much, you can return to the city. Just please keep the house safe and ready for Olivia if she needs to come home.' If Abby and Olivia mutually agree to sell, they split the proceeds."

Typical of Stella to characterize a gift beyond all proportion as an obligation, so that I will accept it. But a house? I am a homeowner?

Johnson continues. Personal effects are next. Most go to Olivia, a few treasured objects come to me, and some will be donated to local charities. "This brings us to the final clause: 'Olivia and Abby, in the attic are two master cartons, one for each of you. In each carton are twelve packages. You are to open these in order, one per month, in each other's presence. No cheating, no peeking, no jumping ahead. You can pick the day of the month—most of the time. See, I don't need to control *everything*.'"

Johnson grins at us. "Any questions?"

We all sit, blinking at him. So much for no surprises.

"Terrific," he says, pulling the papers together, tapping them on each side for maximum alignment, shoving them into the accordion folder. "My assistant has certified copies for each of the parties named herein. Ms. St. Claire, I'll be in touch regarding the title transfer of the house. Thanks for coming in today, and, again, I am sorry for your loss. Stella was . . ." For the first time, his voice wavers slightly. "A special person."

Rob extends a hand to Johnson, thanks him for his time. Olivia and I follow suit, and two minutes later we find ourselves in the bright sunshine of a beautiful end-of-June day. Warmth is finally returning to our forsaken corner of New England.

Wife #2 opines on the house matter. "That's quite a gift, if you ask me."

I am about to point out that no one did, indeed, ask her, when Olivia interjects. "I told Mom it made sense."

We all look at Olivia in surprise.

"We spent hours talking about how to keep the house."

"I would have kept it for you," Rob says.

"Of course!" chimes in Wife #2.

"I mean," Rob says quickly, "I understand—it's typical Stella."

This does not help.

"What does that mean?" Olivia and I say in unison.

"He means," Wife #2 cuts in, "Stella was impulsive, particularly when it came to you," she says, dagger finger pointed at my chest.

"Meaning?" Olivia asks, but I know what Savannah means.

"Meaning she thinks there was more than friendship between us. Let me assure you," I say, directing my words to Savannah, "I loved Stella more than anyone on this earth. Always have, always will. If you'd ever had a best friend, I would not need to explain this to you. I promised my best friend I would take care of her daughter. I have loved Olivia since the day she was born. She is as close to Stella as I can get. I will stay with Olivia as long as she needs me, for her sake, for Stella's sake, and for my own." I step closer, looking from Savannah to Rob. "Any questions?"

Rob puts his hand up in a conciliatory gesture. "Abby, I'm sorry. We're all tense. This came as a surprise, but it's a good surprise." Savannah pierces him with a deadly stare, which, to his credit, he ignores. "It's a big responsibility. If you have any trouble, call me any-time." He adds, earnestly, "Abby, it's the least I can do."

The connection between Rob and me, severed ten years ago in the bitter divorce, flashes on briefly. For all his flaws, he always loved his daughter—and Stella.

"Okay. Thanks, Rob." I turn to Olivia. "Ready?"

"Yes." She kisses her dad on the cheek, glares at Savannah.

We climb into Olivia's Honda Civic hybrid and drive slowly back to Stella's house. My house. I glance at Olivia. Our house.

In the driveway, Olivia cuts the motor. "Are you okay?" I ask.

"I think I'm getting there. You?"

"I think so, too."

We gather our stuff—Olivia her backpack, I my canvas tote bag—and head into the house. Dropping our bags in the foyer, we glance at each other, then sprint up the stairs to Stella's room. Olivia flings open the closet doors, pulls down the retractable stairs. She is up in a flash; I'm on her heels.

There, as promised, are two large, square shapes in the darkness. Olivia pats the wall for the switch, finds it. We fall onto the boxes, drag them into the light. Each is the same size, four feet square. Each bears a label. In glitter. Surrounded by gold and silver stars. Olivia and I laugh. Glitter! Stars! Stella, inept at crafts, is poking fun at herself.

Our laughter dims to soft smiles as we regard the boxes quietly.

"So," I say, "how shall we do this? Do we pick the same day each month?"

"Starting today?" Olivia asks, as anxious as I am to tear into the boxes.

"We could . . . But I'm thinking we should be more . . ."

"Intentional."

We think for a moment.

"We could open the first ones on Saturday," Olivia says.

Saturday is going to be tough. This could help. "Olivia, you are a genius."

As we stand, Olivia pushes her box toward the wall.

"Not so fast," I say, holding her arm. "Maybe we can't open the individual boxes, but we sure as hell can open the cartons!"

"Apparently I'm not the only genius in the house."

We work our respective cartons open, peek inside. "Oooh," we both say, then peek into the other's box. "Oooh," we say again, delighted. I pull out all my items, find each one wrapped in different paper, ribbons, and bows. Olivia removes hers, and we find that the wrappings of her bedecked packages match mine—pairs clearly meant to be opened together. Closer inspection reveals clues as to which items go with which month—Christmas paper for December, Easter egg paper for April, autumn leaves paper for October.

"Can we possibly wait until Saturday?"

"I can, but only if you can," I admit.

"Okay, I promise." Then, in an act that sears my heart, Olivia extends her pinky toward me. I entwine my pinky with hers and say, a mere echo of a pledge made to Stella not so long ago, "Promise."

$\sim$

Dawn edges into my room as if sensitive to the significance of this day, waking me gently to what should have been Stella's thirty-eighth birthday. Crying quietly, a ritual these days, I gaze out the window over maples and pines as the palest pink rises into the gray horizon only to be overtaken by a paler blue, ever-widening ribbon of sky.

I heave myself out of bed and head for the kitchen.

A year ago, we girls started making big plans for our fortieth, a weekend Caribbean cruise. Three months ago, Stella said, "Of course you'll still go," before coughing violently into a handkerchief then collapsing into her pillows, exhausted.

"It won't be the same," I said.

She answered, "It'll be fabulous. Just a different fabulous."

By the time I get my coffee, Olivia enters the kitchen, shower-fresh. We sit opposite each other at the bistro kitchen table, gazing out the lace-curtained window onto Stella's rose garden—once a magical place, now a tangled mess needing serious attention before the Fourth of July and our next Stella milestone.

We finish a light breakfast, then head upstairs to the attic. From our respective cartons we pull identical packages: slender jewelry boxes wrapped in paper that has HAPPY BIRTHDAY TO ME printed all over it. Very Stella.

A charm dangles from the ribbons on each box. Wrought from fine silver, each one is a delicate outline of a star with a tiny rose inside. Stella Rose.

"You first," Olivia says.

"Okay." I slide the ribbon from the box and open it to find a letter, neatly folded. Beneath it lies a fine sterling bracelet that, I suspect, will eventually hold twelve charms.

Olivia scoots next to me to read the letter over my shoulder. The script is in Stella's hand, recognizable despite the shakiness apparent in each stroke of her pen.

My Darling AbbySol,

My dearest friend, how are you doing? I hope you didn't behave yourself at the funeral. I wish I could have been there with you. I know it was a tough day.

I cannot accept taking my leave of you all at once. I have put together these boxes so we can stay in touch over the next year. Though I am the cause of your grief, I can't bear not helping you through this. I hope these letters help. As you know better than anyone, my attempts to help often make things worse, but that's never stopped me from plowing ahead. Because you love me, you will indulge me, as always. I love you for that.

Know that I feel your emptiness and loneliness. Was it worth it? Should we have grown so dependent on one another? If you had leukemia and I was watching you die, wondering how to fill the void your death would leave—it is nearly enough to make me glad that I am leaving us first. If not for Olivia . . . But that is her letter, not yours.

There is so much, too much, to say, and I promised myself to keep it to one page, to keep it to the barest, truest truth. See the size of my writing shrinking? But I will sign off now, save some for the next letters. A dozen opportunities to show what you mean to me and how I want the best for you.

> *It won't all be pretty, AbbySol, and I am sorry for that, but*
> *I trust in the love of our friendship to survive truth and death.*
> *In undying friendship and enduring love,*
> *Stella Rose*

"Wow," Olivia whispers.

"Wow." Guilt taps my shoulder, pointing out that while I was AWOL, Stella was preparing for her departure in this moving way. I draw a ragged breath. "Your turn."

Olivia slips the ribbon off her box, removes the cover. As expected, there is a letter, though in a different stationery, gardenia scented—Olivia's favorite. Below the letter lies a delicate sterling bracelet, twin to mine. Olivia's hand trembles slightly as she reads.

> *My Darling Olivia,*
>
> *My sweetheart, I can only imagine how the past few days have been. If there is any way in the afterlife that I can touch you, hold you, protect you, I will find it. Before I'm measured for my wings (or horns, as the case may be), I will demand the "How to Love and Protect Loved Ones on the Other Side" manual.*
>
> *Thank you, Olivia, for helping me prepare for leaving you.*

Olivia's voice breaks. Her eyes, misty for days, spill over. Her shoulders heave as tears land on the letter, stains spreading rapidly across the delicate paper. I lay a hand on her shoulder, and she leans toward me until her head rests in my lap. Gently, I take the letter from her hand and stroke her hair as I finish reading Stella's letter aloud.

> *Thank you, Olivia, for helping me prepare for leaving you. I could not have done this with any dignity and grace without you. However, I suspect this cost you dearly. You never let me see the depth of your sorrow, your fear, your anger. I know there is anger. I'm angry, too, but I bet it pales against yours. Please,*

now that I am gone, don't hide your sorrow, anger, or loneliness. Promise me you will talk to someone—your dad, Abby, a counselor, friends. Find someone to help you.

I want to help you, too, by giving you these twelve boxes. While there are painful times ahead, some of them exacerbated by these boxes, surely, I do hope they bring understanding, hope, and love to you as you embark on the rest of your life.

And what a life it will be. I will be cheering you on from wherever I am—nothing can keep me from you, Liv. In those quiet moments—the few you may encounter when you're not hooked up to an iPod or IM-ing or hanging out with fifty of your closest friends—you may be able to hear me shouting, "Woo-hoo!" I'll be discreet, though. I don't want to embarrass you. ☺ I know, fine time to start worrying about that, eh?

Olivia, I love you always and always. As do so many others. Let them love you, starting with your dad. Rob is a good man. I wouldn't have married him or had his child if he weren't wonderful. Sometimes he forgets how wonderful he is. Help him remember.

Take care of Abby. Make sure she gets out once in a while.

Know that Abby loves you and has since the day you were born. Being loved by Abby is a blessing. Bringing her to you is my last, best act as your mom.

Love, love, love to you, my sweet Olivia.

Mom

July

ood riddance to June, Stella. Olivia and I survived in a hazy numbness, tripping through each day. Inexplicably, a fresh calendar page, a month without hospice, death, funeral arrangements, wills, or casseroles, seems reason enough to feel better, if only in those small snatches when our hearts aren't poked raw by awkward phrases from acquaintances in the grocery store who lament about how awful it all is.

Olivia and I worked out the details of your ashes, all per your request. Remember how you said you were grooving on the notion of lingering in the garden, and how, just maybe, you could actually help something grow for a change? I laughed because it was funny, but Olivia's eyes welled. "Aw, Liv," you said, "it's been too long since I've heard you laugh. Come here." You crooked your finger; she came obediently. You poked her in the ribs and tickled her, and she collapsed onto your bed, giggling like she used to when she was six, until she was out of breath, perilously close to tears. Then you said, "Think of a great send-off, girls. I trust you to come up with the perfect words to send me into what's next."

No pressure, Stell. You were the wiz with words, not I. You never understood why others couldn't keep up with you, never understood that what flowed from you didn't flow from everyone else.

The Fourth of July dawns fiercely red. My eyes open slowly as I rise on my elbows, squint into the early sun. The trees at the edge of the woods look like they are on fire. I can see no houses from my window, or from any window in the house, for that matter—a thought that makes me feel at once free and incredibly exposed.

This is the day we set Stella's ashes free. Her words, not ours. She said "scattered" sounded too unorganized, too prone to chance. She did not want her final resting place left to chance. "If it works out, Independence Day would be an appropriate day." If it worked out, as though dying before July 4 would be a good thing.

Ten minutes of meandering path through Stella's woods—157 acres of sugar bush—leads to a small back bay of Lake Champlain, quiet, protected on three sides by spindly stands of birch and beech that eventually give way to sturdier maple and oak. As the backdrop of so much of what we did growing up, the lake is part of who we all are. Now Stella will be part of the lake. Half of her ashes, anyway.

The other half will rest in the rose garden, the backdrop of Stella's adult life, an island of aromatic color that lies between the house and the sugar bush. Though Stella felt cozy in her backyard, I've always felt claustrophobic. In my third-story apartment on High Street, I could see across Lake Champlain, all the way to Canada. In Stella's backyard, the world shrinks to a half-acre oasis guarded by trees lined up like soldiers standing sentry in a tight semicircle, protecting and forbidding.

Stella always said I couldn't see the garden for the trees. Stella saw only her garden, and she was not alone. Because the truth is, in the middle of the clearing between the army of trees and the back door lies the most incredible rose garden in the entire state of Vermont.

Fifteen years ago, Stella's garden grew from clearance-sale roses from a local nursery. Each year she added new ones. Stella cooed and cajoled the paltry specimens to bloom, but she lacked the green thumb to manifest what was vivid in her mind's eye. After five seasons, she could not keep up with the ever-widening garden and run her law practice. She declared she owed it to her roses to hire an honest-to-goodness gardener.

She embarked on a search that led to the Rose Whisperer, and so he was. He transformed her emaciated cuttings into a forest of fragrance and color. Whenever Stella spoke of the Rose Whisperer, it was as though she were describing a Zen master or a saint.

Each June and July, on weekend afternoons only, Stella opened her backyard to the public. People would drive for miles to see the spectacle. But Stella and I enjoyed the first blooms of spring and the pungent blossoms and rose hips of fall best, when we had the space to ourselves. We spent hours drinking tea or wine or—on those bad days—pitchers of margaritas in her rose forest, inhaling the strong perfume of the hardy Albas and Gallicas while feasting our eyes on the fleeting boldness of red and yellow Hybrid Teas. Sometimes I even forgot about the encroaching trees.

No one has seen the Rose Whisperer since Stella died, and the garden is a mess. Panic set in as I realized I did not even know the gardener's real name; neither did Olivia. While Stella's search was intentional, finding the Rose Whisperer happened by accident, through a "friend of a friend who had this incredible gardener" connection. Stella surely mentioned his name, but she generally referred to him as TRW. Over the past week, I've checked the local greenhouses to see if Stella was a client. No luck. TRW must be a free agent. Scrolling through Stella's address book, bills folder, and checkbook, I found nothing.

So now it is left to Olivia and me to get the garden ready for Stella's arrival. We stand in Stella's potting shed, consider various articles of clothing hanging on pegs just inside the door. I grab a pair of ridiculously large, faded denim overalls, plunge one foot, then the other into ample pant legs, and hike the straps over my shoulders. Olivia hands me a red-and-black-checkered flannel shirt the size of a parachute.

"Really?" I ask.

Olivia grins. She looks hip in her own gardening clothes, which consist of ripped and grass-stained fitted jeans and a worn T-shirt with the logo GARDENERS DO IT DIRTY, which she says she bought two years ago in protest when Stella established weekend garden dates as mother-daughter time.

I shrug out of the straps, pull on the shirt, button the three middle buttons. Olivia pulls the straps back into place, steps back to inspect me. That look crosses her face again.

"Christ, I look like a scarecrow, don't I?"

"No," Olivia says, "you look like Mom. I mean, you don't look anything like Mom, but those clothes . . ." She shrugs, then smiles. "Let's go play in the garden."

Olivia tosses me a pair of gloves, dons her own. She grabs a canvas bag full of implements of dubious purpose and heads for the backyard.

As I wrestle with my own gloves, I nearly bump into Olivia, who is standing stock-still just outside the shed.

"What is it?" I ask, looking in the direction Olivia is staring, and at once I see.

The Rose Whisperer has returned.

Walking along the fieldstone path, Olivia and I soak in the rose beauty—the reds and the pinks accented by yellows, punctuated by whites, all against lustrous green and burgundy foliage. We pause and breathe in the fragrance, thick and heavy, as though all the pruning and digging and watering has stirred the roses into a cacophony of scent at once diverse and unified. Squadrons of bees buzz amid the blooms; millions of buds are already forming among the later varieties. All that potential beauty tightly wrapped, just waiting for the right time to be seen.

Like Olivia.

This thought, out of nowhere, roots me to this spot near the garden bench, which happens to be where we will bury half of Stella.

"Abby, what's wrong?" Olivia eyes me apprehensively as I sit on the bench.

What's wrong? In my head is a trash heap of all that is wrong right now, all that was wrong and will be wrong for a long, long time. Before Stella's death, I could obsess in the comfort of my home, curl up in a ball with my journal, explain to myself all that is wrong in my world and just how I would pull it all back together, starting tomorrow.

Where the hell is my journal, anyway?

After a heartbeat, I say, "We owe the Rose Whisperer big-time."

"We sure do," Olivia agrees, sitting next to me. We listen to water gurgling in the tiny pond next to the bench. Last week, this was a mud puddle. Today, a half-dozen marbled koi chase each other through the roots of pink and white water lilies.

To our left are three stacked rocks, a formation Olivia created when she was ten years old that, according to Stella, hinted at Olivia's artistic genius. It consists of two large, flat rocks, one on top of the other, upon which sits a third rock, perfectly round and smooth—a rare find in this land of shale and limestone. Olivia fashioned this work of art for Stella's first garden, in the front of the house. Three years later, she and Olivia painstakingly lifted the creation and, step by heavy step, relocated it to the entrance of the wild-rose area. Stella thought this was most appropriate. Though wild and untamed in appearance, these roses had the most intoxicating scent, just like Olivia, she said.

We will inter half of Stella's ashes under Olivia's rocks.

"Well," I say, "should we . . ." I leave the rest unsaid, and there is a long pause.

Finally, Olivia says, "I . . . just need a little more time." She heaves herself off the bench and walks back to the house. I resolve to leave her alone until she is ready.

At 10:00 p.m., Olivia appears in the doorway to the guest room— my room—the urn tucked under her arm. "Ready?" I ask.

"Ready," she says.

~

Clouds blanket the sky, deep and impenetrable, like a lid on a pot. Olivia clutches the urn to her chest as I sweep my Maglite from her feet to mine and back so neither of us trips on the uneven path. As we get closer, the rhythmic slapping of waves against bank begins to accompany the crunch of our feet. Clopping down the dock, we steady ourselves within its gentle sway. Dark against darker; it's as though we are walking the plank to the end of the earth. We remove our shoes and sit at the end of the dock. Our toes skim the cool surface of the lake.

"Did you come up with the perfect words?" Olivia asks.

"Nope. There are none." I place my hand over hers. "But we can come close."

We close our eyes, and my mind is as blank as the sky above us. The waves lap against the underside of the dock. Across the lake a loon cries—no reply. A woman's laughter, soft and distant, floats across the water. I feel Olivia's heart beat through the pulse in her hand.

"Stella," I say, the words coming from nowhere, "as long as this lake is here, and longer, you will be my best friend. I will miss you always."

Olivia's fingers curl over mine. "Mom," she says, "as long as this lake is here, and longer, you will always be my mom, and I will miss you always. Amen."

Olivia rests the urn on her knees, slowly removes the top, and places it between us on the worn wood of the dock. She looks to me; I nod assent. We check the breeze to ensure it is blowing away from us. Thankfully, it is.

Olivia tips the urn to the water and shakes it gently until the fine gray powder drifts down into the lake. She checks the contents, shakes a bit more into the lake, says, "Close enough." So Stella-like. She places the cap back on the urn. Without pause, she clambers to her feet and looks at me expectantly.

Though I would prefer to linger a moment, I sense Olivia needs to get to the next step. I close my eyes a moment, nod, rise to my feet. We pick our way carefully back up the path, through the dark woods, to the house.

In the backyard, we turn on the floodlight I rigged up earlier in the day. We find our way to the wild-rose bed, gently lift the three rocks as one, and set them out of the way. Olivia grabs the shovel and makes some test stabs in the soil for a soft spot to dig.

"What if a dog comes along and digs it up?" I ask.

"More likely coyotes," Olivia says.

"Oh, right," I say, looking around nervously. I had forgotten about those.

We alternate digging, removing sod, digging more, removing rocks and stones, digging deeper. At three feet deep and wide, we agree we've dug enough. Sitting at the edge of the hole, we contemplate the urn clasped in Olivia's lap one last time.

"We should say something again," Olivia ventures.

"Yes."

"What if we say what we will miss most about her?"

This pains me, as it's all I've been thinking about, the likely causal link to my crying jags. Prioritizing the things I'll miss most about Stella is like thinking about what I'd miss most about my right arm; my legs; my sight.

But I say, "That's perfect."

After a pause, Liv says, "French toast!"

I glance at her in surprise.

"That's so stupid!" she cries, face in hands. "That can't be the thing I miss most!"

"First, that's a fine thing to miss. Second, we can make a list; it doesn't have to be in any particular order."

Olivia brightens. "Okay, we can make a list, but at the end, I think we need to pick one from the list." Pause. "And we say that one thing silently to Mom."

"You are good at this."

"I am," Olivia agrees. "Your turn."

"I will miss—"

Olivia interrupts. "Let's tell her directly." "Directly" with a long "i," like Rob.

I begin again. "Stella, I will miss your smile. Your smile always made me smile, no matter how bad things got."

"Me, too," Olivia agrees. "Mom, I will miss your hugs."

"Your sense of humor."

"Your guidance."

"Ah, good one. That's on my list, too, Stella. Your guidance."

"So that doesn't count," Olivia says, bumping my shoulder.

"This is complicated."

"Continue."

"Gosh, you sound just like—"

"Mom." Olivia flashes a smile, genuine and Stella-like.

Tears run hot down my face as I continue. "I'll miss your advice."

"Really?"

"Well, I know that I was often better off with Stella-speak in my head."

"Me, too. And I will miss your eyes, Mom."

Who will not miss Stella's eyes? "Stella, I will miss your insight."

"Your laugh."

"Your understanding."

"Your editing."

I glance sideways at Olivia. "Don't expect that from me."

"I know. Mom warned me."

"Nice!" I say. "Loyalty."

"Love."

"Love."

"Amen."

I am surprised by Olivia's second use of the word in one evening, struck by its appropriateness. "Amen," I say. We sit for a moment, offering up our one best thing. Mine is not from the list but the word that is a symbiotic sum of the list: *friendship*.

I spread a soft, faded quilt across the bottom of the hole. Gently, Olivia lowers the urn onto the quilt and we fold it once, twice over. We each toss a handful of dirt over the quilt; then I shovel the rest of the dirt into the hole. We tamp it down with our feet, and Olivia spreads mulch over the area. We carefully place the stacked rocks back in their spot, now marking so much more than the entrance to the wild-rose garden.

Olivia kneels next to the square of freshly turned earth, places her palms flat on the ground, and whispers, "I'll visit often, Mom."

I tip my head back, move my lips to the stars. "Me, too, Stella Rose." I click on the flashlight; Olivia turns off the floodlight. Hand in hand, we walk back to the house.

~

Olivia and I find a rhythm to our days. I resume my post at the museum; Olivia returns to her job as counselor at Kill Kare Summer Day Camp for tweens. We work long days, order in most nights, watch movies by the dozen. Reading is too slow, and leaves too many opportunities for our minds to drift to sad places. Movies are safer, though we avoid films about dead friends and mothers. We divert ourselves with romantic comedies, black-and-white musicals, and the occasional horror film.

As the weeks wear on, I realize it has been Olivia and me alone for more than a month, since her dad left. I make a mental note to ask about her friends. I also renew my intention to track down the Rose Whisperer and thank him for keeping Stella's garden in order. All month I have expected a bill for his services. Nothing.

On Wednesday, I leave the Harmony early for an appointment at Keller, Keller, Beech, and Rose. The office is two blocks away, so I walk in the sun, nearly at its hottest, letting the rays warm my bones. I can't shake this chill from the damp days of June that followed a chilly April and May, preceded by the bitter cold of a long winter watching Stella die. I shiver in the heat, rub the goose bumps on my arms.

Inside the foyer of the law office, the AC is on full blast, and I regret leaving my sweater at the museum. Ashley Rainville, the assistant ensconced behind a mahogany desk in the center of the foyer—equidistant from the partners' offices, like the hub of half a wheel—smiles brightly. "Let me buzz Mr. Keller and let him know you're here."

Unsure if I should sit or remain standing, I finally decide to sit just as the door to Johnson's office flies open and he beckons me. I pop back up and walk past him into his dark but warmer office.

"Can I get you . . . a coat?" he asks, eyeing my goose-fleshed arms.

"I'll be fine. The AC gets to me." I'm not only cold but nervous. Johnson is much more put together today than last month, and quite handsome. I hear Stella from the heavens: "Johnson Keller, jock of the firm, thinks every day is homecoming."

"I don't like AC, either," he says, snipping the psychic string to Stella. "So I don't have it piped in here. Some days I regret it, but I guess today won't be one of those days. You'll warm up in a minute." He smiles.

Wow. I barely remember him from our high school days. He went to boarding school in New Hampshire, but I recall seeing him at summer parties and holiday gatherings. How did Stella work with him all these years and not want to jump his bones?

But that was Stella. Rather than be turned on by all this charm, she took it as a personal offense. That anyone could wear conceit like a Gucci suit was enough to totally piss her off. She couldn't stand Johnson Keller personally, but grudgingly admitted he was a damned good lawyer.

Eyeing me as I take one of the plush seats before his desk, he shrugs off his suit jacket. "Do you mind?" he asks, and delicately lays the jacket across my shoulders. My skin warms instantly, absorbing his body heat.

"So," he begins, settling into the chair next to me rather than sitting in the large leather beast across his desk. "Do you know why I asked for this meeting?"

"It's about the mortgage."

KKB&R sent a request for a meeting ten days after the funeral. The whole mortgage situation makes me uncomfortable. I just couldn't talk about it. But after the second request and follow-up call from Ashley, I knew I couldn't avoid it forever.

"I'm sorry about not coming sooner."

"I understand. In fact, I apologize for the firm not waiting a more appropriate length of time to set this up. We shouldn't have called until about this time anyway. This is not a typical circumstance, and the clerk handling this file was not fully apprised of the background. She assumed because you were not a blood relative, you would not be . . ."

"Grieving?"

"Yes," he says, then adds quickly, "Not that grief is reserved for family only."

"Of course," I say. "Any more than property rights."

"Indeed," Johnson says, nodding. "This certainly raised some eyebrows."

"So, stuff like this doesn't happen every day?"

"People like Stella don't happen every day."

Johnson explains the broader points of mortgage transfers. The way he fills the overstuffed leather chair makes me feel like he has the situation under control.

"After thirty days, everything becomes final. You own the house."

The gigantic oak grandfather clock in the corner gently thrums four o'clock.

"It just seems so . . . weird."

"Frankly," Johnson says, "this is unorthodox, but when Stella explained it to me—five different times, five different ways—it made perfect sense. Stella trusts—trusted—you implicitly. If that trust was warranted . . ."

This irks me. "Do *you* trust me?" I ask, eyeing him steadily.

Though clearly caught off guard, Johnson smiles. "It's not my job to trust you."

"You're stalling."

"Okay, yes, I do trust you." He laces his fingers together across his broad chest. "Stella told me a lot about you. I feel like I know you, and I'm glad you're there for Olivia. What scared Stella most was leaving Olivia, and the only thing that saved her from losing it was knowing you would take care of her daughter."

"No pressure."

Johnson laughs and sits farther back in his chair. "Stella had a way of ratcheting the pressure up on everything. She never meant to . . ."

"But there it was." I'm surprised at Johnson's insight. Not many folks picked this up about Stella.

"So, how are things going?" He tilts his head to the side, looking serious.

"Olivia's doing okay."

"I'm glad. But I was actually asking about you. How are things with you?"

"I . . . I guess I'm fine. Busy, back to work, figuring things out at the house. . . ."

Nodding, Johnson leans forward, his hands nearly touching mine. "If Stella meant half to you what you meant to her, you must have quite a hole in your life."

Without warning, my eyes go from misty to overflowing in an instant.

"Damn, I'm sorry," Johnson says, scrambling across his desk for a box of tissues. He pulls out three at once, hands them to me.

"I'm sorry," I say, sniffling in a most indelicate way. "Perhaps we should get started on the paperwork."

~

"So," Johnson says, as we walk to the door, paperwork completed, "have you been getting out?"

"Actually, I haven't been out in ages. There hasn't been much opportunity."

"Stella said that would happen."

"Is there anything Stella didn't tell you?" I ask, laughing, but it seems to take a long moment for Johnson to realize I am kidding.

"I'm sure there is plenty Stella kept to herself," he finally says, then smiles at me. "Knock, knock."

"Who's there?" I ask, looking at him quizzically.

"Opportunity."

"Ahhh," I say, smiling. "Nice to meet you." I hold out my hand. Both of his large, square hands close over mine, warm and strong. After exactly three shakes, I remove my hand before losing my senses. I slip his jacket off my shoulder, hand it back to him.

"Dinner? Tomorrow night? Seven?" He looks at me, eyes hopeful.

My insides are all over the place; my brain screams, *Are you crazy? This is the last thing you need right now!* My mouth says, "That works for me."

He smiles; I smile and reach for the door. He steps so close I can smell ridiculously expensive bath gel as he reaches past me for the door and opens it with a flourish.

Laughing, I nod and say, "Thank you, Johnson." *Turn around now*, I say to myself. My body actually listens. Rotating toward Ashley, who's eyeing me from the helm of her desk, I smile as I leave the offices of KKB&R, no longer needing a sweater.

~

"Why are you humming?" Olivia asks. She squints at me, standing in the shaft of light entering the kitchen through the grilled window over the sink.

"Oh, I hum sometimes." I smile, returning to the scrambled eggs, which are perfect. I spoon half onto a plate for Olivia, the rest onto a plate for me, just as the toast pops up.

"Eat up," I say. "You have to leave soon for camp."

Olivia picks at the eggs.

"You don't like scrambled eggs?"

"I've never liked scrambled eggs," Olivia says, looking past me through the French doors out into the backyard. "Mom always cooked them too fast, so they were like rubber and made a mess of the pan." Her eyes wander around the kitchen, her words picking up momentum. "That is, when she made breakfast. Mostly she didn't have time. Sometimes she'd bring me toast and juice in the bathroom while I was getting ready. She always brought it after I brushed my teeth. Do you know how much orange juice sucks after you brush your teeth?" Olivia is shouting now, looking at a spot over my shoulder.

"I'm sure she was trying . . ."

"She was always trying, but she never got it right! She could have made it five minutes earlier—just five minutes—but no, she was always doing ten things at once, squeezing the Mommy thing inside the ten other things. Maybe if she had taken the time and just cooked the frigging eggs, just cooked the eggs and nothing else, then they would have tasted like this. I would have liked scrambled eggs, and . . . and . . ." Olivia's face is scarlet as she pushes the plate away and bolts from the table. I can feel the heat of her as she pushes past me and out of the kitchen.

Frozen, I stare at the scrambled eggs and toast. Seconds, maybe minutes, tick by. Then I hear feet pound down the stairs, the front door open and slam shut. I hear Olivia's car start up, engine wind in reverse the length of the driveway, and fade as she drives away.

∿

All day my stomach churns. I try Olivia's cell multiple times, get voice mail. I'm fully panicked by noon.

I call KKB&R and leave a message for Johnson to call me. He calls within the hour, and I beg off our dinner. He says he understands, asks if tomorrow or Saturday would work. I think, *Dinner on Saturday night screams "date"; tomorrow night will do.*

∿

When I get home from work, I remove my shoes and hang my bag in the foyer, then head to the kitchen. I hold the kettle under the tap and watch cool water flow in, feeling the kettle grow heavy in my grasp. I set the kettle over the blue-tinged flame, then tap my fingers on the counter as I wait. Hearing the steam gathering inside the pot, I close my eyes until finally, finally, a soft whistle erupts into a full-blown scream of release.

Curling up on the sofa, I gaze out the window, watching for Olivia's car. My gaze drifts across the room, settles on the oversize chair and ottoman just a few feet away. A now-familiar feeling washes over me: I'm marooned. I'm in my usual spot on the sofa, my usual cup of tea in hand. Stella should be curled in her cushy chair, eyeing me over her own cup, ready to weigh in on my latest crisis. None of those crises compares to how I feel right now. "You told me I could do this," I say aloud.

Silence.

"You told me I could do this!"

I hear the echo of Stella's voice in my head. "You *can* do this, AbbySol."

"Things are never as easy as you say they are, Stella Rose," I say reproachfully.

"You always tell me that."

"You never listen. You don't get it that not everyone thinks like you. This is unfair, Stella. You've put me in an impossible position!"

Silence. There is no echo for this. We never got to this point. How could I tell my dying friend she was asking too much from me? How could I be honest and tell her she should let Rob take Olivia, be the father he should have been? Be the father, truth be told, that Stella never let him be.

"It's too much," I whisper, looking into my cup.

"Who are you talking to?" Olivia asks from the foyer.

Startled, I slosh my tea as I turn to face her. "I—I didn't hear you come in."

"I just walked in. Sounded like you were talking to somebody."

"Myself."

"So you talk to yourself, too?" Olivia asks with a small smile. "Hey, I'm sorry about this morning."

"Me, too," I say, setting my tea on the end table.

"You didn't do anything. I know I made you worry." She considers the overstuffed chair, then plunks down next to me on the sofa. "Mom would freak out every time we argued, too."

"She would?" I glance at the empty oversize chair.

"Oh my God, yes!"

Olivia curls her legs up under her, and I flash to Stella just for a second. "She would cruise by the school or by Pizza Pie when I was working there. If we had a fight and I stormed out, she'd panic and think I'd just take off. She was such a spaz."

"She worried constantly, but I can't imagine she thought you'd run off."

"She wasn't as together as everyone thought. I think she faked it a lot to help me, like if I didn't think she had it together, I'd be freaking out all the time."

"She probably felt the same about me."

"No. She envied how you went your own way—no matter the consequences. She didn't agree with everything you did!" Olivia grins at me, and I laugh. "But she always agreed with the why. She'd say, 'I may not agree with such-and-such, but Abby did it because not doing it would diminish her personhood,' or something deep like that."

"If she only knew."

"She did. She knew how hard you struggled. She knew she pressured you, like she pressured me. She couldn't help herself."

We are silent for a few moments. I take a sip of rapidly cooling tea. "So, Liv, about this morning . . ."

"I just lost it for a second. I'm sorry."

"I don't need an apology, Liv. I need to know what's going on." I touch her arm.

She flinches, turning her face away from me to look out the window. "It's nothing, Abby. Some days I'm just . . ." She turns back to me and shrugs her shoulders. "Angry. Some days I'm just totally pissed off at the world."

"You seem to be angry with someone pretty specific," I say quietly.

"So," Olivia says, ignoring my comment and settling into the corner sofa cushions, "why were you humming this morning, before my little meltdown?"

I let her off the hook. "Oh, nothing," I say, looking into my teacup.

"Oooh," says Olivia. "A guy."

"No!" I say, too quickly. "Well, kind of. Just dinner."

"It's a date," Olivia says with that teenage know-it-all-ness. "When?"

"Tomorrow night."

"Who's the guy?" She sits up eagerly, hugging a throw pillow to her chest.

"As a matter of fact, it's Johnson Keller."

Olivia stiffens; her gaze shifts to the empty oversize chair. "You're kidding."

"What's the matter?"

"I don't like him," she says flatly.

"Why not?" I ask, and am instantly sorry. Of course she does not like him. He is too closely related to Stella and her death. "Olivia, I guess I understand why."

She looks surprised. "You do?"

"Of course."

She looks truly uneasy, so I say, "He worked with your mom and handled her arrangements and everything. I see why this is hard. It was uncomfortable for me, too."

"But you got over it," Olivia says bitingly, tossing the pillow to the floor, then folding her arms across her chest.

Sighing, I squeeze her arm. "Olivia, if you aren't comfortable with this, I'll cancel. No big deal."

Olivia refuses to meet my eyes. I wait. Finally she looks up. "Just dinner?"

"Yes."

"Maybe you won't like him. Maybe you'll realize he's a big, rich jerk."

"Quite possibly."

"Okay."

"It's okay if I find out he's a big jerk?"

She smiles. "It's okay if you have dinner. You haven't been out for a while. Maybe you'll meet someone else at the restaurant."

"Right, because that's how it works. So what will you do while I'm out? Why not go out with your friends? You haven't been out for a while either."

Olivia rolls her eyes as she twirls her ponytail around her index finger. "Everyone is so uptight. Nobody knows what to say. It's just not worth the effort."

"Olivia, I'm sorry. When school starts . . ." I'm not sure how to finish.

"When school starts, things will be better," Olivia says reassuringly, though I suspect she is saying this for my benefit and doesn't believe it herself.

~

The next evening Olivia lies on my bed, watching me apply finishing touches to my makeup. My fingers tremble slightly, and she teases me for being nervous. "It's like you haven't been on a date in months!"

"Try years."

"That's not true. Mom said."

"Did your mother tell you every detail of my life?" I ask, irritated.

"I'm sure she left out the juiciest details, so feel free to elaborate."

"Not a chance. It's been about a year since my last date."

"Me, too," says Olivia. Our eyes meet in the mirror. Of course it has. Just before the Big L entered our lives and swept everything else aside.

All day I've battled emotions around this evening with Johnson. Why bother going out when I can't come home and tell Stella all about it? Then again, what would I have told her, considering her disapproval of Johnson? He isn't artsy and edgy enough for me—not like Luka. Stella totally loved the idea of my having a torrid affair in the Greek Isles with a handsome local. Johnson is too stuffy for me, not to mention all his other sins: filthy rich, womanizing, arrogant, privileged. *Christ*, I've thought more than once today, *why* do *I want to go out with him? Is it too late to cancel?*

But now, looking into Olivia's eyes in the mirror, I know the true source of my reticence: How dare I go out and have fun when Stella is dead?

And now, too, I know it's time to make my way back to the living. It's what Stella wanted, and it's what I want. And I should show Olivia the way.

"Where are you going?" Olivia asks.

"Puccini's."

"Nice," Olivia says, drawing out the word.

I straighten and turn to Olivia, hands on hips. "So, how do I look?"

"Smoking hot," says Olivia, and her appraising look tells me she's not just saying that. "I like your hair that way."

I have swept my hair up at the sides and fastened it with a rhinestone clip in the back, leaving the rest to fall loosely past my shoulders. The copper eye shadow and smoke gray eyeliner make my eyes pop; a subtle shade of base makeup helps conceal months of stress and sleepless nights.

Olivia leaps off the bed with a quick "Be right back." In two minutes she returns with a handful of lipsticks. She drops them onto the vanity and paws through them. "These were Mom's." She twists one open to reveal a shade the color of fresh blood.

"No way," I say, holding up a hand. "Your mom could get away with colors like that. I need something more subtle."

"Oh, no. Mom wins this argument. For one so artsy-fartsy, your taste in lipstick has always been too conservative. Live a little. I don't think you can get into Puccini's unless they can see your lips from two blocks away. Here, try this one." Olivia holds up another tube, this one a disturbing blend of red, purple, and black.

I strain to read the label. "Indigo Moon. I don't think so."

"First put on some lip balm or something to soften your lips."

I do as I'm told, then take the dreaded Indigo Moon in hand. I smear it on my bottom lip, then the top, smush my lips together, smile at myself in the mirror.

"Okay, too much," Olivia says quickly, handing me a tissue. I wipe off the gunk. "Repeat the lip balm," Olivia instructs, then hands me Steamy Rose. This is a bit more subtle, though not much.

Slowly, I apply the creamy lipstick, purse my lips to spread the color evenly.

"Blot." Olivia hands me a tissue.

I press the tissue between my lips and remove. Surprisingly, it doesn't look that bad.

"Here," Olivia says, handing me another tube. "Intensity controller."

I smooth it on, glance in the mirror to gauge the effect. I smile in spite of myself.

"Perfect," Olivia says, satisfied, arms crossed.

The doorbell rings.

"I'll get it." Olivia sounds grumpy, and I realize she may be happy about me going out but not happy it's with Johnson Keller. At the bedroom door, she says, forefinger raised, "You wait here."

She takes her time down the stairs. Then I hear the door open and voices exchange greetings.

"AbbySol?" Olivia yells up the stairs.

"I'll be just a minute!" I say, then stare at myself for three full minutes. What do I talk about with a lawyer? What could I possibly have in common with Johnson Keller, whose name is mentioned as eventual state's attorney, governor, maybe even senator?

It's just dinner.

Johnson stands in the foyer, making small talk with Olivia. The look on his face when he spots me is priceless.

"You look great!" he says.

"So do you," I say, and mean it. He is hot. Olivia spears me with a glare.

"Are you ready?" Johnson asks.

Dear God, no. "Yes, of course." Impulsively, I kiss Olivia on the cheek, and she hugs me before ushering us out the door.

~

Puccini's is crowded, but Johnson has reserved the best spot in the house, a table for two in front of an open-air window. I've had lunch here a few times, but never dinner. It doesn't suit my wallet or my last-minute lifestyle. The menu is diverse and complicated. I surrender at once to Johnson's suggestion that he surprise me. Johnson makes conversation easily. I relax, enjoying myself for the first time in months.

I try to recall everything Stella said about Johnson. For years she made derisive comments about his privileged background, his Ivy League education, his money, trophy wife, rumored string of mistresses. But she said stuff like this about nearly everyone at the firm, and she was particularly hard on the fiscally fortunate. And deep down she must have liked Johnson. If she hadn't, she would not have allowed him to handle her estate.

On the day he visited the house to discuss Olivia's guardianship with Stella and me, tension strung between them like a tightrope neither wanted to cross. Finally Stella asked me to leave them alone for a few minutes. When Johnson left twenty minutes later, Stella was too tired to talk about it right then, and, of course, the opportunity never presented itself again. Until now.

"Johnson, that day you stopped by Stella's to talk about my being Olivia's guardian and Stella asked to speak with you alone . . . What did you talk about?"

Johnson looks uncomfortable. "Stella didn't tell you?"

"No," I say. "She was tired when you left. If you'd rather not tell me, that's fine."

"I don't mind telling you," he says, looking at me thoughtfully. "She grilled me about my marriage."

I blink at him three times before forcing a smile. "Was she being nosy?"

"A little." Johnson smiles back. "She . . . she was not happy that I left Shayla."

"Stella often thinks she's the only one who had a good reason to divorce. Everyone else should try harder. She's a sucker for happy endings."

"She was," Johnson says stiffly.

"She was," I agree, and for the first time all evening, awkwardness lingers. "So," I say brightly, fully meaning to say something clever to change the subject, but instead my filter fails and I say, "why *did* you leave your wife?"

It's Johnson's turn to blink three times as heat infuses my face, surely reddened to a shade somewhere between the Bolognese I had for dinner and the port currently staining the bottom of my glass.

"Johnson, I'm sorry. That was rude. You don't have to answer."

"I will have to answer, at some point," he says, and I experience a small rush at this indication we will see each other again.

"But you don't have to tell me tonight."

"Okay," he says, "but just so you know, my hesitation is because this is a tough question and I'm not always sure." My puzzlement must show because he smiles and says, "I mean, I know it was the right thing to do, and so does Shayla. Now, anyway. The reasons are many, but the catalyst that caused me to finally leave six months ago is trickier to articulate. You can appreciate what a strange year this has been."

Oh, yes. But my mind catches on one phrase. "It's been only six months."

"And five years. It was a long time coming," says Johnson, "but the separation was official six months ago. The divorce will be final within the year."

That's right. I'm having dinner with a married man.

I excuse myself to use the ladies' room. As soon as I stand, I realize with alarm that I am more than tipsy. It takes all my frayed faculties to make it to the bathroom without incident. Once inside the beautifully tiled, luxuriously appointed lavatory, I slump against the wall, feel my way to the toilet stall. I sit for a long time to get my bearings, then run cold water on my wrists before heading back to the table.

Johnson looks at me, amused.

"This is all your fault," I say.

"What?" he asks innocently.

"Not funny. I haven't had this much to drink in a long time. I'm embarrassed."

"Don't be," Johnson says, suddenly serious. "You deserve to relax."

"Well, I think I need to relax my way home, if you don't mind."

Johnson looks disappointed.

"I've had a great time," I assure him quickly.

Johnson smiles and waves to the waiter for the check.

He escorts me to the car, settles me inside. His face brushes against mine as he fastens the seat belt for me. I hold my breath as he lingers after the belt clicks into place. He turns his face a fraction of an inch toward me, and our lips meet softly, then deeply.

"Coffee at my place?" he mumbles against my lips.

"Sure," I mumble back. He takes his sweet time getting around the car and into the driver's seat. As he pulls away from the restaurant, I crack the window for air.

At his apartment, I slip into the bathroom and carefully reapply my decidedly unconservative lipstick, admiring the effect through hazy eyes. For a moment, my mind goes back to Greece and another man's place, his soft-gray adobe flat facing a crashing sea. We made love to the sound of relentless water against rock and screaming sea birds, a warm breeze through an open window tickling our bare bodies. Luka.

As I leave the bathroom, I hear the chugging of an espresso machine in the vicinity of the kitchen; soft music flows from a complicated entertainment system that commands the farthest corner of the living room. I walk to the picture window, gaze out over our sleepy town. It's only ten o'clock, but already traffic is a trickle, pedestrian activity is nearly nonexistent, and lights are blinking off all over the city.

I feel Johnson, smell the scent of his cologne tinged with garlic and red wine.

"Nice view," I say.

"You're telling me," he says, though he's obviously not looking out the window. He places a palm to my shoulder and I lean back against him. His hand travels down my arm, and goose bumps rise instantly.

"Cold?" he murmurs into my hair.

"No way," I say drowsily.

"Excellent." He runs both his hands down my arms, and we sway to the music. He tucks my hair aside, kisses me softly at the nape of my neck.

That's all it takes.

I moan and twist around, find his mouth, crush myself against him. He cradles my head in his hands, meets me more than halfway, backing me toward the sumptuous sofa at the center of the room. Gently he leans me into folds of soft leather, his lips never leaving mine. I sink into the cushions, feel his body pressing onto mine, and I'm sinking deeper and deeper until suddenly I'm drowning.

I flail against him, push him up and away from me as I gasp for air.

Johnson grabs my arms and lifts me to a full sitting position. "Are you okay?" he asks, breathing heavily and looking concerned.

"I'm okay," I say, hand to my chest. "I just got a little . . ."

"Overheated?"

"Overwhelmed," I say, smiling and placing a hand to his cheek. "I'm sorry. It's been a while, and it's been—"

"A tough year. Should we start with an espresso?"

"That would be great," I say, relieved. Watching Johnson's broad back retreating to the kitchen, I check in with my racing heart. Against all odds, I like this guy; he likes me. I felt it that day in his office, in the way he looked at me all evening. This connection, rooted in respective relationships to Stella, solidified in that amazing kiss.

So why the panic attack?

I have experience with men. Plenty, actually. But I have never managed a relationship on my own. I've always had Stella there to help me tease out every detail, assess risk, cut losses, mend fissures in my heart, move on.

I'm on my own now.

As I watch Johnson meticulously wipe down the espresso machine before serving the coffee, a realization strikes.

I don't have to be scared.

I may not have the guardian thing down yet, and I may not wield a spade like the Rose Whisperer, but I know how to make things happen at the Harmony Museum, I know how to duct-tape an exhaust pipe well enough to pass inspection, and I know my way around men.

"Here you go," Johnson says, offering me the tiny cup.

"Thanks."

He sits close to me on the sofa. I still smell his aftershave, fainter, yet still enough to make me press my knees together.

"So," I say, then blow on my coffee before asking, "Why did you ask me out?"

Johnson pauses, takes a sip of his espresso. With great attention, he places the cup back on the saucer. "I've asked myself the same question."

Not the answer I was expecting. Disappointment must register on my face, because he immediately says, "Since, as a rule, I don't hit on my clients. Poor protocol."

"I hadn't thought of that."

"Exactly. Neither did I. It's like you weren't my client. Stella was my client, and you were . . . something else."

"Meaning?" I take another sip of espresso.

"That day in my office. You were everything Stella said you were, and so much more. I couldn't take my eyes off you. I wanted to . . ."

I place my hand on his knee, look him in the eye. "What?"

"This," he says, kissing me gently on the lips. Then he takes my espresso cup out of my hand, places it next to his. "And this," he says, kissing me again, harder this time, his right hand pressing against the small of my back.

I return his kiss hungrily, rising onto my knees on the sofa, pushing him back against its soft leather arm. As I collapse onto him, his arms wind around me, pull me in. I bury my hands in his dark, curly hair as his hands roam the back of my dress, deftly unzipping me so that soft rayon falls down my shoulders. He places his palms to my cheeks, gently pulls my face from his.

"Okay?" he asks, his eyes hungry yet cautious.

"Okay," I say, my voice husky, and I am kissing him again. He lifts me, carries me into the next room—his bedroom, judging from the king-size bed he places me on. I yank off his tie as he fumbles with his belt and trousers; our tongues explore each other's mouths. I work through the buttons on his soft white oxford shirt as he pulls my dress down low, unclasps my bra. I tug his shirt off, free myself from my dress, and he is on me, pushing me back onto a pile of satin pillows.

Staring, a hand planted by each of my shoulders, he says, "You're gorgeous."

"So are you." Clasping my hands around his neck, I pull his face to mine. "And if you keep me waiting one second longer, I will never forgive you." I pull his body to me, into me, and he fills me. I feel like I am floating above us, watching this woman emerge from the depths, coming, coming into the light, in a shuddering, shattering, glorious reentry.

~

Later—much later—I awake from a doze and bolt upright in the middle of Johnson's yacht of a bed. Fuzzy details slowly shift into focus as I glance around wildly, putting the pieces of the evening together. Johnson stirs; his hand reaches up to cup my breast. "I gotta go!" I say, squirming away, groping around the bed for my clothes.

"It's one o'clock in the morning," he says sleepily.

"Exactly. I gotta go. Olivia—"

"Has surely figured it out by now."

"Exactly. I really gotta go."

"Okay," he sighs, heaving himself out of bed and into his pants, a practiced move.

I run into the bathroom, hurriedly dress, apply a dab of toothpaste to my finger for a quick rinse, then meet Johnson at the door. He's smiling, but I'm in no mood.

"I've left a sixteen-year-old all alone in that house, and it's a one o'clock in the morning!"

"It's not like she's a toddler," he says, chasing me down the stairs, pointing his remote at the BMW.

"I'm her guardian," I say, whipping open the passenger door, "and, though I haven't read the entire guardian manual yet, I assume there is a section about not leaving her unattended, especially with no warning."

Johnson frowns as he slides into the driver's seat. "You may have a point."

Fifteen minutes later, we're in my driveway. A quick peck on the cheek before I vault out of the car, up the front porch. I wave quickly before ducking inside the house.

Inside it's like a tomb. I take off my heels, carry them in hand, tiptoe up the stairs.

"Abby?"

I freeze halfway up. "Yes?"

"Glad you made it home in one piece."

Not quite sure how to respond, I say, "See you in the morning," and continue up the stairs and to my room. Soon I hear the door to Olivia's room close. I stare at the ceiling, wishing there actually was a manual that included the protocols of dating when you are the new guardian of a teenager.

~

Despite my pounding head, I'm up early, busying myself in the kitchen, waiting for Olivia. At around eight o'clock she wanders in, stretching and yawning. "Morning," she drawls.

"Morning," I say. "Breakfast?"

"I'll just have some cereal."

"I'm pouring some for myself. I can make you a bowl."

"Fine," she says, picking up the paper from the table and flapping it open.

"So, about last night," I say, trying to sound casual. Olivia looks up at me expectantly. "That's unusual for me."

"What part?"

"All of it, actually, starting with wearing makeup and dining at Puccini's."

Olivia puts the paper down. "So, how was it?"

I go for broke. "I had a good time."

"Good," Olivia says, and she seems to mean it. "So, what did you talk about?"

"Mostly stuff about his job."

"Figures."

"Olivia . . ."

"I'm just saying . . ." *God, she sounds like Stella.*

"I'm shy, in case your mom didn't tell you that."

"Do you like him?"

"So far."

"Fine," she says, snapping her paper open again. "Maybe he'll let you get a word in edgewise next time."

I sense an uneasy truce.

～

Johnson calls me in the afternoon. "So," he says, "how are you doing?"

"I feel awful. Hung over awful. I don't feel awful about what happened. I mean," I say, groping for the right words, "it's not like I had planned to . . ."

"Me, too," he says hastily.

There is a long pause.

"I'm glad you called."

"Of course I would call. I'm not that kind of guy, Abby."

Thank God, I think. "Of course, Johnson. I wouldn't sleep with that kind of guy."

"Of course," Johnson says quickly. "Are you free tonight?"

After exactly three heartbeats, I say, "Yes, I am. What do you have in mind?"

"Dinner."

I groan. "Is that a new code word?"

Johnson laughs. "No, it still just means dinner. Anything else will be called out explicitly if and when the moment arises. The Red Room?"

"Sure," I say, mentally reviewing my wardrobe. If we keep this up, I'll definitely have to go shopping. "Six thirty?"

"Sounds great. I'll pick you up then."

The evening ends predictably and deliciously in his bed, though I am home by eleven o'clock and Olivia is in a better mood this time.

~

On the evening of the twentieth, Olivia and I bring cups of tea to the attic, haul out our cartons. Inside we retrieve the boxes wrapped in red, white, and blue, clearly signifying July. Our charms are tiny, silver trees; upon closer inspection, we surmise they are olive trees: Olivia. Silently, we attach the charms to our bracelets.

My box is small, like a jewelry box. I gently remove the ribbon, peel off the striped paper. Inside the box is a gift certificate for Introduction to Orienteering lessons. I hold it up for Olivia; we exchange confused looks. Beneath the certificate lies a letter. I take it out and unfold it carefully.

> *Dearest AbbySol,*
>
> *My dear friend, I do hope you are holding up well. I know you miss me. Dammit, I wish I was there so you could tell me how much. I always loved it when you would call and leave me irritated messages on my answering machine, like "Where the hell are you, Stella Rose? I need to talk to you. It's an emergency! Okay, not an emergency. I just want to talk. So call me, because I miss you. It's been, like, two days since we've talked already." No matter how crazy busy my days were, hearing your voice always made me smile. How many meetings was I late for because I would call you on the spot, just to tell you I got your silly message and didn't have time to talk right now but wanted*

to let you know I hadn't been hit by a bus since yesterday, when we last talked? Those were the days, weren't they?

I know how lost I would be without you, my dear, sweet friend. I don't want you to feel that lost. So I would like you to take orienteering lessons. Remember how I always wanted to do this? You always teased me for my sorry sense of direction. Well, though you spent lots of time studying stars and pretending to know where you were all the time, I sensed you were lacking some basic skills. So I have signed up you and my darling daughter for orienteering lessons in Stowe. The guy who runs the program is good—and cute (hint, hint). Check him—I mean, check it—out. You won't be sorry.

Love to you always, my dear friend.

Stella Rose

I smile at Olivia and nod toward her box. "Your turn." Olivia ponders her box, carefully removes the ribbon, places it aside. She pulls the tape from the paper with such care, I think I'm going to lose my mind. Slowly she lifts the lid from the small, perfectly square box. She cocks her head slightly, and her look of curiosity turns to one of puzzlement. She lifts a small, round object from the box and hands it to me. "A compass?" she asks.

I take the object from her hand and inspect it closely. It is indeed a compass, but one more exquisite than any I have ever seen—not that I've seen many, I realize. This one has a delicate gold case and gilding along the face frame, and the face itself is ivory in color, with Old English letters indicating north, south, east, west, and several degrees among them. "Yes, it's a truly lovely compass."

Shaking her head, Olivia extracts her letter from the box. She takes a deep breath.

"Do you want me to read it for you?" I ask, my voice gentle.

"No. Thanks, but I can do it." Straightening, she begins.

Darling Olivia,

I am sure you are wondering why I'm giving you a compass. This is another one of those goofy Mom gifts that you're embarrassed to tell your friend Liza about! I'm giving you this compass so you'll never be lost.

I suspect you will be hurting for a long time. You will make lots of decisions in the next year that will affect the rest of your life, not the least of which are what college to attend and what you want to be when you grow up! Other decisions, too—the continued challenges of drinking, drugs, boys, sex, deciding whom you want to be friends with and who your true friends are. I trust your instincts completely, but one thing is certain: you won't always take the right path. There are just too many to choose from, and with all this "stuff" going on, your center will be off at times.

I won't be able to help you choose the path (and you don't listen to me half the time anyway), and even Abby won't always be able to tell you. Some paths you must choose yourself. I am hoping this compass helps orient you. If you know where the North Star is, you'll know where your center is and you will find your way home.

I love you always and forever, my darling Olivia.
Mom

Still staring at the letter, Olivia murmurs, "How did she know?"

"Know what?"

"How lost I'd be?"

Pulling Olivia to me, I hug her tightly.

August

Your "All Things Olivia" files have saved me. How else would I have known Olivia likes Nutella-and-jam sandwiches? Prefers Colgate to Crest? That she's grumpy in the mornings, so keep conversation to a minimum? Actually, I learned that the hard way but later found the index card titled "Moody in the Morning" in the EMOTIONAL RESCUE folder. It is like living with a thundercloud, never knowing if it is going to storm or blow over.

I thought I knew Olivia so well. Despite years of hanging out together, sharing common passions, staying up too late during sleepovers when you were on business trips, we're strangers now. School starts soon. I hope Olivia reconnects with her friends, especially Liza. She needs her friends to help her.

I know, Stella. I need my friends, too. I promise I will call the girls as soon as school starts. We'll do something fun—go to the movies, or close down McAdams, or check out *Rain* at the Flynn—oh, right, that's not their thing. That was our thing.

August begins hot, close, and pollen-packed. Thankfully, the Rose Whisperer is keeping up with the garden, despite my fruitless attempts to identify and pay him. Does he garden at midnight? No matter. My allergy eyes are grateful.

It's back-to-school season—heretofore meaningless but now vitally important. "Should we go school shopping this weekend?" I ask Olivia over breakfast.

"Nah, we still have time—no big deal."

"School begins in two weeks."

Olivia starts, as though this is news to her, but recovers quickly. "No hurry."

"We could go to Montreal if you want," I say, regretting the suggestion the second it hits the air.

"No." Olivia stands and takes her bowl to the sink, leaving me alone, biting my lip. Every year Stella took Olivia and her friends to Montreal for a weekend of clothes shopping. It was easy brownie points for Stella. She read novels while the girls ran wild in the malls, and they thought she was the world's coolest mom. They got the trip in last year just before everything fell apart.

Olivia's moods are increasingly volatile, swinging more toward withdrawn but occasionally downright hostile. I suspect this is beyond anything Stella witnessed or could have anticipated. Olivia is all Stella believed—smart, sassy, beautiful, and tough as nails. But she is also human, something Stella never quite understood, and she is in pain.

And, at times, very pissed off.

In an effort to regain control over the deteriorating situation, I've read two books on teen grief and am following several grief blogs. How did past generations manage grief on their own? Now resources abound. Online courses for grief management, grief gurus with ten easy steps to moving on, chat rooms for the bereft.

But honestly, I'm hung over from this bereavement binge. Even after I scored high on the Will I Get Through This? test, my heart repeatedly reminds me that Saturday mornings will never be the same, not without Stella to pour the tea and ask about my week. And if I can't figure this out for my own recovery, how can I help Olivia?

Finally, after a painful exchange over where to order sushi that leaves Olivia in tears, I gently suggest she see a therapist.

Major mistake.

"You think I'm nuts?"

"You've been through a tough time, Olivia. Everyone needs someone to talk to."

"It's not like my mother was hit by a bus, Abby. I had plenty of time to get used to her death before she died."

I gape at her.

"What?" she snaps.

"Liv, just because you were prepared doesn't mean your mom's death is something you should have, or even could have, gotten used to."

Olivia's lower lip starts to quiver as she casts her gaze up the stairs, surely wishing she was safely hunched over her computer, earbuds firmly in place.

I place my hand on her arm. "Honey, grief doesn't work that way."

"How does it work?" she whispers, still looking upward.

"Well, I happen to be an expert."

This pulls her gaze to me. I give her a little smile.

"Based on my scientific research, grief works like most processes in life—one step at a time. The first is acknowledging its existence."

"I know I'm grieving." Eye roll and dismissive flick of the wrist.

"Knowing is only a part of acknowledging." I pause until she looks at me again. "To acknowledge grief, you can't just know it; you have to feel it. Right here." I place a hand to my stomach. "When you feel it right here, and own it, then you can move on."

"Where do you move on to?"

"To life after."

Olivia ponders this, then says, "Textbook woo-woo" before heading up the stairs. At the top, she pauses. Without turning around, she says, "No shrinks," then disappears into her room.

This will be the longest year of my life.

~

The next day I head to the mall. Johnson and I have been on so many dates, I have officially run out of appropriate attire.

Making my way through the sprawling complex crowded with lunchtime shoppers, I literally bump into Jason Riendau, Olivia's ex. "Excuse me," I say, disentangling my plastic-wrapped dress from his American Eagle shopping bag.

"No worries," he says, glancing at me shyly. He looks older than he did a year ago, when he and Olivia were inseparable, and happy.

"Ms. St. Claire?"

I turn back. "Yes?"

"Um . . . Can I ask . . . I mean, can you tell me . . ."

"Yes?"

His shoulders drop as he sidles closer. "How is Olivia?" He fixes his gaze on me. I have been angry with Jason for months for leaving Olivia when she needed him most. Now I see a young man in pain.

"She's . . ." I realize I don't want to lie. "It's tough, though she won't admit it."

"That's Olivia, all right," he says with a sad smile, looking down at his Nikes. "I wish there was something I could do."

My sympathy vanishes. "You could have done something months ago," I say sharply.

His gaze returns to me, hurt and confused. "I . . . I . . . Ms. St. Claire, I tried my best . . ." His voice trails off. "I've got to get back to work." He shuffles toward Hollister, disappearing into its dark interior.

Something in Jason's demeanor nags at me. I met him several times over the years, and he was always nice and seemed devoted to Olivia. I was shocked by their breakup. Stella was outraged, and Jason became the Antichrist.

Now, for the first time, I wonder what exactly happened six months ago.

~

My days flow by in a blur of taking care of Olivia, worrying about Olivia, and fighting with Olivia while working long hours at the museum or in Stella's home office, developing plans for the Spring Fling, punctuated by an occasional date with Johnson. I have myself nearly convinced my life is getting on track.

Then I ignore one too many texts from Paula.

In my darkened office, I am studying our latest grant proposal by lamplight when loud voices erupt from the foyer. They grow louder, more familiar, as they draw closer.

"For Pete's sake, Lloyd, we're gonna liven this place up in a hurry," says Paula in her indoor-my-ass voice. Poor Lloyd. I roll my chair back to stand when she barrels into my office, Cecile dangling off her arm like a chimpanzee off a tree limb. "What the hell are you doing here?" Paula demands.

"This is my office," I say, matching her tone. "What the hell are *you* doing here?"

"To see what's so effing important you would blow us off on Cecile's birthday."

Oh, shit. I turn to Cecile. "I'm so sorry."

"It's okay," she says, her gaze ping-ponging between Paula and me.

"The hell it is!" Paula yells, stepping up to my desk.

"Paula, please," Cecile pleads.

And we're all ten again, standing by the monkey bars in the school-yard. Bobby Trudeau just knocked Cecile off the slide, and Paula chased him all the way to the monkey bars, where he sits perched at the top, looking more scared than triumphant. Stella and I urge Paula on in her verbal assault of Bobby, but Cecile begs Paula to quit. So she does, and we walk away. But after school she corners Bobby at the bus stop, bloodies his nose. Paula lets Bobby say he fell out of a tree only because she doesn't want Cecile to know, but she tells Stella and me the truth. We are in awe as we swear to keep her secret.

Now I'm Bobby Trudeau.

"You're not getting off that easy," Paula says, ignoring Cecile this time.

"I'm sorry. I mean it," I say, "I—I was so wrapped up here, I lost track of time."

Paula places her hands on my desk, leans close to my face. I smell tequila. "You completely forgot."

I cannot look either of them in the eye, so I look at my desk blotter.

"This is so Stella. She was always *so* much busier than everyone else," Paula shouts, waving her arms. "She was always late, when she deigned to show up at all. Do you know how many precious hours of our lives we wasted waiting on her?"

"Paula, that's enough," Cecile says quietly.

"So now that she's gone, are you taking her place? Do you feel like the world is so awful without her that you have to be just like her?"

"I'm not Stella!" I yell back in Paula's face.

"You could have fooled me!" she yells back. "You're living in her house, raising her kid; now you're businesswoman of the year, keeping her long hours in the office! If you're not trying to be Stella, who the hell are you trying to be?"

I open my mouth, then hear a choking sound. Paula and I both turn toward Cecile in time to watch her whirl on her heel and run out of the office.

"Christ, Abby!"

"Me? You started this!"

"You were supposed to stop me before it got this far."

"You bitch!"

"That's better," Paula says, clearly relieved. "Jeez, Abby, who are you are these days? You wouldn't have let me get away with that a year ago. I wouldn't have had to *do* that a year ago. I gotta check on Cecile." She heads for the door. Pausing, without turning around, she says, "You lost your best friend, but you didn't lose your only friend."

Then she is gone.

~

My birthday comes without the usual wake-up call from Stella. However, gaudy HAPPY BIRTHDAY, ABBY paper indicates not only which boxes are for August but also that Stella and I will share this day one last time. Olivia and I agree to open them right after dinner.

Flowers arrive at noon, a large bouquet of orchids, freesias, and lilies too fragrant to be sequestered in my tiny office. I hide the card from Johnson in my desk before taking them to the cafeteria. No need for razzing from the team.

Paula and Cecile call from a single phone and sing "Happy Birthday" to me, which touches me deeply. I stopped by Paula's house earlier this week to apologize again for missing Cecile's birthday celebration. She hugged me in her gruffest manner and made me promise not to speak of it again. "Too much tequila, not enough filter," she admitted.

"Too much truth, not enough time with my girls," I said, and we were good.

They want to take me out, but I tell them I have plans with Olivia. I suggest we get together later in the week at McAdams for margaritas, and it's a date.

~

After a dinner of my favorite, fettuccini Alfredo, Olivia surprises me with a supermarket birthday cake. She lights thirty-eight candles on it and makes me wish. Given the tension that's built between us, I've already gotten my wish, but I keep this to myself.

Up in the attic, Olivia and I draw out the August gifts. My box is large and square; Olivia's package is large, flat, and floppy. Dangling from the ribbons are identical tiny silver globes. I open my box, and inside is a large, colorful globe, complete with a teak stand. A letter in Stella's hand is taped to the packaging.

Happy Birthday, AbbySol!!!!

For your birthday, I give you the world. Ha! You always envied my traveling for work. Since it was part of my job, I could have been jaded, focusing on the less glamorous parts: jet lag, countless hours stuck at airports, culinary misadventures. You never let me get away with that. Your envy kept me engaged in travel, helped me see I was privileged to visit different parts of the world. I would push myself to leave the hotel, interact with people, check out the tourist spots and the local hangouts, often just so I could share them with you when I got home.

If I had known my last trip to London would be my last trip anywhere, I would have done even more. I'm glad I saw Big Ben, Westminster Abbey, and Buckingham Palace, but I would have visited English gardens, rented a car and gone to Stonehenge and the coast and, just for you, Jane Austen's birthplace and where she wrote your favorite books.

Please spend some time with this globe, and encourage Olivia to do the same. Talk about places you'd like to go, then pick one. Give the matter due consideration, and I promise you will get there. Okay? And when you go, go deep.

Wherever I am, I miss you terribly.

Love to you always,

Stella

We are quiet for a moment; then I say, "Your turn." Solemnly, Olivia removes the ribbons and tears the beautiful cellophane wrapping from a large Rand McNally road atlas. Another theme. Olivia removes the letter taped to the atlas.

Darling Olivia,

I do hope you are getting along all right. I can't imagine life without your funny laugh and radiant smile. I hope the rest of the world isn't missing out.

Olivia pauses, but doesn't look at me. Suppressing a smile, I look up at the ceiling and wink.

So you're probably thinking this road atlas is pretty lame. It was an impulse buy. I had a flash the other day about what I was doing when I was your age, and I remembered the theme of my last two years of high school: How could I get away?

Abby, Paula, Cecile, Laura, Jo, and I spent hours poring over a worn road atlas, plotting our course all the way to California. We were going to buy an old VW van, load it with all the essentials—clothes, coffee, hair spray—and take off the day after graduation.

Every time I opened the atlas, I saw possibility. Change. Potential. I saw the future. It's a big world out there, Olivia. You're gonna need a map.

Of course I didn't make it to California until I was twenty-eight, and I arrived somewhat more auspiciously than in a VW van—I flew in a 737 and stayed in a great hotel and walked the beach with a glass of chardonnay in my hand. I recall looking out over the waves and remembering, for the first time in years, how I was supposed to have gotten there. It wasn't nearly as much fun as it should have been.

When you are ready to hit the road, Olivia, don't let anyone stop you.

Love, love, love always,
Mom

Olivia reads the letter again to herself, drinking in every word. I reread mine as well. Our tea gets cold. Olivia finds a screwdriver, and in the living room we put together the teak stand. I rewarm our tea, and we admire our handiwork.

I spin the globe. Olivia places her index finger on the smooth, colorful surface, and it stops at her touch. She rolls her finger back, and we peek at the spot. "Uze . . ." she begins; I struggle with the name, too.

"Rule number one: If we cannot pronounce it, we probably shouldn't go there," I declare.

"I suppose we should be more . . . intentional."

"Perhaps."

"Mom always wanted to go to Africa."

"I know." I rotate the globe until we are staring at the vast African continent.

We sip our tea in silence.

"Abby, Africa's not feeling right."

"I totally agree. Why do you think that is?"

"I think because it's too . . . big. And it was Mom's dream, not ours. I think this is supposed to be about all of us, maybe, not just Mom."

"Wow, that's good," I say. "Let's think on it. The right place will come to us."

∼

I have just reached that blessed point of REM sleep when my phone starts buzzing its way off the nightstand. Groggily, I slap it to my ear. "Mom?"

"Happy birthday, Abby! Did you get my gift?"

"Not yet, Mom. Did you send it to my new address?"

"No, I did not, but I knew Charlie would make sure it got to you."

Charlie is Mom's personal postal worker who runs the Franklin County district office. "I'm sure it'll be here any day," I say.

"What time is it there?" she asks, this clueless mom of mine.

∼

The next evening, Paula and Cecile are waiting outside the Harmony. "We're kidnapping you and bringing you to McAdams for that birthday drink," Paula says.

"That's so sweet, girls, but—"

"But nothing!" Cecile exclaims. "You're coming with us."

I blink at the usually docile Cecile and shrug my shoulders. "I thought we were going later this week . . ."

"It *is* later," Paula says.

"Good point. Let's go," I say, smiling in spite of myself. I leave a voice mail on Olivia's cell saying that I'll be home by ten o'clock. We swing by Paula's house to put on party faces. Cecile ushers me up to Paula's bedroom. She removes my tweed blazer and places it, carefully folded, into a large Macy's bag. Zinging coats across the rod in Paula's closet, she finds what she is looking for, wrestles it off a hanger. It's a tiny red leather blazer that will never fit me, but Cecile thrusts it at me nonetheless. "Put this on. I'll be right back." She disappears across the hall, into one of Paula's four bathrooms.

As I walk back down the stairs, I find my arms slide easily into the sleeves of the jacket. Apparently I've lost weight. I observe the effect in the foyer mirror.

Paula pounds down the stairs and pauses at the bottom. "Damn, I guess that's yours now. I'll never fit into it again," she says dryly. "Happy birthday!"

"Thanks! I think I will keep it," I say, surprised at how much I like the look.

"Feel in the right pocket," Paula yells as she heads to the kitchen.

Dipping my hand in the tiny pocket, I feel a small, round tube and pull it out. It's lipstick, and it's the same dangerous shade of red as the jacket.

"Put it on!" Paula yells.

"I don't . . ."

"Put it on!" Paula and Cecile yell in stereo from their respective locations.

~

The interior of McAdams is dark, noisy, and familiar, a rumpus room for adults. The Rainbow Room, a posh, eclectic restaurant owned by the same family, is right next to McAdams, separated by swinging saloon doors and higher standards. Some folks wait in McAdams for a table to open up next door, but we're tucked in McAdams for the night.

Perhaps it's the fact that it's my birthday, or my first birthday in memory without Stella, or perhaps it's simply from being at McAdams with the girls and without Stella—regardless, my eyes fill instantly. Paula shouts to Chantal, who has run this bar for a decade, "Pitcher of margaritas! Stat!"

"Sure thing, ladies," Chantal says, waving us toward a table by the window.

"You *have* been planning this!" I nod toward the RESERVED sign on the table.

"Duh," they say as one, and we laugh.

It feels good to be with these women who have shared so much life with me, and my eyes fill again. "Where the hell is that pitcher, anyway?"

Looking for Chantal, we all glance toward the bar. My gaze catches a familiar figure sitting near the end, her auburn hair perfectly coiffed, her tiny porcelain face tilted up to her companions—a group of well-dressed men standing in a tight, homogenous semicircle around her. Ashley laughs at something one of them says, touching an expensively suited arm briefly, coyly. Her gaze roams in my direction, but, she doesn't acknowledge me.

Then, like a flock of penguins, the men turn as one toward the door and wave. I turn, too, and see Johnson. He waves back to the group. They make room so that he is standing next to Ashley, her smile now a blinding one thousand watts.

I'm tempted to wave to get Johnson's attention, when Becky, the hostess from the adjacent Rainbow Room, pokes her head through the swinging doors and motions to Johnson's crew to come in. Their table is ready. Of course they won't be spending their evening on the McAdams side, and I feel a pang of envy. What would it be like to be comfortable on either side?

To my surprise, only Ashley and Johnson leave the bar for the

Rainbow Room. The rest of the guys remain, glued to the baseball game. My blood pressure creeps up.

"I'm going to check on those margaritas," I say, standing abruptly.

I wedge my way through a throng of locals to get to the bar. "Excuse me, gentlemen," I say, squeezing between two of the suits.

"You are excused," one of them says, leaning in close.

"Thanks," I say, throwing him a Dangerously Red smile.

"What can I get for you?" he asks, flashing a dangerously white smile from a dark and handsome face. "By the way, my name is Phil."

"I'm all set, Phil," I say, tossing my head back toward our table. "Just checking on drinks for our crew."

"Are the other women as pretty as you?"

"Oh, prettier. Are you guys joining your friends in the Rainbow Room soon?"

Phil gives me a vague look, but one of his buddies is quicker. "Oh, no, that's a private meeting, if you know what I mean."

"Private?"

"Oh, yeah," one of the other guys says. "We don't horn in on the boss's private meetings. They have a lot of work to get done." They all laugh.

I am not amused. At that moment I catch Chantal's eye and she lifts the pitcher she has in her hands, mouths, "I'm on my way." I nod to her and turn to leave the bar.

"Hey, where are you going?" Phil asks, placing a hand lightly on my arm. He is older than I originally thought, pushing forty, with mischief in his grin.

"Back to my girls," I say.

"We're going to be here awhile," Phil says. "Mind if we join you?"

"Sorry, girls only tonight. A celebration."

"What are you celebrating?"

"Same-sex marriage."

Phil releases my arm, holds both hands up in surrender. I give the men my best smile, considering my insides are in rebellion, and head back to the table. I'm fixed on Ashley and Johnson meeting just a few feet away, though they might as well be on another continent in the Rainbow Room. Luckily, Chantal arrived before me, and there is a margarita waiting with my name on it.

"To Abby!" the girls cheer loudly.

"To Abby!" the guys cheer from the bar. I turn to them, raise my glass, and smile. Then I clink each girl's glass, and we chug down the first of too many.

Within an hour, and well into the third pitcher of margaritas, I am full-on tipsy. "Let's go to the Rainbow Room," I declare.

The girls stare at me.

"I'm serious!" I say. "Let's go order martinis!"

"Martinis?" Cecile's head swivels unsteadily as she looks from face to face to face. We are all seriously out of drinking practice.

"Whatever you want, Abby," Paula says, looking dubious.

"Great!" I say. "Let's go!"

We flag down Chantal and declare our intentions. She looks at us like we've just crawled in from the hinterland. "It's Friday night, ladies. You gotta have reservations."

The girls can see I'm crushed. Holding up an index finger, Paula turns and heads for the bar. She's back in five minutes to report we will have the next open table.

"How?" we ask.

"Bruce is the GC on their patio project out back. I guaranteed the project will be complete by the end of next week if they get us a table in the next ten minutes." Paula's husband is the most reputable general contractor in Franklin County, and everyone knows it's because Paula runs him hard. If she says the job will be done by the end of next week, it will be done by Wednesday.

We pay our tab, and, sure enough, in ten minutes we are walking through the swinging doors to the Rainbow Room. The place is dotted with couples, some leaning toward each other in private conversation, some focused on sparsely occupied plates. Most look up as we tumble into the room, speaking in our McAdams voices. We adjust quickly, but not quickly enough to avoid glares from some of the more reserved guests.

Instantly I regret dragging the girls over here.

We situate ourselves around a tiny table, and Paula can't stop herself from remarking how much more room we had in McAdams. She's right. I'm about to admit as much, when I spy Johnson and Ashley with their heads together, looking over paperwork spread between them. Johnson has his back to me. All Ashley has to do is look up to see me, and, just like that, she does.

Her gaze slides over my inebriated crew, and a look of satisfaction settles on her face.

I avert my gaze so she cannot start waving to me and thus direct Johnson's attention to our table. If I work fast, I can get us the hell out of here.

"Hey, girls, my mistake. Let's blow this pop stand and head over to Julio's!" I grab my purse and attempt to stand without knocking over the flimsy bamboo chair.

"No way—I wanna martini!" Paula whines.

"We can get you one at Julio's!" I say, tugging at her arm.

"They don't have martinis," Paula says, folding her arms across her chest.

"Sure they do. Anyone who has vodka can make a martini," I say, trying to get both my hands under her locked elbow.

At this moment, Cecile—docile as summer rain, and to her own horror—lets loose a man-belch of monumental length and depth. Paula and I freeze, half in shock, half in awe.

Cecile's hand flies to her mouth. Paula pounds her on the back with a resounding "Atta girl!" and I turn to see Ashley grinning in amusement while Johnson stares wide-eyed at Cecile. Slowly his gaze shifts to me and recognition dawns in his eyes.

Just as he puts it all together, the saloon doors bang open and Phil and his boys burst in singing, "Happy birthday to you, happy birthday to you, happy birthday"—and here they gather around me, each on one knee—"dear Abby, happy birthday to you!"

Phil holds up a cupcake with one candle nearly burned down to the frosting. "Make a wish!"

I glance over Phil's head toward Johnson, who is now turned completely around in his seat, taking in the entire scene, bemused. This throws me for a moment, but then I look at these nice men in their suits, and at my girlfriends grinning crookedly at me from their seats. They have worked hard to make tonight special for me, their friend who has been absent too much over the past year. I owe them this little wishing ritual. Who cares what Johnson Keller or his conniving little assistant thinks?

With an exaggerated wink at Phil, I say, "I'll put your fire out." Closing my eyes, I wish for peace in my little universe and blow out what's left of the tiny pink candle. Whoops go up around our table; polite applause surfaces from dark corners of the room.

"How did you know it was my birthday?" I ask Phil, placing the cupcake on the table, where Paula deftly hacks it into bite-size pieces.

"Joe was lamenting to Chantal that the prettiest women this side of Burlington happen to be lesbians, and, after laughing her ass off, she set us straight about the true nature of tonight's celebration."

The maître d' materializes and advises the suit boys that unless they have reservations, they must return to McAdams or leave the premises. It is at this moment that Cecile, still docile as summer rain, still aghast at her earlier man-belchability, and still clutching her margarita from next door, lurches hard to her right and vomits on the maître d's shoes.

Oh, shit.

"You idiot!" squeals the maître d'.

Tears immediately leak out of Cecile's eyes as she presses a white linen napkin to her mouth. "I'm so sorry," she moans, unable to take her eyes off his shoes.

"Sorry!" He points pointlessly at his shoes. "Who let you in here, anyway?"

Whirling around, I am ready to take him on, but Phil, a dashing prince in Brooks Brothers, already has him by the lapels. "The lady," he says slowly, nose to nose, "said she's sorry. Now take your eyes off your cheap, fake-leather shoes and look at her."

The maître d' looks to Cecile, who is hiccuping into her napkin, still unable to take her eyes off the oozing mess on the floor.

"Does she look sorry to you?"

"Yeah."

"That's because she is. Is that good enough for you?"

"Uh, yeah. Yes."

"Excellent," says Phil, releasing the maître d' with a shove. "Now throw an extra two hundred and fifty bucks on my tab next door for new shoes. You can get some real leather kicks for that and can consider this your lucky day."

Two busboys appear, one with a mop and bucket, the other with a bottle of disinfectant and a plastic grocery bag. The maître d' removes his shoes and places them gingerly into the plastic bag. As the busboys clean up the mess, all the suits except Phil head back into McAdam's.

I thank Phil for stepping in. "I'll cover the shoes. It's the least I can do."

"The best two-fifty I've spent in a year," he says. "Your friend looks mortified."

We both look at Cecile, crumpled against Paula, who is dabbing at her with a fresh napkin and stroking her strawberry-blond hair.

"She's never done anything like that, ever," I say. "She's the quiet one. She will relive this as the worst moment of her life, and she'll think she's ruined my birthday."

"Well, if there's anything I can do . . ." Phil says, gazing at Cecile, his eyes soft.

"Phil, are you a nice guy?" I ask, squaring to look him in the eye.

"Phil is a nice guy."

I glance around to see Johnson standing there, a big grin on his face.

"Really?" I ask, "I'm serious, Johnson. Because Cecile is amazing, and before I—"

"He's really, really nice. He's kind of a geek. Tries to act like a ladies' man, but he's not, and deep down, he doesn't want to be."

"Hey, I'm standing right here!"

I turn back to Phil. "So, do you agree with Johnson's assessment?"

"Well," Phil says, thinking it over, "yeah, he pretty much nailed it."

"Excellent. Then you can call my friend Cecile tomorrow." I reach into my purse for paper and a pen, scribble Cecile's first name and number on it. "Ask if she's feeling better and, if so, if she would consider going out with you tomorrow night."

"Will she go out with me?"

"I have no idea. Just your asking will make her feel better, and that's all I care about. No guarantees. Is that okay with you?"

"Yes."

"Good." I hand him the notepaper.

"Okay," he says, standing awkwardly with the note his hand. "Well, it was nice meeting you, Abby."

"The pleasure was all mine. Thank you so much for the cupcake and chivalry."

Phil bows deeply in my direction, then in the direction of my two friends, who are still wrapped around each other. They glance up vaguely and wave to Phil, then he exits the Rainbow Room to rejoin the suit boys next door.

Sighing, I turn toward Johnson, and all the events of the evening flood over me, leaving my face hot with embarrassment. Johnson steps closer, and I hold up my hand. I have no idea what he's going to do, but I don't want a scene in front of the girls, who don't know who Johnson is or what he is to me. Hell, *I* don't know what he is to me.

"Johnson, look, I'm going to go home now with my friends."

"Okay, sure. What time shall I pick you up tomorrow?"

I blink at him.

"Dinner?"

"Are we still on?" I ask.

Johnson laughs. "Hopefully you'll have two entertaining evenings in a row." And before I think to stop him, he plants a solid kiss on my Dangerously Red lips. "You are *smoking* in that leather jacket," he whispers before turning on his heel. I watch him head back to his table, and enjoy Ashley's obvious displeasure.

Then I turn back to my table to see my wonderful, tipsy girlfriends staring at me, jaws dropped, eyes bugging out of their respective heads. I've got some explaining to do.

~

The next morning, Olivia and I get up early to be at the Adventure Center in Stowe by eight o'clock. We're groggy and grumpy, but game for our orienteering lesson. Stella wasn't kidding—Drew Davis is drop-dead gorgeous, with a brilliant smile and a head of thick, gel-spiked blond hair. He is also gay, a detail Stella could never spot.

We spend the first hour receiving instructions and watching a twenty-minute video on what happens if you don't listen to your instructor. Then we are ready to head into the woods. Drew hands us each a compass. Olivia hands hers back, takes out the one Stella gave her. Drew whistles softly. "May I?"

Olivia hands over the piece for Drew's inspection. "This is superb," he says, and Olivia beams.

Drew hands us a map with various locations highlighted. We have two choices: compete or collaborate. We agree for this first foray, collaboration is best. For the next ninety minutes, we alternate between bumping heads over the map, arguing about how west you can go before you're going east, and high-fiving over found landmarks.

On the way home, we snort over the cheesy course-completion certificates Drew gave us. But I know I will save mine in my keepsake box, a token of a fun day spent with this cantankerous and complicated girl.

~

We celebrate our orienteering success with a huge plate of pasta. The phone rings on the kitchen wall, and we let it go to voice mail. It's Liza again. Olivia avoids my gaze as her friend leaves yet another message. "Olivia, it's me. A bunch of us are heading to the movies. Just wanted to know if you could join us." There is a short pause. Olivia feigns inattention. "Okay," Liza continues. "Well, we're going to the nine o'clock if you want to meet up." Another pause. "I miss you, Olivia." The machine clicks off.

Olivia twirls her pasta without looking at me.

"Olivia," I say gently, "why don't you call Liza back, tell her you'll go?"

She looks up. "I'm exhausted, Abby. We've been up since the crack of dawn."

This is true, but it's not the reason she won't go.

"Why don't you call her and tell her what you did today?"

"She won't get it."

I open my mouth to protest but sense I am in dangerous waters and could drown in my own words again. I try another tack. "I have a date tomorrow night. Maybe you can have Liza over, order pizza or something."

"With Johnson Keller?"

"Yes, actually. For a birthday drink."

"You've been seeing him a lot."

I smile involuntarily; my face warms at the thought. It has been a long time since I felt this way, and who would have thought it would be about Johnson Keller? "Yes, we've been spending time together. Does that still bother you?"

Olivia rolls her shoulders. "His family is just . . . well, they're different from us. Mom always said they were."

"Well, your mom—"

"What about my mom?" Olivia says, suddenly defensive.

"Your mom didn't like anyone with money, even after she had money," I say with exaggerated seriousness, trying to lighten things up.

"She especially didn't like Johnson Keller," Olivia says, standing up. She takes her plate to the sink, rinses it, and places it in the dishwasher. This practiced end-of-conversation move of hers is getting on my nerves.

"Why did she trust him with her will?"

Olivia pauses, then shrugs as she turns back to me. "Who knows?" she says, leaning against the counter. "I just don't want you to think that because she let him handle her will, she would have approved of you seeing him."

"I wouldn't need her approval, Liv. Besides, it's just been a few dates."

"It's more than that!" Olivia yells, taking me off guard. "How stupid do you think I am? You're not just sleeping with him; you're falling for him!"

"Olivia, that's . . ."

"Tell me it's not true!" She stands akimbo, glaring. "It's just a matter of time."

I spread my hands. "What's just a matter of time?"

Olivia clamps her mouth shut and stalks out of the room.

Bolting from my chair, I follow her up the stairs. "Olivia, talk to me."

"Leave me alone!" she screams, slamming her door in my face.

I place my palm to the door. "Olivia, please."

"Just leave me alone!"

Something clicks in my head. "Olivia," I shout at the door, "I won't leave you!"

But I know she already has her earbuds in place. Pressing my back to her door, I slide to the floor. I sit long enough to go stiff, then rise slowly to go clean up the kitchen.

Monday morning I sit with Jaime Thauvette, plotting ideas for the Spring Fling, Harmony's annual fundraising event. He wants to stick with a garden party. It's been successful for seven years, so there is no reason to change, but I am hell-bent on doing something different. I just don't know what. Jaime is chiding me for being stubborn when Rothschild enters my office.

"Hello!" I smile and get to my feet.

Rothschild waves me back into my chair. Standing awkwardly, he clears his throat, pulling at the thin skin of his Adam's apple with his thumb and crooked forefinger.

Jaime and I continue to smile at Rothschild, our lips growing strained with the sustained effort. Finally I say, "Mr. Rothschild, what can we do for you?"

"Oh," he says with a start. "Your paper has been published in *Museum*." He drops a copy of the glossy magazine on my desk. On the cover is a reference to my paper "Ode to Grecian Urns: A Journey Across Time in the Greek Isles."

I sit in stunned silence.

Jaime does not. "'Ot damn!" He leaps up and runs around my desk to give me a bear hug. "That's fantastic!"

I pat Jaime on the back, too stunned to speak. I blink at Rothschild. "But how—"

"I hope you don't mind. I submitted your work for consideration about eight weeks ago. You were distracted at the time," he says delicately, avoiding my eyes, "so I took it upon myself to submit on your behalf. We did fund the research, so I thought it would be appropriate. Perhaps I should have—"

"Oh, no, no. Thank you so much!" I say, rising to my feet again. "I'm pleased you thought it was worth submitting."

"Well," Rothschild says, looking perplexed, "of course it was worth submitting. It was a great piece of work, Ms. St. Claire. Top-notch."

Guilt floods my veins, but this is not Rothschild's fault. How could he have known what this would mean? "Well, thank you," I say, extending my hand.

Rothschild accepts my gesture, shaking my hand with a surprisingly firm grip. "It was my pleasure, Ms. St. Claire. We are honored to have your piece represent our establishment's commitment to history and the arts." Rothschild releases my hand, then turns smartly on his heel and disappears down the hall.

I turn to Jaime. "Wow."

"*Oui!*" Jaime exclaims as he picks me up and swings me around.

After shooing the sexy Frenchman out of my office, I sit, head in hands, taking it in. *Museum* isn't just any magazine. It is *the* magazine of our industry. I should be heady with excitement, telling all my friends. Instead, I feel like a pile of dog crap.

My trip to Greece was the adventure of a lifetime, complete with a blog that had one faithful daily follower among a few intermittent readers. Stella showed up every day to read about my latest exploits, from artwork to food to ruins to ocean-side revelations. She posted comments regularly, encouraging me to go deeper, get out more, talk to everyone, write everything down, go to Crete while I was at it. So I did all that, and took great notes, and my sojourn to Crete became the foundation for my paper. All the way home, I worked out in my head how I could pull all that together into a paper worth publishing.

Then Stella got sick and I got scared. As Stella declined, my paper became my get-out-of-Stella's-death-free card, and I used it to avoid the ugliest days of those nine months. Through all of it, Stella cheered me on. On those days when guilt drove me to her bedside, she waved me away, refusing to speak so I would leave and work on the project. We were in this ruse together. She knew I couldn't handle her death. She didn't just let me off the hook; she pulled me bodily off the hook. And in the end, I simply let her.

Now this paper, produced at the expense of my best friend's dying days, is published in *Museum*. How can I enjoy this?

"You just say, 'I'm going to enjoy this.'"

I shut my eyes tighter, press my hands over my ears. Shaking my head, I moan, "It's wrong, Stella."

"Like I want this on my conscience too, Abby. Come on, sweetie, look at me."

I look up involuntarily, blinking away tears clouding my eyes. "I can't see you."

"Okay, that's true. So just listen to me."

My hands slide down to the back of my neck. "Okay. What do you want to say?"

"We were two friends tossed into a shitty situation and did the best we could. Was I supposed to sit through those months watching you watch me die? Seriously? So stop feeling bad. You worked hard and deserve to enjoy it. That's all I have to say."

She is gone, if she was ever there. I sink back into my chair, my head back in my hands. Am I hearing Stella? Or telling myself what I want to hear? What is the truth?

The truth is, I kicked ass in Greece, wrote a quality piece worthy of publication, and deserve this moment. Though Stella grounded me, holding my fingers to the keyboard for revision after revision when I would have preferred to dream about my next adventure, I did the work.

Going forward, I need to ground myself.

"Abby?"

I blink a few times to get my bearings.

"Am I disturbing you?" Penelope, the new intern, asks from the doorway. Her tiny frame seems barely able to support the mass of wavy, dark hair surrounding her lovely olive face. Her dark eyes are apprehensive.

"No!" I say, smiling at her. "What can I do for you, Penelope?"

"Well, I just wanted to say I read your piece in *Museum*."

"What did you think?"

"It was awesome," Penelope says, stepping into my office. "The way you wove in the logistics, nobody ever talks about that, and your descriptions were so vivid, and, well, I felt like I was right there with you."

"That's nice to hear."

"Going to Greece has been a dream of mine. My ancestors are Mediterranean."

No. With that hair and skin? My smile widens.

"Now I feel like I've almost been there. I just wanted to tell you that. And, well, this is lame, but I have a copy and I was wondering . . . would you autograph it?"

I burst out laughing, and Penelope immediately flushes, casting her gaze downward. I reach for her free hand, hold it in both of mine.

She looks up, and I smile at her. "I would be honored to sign your copy. Thank you for asking."

Her face is like sunshine as she hands me the magazine, already open to my article. I drink in my own words printed across the page. I place the magazine on my desk, take the pen from Penelope's hand. *For Penelope*, I write in big, swirling letters. *Thank you for reading my piece and sharing your thoughts with me. But don't take my word for it. Go to Greece one day, see for yourself. Best always, Abby Solace St. Claire.*

Penelope is too shy to read it in my presence, so I give her a quick hug and send her on her way. Collapsing in my chair, I look up to the ceiling. "Nice touch, Stella Rose."

Part Two
Autumn

You say I am repeating
Something I have said before. I shall say it again.
Shall I say it again? In order to arrive there,
To arrive where you are, to get from where you are not,
You must go by a way wherein there is not ecstasy.
In order to arrive at what you do not know
You must go by a way which is the way of ignorance.
In order to possess what you do not possess
You must go by the way of dispossession.
In order to arrive at what you are not
You must go through the way in which you are not.
And what you do not know is the only thing you know
And what you own is what you do not own
And where you are is where you are not.

"East Coker," Verse III
Four Quartets, by T. S. Eliot

September

Another nightmare, Stella. I was flipping the calendar page to September and found every day captioned "Leukemia Day." Every single day. As though each day I had to remember all over again, and in that month I saw you diagnosed, getting sick, and sicker, until finally, on September 30, you died, even though you didn't die until June.

Some nights I dread going to bed.

Stell, I can't shake this feeling that everything could fall apart at any moment, and when I look at Olivia, the sensation intensifies. How could you stand knowing all that happens to young women these days? You're smirking, aren't you? Recalling all the times I exhorted you to stop worrying so much, told you your worry was manifesting every bump or bruise Olivia came home with. Yes, you were right all along.

On to lighter fare. Paula and Cecile kidnapped me on my birthday. We pulled up a chair for you at McAdams and took turns sharing the latest. You would have loved it, Stella. Our Cecile had quite an evening: she got drunk, vomited on an asshole's shoes, and wound up on a date with a nice guy.

Speaking of love lives, why did you never tell me Johnson Keller was even more handsome up close than at the distance you seemed to prefer? Though he likely crosses that line between confidence and arrogance at times, he is also thoughtful, kind, and always a gentleman. You might have underestimated him, Stella Rose.

September arrives balmy and brilliant. A wet August assured our maple, oak, and birch will reach a zenith of color as their pallet of orange and yellow, accented with scarlet and plum, spreads across the mountains north to south. "Man, it's like we live inside a postcard," Olivia, not moved by much these days, admits grudgingly as we drive in for the first day of school. With her mass of dark hair pulled back in its perpetual ponytail, summer freckles splashed across her nose, she looks like she's heading for kindergarten instead of her last year of high school.

As we drive down our winding road, maples arc over us, a kaleidoscopic tunnel toward the city. Over the next four weeks, the leaves will transition from canopy to carpet, the branches will resemble thin hands grasping for each other. I never look forward to our long winters, and this one looms interminable and desolate.

Dropping Olivia off near the entrance of Fairleigh High, I wish her a good day. "You, too," she says, before disappearing into the throng of students wearing expressions of detachment, too cool to be interested in life.

As I maneuver the car around the driveway loop, I see Jason Riendeau leaning against the brick wall of the school. He is surrounded by other boys, but his gaze is locked on the entrance to the main campus building. I glance in that direction, see Olivia and Liza facing each other near the large double doors. Liza is talking; her hands move energetically. Olivia nods and backs away a step. More chatter from Liza. Olivia shrugs, turns, and heads inside, leaving Liza standing alone, looking deflated. I feel a pang of sympathy for her; she has obviously not moved beyond this best friend she has lost.

Glancing back at Jason, I see his gaze linger on the entrance door a moment then return to the boys, seemingly half-listening to the conversation. I close my eyes. "Stella, what is going on with Olivia? Why is she shutting out her best friend, and why is this boy who dumped her obviously still crazy about her?"

I look to the passenger seat, picture Stella sitting there, her brows furrowed. "Abby, who the hell knows? But we need to figure it out, so pay attention!"

~

After work, I head for the mall. I hesitate outside Hollister, then enter its dim interior and immediately feel ancient and large. Two stick-figure girls call out to me in singsong, "Welcome to Hollister!" When they see I'm old enough to be their mother, they lose interest and busy themselves refolding tiny tank tops.

Walking deeper into the store, I feel like I've entered a cavern far from the mall, with music pulsing from the walls and large, illuminated pictures of tanned young men perched on surfboards inside blue-green tubes of curling water—absurd to me in landlocked and soon-to-be-snow-socked Vermont. I find the men's/boys' section and accost the first guy I see, a West Coast transplant whose wildly coiffed 'do must look outrageous anywhere outside this store. "Is Jason Riendau working today?"

"He's in the back, getting polos," he says, flashing a too-white smile.

At that moment, Jason appears with a stack of polo shirts. He spots me and stops, places the stack on a table. We stand awkwardly until California Boy excuses himself to stand elsewhere.

"Jason, I was hoping we could talk."

"Sure. What about?"

"Olivia."

"Ms. St. Claire," he says, looking around the noisy store, "I can't talk about anything but clothes while I'm working."

I suppress a smile. "Do you get a break?"

"Twenty minutes, at seven o'clock."

"Do you mind meeting me at Starbucks?"

He pauses. "Sure, I guess so."

"Thanks, Jason. I'll be waiting for you."

Jason arrives promptly at seven. We order lattes and find a table in a quieter corner.

"So, Jason, what exactly happened between you and Olivia?"

Jason, clearly uncomfortable, grips his heavily creamed and sugared coffee.

I press. "Everything was fine; then, when Stella got sick, you disappeared."

"It wasn't quite like that."

"Then how was it?"

"I admit I was freaked out by Ms. R's illness. It was bad, and Olivia was, well, different."

"She was going through hell, Jason."

"I know that. I do. I told her I understood, or was trying to. But she wouldn't open up. She just kept pretending everything was okay, and that freaked me out even more."

I blow on my coffee but maintain eye contact. The kid looks sincere.

"So," he continues, "I tried to pretend, too. Things were going along normal and all; then, well . . ."

"Then what?"

He looks around the crowded café, then leans across the tiny table, inches from my face. "Then she started talking about wanting to have sex."

I give him a sideways *oh, come on* look.

He leans back in his chair. "I swear." He crosses his heart. "I'm not saying I hadn't been heading down that road. Ms. St. Claire, I've loved Olivia since the sixth grade. I'd been dreaming about—"

"Jason, I get it."

"Right. So I backed off once Ms. R got sick. I figured the last thing Olivia needed was pressure. When she started coming on hot and heavy, I didn't know what to do."

"You didn't know what to do," I repeat, deadpan.

"Yeah," he says, defensive. "Look, I don't know what she's told you."

Not much, I admit to myself, but say nothing.

"But that's what happened. I didn't know what to do. I said I didn't think it was a good idea with her mom sick and all." He runs a rough hand through his buzz cut. "I said it should be about us loving each other, not some reaction to her mother's illness."

"That's a mature assessment," I say, unconvinced.

"Well, that's what I said, more or less, and she freaked out. Totally freaked out. She told me to get out of her life, she never wanted to see me again."

"So that's that. You let her go because she got mad and told you to get lost. She was upset. You could have checked back in a few days to see if she got over it."

Jason shook his head. "I did check back. Every day for two weeks. I left voice mails, text messages, I tried to talk to her at school. She unfriended me on Facebook. She avoided me like the plague."

"Still, she needed you, Jason."

Jason sputters, "Needed me? Needed *me*?" Now he is angry. "She made it clear she didn't need me when she—" He stops, takes a gulp of his coffee, then glances out the window at pedestrian traffic.

Something inside me goes cold. "When she what?"

"Nothing. Look, I hope Olivia gets past all this." He stands.

I grab his wrist, implore him. "When she what?"

He sits back down, looks hard at me. "You're taking care of her now, right?"

I nod.

"Then you should know. After a couple of weeks chasing her around, I found out from one of her friends that she'd started sleeping with some guy at another school."

My heart stops. I realize I shouldn't have assumed Olivia was a virgin at sixteen, but this news shocks me.

"Who?" I ask automatically.

"It doesn't matter."

"Who?" I glance around the crowded café as though the culprit could be any of these pierced, tattooed, tie-dyed punks. Suddenly I despise them all.

Jason takes a deep breath, then shrugs. "A kid named Matt Keller."

My heart stops again, and I wonder how many times this can happen before I have a full-on heart attack. "Matt Keller?"

"Yeah, you know him?"

"I know of him."

"Then you know his father and grandfather are hotshot attorneys. Loaded. He spread it all over his private school and our school, the stuff Olivia was into." Jason struggles to keep his composure. "I wanted to kill the guy. The only thing that stopped me was thinking that maybe this was what Olivia wanted. So I let her go."

Jason's loss is palpable.

"I'm sorry, Jason."

"Me, too," he says shakily. "I'm sorry I couldn't be what Olivia needed."

We are quiet until Jason excuses himself to return to work.

～

My next date with Johnson is a disaster. We barely speak over drinks, and when he asks what's wrong, I ask him to take me home to nurse a headache. In the driveway, he leans over to kiss me on the cheek.

"Matt slept with Olivia," I say.

Johnson stops inches from my face. "What?"

"You heard me."

"How do you know?"

"Everyone knows—everyone at FHS, anyway, though I suspect lots of kids at Camden Academy know as well," I say, my hand on the passenger-door handle.

"And you're just bringing this up now, after weeks of—"

"I just found out this week. You didn't know Matt slept with Olivia?"

"Christ, Abby, I don't keep track of who Matt sleeps with!"

I stare at him, incredulous.

"What?" he says, spreading his hands. "Abby, he's seventeen. He's having sex. It's what kids do. Look, you're in way over your head here. You haven't spent the last seventeen years raising a kid."

"Screw you, Johnson."

"Abby . . ."

I wrestle with the door of his BMW, finally make it out and onto the driveway.

"Abby!" he shouts from inside the car.

"Don't bother to call," I say, slamming the door.

∼

Over a breakfast of bagels and low-fat vegetable cream cheese, Olivia says nothing about my puffy eyes or lack of humming. I am grateful for her discretion. I simply don't know what to say to her about anything, and for the first time in a long time, I'm content to let silence prevail. Olivia is driving herself to school, so I excuse myself and put my dishes in the dishwasher before heading out.

"Have a good day, Abby."

"You, too." I pause at the swinging door, then continue without another word.

Johnson was right. I *am* in way over my head.

∼

On my way home from work, my phone dings, and at the next red light I read a text message from Olivia. She is going to Pizza Pie with some friends. Really? It's about time. I pull into the shopping center and text her back, "See u later."

Deciding friendship is contagious, I call Paula, chide her into joining me at McAdams for a beer. She calls Cecile, and within the hour we are all sharing a pitcher of Magic Hat #9 and heaping plates of nachos and potato skins. Cecile confesses she has seen Philip twice a week since that fateful night in August and she likes him. A lot. Sloshing our beer mugs in a lusty cheer, we spend the next hour gleaning details.

Finally, and surely in an effort to divert attention, Cecile asks, "So, how is Mr. Johnson Keller, Esquire?"

Paula and Cecile put their pretty chins in their respective palms, elbows on the table, and lean toward me in anticipation. I was dreading this moment, but now that it is here, I am relieved.

"I have no idea," I say, taking a long sip of my nearly drained mug.

"Oh, shit," says Cecile, grabbing the pitcher, refilling my mug and theirs.

"Oh, yeah," I say, taking another long sip.

"Fuck him," Paula says succinctly, raising her mug.

"Fuck him!" Cecile and I cheer, sloshing our mugs together once again.

"Fuck him!" cries Chantal from behind the bar, raising her club soda in solidarity.

"Fuck him! Fuck him!" comes a chorus from around the crowded pub as glasses are raised to me and my predicament.

I love this place.

~

I enter the house just as Olivia pulls into the driveway. "How was your evening?" I ask as she comes through the door.

"Fine. Yours?"

"Great. I met the girls at McAdams for a bite to eat. How's Liza?" I ask.

Olivia looks confused, then says, "Oh, I didn't go out with Liza."

"So who?"

"Cherie. She's in my chem class."

Chem class? "Just the two of you?"

"No, a group of kids, but she's the only one I really know."

I don't push by saying how nice it is that she's getting out. I am figuring out that less can be more, that more can be too much.

⌒

Rob missed a visit in August, and though she said it didn't bother her, Olivia was thrown. So when he calls to say he is coming for her birthday, I can see Olivia girding herself for disappointment. I call Rob later that evening to make damned sure he will follow through, and he assures me he will. He sounds sincere, and contrite for missing August.

"I do love her as much as Stella did," Rob says.

I know this is true. It was hard to outlove Stella. Without her here, it is easier to see that others do love as much, perhaps just not as overtly.

Though I invite Rob to stay at the house, he insists on getting a room at the new Hilton downtown. I suspect this has less to do with his professed sensitivity to our routine and more to do with Wife #2's jealous tendencies. Her concerns are unfounded, but appearances are everything to Savannah. Grudgingly, I admire Rob's consideration of her feelings. She got a good man, that's for sure, and Stella helped make him that way.

Rob commits to driving Olivia to school each day for the five days he is in town, and to taking her out to dinner each night—except Wednesday, which is Olivia's birthday. Olivia's mood visibly lifts when Rob arrives. I am glad for this, but that small, jealous person inside me chafes. On day three I realize this is how Stella felt every time Olivia was around Rob. Now I get it.

⌒

Wednesday morning I am up early, preparing a breakfast of all Olivia's favorites: my special eggs in toast, pancakes, Vermont maple syrup, sausage and bacon—why choose on your birthday?—and fresh fruit, for color. Beside her plate is a small gift box. I agonized all week over what to get. Surprisingly, my mother bailed me out.

"Music," she replied simply to my instant message expressing consternation at what to get a seventeen-year-old who is becoming more of a stranger every day.

"Music? What kind?" I typed back.

"Your kind."

"She won't like my kind."

"You don't know that, and that's not the point. Gotta run!"

Then what is the point?

Olivia shuffles into the kitchen, stretching and yawning off sleepiness from a late night spent on her computer. The incessant dinging of IMs let me know she was not studying, but I'm glad she's communicating with friends again.

Her eyes brighten at the sight of the table, and she gives me a quick hug before taking her seat. I sit across from her and start in on my own, smaller version of breakfast. Halfway through, she picks up the gift box, eyeing it critically.

"It's no big deal," I say quickly, suddenly sure my mother was completely off base. Why ruin a perfect track record?

"I'll be the judge," Olivia says with a Stella grin, tears open the package. She lifts the gift card, reads the accompanying note. *The Beatles: The Complete Box Set.*

Suddenly I don't care if Olivia likes the gift or not. I want her to have this piece of her mom's history with me. It's more than music, this complete box set. It's—

"Cool!" Olivia says, getting to her feet. "I'm going to download it right now!"

"But your breakfast . . ."

"Thanks, Abby, I'm stuffed. I want to get this in my iPod before school, okay?"

"Sure," I say, and smile to myself as she dashes out of the kitchen, leaving the door swinging in her wake. *Nice going, Mom.*

~

That evening, we all have dinner together at the house, followed by chocolate cake with chocolate frosting and chocolate ice cream. Rob then presents Olivia with a brand-new snowboard, boots, and bindings, and she is over the moon.

When Olivia goes upstairs to study for a history test, Rob and I retire to the living room with a glass of wine.

"She seems good," Rob says, pointing to the ceiling.

"She's better now that you're here."

"Really?"

"Really. It's going well, but she—we—have our ups and downs."

Rob smiles. "It's a lot to take on."

This snags me, and I get defensive. "It's not so bad."

Rob's smile turns sympathetic. "I just know what a handful she is."

I relax. "Funny how you and Stella always raved about how perfect Olivia was, and now you tell me all the flaws!"

"Ah, that's being a parent. We want everyone to see only the best in our kids, and we keep all the weirdness and demon-seed tendencies to ourselves."

"Some days I do feel overwhelmed," I admit.

"Me, too," Rob says, leaning over to clink my glass. "Me, too."

~

Rob leaves around eight thirty, and by nine Olivia and I are seated in the attic, holding our respective boxes, Olivia's festooned in HAPPY BIRTHDAY paper and bountiful ribbons. The charm on my box is a tiny ballet slipper. A delicately wrought, sterling silver, beautiful ballet slipper.

Inside the box lies a sheet of stationery, neatly folded to fit perfectly. I pull out the letter, and below lie four theater tickets. I don't need to read them; I know what they are.

"What are they?" Olivia asks, peering into the box.

"Tickets. To *Giselle*."

"Oh. That sounds like fun," Olivia says uncertainly.

"Yes, it does." I unfold the beautiful, rose-scented stationery. My eyes well at the sight of Stella's handwriting, growing more wobbly, evidence of the weakness settling into her bones, but it's Stella. I hear her voice echoing mine as I read aloud.

Dear, dear AbbySol,

Giselle. Have fun. That's an order! Okay, more like a strong suggestion, even a plea. Whatever it takes. Though it's not what you are about right now, it is what you were about at one time, and that piece of you lives on. Reconnect. It will guide you.

When I think of the last time I saw you in toe shoes, I always smile. You didn't get to see yourself. Hopefully this Giselle will be half as inspiring. If she is, keep the vision of her with you, as I keep your image with me.

And if not for your own sake, then for the sake of our girl, who is turning seventeen. Remember when we turned seventeen? What an amazing year! We saw our first Beatlemania, remember? We sang and danced in the aisles, knew all the words, impressed those a generation older with our adoration for these musicians who changed the world. This is what I would give to Olivia if I could—that feeling of passion and limitlessness, sheer inspiration. This is what I would reflect back to you, my lovely friend, the limitlessness I've seen in you so many times—not just in toe shoes. Show our girl that dreams don't have to die; they just morph, if we are lucky—and vigilant—into our real lives. We can't stay seventeen forever—thank God. But we can stay inspired and passionate. We can sing—and dance.

Love always to you, my lovely friend.

Stella Rose

Olivia stares at me, mouth agape. "How did you know?"

"I didn't." The real question is, how did my mother know?

"How many tickets?" Olivia asks.

I extract them from the box and fan them out. "Four."

"Who will you bring?"

"Well, you, for one, if you want to come."

There is a short pause. "When is it?"

"July."

"That's so far away."

"Yeah, you have to get tickets way in advance, Olivia. It's kind of a big deal."

"Well, sure, I guess I'll go. I don't have anything planned for July right now."

"Great. Okay, Liv, what have you got there?"

We examine Olivia's charm. It is different from mine. It is a tiny sterling silver depiction of the comedy/tragedy masks. "I detect a theme," I say.

"Uh-huh," Olivia agrees as she removes the ribbons from her box. Inside lie an envelope and a letter from Stella. Olivia grabs the letter and unfolds it hungrily, clearly yearning for her mother's presence, even in words on a piece of paper. She reads in a whisper:

> *Dearest darling birthday girl,*
> *Herein lies . . .*

Olivia breaks off and looks at me. "Always a lawyer," she says, rolling her eyes.

> *Herein lies a registration form for acting lessons with Hector Patrizzi. He is here for an eighteen-month run of Shakespeare Theatre at the Flynn, and also he will be working with two area schools, including yours, on their drama programs. He will work with you in individual sessions twice a week from now until you leave for college. If you work hard and meet his expectations (which should be a snap if you meet your own, which are always higher than anyone else's), he will write a letter of recommendation for entrance to the performing-arts school of your choice.*

This is a gift you may choose to accept or decline. I respect your right to decide. I know it seemed at times I discouraged you from pursuing this path. But, as we have discussed in recent months, I want you to live your dreams. It's unnerving how many clichés crowd my mind these days with truth written all over them. Life is too short to spend it doing what your mother thinks you should do.

Be happy, my darling. If acting makes you happy, then, by all means necessary, ACT. I will be in the balcony at all your performances, leading the standing ovations.

Because this is a special day, you have two presents. Putting this DVD together helped me deal with the fact that I won't see you leave your teens, grow into your twenties, become all of who you are in your thirties. Spending time with these memories helped me see so clearly the amazing woman you already are, and are destined to be.

Love now and always, always,
Mom

Slowly Olivia refolds the letter and places it reverently on the floor under her crossed legs. She removes the registration form from the envelope. "This must cost a fortune."

"Stella made sure that won't be your concern," I say confidently, knowing my best friend has taken care of this, along with so many other things.

"How did she afford all this?" Olivia looks at me.

I don't want to tell her that death has its financial benefits when you're a lawyer for an insurance company.

"I mean, we weren't poor, but Mom was always telling me we weren't made of money whenever I asked for stuff."

"Your mother was good with money," I say, hoping this will suffice, and for now it seems to satisfy Olivia. "So, when will you start?"

"I don't know," says Olivia. "I'm pretty busy."

This is a lie, but I let it go. She probably doesn't feel much like acting these days. Time is relative when you're dealing with endings and a new, unasked-for life.

"When you're ready," I say, and leave it at that. "Do you want some privacy opening your other gift?"

Olivia pauses, then nods slightly. "I think so," she whispers.

"Okay," I say, patting her shoulder as I get to my feet. "I'll be right downstairs if you need me."

Ten minutes later, Olivia steps into the kitchen, where I am heating water for tea. "Can you make some for me and bring it to my room?"

"Sure, hon."

Turning out lights en route, I make my way to Olivia. She is in bed, propped up on pillows, and has made a nest for me right next to her. I settle in as she points her remote at the small flat-screen in the corner of her room.

For the next two hours, we watch clip after clip of Olivia's seventeen years. Stella didn't miss a milestone. There's Olivia sleeping in Rob's arms in the hospital, creeping across a crazy quilt, naked in the tub, splashing water onto the camera lens; her first steps, her first words, her first day at nursery school, kindergarten, elementary school; her Brownies debut, t-ball, soccer; her first school play, her second school play, every single school play; dance, eighth grade graduation, a sports banquet; a school trip, a camping trip, a trip to Europe, to California, to Wichita.

Of course we never see Stella—she is always behind the camera. But we hear her voice, clear and strong, cheering Olivia on, marveling at each achievement, in a thousand ways telling the world how proud she is of her little girl, who is seventeen years old today.

∼

The next day I'm deep in the details of a key estate when Johnson calls, just before noon. "Can you meet me today to talk?"

I take a moment to breathe. It has been more than two weeks since I've seen his face. Smelled his skin. Felt his hands . . .

"Abby?"

"Today's pretty busy."

"I want to set some things straight."

"About Matt?"

"About . . . a lot of things."

In spite of my reservations, I'm intrigued—and, I admit only to myself, suffering massive withdrawal. "Lunch?"

"TJ's?"

"Fine. I'll meet you there in fifteen." My hands tremble slightly as I place the phone in its cradle.

~

I'm right on time, but Johnson already has an iced tea sitting in front of him when I'm shown to the table.

We both know what we want, so we order right away. The waitress takes our menus and leaves us to an awkward silence.

"So," I say finally, "you called."

Johnson tents his fingers under his chin, his lawyer pose. "I talked with Matt."

"And?"

"And he responded predictably. Denial, then bravado. 'None of your business, Dad. We're not hurting anybody, Dad.' All that stuff."

"And?"

"He says this was all Olivia's idea, and—"

"Olivia's idea?" I fairly yell, leaning back from the table.

"Listen to me."

"Listen? Listen to you repeat Matt's lies? I may not be a parent, but I know men's bullshit when I hear it, Johnson."

"I want you to know I took what you said seriously. I didn't just let it go."

"No, you just listened to his side of the story and want me to think he's some kind of angel in all this!"

"No, Abby. This is a difficult situation; please don't make it harder."

I hate that he's right. I am picking a fight because I don't want to hear what Johnson is saying. I take a breath. "All right. I'm listening."

"Okay," he says, eyeing me warily. "Matt didn't go into detail, which is just as well. He just said Olivia was well aware he was telling folks about them and that she was okay with it. He swore she actually started it. He also said it's over, has been over for months. Apparently it was a short . . . relationship."

Taking this in, I nod for him to continue.

"I asked if he embellished. He shrugged his shoulders. We had a . . . lively discussion about how men should talk about women, about propriety, reputation."

"Sounds civilized," I say.

"Well, it wasn't, actually. I'm paraphrasing. There was a lot of shouting and yelling and f-bombs—on both sides."

This gets to me. I see the pain of a father facing facts about his son, about himself. Grimacing, I reach for his hand and give it a brief squeeze. "Thank you," I say, "for having the conversation."

"It was long overdue. I will be spending more time with Matt over the next few months, Abby. I want to thank you for that."

Awkwardness stretches between us again, and we're both grateful when our sandwiches arrive. After a couple of bites, I ask, "What else did you want to talk about? You said there were a lot of things to set straight."

Johnson becomes visibly uneasy, and I think for a moment he is going to choke on his sandwich. Taking a long draft of his iced tea, he clears his throat. "Stella . . ."

"Stella?"

"Stella had a way of, well, getting her way."

I feel my stink-eye coming on, and Johnson can see it coming, too.

"Listen to me, Abby. I want to explain my relationship with Stella."

"Good, because I've been wondering—why you?"

"Why me?"

"Yes, why you were the partner she asked to handle her estate." Johnson looks perplexed, which irks me, so I add, "Considering how she felt about you."

"How she felt about me?"

Sighing, I lean forward to whisper, "You weren't her favorite lawyer at the firm."

"Oh," Johnson says, suddenly smiling, "that was probably true."

"So why did she have you handle her estate?" I ask.

"That caught me totally off guard," Johnson admits. "Stella asked a lot from the people in her life, and some things we never saw coming. Your situation, for example. A year ago you were single, free, unencumbered, traveling to Greece—"

"How did you know about Greece?"

"Abby, my point is that Stella asked a lot from you. I told her it was too much to ask, in my opinion."

"In your opinion. In your *professional* opinion?"

"In my professional opinion, in my parental opinion, and now in my personal opinion, yes," Johnson declares, placing his napkin over his half-eaten sandwich.

And it hits me. All the doubts, all the fear, all the feelings of inadequacy and resentment crash over me like a tsunami. Finally somebody gets it; somebody knows how I felt. Had the guts to tell her, to tell Stella Rose it was too much to ask, too much to expect, too much to pull off. Johnson knew it before he even knew me. But then . . . then he got to know me. And now he is convinced he was right all along.

And this pisses me off.

"So." I slowly place my own napkin over the corpse of my Monterey chicken sandwich. "You told Stella this was too much to ask, without even knowing me?"

Johnson blinks at me.

"And after the last few weeks of getting to know me and watching me struggle with Olivia, you are convinced you were right, Stella was wrong, and"—I look him dead in the eye—"I am unfit to take care of Olivia."

"Abby, that's not what I'm saying!" Johnson reaches for my hand, which I snatch out of his grasp as I lean forward.

"That's exactly what you're saying. I'm glad you set that straight. I might have missed it otherwise. So while we're thanking each other right and left here, thank you, Johnson, for that vote of confidence in Stella's maternal instinct and in my ability to take care of the most precious thing in my life right now." Johnson opens his mouth to protest, but I put up my hand. "While I'm sure there are plenty of other things you want to set straight, I've run out of time." Rummaging in my purse, I pull out a ten-dollar bill, toss it on the table. "You'll have to find someone else to straighten out."

As I stand and turn to leave, something in the way Johnson says, "Abby, wait!" makes me turn around. His face is contorted, and for the first time I see him struggling for words. Finally he says, in a voice so defeated my resolve begins to crack, "I'm sorry."

"Me, too," I whisper, and through blurry eyes find my way out of the restaurant.

October

She *lied* to me, Stella Rose. She said she and Cherie were going to the movies. Nope. They got piercings. Cherie sports a belly ring, Olivia an industrial—a fourteen-gauge *spike* driven through the cartilage across the top of her left ear. I was nauseated at the sight. And how did I see it? Well, that's the best part.

Post-piercing, Olivia called for permission to spend the night at Cherie's. I said yes, because that's what I do these days—say yes, yes, yes. When she came home from school the next day, she went straight to her room. At dinner, I noticed her hair was down and remarked on the nice change from her perpetual ponytail. She shrugged her shoulders in the new Olivia communication style.

Days went by, Stella—a week, even—before I caught sight of metal through the curtain of her hair. "What's that?" I asked, reaching toward her.

"Nothing!" she shrieked, smacking my hand away.

"What is it?" I demanded, hands on hips.

"Just a piercing."

Just. A. Piercing. Like an anaconda is just a snake. Finally, she confessed to lying about the movie and setting up poor Trish Shoreham, Cherie's mom, as an unwitting participant. Rather than act contrite, she became defiant. "It's my body, and I can do what I want!"

"Maybe, but you shouldn't have lied about it."

"You wouldn't have let me do it."

"You'll never know now, will you?"

This stopped her in her tracks. Of course I would not have let her mutilate herself like that, but she didn't even give me a chance to be the bad guy. Until now.

"You're grounded."

"What?"

"You heard me."

Then she said something I could not believe: "Mom never grounded me. Ever."

Stella, you raised this girl to sixteen and never once grounded her? So now I am the guardian from hell.

The trees, so brilliant a week ago, stand nearly naked and shivering in the strong gales of October. I'm never ready for winter—ridiculous, after nearly forty years. Even the rose garden is more ready than I; the Rose Whisperer has seen to that. He has pruned several bushes to nubby sticks, covered others with snug burlap sacks. The rest look dangerously thorny, forbidding in their increasing leaflessness.

While Olivia remained stoic throughout her groundation, I couldn't wait for that week to end. I wish we hadn't decided to open Stella's boxes just before Halloween. Opening Stella's boxes seems to bring us closer, and we could use an excuse for closeness right now.

I'm discussing the latest ideas for the museum's Spring Fling with Jaime when I receive the customary text message from Olivia: she and some friends are going to the mall after school. Olivia's friend aversion is a distant memory. I've encouraged her to bring these new kids to the house to hang out, but she always demurs. I'm particularly concerned about Cherie, the new BFF in Olivia's life. She's no Liza.

Paula calls to check in and, when she hears I'm on my own, invites me to dinner. Though I would rather get more work done, I realize this could prompt another intervention, so I accept.

Over plates of steaming shepherd's pie, I do my best to track the dramas of two teens, a tween, and a weary Bruce, who has spent fourteen hours at his latest project, for a particularly difficult homeowner. By the time they all wander off, I'm exhausted, but Paula bounces to her feet and pours us each a glass of pinot, fortification for cleanup.

Somewhere between loading the dishwasher and wiping down the countertops, this intrepid mother of three energetic but seemingly normal kids helps me reach the conclusion that I cannot control Olivia's relationship with Cherie—or anyone, for that matter. Her exact words: "Total freaking waste of time."

"Focus on you," she says before downing the last drop of her second glass of pinot, "and *your* time with Olivia."

"Developing my relationship with her," I say, nodding.

"No, no, no," Paula says with a snort. "It's about spending time with her. All that quality-over-quantity crap is just that—it's bullshit. With kids this age, it's about quantity. They can smell a setup from a mile away, so don't force anything; don't try to develop a relationship or get inside her head. Just be there. Be the sponge."

"Be the sponge?"

"Absorb everything she says, does, doesn't do. So when she squeezes you all that stuff will come out and she'll know you've been paying attention. That's all they want. To be heard, seen, understood, loved. In that order."

I blink at Paula, gaze out the steamy kitchen window, and vow to be the sponge. I remain concerned about not having met Olivia's new friends, but I tell myself to trust her judgment, even when her room smells faintly of cigarette smoke and even though she never leaves her purse lying around anymore.

$\sim$

My resolve is sorely tested when I get a call from the school. "Ms. St. Claire? This is Owen Montagne, Olivia's faculty advisor."

"Yes?"

"Are you available to talk at some point this week?"

"Is something wrong?"

"I'd like to talk about Olivia's progress so far this year. A successful senior year is critical to getting into college and laying the ground-work for—"

"The rest of her life. Yes, I understand. You sound concerned."

"No specific concerns. I would like to touch base, considering everything that has happened in her home life." His voice is steady and reassuring, but I cannot relax the knot forming in my stomach.

"Of course, Mr. Montagne. I'm sorry if I sound . . . difficult."

"I'm sure it's been a difficult time. Are you free any day this week?"

It's the worst possible week. "I'm afraid we have class trips every day this week. Everyone is getting their field trips in before the budget vote next month."

His laugh makes me smile in spite of my anxiety. "Well, I can be flexible," he says. "We could meet over coffee after work one day, if that's better."

"That would be great. Can we meet tonight at five fifteen, or is that too soon? To be honest, you have me worried."

"I don't mean to worry you. Tonight would be fine. You work at the Harmony right? Would you like to meet at the Coffee Pot?"

"Perfect," I say, and hang up. I take five deep breaths before heading out to greet Ms. Rainville's second-grade class.

~

Rothschild calls an impromptu staff meeting right after lunch, setting the museum staff buzzing. "I give him two months," declares Peggy, the staff accountant.

"Two months for what?" I ask, settling into the chair next to her.

"Retirement."

"Who?" I ask, glancing around the table. They all stare back at me as though I have just returned from Pluto.

"Rothschild, of course," snorts Dave, head of Shipping and Receiving.

I turn to Peggy. "Why do you say that?"

"It's been going around for months," Peggy says, then stage-whispers, "Then Ann left paperwork in the copier . . ."

I hate it when that happens. "And?"

"And," she says, drawing in the room with a conspiratorial glance, "it was a draft of a resignation letter to the board."

A collective "oooh" travels around the table.

"Signed by Rothschild?" I ask.

"No, but it was clear who the author was. And here's the kicker," Peggy says, leaning across the table. We all lean in closer. "He is recommending his successor." She sits back in her chair, a look of satisfaction settling on her broad, putty face.

Jaime can't stand it. "Who is it?"

"Well . . ." Clearly, Peggy lives for moments like these. "That's the big mystery. The sentence went something like, 'After careful consideration and months of preparation, I recommend *blank* take over the role of head curator of the museum.'"

As one we chorus, "Blank?"

"Yup, a big blank. My guess is, either he's playing it close to his chest—"

"Or," Janice says, cutting Peggy off, "he hasn't made up his mind yet."

We all glance at each other in consternation. Then Peggy hisses, "He's coming!" We straighten in our chairs as Rothschild walks in.

"Oh!" Rothschild says, looking surprised to see everyone gathered.

Jaime is on his feet in an instant, generously offering his own chair for the head curator. "Please," he says, almost bowing, "Monsieur Rothschild, you can sit 'ere and I will find another chair."

"Thank you," Rothschild says absently, holding the back of the seat but not sitting down. In a moment Jaime returns, rolling in another chair and seating himself close to Rothschild. I catch his eye and wink; he winks back with a wide grin.

"So," Rothschild says, clearing his throat, "I called this meeting to discuss a few pressing matters. First, I wish to recognize again Abby St. Claire's recent contribution to *Museum*. Fine writing and excellent publicity for our enterprise." Anemic applause. "Second, we are looking forward to the Spring Fling. How is that coming?"

I don't even bother to open my mouth. Jaime is already on his feet. "Coming along well, Monsieur Rothschild. I . . . I mean, *we*"—indulgent smile my way—"have several great ideas. Perhaps too many!" He laughs, and the women in the room oblige him with their own giggles. "This will be our best event ever."

"It'll have to be," says Rothschild, all frivolity lost on him. I sit up, attuned to the solemnity in his voice. "The board has enhanced expectations for this year's revenue targets. If we don't double our fundraising intake, we will be shut down."

We all gape at Rothschild.

"I'm not worried, though—this team can make it happen." With that, he turns to leave.

"Sir?" Peggy asks, unable to contain herself.

"Yes?" Rothschild asks, turning back to the table.

"Was there . . . anything else?"

Rothschild considers this carefully. "Oh, yes. I'm retiring in June."

~

At five fifteen, I walk into the Coffee Pot and scan the array of tiny tables. I spot a young man in black-framed glasses, short yet disheveled auburn hair, and a gray overcoat smiling and waving at me. Something in his friendly manner soothes me instantly. My shoulders relax as I head for his table. I smile and extend my hand. "Mr. Montagne?"

"Yes, it's nice to meet you, Ms. St. Claire." His handshake is firm, two-handed.

"Likewise." Shrugging off my coat, I hang it over the back of the lightweight chair, along with my handbag, and the chair tips over with the weight.

"I'll get that," Mr. Montagne says, leaping to his feet. He bends over for the chair at the same time I do, and our heads bonk with an audible smack.

"Ow!" we exclaim, each with a hand pressed to our forehead.

"Sorry," he says.

"No, thank you for trying," I say with a laugh as I right the chair. "Can I order you some coffee?" I ask, turning toward the counter, still holding my head.

"I was waiting for you, and I'm happy to buy," he says, holding my chair out.

"It's on me. It's the least I can do for keeping you after hours. What would you like?"

"Actually, I'd like some hot chocolate."

"That sounds really good. I'll have some, too. Whipped cream?"

"Of course."

I return in five minutes with steaming mugs of hot chocolate, whipped cream piled high and melting down the sides. We blow on our mugs. "So," I say, "what's going on with Olivia?"

"I'm not sure," Mr. Montagne says simply, his clear hazel eyes pensive. "I've known Olivia a long time, and she's been in my advisory group for three years. Ms. Rose never missed a parent-teacher conference."

"I won't either," I say quickly.

"Actually, the first rounds were held earlier this week."

"Already? I didn't . . . Why didn't the school contact me?"

"You should have received a notice in the mail."

I look at him blankly. Then I think, *Olivia.*

"Perhaps it got lost. This was a post-orientation/pre-parent-teacher conference anyway. We're a little anal about communication," he assures me, taking a sip of his hot chocolate. "Damn!" He mumbles something that sounds like "*I um eye ung.*"

"I hate that," I say. "Are you okay?"

"Fine, sorry," he says, running a tanned hand through his hair, sending it straight up in spikes. I suppress a smile as he continues. "Ms. Rose spoke highly of you."

"You talked about me? When?"

"Ms. Rose had me come see her near . . . I mean, close to . . ."

"The end."

Mr. Montagne nods. "When I see certain behavior in a student who at one time was very clear on her goals, particularly considering what she has recently gone through, and considering her mother's explicit request of me—I found myself dialing your number."

He clears his throat and continues. "Don't get me wrong—Olivia is a great kid. Her grades are holding, with only a slight slip in Calculus. Given her aspirations, this should not be a problem. That is, if her aspirations are the same as they were."

I raise my eyebrows but keep a fragile hold on my tongue.

"Have you talked to Olivia lately about what she wants to do next year?"

"Um . . . recently? Well, honestly, no," I say, sounding lame.

Mr. Montagne tries to bail me out. "Of course. With everything going on."

Something inside me snaps. "You know, I am so sick of everyone saying that! 'With everything going on.' Like that absolves me of my responsibility to know what the hell is going on with my . . . with Olivia. I don't know who she's hanging out with these days, I don't know how she's feeling, I don't know what she wants to do with the rest of her life. Hell, I don't know where she is right now, do I?" Pausing for breath, I see the look on Mr. Montagne's face and stop.

He says nothing. Instead he takes a tissue from his pocket, reaches across the table, and presses its softness to my cheek. Sitting stock-still, I let him press the tissue to the opposite cheek. I hadn't realized I was crying. Then he presses the tissue into my hand. This act of kindness unhinges me completely. I thrust my face in my hands and sob.

He gives me a fistful of napkins, and I go through each in a noisy, unceremonious manner.

"Will you excuse me a moment?" I say, my face still buried in sodden napkins.

"Take your time."

I rush to the bathroom and splash cold water on my face. Looking in the mirror, I see the truth. I am failing at raising my best friend's daughter. It's not like I had to raise her from scratch, for Christ's sake. It's just one year. And I'm going under. More cold water as I prepare to rejoin this patient school advisor, who is probably jotting down notes for Social Services or worse: looking up Rob's telephone number.

Mr. Montagne stands politely when I return.

"So, where was I?" I smile with flagging brightness.

"You were telling me something I hear from every single parent I talk to all year. You're experiencing distance from your teenager."

"So, you're telling me this is pretty common."

"Universal."

"What a relief. I'm a little new at this teenager thing."

"Yes, Ms. Rose told me you might need some . . . reassurance."

"I'm sure she also mentioned guidance, if not downright intervention."

He has the good taste not to answer, but the smile in his eyes assures me I am correct. "Ms. St. Claire."

"Abby."

"Ms. St. Claire—my policy—I met with Olivia last week about college tours, and she said she had no plans to date."

College tours—yes, this was on Stella's list of things to do this fall. But it's only . . . October. Christ, it's fall already. I flush a bit. "That's right, but it's on my to-do list."

"I can help with that. In fact, I've already pulled information on schools I thought would interest Olivia, mostly performing-arts schools, NYU in particular. But when I showed them to her, she said she was rethinking her plans."

"What does that mean?"

"She wouldn't get specific. I asked if she was going into a different area of study, and she said she might take a year off."

Shit. This was Stella's worst nightmare. "But they had it all planned out. I would take Olivia to NYU this fall, and maybe to Juilliard and UCLA. There's a special 'college visit' fund in the will. I know I'm a little late getting it going, but I never thought Olivia was actually losing interest in theater. And the lessons . . ."

"Lessons?"

"Stella gave Olivia acting lessons. Hector Patrizzi is in town, working on a Shakespeare series with the Lyric group at the Flynn. Stella arranged for weekly lessons. I bet Olivia hasn't even called yet. Why haven't I followed up with her? It completely slipped my—" I stop suddenly, realizing I've been rambling. This man must think I'm a lunatic. Why can't I stop talking? "I'm sorry," I say. "I'm babbling like an idiot."

"Not at all."

I eye him critically.

"Well, perhaps just a little. It's okay, Ms. St. Claire. Between the two of us, I'm sure we can figure out what's going on with Olivia."

"Do you know a student named Cherie? Olivia has been hanging out with her."

"There are a couple of Cheries. What's her last name?"

It escapes me.

"Do you know what she looks like?"

Each question reveals how little I know about Olivia's life. "I have no idea."

"Well, I'll keep my eyes open. One of the Cheries is quiet; I don't know much about her. The other one . . . well, not so quiet."

"Shoreham!" I blurt, recalling Trish's voice on the phone during that fateful piercing incident. "She's the latter, isn't she?"

Mr. Montagne smiles. "Olivia is a great kid going through a tough time. She'll be fine no matter who she hangs out with. And so will you. Maybe we should both do a little research this week and compare notes next week."

I appreciate his reassurance. "Great, Mr. Montagne. We can talk over the phone, and I'll call you from work so I don't take up your personal time."

He shrugs. "I have no social life."

"Me neither," I say. "But it's a personal choice."

"Same here, I suppose. I used to be fun." He smiles again. "Then I broke the cardinal rule . . ." His eyes widen as he suddenly realizes what he's just said out loud.

"Oh, dear." I smile to let him know it's okay. "What happened?"

There's a pause, then he says, "She died." He holds my gaze for a beat. "Well, I have to go. Let's talk Monday by phone and see where we are. If anything urgent comes up in the meantime, I'll call you. Thanks for meeting with me. Olivia is lucky to have you."

I automatically take his outstretched hand. He leaves me sitting in the café, my head spinning. *Stella, you do have a way of impacting everyone around you, don't you?*

~

At home, I find a note from Olivia saying she'll be home by nine o'clock. I warm up leftover tofu stew and plot my strategy. I don't want to overwhelm Olivia with questions and demands, but something must be done. I review notes from those last talks with Stella. Seeing my hurried scrawl, I remember those discussions like they were yesterday.

"Abby, I know you don't agree."

"I just feel that if you push Olivia too hard, she'll rebel."

"Personal experience, right?" Stella said, a slight edge in her voice. "Rebellion is so sexy, so much cooler than 'compliance' or 'planning' or 'doing what's best.' What if she goes too far, makes too many bad choices, closes too many doors?" The panic in Stella's voice seared my consciousness.

"Olivia is your daughter. She won't go too far."

"Abby, sometimes she is so stubborn. I swear she will take the opposite side of an issue just to get me going."

"Like I said, she is your daughter."

Stella was in no mood. "It's not funny. It's dangerous."

"She's sixteen years old! What can be so dangerous?"

"God, Abby! She could fall in with the wrong people! Meet the wrong guy! Drink one too many beers, have Ecstasy slipped into her drink, walk in the wrong part of town at night, decide to take a year off before college to *find* herself . . ."

"I get it, Stella. I'm sorry. Please stop," I pleaded, taking her hand in mine, stroking the damp hair from her eyes.

"I'm afraid I didn't do a good enough job. Does she have the right equipment? Is she who I think she is? Or has she been showing me what I want to see, humoring me, and deep down she's this whole other person?"

"Stella. I've known Olivia since the day she was born. I've watched you raise her. I may not have agreed with everything you've done"— Stella snorted at this—"but it doesn't mean you were wrong. It's much easier to raise a kid when you don't have one."

Stella smiled at me, her eyes full. "You are going to be a great mom."

"Stella, please. Olivia doesn't need another mom."

"Promise me one thing."

"Does this replace something else on the one-thing list, or do I squeeze it in somewhere?"

"This is one more one thing: help Olivia build a foundation of joy for her life."

I stared at my best friend. "Oh, okay, let me write this down. 'Help Olivia build a foundation of joy for her life.' And I am qualified to do this because . . . ?"

"Because you've done it, so you can show her how to do it."

"Stella, that's crazy!"

"Just write it down, okay?" Stella waved her impossibly thin hands at me dismissively. "You'll figure it out. You always do."

"Stell."

"I trust you, Abby. That's all you need to know." With that, Stella closed her eyes and the conversation was over.

~

Olivia comes in at exactly nine o'clock and catches me in the kitchen with my notes spread across the table. Hastily, I gather them up and shove them into the All Things Olivia file.

"What's all that?" Olivia asks, opening up the fridge and pulling out a Sobe.

"Notes."

"Oh," she asks, not interested. "I'm going upstairs. Homework."

"Olivia, can we have dinner tomorrow night, here, so we can talk?"

She turns at the kitchen entrance and asks warily, "What about?"

"It's nothing heavy. I just want to catch up with you. I miss you."

"Well, I had plans." Olivia sees my face and reconsiders. "But I can postpone them. I'll be here when you get home from work."

"Thanks," I say, and Olivia leaves me with my portfolio of notes and uncertainty about where to go next.

~

Olivia and I eat our pork chops and mashed potatoes in silence. "Tea?" I ask when we are both finished.

"Sure," she says, picking up both our plates. She scrapes crumbs into the trash before rinsing and loading the dishes into the dishwasher, and I get the tea started.

Steaming cups in hand, we resume our places at the kitchen table. "So, Olivia," I begin, trying to sound casual and not succeeding.

"So, Abby," she says, ready to spar.

"How are your grades?"

"Fine."

"Good. Do you like your teachers?"

"They're fine."

"That's good." I am not sure what to say next.

"You're supposed to ask me if I've made any new friends this year."

I look at her blankly. "That's in the *New Parents of Teenagers* handbook," she says sarcastically.

"Funny, Olivia."

"Abby, just say what you want to say, for Christ's sake."

I am stung by Olivia's attitude, but this is not about me. It's about Olivia and the rest of her life. My feelings stay at the curb. "Okay, Liv. What is going on with you?"

"My mother died four months ago."

"Olivia."

"That's what it comes down to, Abby—every conversation, every look, every day in the cafeteria. I just want to be normal again."

I remain quiet.

"I don't know what you want from me. You and everyone else. My grades are fine, I'm not falling apart, I'm doing the best I can. Why can't that be good enough?"

"Have you called Hector Patrizzi yet?" I ask, changing the subject.

"No."

"Why not?"

"Because I don't want to act anymore." She sees the shock on my face. "Seriously, Abby. Acting is for kids. I'm over it."

"But it's all you ever wanted to do!"

"When I was a kid! I think about it now, and I just think . . . it's not enough."

"Enough for what?"

"For a life!"

"And taking a year off to think about it is?"

"Who said I was taking a year off?" Olivia asks, eyes narrowing. I say nothing but hold her stare. "Who have you been talking to?" she demands.

"Not to you," I say. "But there are lots of people who know more about you than I do."

"Oh, so this about being the last to know? Am I making the wonderful best friend–slash–guardian look bad?" This hurts, doubly so because it is pretty close to the truth. "Look, Abby, I'll make you a deal. I'll tell everyone you're the best thing since my own mom, and you just leave me the hell alone. I can figure this out for myself." She pushes back from the table and stomps out of the kitchen, leaving the swinging door flapping.

"Like you figured out how to get rid of Jason?" I shout after her, unaware of what I am saying until the words hang in the room like thick smoke.

The kitchen door bangs back open and Olivia stands there, hands on hips, pale and furious. "What the fuck does that mean?"

My head snaps back at the f-bomb, but I hold my ground. "You know exactly what I mean."

"You don't know what you're talking about."

"Oh, yes, I do, and you know it."

"It's none of your business."

"The hell it isn't."

A shadow passes over Olivia's face, and fear creeps into her eyes. "Did Mom—"

"She didn't know." Her body relaxes, and I am incensed. "That's not the point!" I say, getting to my feet.

"Yes it is!" she cries.

"You could have gotten pregnant! Or caught some disease!"

"That wouldn't have happened."

"How naive are you?"

"It doesn't matter, as long as Mom didn't hear about it."

"So, as long as Stella never knew, then it's okay. As long as Stella didn't have to deal with this crap, it's all good. She got to die thinking her daughter was all that, and I have to figure out what to do with who you really are!"

Olivia staggers back, hands to her face as though I've struck her. She wheels around and flings herself through the door, leaving me alone with my hateful words.

~

On my way to my room an hour later, I stop at Olivia's door and knock. "Olivia?" I say softly. I expect no answer and get none. She probably has her earbuds in. I try the door, and it is unlocked. I knock again and slowly open the door. Olivia is sitting on her bed with a schoolbook open in front of her. She is looking at me, no earbuds. Her eyes look puffy but dry. "Olivia, I'm sorry for saying that."

"I know."

"Okay," I say awkwardly, and start to close the door. "Do you need anything?"

"Like?"

"Like, you know, birth control or anything?"

"I'm not seeing Matt now," Olivia says.

"Oh. Well, just in case . . ."

"Just in case I want to have sex with anyone else?"

I can only stare at this girl who is becoming a sullen, unruly woman before my eyes.

"I'm covered."

"Okay," I say, and close the door. When did I lose control of this situation? Did I ever have it? Did Stella?

~

The next morning I awake with resolve coursing through my veins. When Olivia enters the kitchen, I ask if she wants breakfast. She says no, she'll just grab a vitamin and juice. "Fine," I say. "I'll talk while you take your vitamin."

Olivia shrugs as she leans into the fridge for the orange juice.

"I want you to call Hector Patrizzi today and set up your acting lessons."

Olivia straightens, juice carton in hand, and stares at me. "It's a waste of money."

"It's not yours to spend or waste. It's your mom's."

"Mom said clearly in her letter that it was my choice."

"I'm overruling your choice."

"You can't do that! Mom would—"

"Support me one hundred percent on this. Olivia, she wanted this for you. She knew what made you happy. Even if you don't become a professional actor, you can still have acting in your life."

Olivia turns to me, her face a series of expressions before it finally lands on pensive. Her voice is quiet, tentative. "It's just that my head is so full right now. I don't know if I have room."

Though I want to ask what is making her head so full, I sense it is not the time to dig. I am just grateful she is talking.

"Tell you what," Olivia says, filling her glass with juice and popping a vitamin into her mouth. "Let's split the lessons."

"What?"

"Mom set up lessons for twice a week. I'll go once a week, you go once a week."

"Olivia, that's ridiculous. I don't act."

"Why not?"

"It's just not my thing."

She crosses her arms and stares me down.

"You're going to be late for school."

Still staring.

"For Christ's sake, Olivia."

"You always said you admired me for getting up onstage and speaking. It was always something you were afraid to do. Here's your chance. Why don't you just do it?"

"Damn, I hate it when you sound like your mother." I chew on a cuticle.

She's still staring.

Groaning, I throw my hands up. "Okay. I'll do it."

Olivia smiles, the wattage warming my heart and misting my eyes. Whatever hell I'm getting myself into is worth this thaw.

"Now get to school before I change my mind."

~

On Friday evening, Olivia and I meet with Hector Patrizzi. He is in his fifties, tall, painfully thin, with salt-and-pepper hair swept back from a high forehead and hanging just past his shoulders. His aquiline nose and smooth olive skin give him an exotic sex appeal. Olivia and I are intimidated out of the gate.

We meet at his studio, a rented space adjacent to the Flynn Theater with a built-to-order stage, a few chairs, and some props spilling out of a steamer trunk. The place is poorly lit—intentionally, I suppose—and we huddle together on three stools in a small pool of light in the center of the stage. Hector's booming voice fills the room, but Olivia and I can barely hear each other, our voices swallowed by the darkness.

I am up front with Hector about Olivia's plan, hoping he will help my cause by claiming I am simply too old to be taught and that Olivia needs at least two lessons a week to get the most out of his teaching. He fails me badly, choosing instead to take my lessons as a personal challenge. He advises Olivia to apply his lessons in the upcoming BFA production of *Annie Get Your Gun*. Olivia seems taken aback by this; surely she was not planning on actually acting in any kind of production, let alone the school's annual play. Instantly I forgive Hector for failing me. This is going to work out perfectly. Olivia looks in my direction. I purse my lips and raise my eyebrows twice. *So there.*

Olivia looks slyly back to Hector. "All right," she says. "As long as she"—she jabs her finger in my direction—"has to try out for one of your Shakespeare productions."

Before I can say anything, Hector wheels on me, beaming, and says, "But of course!"

Of course. I scowl at Olivia, and we turn to the topic of which nights of the week we will be in Hector's personal care. If we wish, we can have him the same evening—carpool, if you will. We will.

~

A week before Halloween, we carve two gigantic jack-o'-lanterns and set them on the front porch, tea lights in each. After admiring our handiwork, we head inside for mulled cider, then upstairs to Stella's room to open our October boxes. We retrieve the autumn leaves–covered boxes, each with a tiny silver leaf charm that we attach to our bracelets. I open my box, and inside rests a single orange sugar-maple leaf. It is starting to curl at the edges but is remarkably well preserved, as, I realize, Stella must have collected this leaf a year ago. I pull out the letter and read aloud:

Dearest AbbySol,

I have picked this leaf just for you. I do hope it survives the long winter, spring, and summer to find its way to you intact. Olivia is getting one as well. I would like you to place these leaves in the pile outside the house. (You have raked the leaves, right? Because if you leave them piled on the lawn, the grass will get a poor start in the spring.)

I cast a guilty glance toward Olivia, and she whispers, "We can rake tomorrow."

Then I would like you and Olivia to jump in these leaves. Why? I don't know. I can't think of anything for October except dressing up in costumes, and that seems too obvious. So I would like you to do with my daughter something I have not taken the time to do in too many years. Indulge me, please, my dear friend. Don't try to save this leaf. Don't keep it preserved somewhere as a morbid token of a dying woman's desire. Toss it into the leaf pile and revel in it, and revel in my daughter.

I do hope you are hanging in there and getting out some. Have you seen the girls? Please give them my best. I am sure I miss them all. Enjoy them, AbbySol. They are special women.

Love to you, my lovely, lovely AbbyFriend.

Stella Rose

I hear Olivia sniffle, but when I glance her way, she is already sliding the ribbon off her box, identical in size and shape to mine. Her leaf is brilliant red fading to burnt red at its own curly edges. Lifting it carefully, Olivia slowly spins it by the stem, the slight breeze lifting tendrils of her hair. "It's lovely," I say. She smiles at the leaf, places it gently back into the box, and takes out her letter.

> *My darling Olivia,*
>
> *I have given AbbySol a pretty autumn leaf as well. Please follow the instructions in Abby's letter carefully. Attention to detail is critical for success of the operation.*
>
> *Remember that last time we jumped in leaves? It was so long ago, too long ago, so you may not recall, but I remember clearly. I see you standing next to the pile, yelling in a lumberjack voice, "Tim-ber!" then falling straight back into the leaves. You fanned your arms and legs and squealed that you were making a leaf angel. Then I buried you in the leaves and you were so quiet, so quiet, and you never knew this, but for just a moment, I was scared. My heart stopped and I stepped toward the leaves to start pawing you out, when, suddenly and spectacularly, you exploded out of the leaves and grabbed me around the neck and pulled me down into the pile with you. I was so happy in that moment, Olivia, I thought my heart would burst.*
>
> *I have made so many mistakes, Olivia. I took things too seriously. I hope you never get too busy to jump in leaves or too serious to be silly or too worried about money to give up what you love to make a living.*
>
> *Love, love, love always and forever,*
> *Mom*
>
> *PS: Have you called Hector yet?*

We have learned our lesson by now and have a box of tissues between us, both of us already on our second round.

"Thank you," Olivia says, after noisily clearing her nose.

"For what?"

"For making me call Hector. This way I can tell Mom I've called him."

I give Olivia a look, and she shrugs her shoulders. "I talk to her sometimes."

"I talk to her all the time."

~

On Saturday we are up early and raking our butts off. By noon we have one huge pile as high as our chests in the middle of the front lawn. We take our gifted leaves and, in turn, toss them into the pile. Olivia runs the rake up and over the pile to mix our leaves in well. Then we stand with our backs to the pile, side by side, mittened hand in mittened hand, and together we fall in. We laugh up into the brilliant blue sky and the soul of Stella above us.

November

The Farmer's Almanac forecasts tons of snow this season. Your kind of winter, Stell. All I can think about is Olivia driving in it. The thought of her navigating these roads has become an obsession. Even Rob is nervous. I've had to assure him in three separate conversations that we had her snow tires mounted and balanced.

If only everything could be solved with snow tires. I don't even want to tell you what's going on with Olivia these days—as if I could, as if I knew. I mean, one minute we're holding hands through this thing; the next we're at each other's throats. But don't worry, we'll get through this. It'll be okay.

What's not okay is this acting business. Olivia is devious, Stella, which you failed to mention. Not one index card on sneakiness or cunning. Isn't it enough I have to act like a guardian? Now I have to act on an actual stage, with an audience, for God's sake. Did you put Olivia up to this, or is this one of those mother-daughter-osmosis things?

It's a monochrome day, Stella. The sky, the clouds, the mountains, the trees, all layers of slate, each heavier than the next, suffocating me. I think, *This is what grief looks like.* My eyes are heavy. I want to sleep all day, finally wake and tell you about a dream I had—how you went on a trip and didn't come home, didn't tell me about the places you saw or the people you met or the food you tasted. You kept it all to yourself.

Two days into November, the snow arrives. At first it's hesitant, huge flakes, intermittent as cell reception on I-89. Four days into November, it's full-on winter. We awaken to eight inches on the ground and trees bowing under the weight of snowy coats. I am grateful for the attached garage Stella loved so much. I never realized what a pain in the ass it was to sweep snow off my car every morning. I'm getting spoiled. I can barely remember the tiny apartment on High Street, with its creaky stairs and leaky foyer roof.

Olivia and I attend our first bona fide parent-teacher conferences. All of Olivia's teachers remark on how well she is doing, "all things considered." Though I knew Olivia was taking chemistry, I am surprised to learn that she has switched out of visual arts to do so. I am even more surprised to learn that Olivia is doing quite well in chemistry. The teacher, Ms. Godin, calls her a motivated student.

Owen Montagne looks dapper in a sport coat and tie and seems bashful in our presence. He shakes Olivia's hand and fumbles with mine as we squeeze into student desks to chat. "So," he says to Olivia, "have you decided which colleges to visit?"

Olivia looks at me, then back at him. "Abby wants to take me to NYU."

"That was one of the schools on your list, correct?"

"It was on the list last year."

An uncomfortable silence descends; I hear the soft shift of the second hand on the wall clock.

"We are going to visit a few in the city while we're there," I offer. "Performing-arts schools and liberal-arts schools."

"I could give you a list of good LA schools if you'd like."

"That would be great."

"Yoo-hoo! I'm sitting right here," Olivia complains.

"What other schools are you interested in?" he asks, attention refocused on Olivia.

"I'm still trying to sort it out," Olivia says. "I don't want to waste everyone's time until I know for sure."

"It's not a waste," I insist. "I love New York. I haven't been in a long time."

"We're going in July," Olivia reminds me.

"Yes, but you need to start applying next month." We get our mutual glare going, and Mr. Montagne deftly interrupts.

"Well, NYU is a good start. You might also want to consider colleges in the Boston area. Excellent schools, closer commute."

Olivia looks skeptical.

"Unless you are set on New York," he adds hastily. "What made you think of NYU in the first place?"

"Because it's where Abby went," Olivia says with a shrug.

This surprises me. "Really?"

"Of course," she says. "I knew that's where you went, so I wanted to go there."

"Is that why you don't want to go there now?" I ask quietly.

"No. Jeez." Olivia pokes me in the arm. "Don't be so touchy. I might still go there, just not to the Institute of Performing Arts."

"When are you going?" Mr. Montagne fixes us with an intent gaze, determined to get a commitment.

"Next weekend," I say. "They're having an open house."

"Excellent," he says. We discuss a couple more options, then it is time to go. He shakes both our hands, his grip sure now, warm and solid, two-handed.

~

Olivia drives us to our first official acting lesson. I am scared shitless, and she could not be happier. By the time we enter the dark studio, I am completely seized up. Olivia is five paces ahead when she realizes she is alone. Peering back into the gloom, she whispers, "Abby! Where are you?"

"Here," I croak, more like a question than an answer.

"For God's sake!" she hisses, coming back for me. I allow her to drag me to the small stage where Hector waits.

"Ladies," he says, and I can hear bemusement in his voice, though I can't see his face at all in the gloom. "Let's get started."

Sweat trickles from my armpits to my bra.

"What is acting?" Hector asks, as though he has no clue and is looking to us for enlightenment. I look at Olivia; she smiles and shrugs her shoulders. Hector looks from one to the other of us. He is willing to wait all evening.

"Okay, fine." I say, "Acting is taking someone's work, figuring out what it means, learning the material, and delivering a presentation to an audience—something along those lines." *That sucked. Serves him right.*

"Okay, and you?" Hector turns his inquisitive gaze on Olivia. She's ready.

"I just want to be someone else."

"Ah, but that is impossible," says Hector, no trace of a smile.

"It's possible. Just reject Stanislavski, Adler, Strasberg, and even Meisner, and go back to acting," says Olivia, warming up. "Stop using other people's words as a smoke screen to expose your own deep, dark secrets; stop injecting so much of yourself into the work—it's not your work. It's someone else's. Be true to their vision; don't let your ego get in the way. That's my definition of acting."

"What do you think of that?" Hector asks me.

"I have no idea what she is talking about or who any of those people are."

"Excellent," Hector says, rubbing his hands together. "Let's get started. Abby, come with me."

I glance at Olivia, then follow Hector off the stage area and behind the curtain, where, if possible, it is even darker.

Hector places his hands on my shoulders so that I'm looking

approximately where his face would be if I could see in the dark. "Okay, Abby, you have just lost a precious necklace, and you know the woman in the next room took it."

I inhale and exhale exactly three times before asking, "And?"

"That's it. That's all you need to know."

"What do I say?"

"Whatever you need to say."

"But—what are my lines?"

"Whatever you need to say."

"Ummm . . ." I'm shaking my head, and Hector opens his mouth again, but this time I repeat, "Whatever I need to say."

"Exactly!" He beams at me, the child who has just learned to tie her shoes.

Two minutes later, I glean a small measure of enjoyment at hearing Olivia exclaim, "But what are my lines?"

This might actually be fun.

My optimism evaporates the second I step into the stage area. There are five strangers sitting in folding chairs so close they're practically on the stage. "Who the hell are they?" I ask, gesturing at the audience.

Hector frowns and Olivia purses her lips. Two points for Olivia. Sweat pools in the small of my back as I tremble in a palsied fashion. My limbs will start flailing at any moment, and my mind is blank as the check Stella wrote for me to take care of her demon daughter, whose smirk is growing larger and larger. I want to strangle her, not because she took some frigging necklace but because she is eating this up.

This I can work with.

Stalking across the stage to where Olivia sits behind a desk in a tiny pool of light, I stab my finger in her face and snarl, "Wipe that smirk off your face."

In an instant, the smirk is gone and Olivia stares at me, a hint of fear in her eyes. She leans back in her chair, holding her hands out in front of her as a shield.

"That's better," I say, gripping the edge of the desk with both hands, leaning across the top and into Olivia's face. "Now, give me my necklace."

Olivia looks at me blankly. She has no idea what I'm talking about, and this throws me, but only for a moment.

"Don't look at me like you have no idea what I'm talking about."

"I have no idea what you're talking about," Olivia says, sounding sincere.

"Bullshit!" I shout. "You took it! I saw you!" *I did? Where? When?*

Recognition dawns on Olivia's face. "It was you!"

It's my turn to lean away.

"It was you!" Olivia repeats, getting to her feet. "In the pool!"

In the pool? What pool? "You . . . saw me?"

"Yes!" says Olivia, nodding enthusiastically. "Yes, you were . . . inspiring."

I step back, hands to my chest. "Me?"

"Yes, you! I watched you lapping the pool, and it was amazing. You were so intense. You never looked up; you kept your head down, stroking, stroking. I thought for sure you'd hit the walls, but you knew exactly where they were and instinctively curled just in time, launching yourself into the next lap . . ." Olivia is breathless, and I am swept up in her story. I smile in spite of my distress over the make-believe necklace.

Then I pull myself together. "I pay to have the pool to myself."

"I . . . wasn't supposed to be there."

"Damn right! What the hell were you doing, spying on me?"

"I was not spying on you! I was . . ."

"You were what?"

"I was running away!"

"To the pool?"

"It's a long story."

"Not interested. Why did you take my necklace?"

"I didn't take your necklace!"

"Of course you did. I saw you."

"You never looked up!"

"That's what you think. I did look up, near the last lap. You were just a shadow, shimmering above the water, and for a second I thought you were . . ."

Olivia steps closer to me. "You thought I was . . . who?"

Swallowing hard, I look into her face. "I thought you were her."

"Who?"

"The woman who gave me the necklace," I whisper.

Olivia touches my arm. "You loved her?"

"Yes," I whisper.

Smiling gently, Olivia asks, "Is it this necklace?" and she touches my throat.

My hand joins hers at my throat, a tear slips from my eye, and I say, "Yes. Oh my God, I always take it off in the pool. What was I thinking? Then I couldn't find it in my bag. Then the pool guy said he saw you leaving the locker room just as I was coming out of the pool area. He said you worked here, so I took a chance . . ."

"I saw it on your neck, in the water, glinting in the light. It was so beautiful, like a part of you, shining in the water."

Still gripping Olivia's hand, I ask her, "What were you running away from?"

"Who, and it doesn't matter. I found you in the pool and realized I don't need to run anymore. You found me, and I'm glad."

At this, Hector leaps to his feet, clapping. "Nice, ladies!" The other five audience members applaud enthusiastically. Olivia throws her arms around me, and I realize I am not the only one trembling.

~

On the way home, Olivia and I play the improv game, taking turns, building our own story one line at time. Though we both admit we were petrified in the beginning, we are fascinated with the process. As we pull into the driveway, I turn to her. "What did Hector give you as a prompt?"

"He said, 'You've seen this woman once before.'"

"That's it?"

"That's it."

~

As the weekend draws near, I sense I am the only one preparing for the trip to New York City on Saturday. Sure enough, by the end of the week Olivia develops a sniffle, and by Friday night she is flat on her back in bed. I cancel our plans and detect relief in her eyes. Suddenly she seems not so sick. With the holidays fast approaching, I doubt we will fit in a trip anytime soon, and I suspect Olivia is counting on this. But why?

~

Rob is flying Olivia out to San Diego for the week of Thanksgiving, so she and I open our November boxes the night before her departure. The wrapping paper sports turkeys—real wild turkeys—and our charms are exquisite sparkling snowflakes. Our boxes are identical, perfectly square, approximately ten by ten by ten inches. I open mine first, and Olivia and I laugh when we see the picture of the contents—a giant snow tube waiting to be inflated.

"Awesome!" Olivia exclaims, hugging her still-wrapped box to her chest. I read the letter taped to my box:

> *Dear, dear Abigail Solace St. Claire,*
>
> *Bet you didn't see this one coming. I know how much you hate winter. Same here. Why have we lived in Vermont our whole lives? I secretly think we love to hate winter. It gives us something other than our fellow man to direct our inner hostility toward. It also makes us hardy, makes us appreciate summer, blah blah blah. But enough of hating winter! Snow tubes are the best—and, incidentally, the least expensive—way to love winter. I invite you and my snow-averse daughter to embrace winter this year!*

Okay, so "embrace" may be too strong a word. Let's shoot for "tolerate" and see how it goes. Enjoy the snow tubes. Enjoy hot chocolate. Enjoy mulled wine with the girls. Enjoy, enjoy, enjoy!

'Tis the season for giving thanks, and I have so much to be thankful for. Don't get me wrong—I'm totally pissed about this cancer thing and often get mired in sadness over how much I will miss. But the truth is, I won't be missing anything, because I will be experiencing existence differently. So, rather than linger in that bad place, I know it is good to have this letter to write to you, a letter you will receive in the month of Thanksgiving.

List of things I am grateful for:

- *Olivia*
- *Abby*
- *The Girls*
- *TRW*
- *My garden*
- *Visiting nurses*
- *Sunrise*
- *Love affairs*
- *Cats*
- *Naps*
- *Travel*
- *Freedom*
- *Opportunity*
- *Art*
- *Music*
- *Solitude*
- *Morphine*
- *Memories*

What are you thankful for these days, AbbySol? Please tell me. I'm right here listening.

Love to you always, my darling AbbySol.

Stella Rose

PS: December's boxes: Please open them on December 10 and at the same time. Don't forget!

Hmmm. What Christmas surprise does Stella have in mind for us?

"What are you thankful for, Abby?" Olivia asks quietly.

Sighing, I lean against the wall, stare at the rafters. "These letters. The girls. This house, my job, my health." I glance at Olivia. "You."

Olivia nods. She pulls her box and letter into her lap.

Darling Olivia,

Is there any snow yet? November is so unpredictable—sometimes tons of snow, sometimes none. I hope the first good dump has you and Abby outside playing with the snow tubes. Just be careful!!! Don't be barreling down Hard'Ack hill—promise me!

I've been thinking a lot lately about what I will miss, which is also a list of all the things I am thankful for. As a mom, I want to write a list of all the things you should be thankful for, but I will refrain. Instead, I've spent the last week making a list from memory of all the things I was grateful for when I was your age. Here is what I recall:

- *Abby*
- *The Girls*
- *Aqua Net*
- *School*
- *The Beatles*
- *Books*
- *Teachers*

- *Whitney Houston*
- *Bon Jovi*
- *Boys*
- *Libraries*
- *School dances*

So, while I won't tell you what to be thankful for, I do implore you to make a list of what matters most to you. It's so easy to think about what is missing or wrong or frustrating, you can lose sight of the blessings right before you. When you are feeling low, that's when you need the list the most. I keep mine with me always now, and your name is at the top.

All my love and gratitude to you, my sweet baby.

Mom

We sit quietly for a moment before Olivia says, "If Mom can make a list when she's dying of cancer, I suppose I have no excuse."

"I know what I'll be doing at bedtime," I say, gathering my wrapping paper.

"You know even when I'm being witchy, I am thankful you're here."

"Sure," I say, getting to my feet. I hold my hand out to Olivia, and she takes it.

~

Sunday morning, I awake to a note from Olivia saying she has some business to do and will be back by ten o'clock to leave for the airport. Her carry-on sits by the door.

Promptly at ten, she comes in, stomping snow off her feet and rubbing her hands together. "Ready?"

I pull on my coat, and on our way to the car I ask, "Where did you go?"

"Had to take care of some things," Olivia says, then quickly changes the subject to tryouts for *Annie Get Your Gun*, which is the week after Thanksgiving. I am pleased to hear it's on her mental calendar, though I'm sure she switched topics to head off more questions about her morning activities.

As we stand outside security, I run down the list of necessities: toothbrush, toothpaste, extra underwear, a book to read on the plane.

"Abby, if I forget anything, I can get it in San Diego," she reminds me.

"Right. And you know what to do in Chicago, right?"

"I've done this plenty of times," Olivia says, impatience creeping into her voice.

"I know, I'm being—"

"A mom."

After an awkward beat, I say, "You need to get through security now. Give me a hug." I wrap my arms around her, and she drops her pack so she can put her arms around me, too. I realize I am going to miss her.

I let her go and help hitch her pack back onto her shoulder. "I'll call you when I get to Chicago," she says, and waves at me as she joins the line. I loiter in the waiting area, discreetly watching her go through security and find a seat in her gate area. She pretends not to see me as I wait until her flight is called. She gets into line, hands over her boarding pass, and heads down the Jetway. Three steps in, she turns and waves at me with that "gotcha" grin on her face. Smiling, I wave back; then she is gone.

~

Standing at the patio doors in the kitchen, I steep my tea and look out into the backyard. That is when I see the tracks—Olivia's—fresh from this morning. Squinting, my eyes follow her progress around the garden, forming a wide arc to the left, coming in near the top, then back out, then . . . I see it. Olivia has formed a huge heart around the garden. A lump forms in my throat, and I blink back tears.

I set my tea on the counter and head to the foyer to get my coat, hat, and gloves. I pull on my boots and trudge out back. Olivia tramped around the garden several times to form a distinct heart shape. Then a single set of tracks enters the garden. I follow them, knowing where they will stop. In the center of the garden, at the entrance to the wild-rose section and Stella's ashes, is a perfect snow angel. I am sure she talked with her mom this morning about this cheesy trip to the West Coast, where she will see Wife #2 and the half brother who is spoiled rotten and seventy-five-degree sunshine on Turkey Day, for God's sake, and she could be snowboarding.

I sit on the garden bench near Olivia's angel and take in the somber landscape. Shadows creep in from the woods, hinting at the darkness that comes early this time of year. My voice, sudden as a gunshot, slices the gray silence.

"Stella, I'm in trouble here." I pause, hoping I have her attention. "Why the hell didn't you tell me what a minefield this would be? I can say all the right things for days; then—boom!—I blow it big-time."

Pulling my jacket closer, I listen to the wind rattling through the naked rose canes. "Seriously, Stell. It's not like I remember every single detail of our teenage years. Was it this bad? If so, our moms were saints—*saints!*—not the monsters we thought they were."

I think about my mom in Arizona with her third husband, Howard, and how she dropped like a stone out of my life after my high school graduation. She barely finished high school, and college was beyond her. She made it clear that my brother and I were on our own when it came to figuring out the college game. She was surprised that we managed to find our way through it all.

But not as shocked and amused as she was about my being saddled with a teenager. "This is perfect!" she said when she called last month. "No grandma angst and all the satisfaction of watching you try to handle a teenager. Instant karma." When I broke down last week and asked her for teen parenting tips, she had this gem: "It's a crapshoot—gut instinct mixed with prayer, faith, and hope. That's all it ever is."

My thoughts roam to Stella's mom, and how young we all were

when she was killed, trapped in a stalled car on a railroad crossing. That was the story in the police report. Stella always believed her mom had picked the day and time of her own death, planned it all out—the before, but not the after. The after was left to Stella—taking care of the household, the finances, and her own dad until he drank himself to death ten years ago. Christ, it's amazing any of us turned out halfway sane.

I sit bolt upright on the bench as it hits me.

"God, I get it, Stell! All the notes, the lists, the letters, the packages! You couldn't control the before, but you would sure as hell control the after." Laughing, I leap from the bench, reach up to the sky, and shout into the bottomless gray, "Stella Rose, I miss you!"

I let myself fall back into the snow, perilously close to Olivia's angel. Initially I feel warmth as the snow cradles me; then coldness seeps in through my jacket and snow melts into my hair and I feel alive. Slowly I fan my arms up over my head, then down to my sides, over and over, creating my wings as I scissor my legs for my angel gown. Satisfied, I carefully get to my feet and hop out of my lovely snow angel. Standing back a pace, I can see my right wing blends into Olivia's angel's left. Holding hands.

⁓

I make my way inside the house, climb onto the sofa, pull the comforter over me, and shiver myself into a tiny ball. So this is what grief feels like. A cold, icy hand squeezing my heart; a red-hot spool of wire scoring my brain, searing my memories, burning images into my soul.

⁓

"What's your name?"

"Abby. What's yours?"

"Stella Rose."

"I've never known a Stella before."

"It means 'star,' for your information." Hands on hips, chin sticking out a mile.

"Well, Abby is—"

"A church."

"That kind of abbey is spelled with an 'e.' Mine's Abigail, like Abigail Adams, John Adams' wife."

"What's your middle name?"

"None of your business."

"Oh, it must be good. What is it?"

"What's yours?"

"I don't have one. Come on, tell me yours."

"You don't have one?"

"Nope. Don't need one. Let me guess yours . . . Hortense."

"No, of course not!"

"I'm going to tell everyone it's Hortense if you don't tell me what it really is."

"No fair."

"Life's not fair."

"Solace."

"What?"

"Solace. That's my middle name."

Silence. Eyes wide.

"It means—"

"Comfort. It's the most beautiful word I've ever heard."

"You're making fun of me."

"I'm not. Abigail Solace St. Claire. Sounds like a movie star."

"Now you're making fun of me."

"Stop being paranoid. I would like to have a friend with a cool middle name like Solace. I can hear 'soul' in your name, like 's-o-u-l.'"

"Soul?"

"Yeah, soul. I will call you AbbySol."

"Don't you dare."

"Well, not in public. You are obviously paranoid. It'll be our secret code."

"What will I call you?"

"I don't have much to work with."

How wrong she was. There were all sorts of nicknames over the years: Starry Eyes; Starlight; Rosie; and my favorite, Stella My Rose. But none stuck for long. Stella Rose was perfect. Her mom got that right. But her middle name could have been Loyalty.

~

As I stare through the darkness to a ceiling I can't see, Stella's face floats before me, shifting over time, her flat hair, pronounced overbite, dark and stormy eyes; her permed and large hair, braces, indigo eye liner and smudgy mascara; her hair parted in the middle and feathered, brilliant smile, eyes that light up a room; her hair pulled back, confidence replacing makeup. Then there is no hair, anywhere. Her eyes loom large in deep sockets without eyebrows or lashes to rein them in, ringed in darkness, dim, extinguished.

"Stell?"

"AbbySol?" A whisper, a croak.

"Yeah, it's me." A hand, light as paper, caught in two hands cold and trembling. "I'm sorry, Stell—"

" . . . Okay."

"It's not okay. Cancer's not okay. Desertion's not okay. Stop saying it's okay."

"Okay."

Two small smiles, one weak, one desperate.

"What color is it?"

"All the colors of the most vibrant rainbow you can imagine."

Color leaps out of the small gift bag, rich, luxuriant, obscene. Eyes flicker with delight, cracked lips part in an exhalation of appreciation. Off with the old, tufts of soft baby hair; on with the new, moon-face in the mirror, eyes that see only color.

"Beautiful."

"Yes, you are."

"You're blinder than I am."

"Maybe, but I know what I see."

Eyes on mirrored eyes.

"I see forgiveness."

"Forgiveness?"

"I know why you've been . . . away."

Guilt, an undertow, drowning. "Stell . . ."

Thinnest of hands waving, a branch in the wind. "I know why, and it's okay. You forgive me. Olivia told me."

Told her? I sit up on the couch, eyes closed, trying to hold the memory. Olivia told her what? I was so wrapped up in guilt at abandoning Stella in those last days, I didn't fully understand the details of that conversation, assumed it was Stella's confused state as she prepared for death. I thought she was talking about forgiveness for her leaving me by dying, which was ironic, considering I had left her way before that. But now . . . now details return, and I wonder: Was there something else?

"Stell, there is nothing to forgive. None of this is your fault."

"Cancer doesn't absolve all sins."

"Cancer is not the ultimate penance."

Relief softens the lines between the hollow eyes. "So this isn't my punishment?"

"Of course not!" Shock punctuates each syllable.

"Because I couldn't bear it if you and Olivia had to share my punishment."

"Christ, Stella, stop this right now. This is just some act of cosmic chaos. It doesn't matter what you ever did—everybody screws up, Stella Rose. Everyone makes mistakes, and we've made our share of serious ones. You are a good person. You have made me a better person. You are better than I'll ever be, Stella. Christ, if cancer is your punishment, I can only imagine what mine is!"

"Abby, don't say that!"

"Then stop it, Stella. Stop it right now. Just be with me, okay? Just two flawed friends trying to get through this. Can you do that for me?"

"Okay." A tired ghost of a whisper.

"Thank you, Stell."

"I love you."

"Always."

"Always."

~

I awake in a fog but make it into work for the half-day before Thanksgiving. Hearing everyone talk excitedly about their plans highlights a key piece of information for me: I have no plans. I always spent Thanksgiving with Stella, since Olivia went to her dad's. The rest of the girls had traditional holidays with their own families or extended families. We were the misfits. We went out to dinner and ordered anything but turkey. We came home with two bottles of good wine and a movie we rarely got around to watching. Hung over on Friday, we would vow to do things differently next year, and never did—until now.

The roiling starts in my stomach.

I could call Paula, but how pathetic would that be? My dad isn't an option because he's still in Idaho helping his girlfriend settle her parents into Assisted Living care. I could call my brother, but I don't feel like driving four hours to Springfield, Massachusetts to listen to all my relatives talk about the ones who are not there. With my luck, they would forget I was in the room and start talking about me. "Hey, I heard since Abby started taking care of her friend's kid, the girl's become a drug-addicted sex maniac who dropped out of school."

The wall of grief and loneliness advances on me, and I start to panic. Am I relegated to watching the Macy's parade by myself?

Then I think of one other person who might possibly be spending Thanksgiving alone. Surely he has family of some sort . . . but maybe not.

I look up his number in the White Pages online and dial. On the third ring, I hang up. What the hell am I thinking? I pace the kitchen, reach for the phone again just as it rings under my palm. I pick it up. "Hello?"

"Ms. St. Claire? It's Owen Montagne. Did you just call me?"

I close my eyes and rap my head against the wall twice. "Yes, I did. I'm sorry about that. I thought no one was home, so I hung up."

"No problem. I was hunting for the phone. Never can find it when I need it. Is everything okay with Olivia?"

"Yes, sure, she's in California with her dad."

"Oh, that's good. I'm sure she misses him."

"Yes, she does." The silence stretches. "Well, I was just calling to . . ."

"Yes?" His voice is pleasant, patient.

"This is silly, but, well, I'm sure you have plans. I have no plans for tomorrow, none. I didn't plan well and don't feel like driving four hours to be with my crazy family, and I was thinking that you had mentioned your family lived quite a ways away, and I thought maybe—though probably not, but maybe—you were also spending tomorrow watching the Macy's parade by yourself and maybe you would like to spend Thanksgiving here." I inhale like an athlete who's just crossed the finish line.

"Sure," he says.

"Sure? What part?" I ask.

"Most of it, but especially the last part. I'd love to come over for Thanksgiving."

"Oh! Okay."

"Should I bring something?"

"Um . . ." I hesitate. I hadn't gotten this far in my head. "Well, I haven't given this much thought, actually."

"Second thoughts already?" he asks, his voice guarded.

"No!" I say, unable to convince even myself. "I haven't done this in years."

"Asked a guy over for dinner?"

"Made Thanksgiving dinner."

"Oh."

"Or asked a guy over for dinner, either, actually."

"What can I do to make this easier?"

I laugh, and he laughs, and we plan our attack on Thanksgiving.

~

All the turkeys left in the store are frozen, and it is too late to unthaw one of these mighty birds before tomorrow morning, so I buy the largest roasting chicken they have, along with stuffing in a box, potatoes in a box, real baby carrots, mixed salad in a bag, pumpkin meat in a can, piecrust frozen in a box, and Bisquick—what every cook needs to make a homemade Thanksgiving feast.

At six o'clock sharp, I greet Owen Montagne at the door and he hands me a bottle of nice merlot. "I understand it is the most over-drunk varietal in America today."

It is. I learned this from Johnson, who sneers at any bottle of merlot, or chardonnay, for that matter. "Well, there must be a reason!" I say brightly, snatching the bottle from his hand. "Let's open it and let it breathe while we get ready."

The pumpkin pie, its crust a bit too dark, sits on the counter. The chicken rests on a platter for the requisite twenty minutes while I scurry to make the stuffing, mashed potatoes, carrots, and biscuits all at the same time. I set the table first thing this morning, thank goodness.

My guest surveys the kitchen appraisingly, a broad smile on his face. "It smells fantastic in here," he says, inhaling deeply.

"Thanks!" I say, wiping my brow with a floury hand. He pulls out a stool at the bar and sits across from me as I wrestle with the sticky dough.

"Try adding a sprinkle more Bisquick," he suggests. I do, and it works.

"Can you reach in the cabinet there and grab me a coffee mug?"

"Sure," he says, sliding off the barstool. He heads for the cupboard I indicate with a jerk of my head. I glance at him from behind, appreciating the way his fine-gauge sweater clings to his lean frame as he stretches into the cabinet. I realize I have never seen him without a heavy overcoat or sport coat on. He smiles as he hands me the cup. I blush and refocus on the biscuit dough. I roll the mug over the dough to flatten it. "Nice rolling pin," he observes.

"Watch this," I say, placing the mouth of the mug over the dough and pushing down, cutting a perfect circle. "Double duty."

"Brilliant," he says admiringly.

"Yes, I am," I say, smiling. "I have some chardonnay chilling in the fridge, if you'd like to start with that before we have the merlot with dinner."

"Sounds great," he says, starting for the fridge, then pausing. "Corkscrew?"

I move aside and indicate the drawer at my hip. He opens it carefully, avoiding contact, and paws through the gadgets until he comes up with the corkscrew. I can smell his cologne, subtle amid the aroma of our food.

He returns to the bar and uncorks the chardonnay bottle while I load the biscuits onto a tiny baking pan and pop them into the toaster oven, set at 450. I wipe my hands on the dish towel and proceed to the stuffing and potatoes on the stovetop. I feel oddly masterful in Stella's kitchen under the appraising gaze of Owen Montagne.

With exactly four minutes before I have to tend to the next item, I see he has poured the chardonnay and is waiting politely. I take up my glass and he takes his. "To Ms. St. Claire and her lovely Thanksgiving feast!"

I clink his glass and sip my over-drunk but wholly enjoyable chardonnay. Smiling, I say, "Today, please call me Abby."

He seems uncomfortable, and I say, "How about Abigail? Is that formal enough?"

"Fine," he concedes, "Abigail it is. I don't have any option other than Owen."

"That's fine with me."

"Terrific. To us," he says, raising his glass again.

"To Abigail and Owen," I say, clinking his glass again.

~

I arrive at the airport thirty minutes early in case Olivia's plane lands ahead of schedule, so I am all wound up by the time it actually does arrive, nearly an hour late. Anxiously, I scan the stream of incoming passengers. Then I see her searching the sea of people waiting with me behind the glass. Our eyes meet; she waves energetically and smiles. I wave and smile back, bringing a hand to my chest, my eyes suddenly blurred. *Get it together*, I instruct myself, as I realize just how much I have missed my girl. I caution myself to be cool, not to overdo it like the family next to me, which is swallowing up their boy. I will not embarrass her like that.

Olivia passes through the gate and I walk over to her casually, reaching for her bag. She, however, deviates from the script. She reaches for me, and before I know it I am crushing her to my chest and rocking her back and forth, telling her how much I missed her. Tears return from their banishment, and I realize I am officially behaving worse than the Cleavers ten feet away. Olivia seems fine with this, smiling indulgently as she hitches her backpack onto her shoulder. "I missed you, too," she says, and I know she did.

On the way home we talk about Wife #2 and how, defying the odds, little Keene is even more spoiled than last year. Olivia is tanned and relaxed, her hair a touch lighter. She's even lovelier than when she left only a week ago.

"I know where I want us to go," she says out of the blue.

"Where?" I ask, picking up the thread. Where in the world will Olivia and I go?

"The last place Mom went is the first place I'd like to go without her. London."

I marvel at how Olivia puts things together, just like her mom. "That makes perfect sense," I say. "It feels right."

She turns in her seat, excited now. "I was hoping you would agree."

And so it is settled. We will go to London.

Part Three
Winter

Men's curiosity searches past and future
And clings to that dimension. But to apprehend
The point of intersection of the timeless
With time, is an occupation for the saint—
No occupation either, but something given
And taken, in a lifetime's death in love,
Ardour and selflessness and self-surrender.
For most of us, there is only the unattended
Moment, the moment in and out of time,
The distraction fit, lost in a shaft of sunlight,
The wild thyme unseen, or the winter lightning
Or the waterfall, or music heard so deeply
That it is not heard at all, but you are the music
While the music lasts. These are only hints and guesses,
Hints followed by guesses; and the rest
Is prayer, observance, discipline, thought and action.
The hint half guessed, the gift half understood, is Incarnation.

"The Dry Salvages," Verse V
Four Quartets, by T. S. Eliot

December

The holidays are here, Stella, and you are not.

I'm worried about Olivia, I admit it. Often she seems so together, but her random outbursts worry me. She's like the teacup I kept on the knickknack shelf in my kitchen. Beautiful yet delicate, and when I lifted it to pack for the move, it fell apart in my hand. I'd never noticed the hairline crack down the side, and the simple act of lifting it split it in two. Sometimes I think I'm driving Olivia nuts trying to find a crack that's not there.

Which is worse: looking for a crack that's not there or missing one that is?

We shiver on the front porch, a tangle of Christmas lights at our feet. "Th-th-this is why M-M-Mom made us put the stinking lights up in Oc-Oc-October."

"Smart woman. Where do we start?"

"I have no idea."

"Your mom told me this was one of your traditions!"

Olivia gives me the hairy eyeball. "I was a *participant*. She worked it out so everything strung together, then she plugged into that outlet." Olivia indicates an outlet by the doorway—the lone exterior outlet; the one I cannot figure out how to run the lights to.

I have an urge to call Owen but squelch it. I haven't told Olivia that I spent Thanksgiving with her high school advisor, or that we went to a poetry reading the following Saturday evening. It's no big deal, and after Olivia's reaction to Johnson, it's best to keep this simple friendship on the down-low.

"We need a man," Olivia declares, eerily picking up on my vibe.

"Absolutely not, and if your mother heard that—well, you better hope she didn't." I swat at her arm, then drag her inside. "Graph paper," I say, doctor to nurse. "Colored pencils. Ruler. Tape measure."

"Yes, ma'am," Olivia says, clicking her heels, dumping snow on the rug. She trots upstairs, rummages through her art drawer, returns with the requisite materials.

We measure the length, width, and height of the porch. Back inside, we spread the pencils, ruler, and graph paper across the coffee table. We create a scale drawing of the porch, each square on the graph paper representing two feet. With a different color for every string of lights, we put together a scenario. Exactly eight wadded-up scenarios later, we strike upon a workable plan.

We return to the porch and execute. We string and restring, invoking salty language along the way. Our plan, it seems, is flawed. But after forty-five minutes in freezing temperatures, I let Olivia insert the plug and, voilà, we have lights.

It was tough, but December is off to a promising start.

~

As directed, we open our December boxes on the tenth. Each box is wrapped in fine, shiny paper covered with angels of all types, and adorned with curly ribbons of silver and gold. The charms are tiny silver angels.

Also as directed, we open our boxes at the same time. In the folds of the paper in each box lies a letter, folded neatly, and a first-class airline ticket good for anywhere in the world. Our eyes lock, and we both whistle softly.

Merry Christmas, my AbbySoulMate,

I hope you and Olivia have selected your destination! If not, you'll have to do it soon, because you leave in less than two weeks!

Olivia will not want to be with Rob, even if she says she does. It's going to be a tough Christmas, and Rob and Wife #2 will not want their little terror subjected to any sadness on the holiday. So Olivia will make up some excuse to stay close to home. The thought of the two of you moping around the house, spending money on cheesy gifts that won't lift your spirits, thinking about me and missing me—well, it depresses me.

I like the thought of you two jetting off to an exotic location, discovering a new place, eating regional food, taking in local sights and culture. So indulge me. Have a wonderful Christmas adventure. I can't wait to hear all about it!

Also, I'm letting you off the hook in the decorating department. I know I always went a little overboard—too many lights, too many corny decorations, too much going on. This past Christmas, you all pitched in and made my home the most beautiful ever. I want to say again how much that meant to me. But I also learned that it was having you all close to me that was most important. So, while I hope you light a candle or two—like you did at your apartment—please don't feel the need to keep up my traditions. Create new ones of your own. If I were there this Christmas, I would be creating new traditions, too.

Merriest of Christmases, my darlingest friend.
Love to you,
Stella Rose

"Well," I say ruefully, "I wish I'd read this before we tackled the damned lights."

Olivia smiles. "I'm glad we did the lights, though."

"Me, too."

Olivia opens her letter.

Merry, Merry Christmas, my darling Olivia-Heart,

If you can tear yourself away from the tradition of visiting your dad and co. this Christmas, I would love for you to accompany Abby to the destination of your choice over the holidays. Your dad will have a fit, but that only gives me more pleasure in insisting that you indulge my latest whim.

I hope you go somewhere fabulous, someplace that will have special meaning for you all of your life. Someplace from which to launch the rest of your life.

Honey, I know this Christmas will be difficult for you. If only you could feel me wrapping my arms around you right now. You have a wonderful life ahead of you, and you have a wonderful life right in front of you. I hope you recognize this and don't wait to get over this thing before embracing all that life is offering you right this moment.

You are not skipping Christmas this year. You are trying out new traditions to see what fits you best. I honor that, and so does Abby.

Be brave, my love. Drink in all that is holy and precious about the season this year. Be open to giving and to receiving.

Love, love, love always and always, forever,

Mom

"Do you think London is good enough?" Olivia asks, her voice small. "It seems Mom has big plans for this trip."

Stella had big plans for everything.

"Why did you want to go to London?" I ask.

"Because it's the last place Mom visited," Olivia says, but it sounds like a question.

"That's what you said. Is that still compelling for you?"

Olivia hesitates only a moment. "Yes," she says firmly. "It is."

"Stella would be thrilled with the choice. She would be honored."

~

As Stella predicted, Rob is incensed. "But I have plans!" he shouts. "Savannah has been working on our agenda for weeks."

I'm standing in the kitchen, holding the phone away from my ear, Olivia grimacing from the doorway. While he gave her a hard time five minutes ago when she broke the news, he was apparently just warming up. "Rob, it's what Stella wanted."

"Always what Stella wants. Always was, always will be, even when she's dead!"

Though I have pulled the phone back to my ear by now, Olivia catches the gist and gasps audibly before storming out of the kitchen, leaving the door swinging in her wake.

"Nice, Rob," I hiss.

"Well, Jesus, Abby—was she listening in?"

"She didn't have to, with you yelling like that!"

"Abby, put her back on, please."

"Too late—she's upstairs in her room now. Listen, Rob, Stella's right. You know it; I know it. The last place Olivia needs to be right now is with your family. It's going to be rough, and she won't want to ruin your kid's Christmas. She needs somebody with nothing better to do than hover over her. We both know I have nothing better to do."

Rob manages a small laugh. "Abby, I appreciate your doing all this, I do. But I love my daughter, and I feel so . . ."

"Me, too, Rob. We all feel so . . . All we can do is the best we can do. We'll call on Christmas, and you can visit her in early January. We'll have a mini-Christmas."

"It just seems so awkward."

"It sure is. Nothing like a cancer death to fuck up the holidays."

~

We decide on a tiny tree, one that can easily be moved to the porch while we are gone so it doesn't drop all its needles inside. Emancipated by Stella from her enormous box of ornaments and household decorations, and unwilling to use my own ratty decorations from years of lackluster Christmas trees in my apartment, we buy a few new ones. Perusing tacky garlands and glass balls of every shape and color, we agree on a few small red and gold balls and strands of red beads for garland, and two sets of clear lights. It takes us all of thirty minutes to finish the job; then we sip tea on the sofa and admire our handiwork as Celine Dion belts out "Silent Night."

"Not bad," I say.

"Mom would be mortified."

"Not enough going on. But she gave us permission, so she must forgive us."

There is a pause; then Olivia says, "She'd forgive us this."

"She'd forgive us anything."

"Are you sure?" Olivia asks, turning to me, eyes shiny.

Laughing, I say, "Of course! Especially you, Olivia." I stop laughing when I see she is serious. "Olivia, what's wrong?"

"It's just . . . Some of the things I've done . . ."

"Like what? Having sex?" Olivia squirms, but I press on. "Seriously, Olivia. Your mom would get that. Everyone has sex. And everyone makes mistakes. She would only hope you had a positive first-time experience. She would have been upset because you were hurt. But she would have said there is nothing to forgive."

"Would you forgive Mom anything?"

"Well, of course," I say, thrown by the change in direction. "Why?"

"I just . . . I was just wondering if there is ever anything that is unforgivable when—or maybe because—two people are family, or best friends."

"Olivia," I say, turning to face her, placing my palm to her cheek.

"'Forgiveness' is a big word, but 'love' is bigger. The three of us are bound by love, and forgiveness is part of love. A given. If we can't forgive each other, we can't love each other, and that simply is not an option." I squeeze her chin in my hand, and she looks down into her lap.

"You sound so sure."

"I *am* sure."

"Mom would be proud of you."

I can't answer with this knot in my throat.

~

Since Olivia has joined the weekly ski-snowboard commuter bus to Smugglers' Notch, I have Saturdays to myself. I hit the mall to power-shop for relatives, feeling way behind on getting my Christmas gifts in the mail.

Though Olivia and I agreed not to exchange gifts, I can't stop thinking about what I would like to get for her. A laptop, a tablet, new music, new books? I spot delicate sterling earrings to go with our charm bracelets . . . but that's too mother-daughter. Besides, they would clash with that hideous industrial she has.

Rounding the bend between Macy's and Pottery Barn, I find myself face-to-face with Johnson Keller. He looks J.Crew in his heavy tan trench coat and matching beret, his hair getting long and curling around the brim, his hands large, encased in smooth leather gloves. I suddenly feel faint. Why don't they keep AC on year-round in malls?

"Abby! How are you?"

His smile is so warm, I melt and say, "Hanging in there. You?"

"Same," he says, holding up his shopping bags. "Overwhelmed."

We smile. And stare. "Well," I say, rousing myself, then walking past him. "Take care."

"Abby?"

I turn back and he steps close.

"I miss you," he says, so quietly I strain to hear him.

But I do hear him, and I take a step back, surprised.

"I was going to call you last week," he says, holding my gaze.

I find my tongue. "But you were tied up with that *Stomp* opening at the Flynn, the event you attended with—what's her name?"

"Brenda Winters."

"Yes, Brenda. I get her confused with Sharon Smyth," I say, naming another of his recent, publicized dates.

"Okay, you win. I'm a heel. That doesn't mean I don't miss you. What are you doing Friday night?" Johnson asks, laying his hand on my arm. I rock under his touch, immediately chastise myself in my head.

"I'd have to check my calendar, though I can tell you right now I am not anxious to rejoin your *people* or be part of the Keller Gallery of Girls."

Johnson laughs, his dark eyes crinkle, and he hugs me. "How about pizza at Papa Mimmo's? Can you clear your calendar for that?"

With my brain screaming, *Are you crazy?* my heart tells my mouth to say, "Yes, I suppose so. I'll meet you there at seven o'clock."

～

I make it through pizza on Friday with no strings attached, but barely. I arrive home all aquiver and get myself to bed early with hot dreams of Johnson's hands all over me. I refuse his invitations to dinner on Saturday and Sunday and Monday. But a girl can resist what her heart—okay, body—wants for only so long. On Tuesday evening, I meet him at Puccini's, site of our first date. We make it through antipasti and pinot noir, pasta primavera and a shiraz. Then he touches my arm as we wait for the dessert menu and a rich cabernet. We enjoy the cab but never make it to dessert. We barely make it to his car. Once inside, we are on each other like teenagers at a drive-in.

～

Flying first class is like not flying at all. Olivia and I have veritable beds, where we doze five out of seven hours of the transatlantic flight. I enjoy a malbec while Olivia gorges herself on fresh roasted peanuts served in a plastic martini glass. Despite the cushy experience, we arrive at Heathrow bedraggled and grumpy, wait an interminably long time at security, and lug our bags through the dingy, crowded airport. We take a cab to our hotel, the Knight Horses Inn, where we are taken aback by the petite size of the suite. Upon closer inspection, however, we find ourselves charmed by details like expensive drapes, bedspreads, and pillows, well-wrought antique furniture, fresh flowers on the dinette and the windowsills, and a real dressing table. It's quite sumptuous, actually, and we collapse on our respective beds in our respective rooms and drink it in. London for the holidays. We will get through Christmas in this marvelous place. Thank you, Stella Rose.

~

Early the next morning, leaving Olivia to sleep off some jet lag, I head to the tiny hotel restaurant for breakfast. Forgoing the buffet, I order off the menu: the American breakfast—two eggs over easy, toast, bacon, and hash browns. When the waitress leaves, a dapper gentleman in his fifties—expensive suit, nice shoes, clipped mustache, and sharp eyes—stops to ask how I am enjoying my stay. He must be the manager.

"Fine," I say. "A bit jet-lagged."

"I do hope you are enjoying the suite. Do you come to London often?"

"It's lovely, and no, but my friend came often and she often stayed here."

"What was your friend's name?"

"Stella Rose."

"Ah! Ms. Stella Rose! She was delightful! Smart, professional, and quite—"

"Lovely." *Here we go again, Stella.*

"Yes, quite. Though the events were across town, she preferred to stay here, where it was quiet, away from the party scene. She commuted in each day."

Really? Stella?

"Of course she would have lovely friends."

I blush in spite of the overt charm machine in motion. "That's kind of you to say."

"So Ms. Rose is not with you, I take it?"

"No, I'm afraid not."

"Well, please give her my personal regards."

"She died." I'm stunned by my own abruptness.

The poor man is clearly rocked. "Oh, my. What a shame. May I ask . . . ?"

"Cancer."

"Oh, I am dreadfully sorry. Please accept my sincerest sympathies." He wrings his hands. "Her husband must be devastated."

"Oh, she wasn't married."

"Oh." The manager looks perplexed. "I just assumed. They seemed . . . married."

"They did?" I ask. The man is too deep in reverie to note my utter shock.

"Oh, yes. He was with her every moment—outside of the conference, of course. They mostly took meals in their suite but sometimes came down for a breakfast before cabbing to Piccadilly. Once he was in here for a drink, waiting for her to join him, and we struck up a conversation. He said . . ."

"What?" I prompt him, hanging on each syllable.

"He said, 'That woman is my undoing—and my doing.' I wasn't sure what that meant, must be an Americanism, but he clearly loved Ms. Rose."

"Yes," I say faintly, "I suppose he did."

"Well, do give him my sympathies as well. My name is Desmond Haversmith. He may not remember me, but I will never forget the look in his eyes when he spoke of Ms. Rose. In fact, I was so moved,

I brought flowers home for my wife that day. Perhaps I'll bring her some today."

"That would be lovely."

"Yes. Yes, it would. Have a wonderful day, Ms. St. Claire."

"Thank you, Mr. Haversmith. I hope your wife enjoys her flowers."

Twenty minutes elapse as I sit in a trance. Finally I leave, my breakfast barely touched, coffee stone cold, and return to the suite to find Olivia showered and ready for the day. I keep the breakfast revelation to myself and blame my distraction on jet lag.

Stella Rose, what the hell were you up to?

With whom?

~

Olivia and I head out armed with a map and no real plan. Contrary to London's reputation, the skies are clear, the air crisp. Circuses, to our angst, are like hubs of various wheels, with no obvious rhyme or reason, and no connection whatsoever to our map. A dozen blocks into our adventure, we shove the map in a trash bin and let fate guide our day.

The streets are crowded with people in trench coats, collars hiked against the wind, faces chapped and chagrined. Olivia and I giggle as we remove layers, enjoying the relative warmth compared with the subfreezing temps we left behind. We become attuned to tourist street signs pointing us to main attractions and find our way to Buckingham Palace, Westminster Abbey, and, most impressive, the House of Parliament. Olivia begs me to ride on the Eye, a glorified Ferris wheel of enclosed capsules that rotate slowly, giving occupants a spectacular (terrifying) view of the entire city. I decline, citing the twofer of acrophobia and claustrophobia. "I don't mind waiting if you want to go with that group of New Yorkers over there."

"It's not a big deal," she says.

I feel guilty, but not guilty enough to go on the damned thing.

Suddenly famished, we enter a tiny, steaming, dimly lit pub just across the Thames from the House of Parliament. Smoke hangs thick as fog above every table in the place, a sight unseen in our neck of the woods. Though Olivia coughs uncontrollably, she insists we stay. "It's part of the experience," she intones, channeling her mother.

"Okay," I assent, coughing a couple of times myself. A waitress appears, delivering the specials of the day in a rapid-fire language that is possibly English. In self-defense, we order the fish and chips in the house beer batter. In two minutes flat, the waitress returns with huge baskets brimming with aromatic golden planks of battered fish resting on a bed of hand-cut steak fries. Two unordered beers appear as well.

Olivia grins at me, and I capitulate. "When in London . . ." We clink glasses and sip our beers, puckering and shuddering.

Eyeing my basket warily, I say, "This cannot be healthy," to which Olivia replies, "Man, I hope not. Dig in!" Within the crispy batter lies the flakiest, lightest fillet of some unknown species of whitefish I have ever tasted.

"Heaven in a basket."

"Mmmmm," Olivia responds.

~

Stepping out of the dim pub an hour later, Olivia and I stop dead in our tracks, staring up, gaping at the spectacle. The House of Parliament and Westminster Abbey glow golden against the navy sky. Though hundreds of pedestrians litter the sidewalks and traffic flows through the streets, the evening is hushed and reverent. Maybe it's just us, quieted inside by the majesty of flawless architecture and a sense of timelessness. Impulsively I squeeze Olivia's hand. She squeezes back, and, as we turn to go, she loops her arm through mine. Arm in arm, we return to the hotel where nearly two years ago Stella rendezvoused with a man she never told me about.

~

While Olivia scouts the hotel amenities, I call the front desk and ask for Mr. Haversmith. I want to know who the hell Stella's guy was and intend to ask all the questions I should have asked this morning.

I'm crushed when the receptionist informs me he left to get a jump on his holiday—something about life being short and his wife being lovely—and that he was unreachable until the new year. When Olivia and I will be back in the States, of course.

How else can I find some answers?

A thought hits me: this could be the news that Stella was anxious to tell me when I returned from Greece, before leukemia eclipsed everything. She'd told me about men she'd met traveling before. What was so different about this one? Was he European? Royalty? Dangerous? Christ, what could it have been?

Another thought hits me: Johnson. He was at the same conference and might know who this guy is. I glance at my watch and do the math. The time is right. Then I realize it's Christmas Eve. Calling him on Christmas Eve might seem . . . girlfriend-ish. Besides, he'll probably be with his kids. And Shayla?

Don't go there. It's best to wait until we're back in the States.

I'm pacing the length of the suite when Olivia returns, disappointed that there is no gym—or pool or sauna. "I thought this was five stars," she grumbles, and I toss an elaborately tasseled tapestry pillow at her.

"It's about the ambience, me duckie," I say, affecting my worst English accent.

"Ambience, schmambience," she snarks, tossing the pillow back at me. Hard.

"What do you want to do?" I ask.

"Nothing." She flops onto the brocade sofa, hangs her feet over the arm.

Sighing, I sit down in an armchair that looks like it came out of the 1700s and smells a little that way, too. "What's wrong?"

"Nothing."

I wait. I've learned to wait.

"She sent us away for Christmas, and now Dad's pissed—"

"He's not pissed at you, Olivia."

"Well, it hurt his feelings. He practically said so when I called him. Mom didn't give a shit about that, but I do. She never wanted me to really love Dad, and now he's feeling awful about me not being there on Christmas. He's mad, Cherie's not happy, Ryan's pissed—"

"Who's Ryan?"

Silence. Then, "Nobody."

"Come on, Liv."

"None of your business."

"It is most definitely my business."

Her eyes are slits. "He is just a guy, and no, I am not having sex with him, and now I will be going to bed in my room, so ho-ho-ho, merry freaking Christmas to you."

Olivia stalks into her room and closes her door with a rattling thud. Goddammit.

~

We wake late the next morning and grumble apologies over coffee, We take our time showering and then linger over a late lunch as we wait for the US to wake up. I give Olivia privacy to talk with Rob and her brother. Fighting the urge to call Johnson, I prowl around the hotel, keyed up from persistent jet lag and all the drama of the past few days.

Months.

In the dining hall there are only a handful of folks, all on their mobile phones. It's too early still to call either of my parents. They don't have a toddler waking them at the crack of Christmas dawn like Rob does. I could call my brother, since he is closer in time-zones, but I won't. I pull out my phone and stare at it. Has my world always been this small? I have the time and inclination and no one to call?

That isn't true. I could call any of the girls and interrupt their various Christmas-morning rituals. They would totally indulge me. They would even be glad I'd reached out to them. But instead I find myself looking up Owen's number. It's still early at home, and he probably hasn't left to visit whomever he sees on Christmas Day.

I pause before hitting the SEND button. Is this appropriate? Would he read too much into a phone call on Christmas Day? As I am weighing the pros and cons, my phone buzzes in my hand, startling me into bobbling it and nearly dropping it on the shiny tiled floor. Squinting to read the caller ID, I smile. "Owen," I say into the phone, "I was just thinking of you!"

~

Olivia and I stumble through the rest of Christmas, wandering the nearly deserted streets downtown. I lead her back to the Eye.

"Really?" she asks.

"Really," I say, girding myself as I hand over pounds to the poor guy stuck with the lousy job of managing tourists on Christmas Day.

Halfway through the ride, I am able to ignore the stabbing pain in my solar plexus where my acrophobia manifests and focus on the 360-degree view of London.

"Amazing," I say, breathing hard.

"Yeah," Olivia agrees, squeezing my hand.

As soon as we disembark, my mobile buzzes.

"Mom!" I say, pleased she called me before I remembered to call her.

"Hello, Abby, how are you doing? Are you enjoying London?"

"Yes, we are! In fact, we just got off the Eye."

"You don't like heights, honey."

"That shouldn't stop me from doing something that makes Olivia so happy."

"That's nice, hon," she says. "You're getting the hang of it now." There is a warmth in her voice I've never heard before. "So, did my gifts arrive before you left for London? Charlie promised they would be there by the twentieth." And we are back on track.

That evening, tucked into our tiny suite, Olivia and I make hot chocolate topped with real cream.

"Abby, I broke the rule."

"Which one?"

"The one about not buying each other a Christmas gift."

"Great! I broke the rule, too!" I exclaim, leaping up from the ancient chair and dashing to my bag. Olivia runs to her room and returns with a box nearly identical in dimension to mine.

"You first," I say, thrusting my tiny square package at her.

"Okay!" she says, smiling as she takes the box. Pulling one end of the ribbon ever so slowly, she takes her sweet time unwrapping the gift, knowing she is driving me nuts.

"No hurry, sweetheart," I say, gritting my teeth.

Mischief in her eyes, she pulls a letter opener out of the desk and painstakingly slides it under each piece of tape until at last the box is free from the paper, ribbon, and bows. "Nothing will live up to this kind of foreplay," I warn, and she looks suitably shocked. I grin wickedly at her.

Slowly she lifts the cover of the box, and I am pleased at the genuine delight on her face as she lifts the delicate silver hoops from their bed of cotton. "They are gorgeous." They are, but I wasn't sure she would appreciate them. Again, I underestimated her. She removes the studs from her ears, tosses them into the box, puts the hoops in. "They go so well with that Old Navy sweatshirt," I say, only half kidding. They look great. Even the industrial looks better in contrast with the delicate hoops.

She steps into the bathroom to get a better look, and she actually squeals with delight. "They are gorgeous, gorgeous, Abby." Running back into the room, she throws her arms around me, kisses me on the cheek. "Thank you!"

"You're most welcome. May I?" I ask, pointing to the package on the table.

Olivia looks apprehensive. "Well, it's not . . . it's not expensive silver earrings."

"Well, I would hope not. That would be so tacky," I say, teasing.

"It's just that, I didn't know what to get, and I wanted something . . . well . . ."

I grab the package and rip the paper, ribbon and all, right off to reveal a thick layer of tissue paper. "Tricky," I say approvingly, and set about tearing that off, too. I glance at Olivia, but her gaze is glued to the package in my hand. I slow down and remove the tissue paper gently, revealing an antique silver picture frame containing a picture of Olivia and me from two years ago. It was taken right after Olivia performed as Dorothy in the school's production of *The Wiz*. Her makeup had rubbed off and her hair was pulled back, but she was still in her Dorothy costume and aglow from her performance. She was holding the flowers I had brought for her. I had just given her a big hug when Stella said, "Look at me, girls!"

I look up at Olivia now and say, "When we saw that your mom had her camera, we pulled close and hammed for the shot."

Olivia nods. "And Mom said, 'Perfect. My two best girls, together . . .'"

"'For always.'"

"She was the real drama queen, you know."

I snort loudly, with relief, tears already brimming over. "Sure was."

Olivia sprints to the bathroom and returns with the tissue box. "Abby, I didn't mean to make you cry."

I blow my nose heartily and say, "Liv, I've received many lovely gifts over the years—most of them from your mom, by the way. Expensive, tasteful—extravagant, even. But this"—I gesture toward the picture—"this is the best present I have ever received."

"Well, it—"

"Ever. It's the best present I have ever received."

Olivia beams at me.

January

The holidays were touch and go for a while, but we managed to squeak out an incredible memory filled with new sights, new insights, old stories, and lots of you, my friend, so much of you.

But I have to ask: What were you up to in London, Stella Rose? Is this what you wanted to tell me when I returned from Greece? How could you be in love and not tell me? Disease or no disease, this would have been a good thing! Who was he? And where was he those last nine months, Stella? Whoever this guy is, I suspect he broke your heart. Otherwise, he would have been there for you at the end.

Sounds pretty judgmental coming from me, eh?

I will get to the bottom of this, Stella, starting with Johnson. He will help me unravel your mystery.

January brings the *brrr* factor to a whole new level, and soon after our return I remember why I detest winter. However, detesting winter in the sticks is harder than in the city. Gone are slippery sidewalks, dirty snowbanks, salt and mud–caked cars snaking through icy intersections and exploding through puddles of slush and sliding perilously close to each other, horns honking, tailpipes pluming exhaust, pedestrians scurrying along, wool hats pulled low, Sorels laced high.

Out here, I stand on the back deck in a down jacket and moccasins, a cup of tea steaming in mittened hands, sunglasses protecting against the glare of pristine snow that sparkles alive under the sun's rays. Fresh snow piles on the trees like heavy coats, and Stella's rose garden is a mere hump in the middle of a vast white lake. My God, it's gorgeous out here. And freaking cold. This is the first bona fide cold snap of the season. "Cold snap": a quaint expression for the evil phenomenon that makes the insides of noses feel raw and ears turn plum-tomato red.

I asked Olivia to join me in the backyard winter wonderland, but she demurred. We have our own little cold snap going on. We returned from London in high spirits, but over the past week our relationship has become frosty as the windowpanes. I blame jet lag in part, but I can't shake this nagging feeling something is not right.

Stella's older Subaru, which is now Olivia's winter car, starts hard when it is below zero. This aggravates Olivia to no end, as I have to jump-start it nearly every morning. I urge her to park in the garage, saying I will park in the driveway. This only irritates her further, as she points out the obvious fact that my Saab will never start if left outside and she would only be stuck jumping me every morning.

Okay, fine, just trying to help.

I ask if Ryan Nobody is handy with cars. A snort signifies her contempt for my total inability to grasp her reality, and she intones, "He is not the grease-monkey type."

My mistake.

Ryan has called for Olivia a few times since we returned. I don't like his voice. This may be unfair, but how can I gauge a guy Olivia refuses to let me meet in person?

Finally I ask Olivia if it's getting serious.

"It's over," she says. "That should make you happy."

"That's not fair. I never met the guy. I don't know if I should be happy or not."

"You should be happy about it."

"Are *you* happy about it?"

Pause. "I should be happy about it."

"That's not the same thing."

"I know."

~

Standing in the foyer of Chez Pierre, I remove the hood of my long red wool coat, shake my head vociferously. I peek around to make sure no one is looking, then eye my reflection in the tiny, grainy entry mirror to inspect the damage. Running my hand through my tousled locks, I endeavor to remove every last snowflake before it melts, taking a solid hour of hair prep with it.

"There you are!" Jacques, the maître d', swoops in, arms outstretched like wings.

Instinctively I step back, then realize he is simply after my coat, which is getting heavier by the moment with melting snow.

"Monsieur Keller is waiting for you! My, how lovely you look this evening!"

"Thank you, Jacques," I say, overwhelmed as always by his ebullient charm.

"Not at all, not at all!"

Walking demurely on the maître-d's arm, I saunter to Johnson's table. A seemingly besotted Jacques nestles me into my chair, and I can barely suppress a giggle.

Johnson stares so long, my hand instinctively goes to my hair.

"What?" I ask, glancing around.

"You look fantastic," Johnson says, a declaration of fact.

"I must agree," chimes in Jacques, beaming at me, bright as a Vegas casino.

"Thank you, Jacques."

"You can stop hitting on my girlfriend now."

"But of course." Jacques smiles broadly as he bows his way from the table.

Girlfriend?

"Let's toast!" Johnson says, taking up his glass.

Raising my glass to his, I ask, "To what?"

"Your return," Johnson says, his dark brown eyes soft and appreciative, making my insides soft and squirmy.

"It's good to be back." I clink his glass softly before bringing the berry-rich shiraz to my lips, realizing it is indeed good to be back.

We catch up on each other's holidays, sharing much but, I'm sure, not all. When our waiter appears, Johnson places our order, and food arrives course by course. I ask about Johnson's father-in-law, who has just been released from the hospital after open-heart surgery and is resting comfortably under at-home nursing care at his estate on the lake in Shelburne.

"How is Shayla holding up?" I ask, eyeing Johnson over the rim of my wineglass.

"She's a trouper."

"So you've said." I detest the sarcasm seeping into my response.

Smart man that he is, Johnson says, "Let's talk about you. How are you doing?"

I smile back. "With Olivia? Johnson, it's so hard. Some days we get along great. She is so smart and funny—even loving and affectionate. Other times she's . . ."

"The devil incarnate?"

"Well, not that bad!"

"Then you'll get no sympathy here. You already know what an ass Matt can be." He looks me straight in the eye, and I am surprised that we can speak this frankly, almost conspiratorially. "But he's a guy, and transparently idiotic and overconfident sometimes."

"That doesn't sound all that different from the man sitting across from me."

Smiling, Johnson continues, "And I'm intolerant and self-righteous and unbearably impatient."

I laugh. "That I can believe."

"Why?" Johnson asks, exaggerated hurt in his voice, but the question is sincere.

"Because that is how Stella always described you."

Johnson laughs, but I see the hurt is now real.

"Johnson." I place my hand over his. "You know Stella was a tough critic!"

"Even by Stella's standards, that's pretty harsh."

"She just sounded harsh. In the end, she had a soft spot for you. She trusted you with her life after death. I told you I was surprised she chose you to manage her affairs."

Johnson grimaces, surely remembering the whole nasty conversation.

I say quickly, "I didn't know you before Stella's death. I was just going on what she told me over the years and, of course, what I read occasionally in the papers. When I heard you were helping Stella in the end—the will, Olivia's care, the house, even the monthly letters and boxes—then I knew Stella trusted you. And that's all that matters."

Cocking his head, Johnson says, "That's all that matters?"

"Yes," I say firmly.

"She was fallible, you know."

This rankles. "I never said she was perfect."

"You didn't say that, but you think it."

"That's not true," I say, but even I can hear the falsehood in my words. "Okay," I say, smiling, "maybe I do think Stella is—was—pretty close to perfect."

We take a few moments to savor our entrées; then I ask the question I have been dying to ask since my trip. "What happened in London?"

Johnson takes his time chewing, attentive to the contents of his plate, then reaches for his wine. "What do you want to know?"

"Who did Stella spend most of her time with?"

"Me."

Pausing, fork in midair, I gawk at him. "You?"

Johnson smiles. "Of course. We were partners representing our firm at this conference; it was a great opportunity to expand our client base, going global, all that. We were launching a new product . . ."

"Boring. Who else did she spend time with?"

"Why do you ask?"

"I need to know."

"You want to know."

"No, Johnson," I say, eyes close to overflowing, "I need to know."

Reaching for my hand, Johnson says gently, "Abby, if Stella had wanted you to know, she would have told you."

"She wanted to! When I was in Greece, she kept saying she had something important to tell me and it couldn't be done over the phone or e-mail. But then—"

"Then she got sick and suddenly all that simply didn't matter anymore."

"How could it not matter, when it was so important at the time?"

"Because cancer changes everything."

Looking into Johnson's eyes, I see he is struggling to help me see these dots that I refuse to connect. "So I may never know."

"That's right."

"I cannot accept that."

"Maybe one day you will. Until then, you have a lot on your plate that you can't lose sight of, Abby." His hand on mine is gentle, his gaze imploring.

I am chastened but undeterred. He may not be able to help me, but someone out there knows what was going on, and I will find out one way or another. But not now. Tonight I will focus on my full plate, which includes a handsome, intelligent, evolving man who seems to be quite fond of me.

～

The next day, after work, I hear the phone ringing as I enter the house. I am pleased to hear Trish Shoreham's voice on the line. We haven't spoken since just after the piercing incident, when she phoned to apologize and I assured her that we had both been manipulated by pros. I liked her immediately, even over the phone.

Now her voice sounds anxious. "Abby, I'm worried about the girls."

I grip the phone harder. "What's going on?"

"Do you know where they are?"

I hate to tell her that if she's asking me, we are both in trouble. "I assumed they were at your house. That's usually where Olivia goes."

"They do spend a lot of time here, but I'm not working tonight. I usually work nights, and, well, I have tonight off and they aren't here."

"Did they leave a note?"

"Cherie is not a note kind of girl," Trish says ruefully. "She won't answer her cell phone. She's under curfew and is supposed to be home by eight o'clock. It's already nearly nine."

"I'm sure they're just running late," I say, trying to sound positive.

"Probably." Trish sounds doubtful. "I just . . ."

I swear I can hear tears in her voice, and I am suddenly sorry for this woman and, truth be told, relieved I am not the only one struggling with a teenage girl in the house.

"I don't mean to be nosy," I say, "but the girls are spending a lot of time together this year, and I'm having some issues with Olivia. May I ask why Cherie has a curfew?"

"Drinking."

"Oh, dear," I say, my heart sinking. "I'm sure she wasn't drinking alone."

"No, she wasn't. But Olivia is a good girl, considering all she's been through."

A lump rises in my throat. "Thanks for that, but it doesn't excuse bad behavior."

"Cherie has no excuse at all, except being seventeen and hanging with degenerate boys."

"What boys?" I ask, not caring anymore how many people know how little I know about Olivia's social life.

"The bad boys I used to like when I was in high school. I even married one. You'd think Cherie would have learned from my mistakes."

At that moment, the door opens and Olivia walks in. "Just a moment, please," I say, putting my hand over the mouthpiece. "Where is Cherie?" I whisper loudly to Olivia.

"On her way home," Olivia says, also in a loud whisper.

"Trish, Olivia just walked in and says Cherie is on her way home."

"Thank goodness. I'll let you go. Thanks, Abby," she says, and hangs up.

I wheel on Olivia. "That poor woman has been worried sick!"

Olivia spreads her hands at her sides. "What's the big deal? We were at the mall."

"Trish didn't know you were at the mall!"

"I guess Cherie forgot to tell her."

"She should have left a note!"

"Yes, she should have! Why are you shouting at *me*?"

"Because I feel bad for that woman," I declare, hands on hips.

Olivia shakes her head and turns toward the stairs.

"Who were you at the mall with?"

"Friends."

"Boys?"

"There were boys there, yeah," she says, turning back toward me. "What exactly did you and Cherie's mom talk about?"

"She said you were hanging out with some boys. Is one of them Ryan?"

Shrug.

"What does that mean?"

"It means I'm not sleeping with anybody, if that's what you're asking," Olivia growls as she stomps up the stairs.

I catch up to her on the landing. "Liv," I say, clasping her shoulder.

"Ouch," she says, reflexively pulling away from my touch.

"What's wrong?"

The worry in my voice seems to soften her. "Nothing, Abby, just …" she pauses slightly. "Somebody slammed into me during indoor volleyball yesterday, and my shoulder is still sore."

Something in the pause bothers me. "Let me see it."

"Jeez, Abby, no way! It's just a bruise. You need to relax."

"Relax? My lack of knowledge about your boyfriend status indicates that I may have been too relaxed."

"Meaning?"

"Meaning if you are irritated with me now, you will be downright aggravated over the next several weeks as I get up to speed."

⁓

"Olivia has been hanging out with some redneck boys," I say to Owen during our weekly check-in call.

"I'll keep my eyes open," Owen says. "Also, so you know, she dropped History for Intro to Psych this semester."

"Hmm. That's probably a good thing, a backward way of getting therapy."

"Maybe." There is a pause; then Owen asks, "Are you coming to the budget meeting next Wednesday?"

The hotly contested budget vote failed in November, but a small group of supporters is working hard to get it included in a March referendum. Owen has been active on the council to get the measure passed. I attended the first meeting but missed the last two, which is every meeting since I started seeing Johnson again.

"Abigail?"

The sound of my name jolts me back to the conversation. No one has called me Abigail since . . . well, ever, actually. It sounds nice.

"Sure. I'll be there, six thirty sharp."

⁓

Our January charms are miniature maple trees, deceptively delicate. My package is the size of a shoe box, and heavy. I tear away the paper, slowly lift the lid. Inside are several paperbacks, and on top of them rests a page of lovely stationery bearing the numbers 1 through 10 in Stella's hand, marching down the left side—the makings of a list.

> *Dearest Abby,*
> *A brand-new year full of possibilities! Despite the fact that*
> *I barreled through my life at ninety miles per hour, my world*

was simple. My passions were few—Olivia, you and the girls, KK&B, my rose garden. Though overwhelmed, I often felt my life was too narrow.

While I ran around like a madwoman, mouthing off to the world about my crazy life, you placidly segued from interest to interest, a devotee of each subject—until you no longer were. The cycle never changed: 1) Internet research; 2) read books—lots; 3) find guru; 4) take lessons; 5) fit new activity/program/notion into your life; 6) move on. Watercolor painting. Quilting. Running. Eckhart Tolle.

I was the maniac; you were the grounded, serene life yogi—the yin to my yang.

Since I've had time, too much time, to think about this, about us, I see things differently. Now I see your restless soul and, I suspect, a gun-shy heart. I wonder if you were so busy looking outside for that bright, shiny object, you never took the time to look inside for what mattered to you. It's as though you stopped just short of letting any one passion settle into your life.

I can say only what I see, not why it is so.

This I know: Passion happens from the inside out. It cannot be any other way. Passion is the quiet, slow burn, exactly opposite of the combustible dramas we concocted over the years, and for which your quiet, thoughtful nature is perfectly suited.

I know this only in retrospect; only now do I see how lucky I was to integrate my passions into my life. Another year, and perhaps I would have cultivated one more.

But that's not how life works. It is precisely because I don't have a year that I am having this revelation. As I sit thinking about life and death and what lies between, I know I would not trade one of my few passions for a thousand interests.

The books in this box earned high recommendations as helpful in mining the soul for passion. For comfort's sake, you can treat this as another project! Maybe you will find that one passion, or a few—that one desire, one vocation, avocation, *place, maybe even that one man. That seed that becomes the maple. The something or someone that doesn't just sweep you off your feet in the moment but takes root in your soul, becomes part of who you are, something that would leave a huge, gaping hole if it were ripped from your life.*

The page of stationery is for your Passions List. Fill with love and joy.

Happy New Year, my wonderful, sweet, passionate friend.
Stella

"That's weird," Olivia says quietly.

"Which part?"

"All of it. I mean, you're one of the most passionate people I know. And Mom always said you were passionate about everything."

Olivia's words take some of the sting out of Stella's well-intentioned edict. I smile and say, "That's your mom's point, Liv. I was passionate about everything—and nothing. Stella discovered what passion means, and it's not what I've been practicing. I've been sowing lots of seeds. Your mom is telling me it's time to weed, water, and commit to the ones that matter most."

"Which ones are those?"

"I have no idea."

Olivia smiles, then pulls her large, square, flat box into her lap and slowly removes the colorful HAPPY NEW YEAR paper. We both gasp. Within is a spectacular collage framed under glass, a myriad of photographs—of Olivia, me, the girls, even Rob and people Stella worked with, including a nice shot of Johnson looking dapper in a navy trench coat. Several shots of the rose garden, the house, the lake. Some photos are recent, some go way back to high school, and countless are from in between. Some pictures are whole, but most are cut—focused, I suppose, on what was most important to Stella. A particular rosebud, a person in the crowd, an expression on a beloved face.

We are so engrossed that several minutes pass before Olivia takes her letter in hand.

Dear, darling Olivia,

The theme for this month is passion. January offers a chance to look ahead toward a future full of hope and promise. There are tough times along the way, but now is the time to think about potential, about turning tough times to one's advantage, to grow, become stronger, more courageous, adventurous. Running through all this must be passion. Not the hot, sweaty kind, the subtle, deep kind—like the growl of a lioness protecting her cubs.

My gift to you this month is this depiction of my passions. I've spent much of the past few weeks looking at old photographs and digitals, highlighting those that resonate deeply with me, signifying passion. Many will look familiar to you; many are you, as you are my greatest passion. Others may surprise you. Whenever you want a glimpse into what made my life so wonderful, look at these.

Clichés are clichés for a reason—because they are true. I'm not sitting here regretting that I didn't squeeze in one more staff meeting to discuss rate indexes. I'm wondering why the hell I didn't go deeper into passion, why I didn't spend more time with my hands in the dirt, why I didn't take that vacation in Maui with your dad, just the two of us, like he begged me to the year before we split. Why I didn't slow down and enjoy being a mom more, be better at the little things, like baking with you or learning to knit with you, or those other details that make a mom a mom. I should have held you more, and longer, and closer, Liv. I made a business out of being your mom and thought it selfish to indulge in the passion of it. What a stupid-ass. But even with these regrets, I have known passion and I know this: passion breathes life into living.

I hope you start your own passion collection. Not with pictures, glue, and glass, but with friends and interests and events that generate the most amazing memories while pulling you forward into each new day with anticipation and delight.

Happy New Year, my sweet—may it be filled with love, peace, and passion.

Love always and forever,
Mom

Looking up at me from her letter, Olivia says, "Scrambled eggs."

I nod slowly. "You were right about that. She should have taken the time."

"No! She's got it all wrong! She was perfect. She was a perfect mom. How can you say such a thing?" Olivia is on her feet now, her chest heaving, eyes ablaze.

"Because she is telling you she wasn't perfect, and deep down she knew that you knew it. She is setting both of you free from the bondage of perfection."

Olivia continues to stare at me, wild-eyed.

"Liv, you know I think your mom was pretty much perfect, right?"

She tilts her head to one side, exposing the bare bulb so that I have to shield my eyes before continuing.

"It's the 'pretty much' part that kept me from hating her. That's where her vulnerability was, what made her human and lovable, our Stella. So we accept that part of her as perfect, too. That doesn't mean she doesn't have a right to her own regrets."

Olivia sinks back down to her knees. "But she tried so hard."

I laugh. "I love the part about making a business out of being your mom."

Olivia laughs, too. "Everything was a business. It just seems unfair that she judged herself like that."

"True," I say, pulling this lovely girl-woman into my arms. "Perhaps we can learn from that, too."

～

Passing by Olivia's room later that evening, I hear the pinging of instant messages and Olivia's voice on her mobile phone. She sounds agitated. I knock softly.

"Yes?" Olivia says, flinging the word over her shoulder as I open the door. "Hang on a minute," she says into her phone, then looks up at me expectantly.

"Is everything okay?"

"Fine. Why?"

"Well, you sounded a little . . ."

"Are you eavesdropping on me now?" Olivia asks, anger instantly flaring.

I keep my voice even. "No, I could hear you out in the hallway. I'm not going to plug my ears when I walk by your room."

"I'm fine," Olivia says, calming down. "Is that all?"

"Yes," I say, and close the door.

~

The next day Olivia comes home right after school and barricades herself in her room. Part of me thinks I should check on her, but a larger part of me enjoys time to myself again. Teenagers need space, as do introverts—especially those tossed into the deep end of raising a teenager. I reason the best course of action is sneaking *Reviving Ophelia* out of my canvas bag as though it's porn, curling up on the sofa, and reading about the mysterious world of adolescent girls—as though I never was one myself.

At around seven o'clock, the phone rings in the kitchen. I take my time, assuming it's a telemarketer. As I approach, it stops ringing, so I lift the receiver to check caller ID. It rings again in my hand. "Hello?"

"Is Olivia there?" Ryan asks—no "hello" first, which irritates me. Kids today.

"May I ask who's calling?" I don't want him to think he is her only male caller.

"Ryan," he says, verbose as ever.

"One moment." Holding the receiver to my chest, I call upstairs, "Liv, it's Ryan!"

No answer.

I climb the stairs to her room and knock loudly. When I open the door, I find Olivia typing away at her computer with her earbuds in her ears, the music so loud I can hear it from the door. "Olivia!" I shout, waving my arms to catch her peripheral vision.

She swings around, pulling the buds out of her ears. "What!" she shouts back.

"It's Ryan!" I whisper loudly. Her lips tighten, and I realize she is screening his calls to her mobile. "Do you want to talk to him?"

"Not really."

I raise the phone to my ear.

"Wait!" she whispers.

I place my hand over the mouthpiece. "I can tell him you're in the shower."

She looks relieved, nods her head.

"Ryan, she's in the shower and can't hear me. I'll tell her you called . . . Okay, I'll let her know." I hit the OFF button and sit on Olivia's bed.

"So, what's that all about?"

"It's just kid stuff."

"Olivia, I don't think you're into kid stuff anymore," I say, looking around her decidedly teenage room. "So, you're seeing him again?"

"Kind of." She shrugs and glances out the window. "Right now he's being a jerk."

I laugh. "That puts him squarely in the ninety-nine percent of teenage boyfriends."

Olivia looks back at me. "He said he loves me."

Oh, boy. "That feeds into his being a jerk . . . ?"

"He's told me that a few times, but then he . . . acts like a jerk. Then he loves me again. Is that how it works?"

This is exactly how it works most of the time, at least in my own experience, and certainly most recently with Johnson. But is that what I tell her? Looking into her troubled face, I think about all she's been through. "Sometimes," I say, patting her hand. "Sometimes not. No relationship is perfect, but I do think a certain level of consistency is required for a sound relationship."

"That's what I think, too," she says.

"If we agree, then it must be so," I say, chucking her under the chin. "Trust your instinct, Olivia. If this guy is bad news, break it off."

She looks down at her lap.

I lift her chin so our gazes lock. "Can you do that?"

She nods. But I have a sinking feeling that Ryan is not out of the picture yet.

~

On Wednesday, Johnson calls me on my mobile and sounds frantic. "Please, Abby. I know this is last minute, but there is this Burlington City Arts dinner on Friday, and I don't want to go by myself."

"Did your date cancel at the last minute?" I ask, dreading the answer.

"No, of course not. This came up last-minute." So far, so good. He continues, "It was on my calendar, but Ashley . . . well, I didn't get the reminder."

"Why don't you take her?"

"Who?"

"Ashley!"

"Oh. Because I'd rather take you."

Best answer ever. "Well," I say, dragging this out, "I don't know. I had plans . . ."

"I know it's short notice, but my parents will be there, and—"

"I will meet your parents?"

There is a pause. "Well, it's not like *meet the parents*."

"Of course not," I say.

"I mean, there's no pressure."

I glance at my calendar. "Fine, Johnson, I'll go. What time should I meet you?"

"Jeez, Abby, I can pick you up!"

I still have not told Olivia about Johnson and am not up to having that conversation right now. "I will meet you, Johnson."

∼

Luckily, Olivia has play practice Friday evening and intends to spend the night at Cherie's. Trish and I now have a system. I secretly call her when Olivia says she's heading over there; she calls me when Olivia arrives. We work it in reverse when Cherie comes here, which is far less often. But at least I can pick her out of a lineup now. Despite her tough-girl exterior, Cherie seems bright and good-natured, and her affection for Olivia is genuine. I'm glad Olivia has Cherie, and I'm glad I have Trish to help me keep an eye on our girls. Trish also has a potty mouth and a killer sense of humor.

I prep as much as I can before Olivia leaves, then kick into high gear once the sound of her car fades. I throw hot curlers in my hair, apply makeup, spray perfume strategically, slip my new gown over my head, take out the curlers, run a brush through the waves, spray with fine-hold, then finish with mega-hold, and I am ready.

I find Johnson in his BMW at the end of the parking lot, and tuck my Saab into the spot on the right. My purse gets tangled on the stick shift, and Johnson watches my ass while I wrestle it loose. As I pop up and around, he encircles me in a bear hug. I slap him with my purse and squeal about messing up my hair. Grinning, he takes my hand and we head into the Hyatt. As we enter the ballroom, flashbulbs pop in our faces. This part is still fun. Olivia doesn't read the society pages, but the girls do—now. I smile widely, my hand tucked securely in the crook of Johnson's arm.

We wander table to table, meeting players in the BCA community. Then a large, balding man with a petite, brassy-blond, middle-aged woman on his arm approaches us. I recognize him immediately as Byron Johnson Keller and realize she must be Carolyn Keller.

"Dad!" Johnson smiles as he extends his hand.

"Son!" the senior Keller booms, shaking his son's hand vigorously. Both are white-knuckled. I can barely control an eye roll.

Johnson breaks free from his father and leans over to kiss his mother on the cheek, "This," he says, motioning my way, "is Abby St. Claire."

"A pleasure to meet you," I say, extending my hand first to Mrs. Keller, then to Mr. Keller. They both profess delight at meeting me, though it's clear they have never heard my name. This smarts, but only momentarily, as I remind myself Johnson and I are not officially anything worth mentioning to either set of parents.

"Are you ready to join us at the head table?" Byron Keller says to Johnson.

Johnson looks at me guiltily, then back at his father. "I'll be right there."

"Head table?" I hiss in Johnson's ear. "What the hell does that mean?"

"I kind of forgot about that," Johnson says sheepishly.

"Forgot the fact you have to sit at the head table? Where do I sit? In the kitchen?"

"Of course not. You can sit right at this table here." He gestures to a round table for eight. "From what I understand, there are some Fairleigh folks sitting here, so I'm sure you'll know someone."

"Johnson. I'm going to kill you."

"You can kill me as soon as we leave, hon. Did I mention you look hot?" He winks, and I struggle to stay pissed at him. I stomp my foot. "Really, really hot," he adds.

I whirl around, plunk into one of the seats at the half-empty table, and flick my hand at him dismissively. I look across the table, straight into the face of Owen Montagne.

"Owen!" I exclaim, then glance guiltily at Johnson's receding, tuxedoed back.

"Nice to see you, Abigail."

"It's nice to see you, too! I was afraid I would be stuck with a bunch of strangers!" I regret my words immediately. How self-absorbed could I be? "I mean—"

"I totally understand. These functions make me uncomfortable. It's always nice to run into a friend."

"This came up very last-minute, and, well, I guess he"—I gesture over my shoulder in the general direction of Johnson—"didn't think this through."

"Johnson can be an impetuous guy," Owen says.

"Do you know Johnson?"

"Yes, I do."

The silence stretches to the point where I am almost ready to say something surely stupid, when I see Ashley threading her way straight toward our table. She's holding a glass of champagne in each hand, a woman on a mission. Johnson must be sending her over with a drink to pacify me. She is never off the clock, which I suspect has more to do with her hunky boss than with a strong work ethic. Despite this conclusion, and despite how stunning she looks in that slinky indigo one-shoulder Armani knockoff, she is a welcome sight. "Ashley!" I say brightly, rising slightly out of my chair.

"Oh, hello, Abby," she says, looking surprised to see me.

"Hi," I say stupidly, and sit back down.

Ashley's gaze turns to Owen, and she brightens. "Here!" she says, placing a glass of champagne by his plate as she shimmies into the chair right next to him.

There is another uncomfortable pause; then Ashley, ever the go-to girl, glances around the table and asks, "Does everybody know each other?" The three other people at the table, a couple and a young man who is likely their son, glance around dubiously. "Let's go around the table, then. I'm Ashley Lafontaine, and I work for Keller, Keller, Beech, and Rose. I run the place, actually, but don't tell the Kellers!" Polite chuckles. "I'm here tonight to support the BCA and"—she lowers her voice to a conspiratorial whisper—"to help Owen drum up support for the school budget vote." She puts her perfectly polished index finger to her lips and smiles.

Today is Friday; the budget meeting was Wednesday. Wednesday was the day Johnson called to ask me to this event. Then I totally forgot about the budget meeting.

I want to sink beneath the table. But I can't, because Ashley is beaming at Owen, urging him to go next, and it would be rude to leave before we've all had our turn.

Owen shyly introduces himself, thanks Ashley for plugging the school budget. He avoids my eyes as he assures everyone he won't pump them too hard for their vote.

The couple next to me are the Howards, Lydia and Donald, and this is, indeed, their son to my left. His name is Preston, and he has been accepted at Georgetown and Skidmore and Northeastern. So many choices, you know. I recognize their name from the Harmony's top-ten-patrons list. Great, just what I need—an opportunity to humiliate myself in front of friends of the museum.

It's my turn. My palms are sweating, my mouth gauzy. I glance at Ashley, and she holds my gaze. She engineered this whole introduction scene to have me go last and be my most nervous. And the school budget reference was intentional. How does she know the significance of my missing it? How does she know I hate this kind of thing, and my palms are sweaty, and I can feel pit stains forming on my own Armani knockoff?

"I . . . My name is . . ." My hands flutter in front of me like aimless butterflies.

"Abigail Solace St. Claire," says Owen quietly but clearly.

Telepathing my gratitude, I say, "But nearly everyone calls me Abby."

"What a lovely name!" Mrs. Howard says. "And what do you do?"

"I work at the Harmony Museum."

"She's being modest," Owen says, leaning toward the Howards. "She actually runs the place, but don't tell Richard Rothschild."

Everyone laughs—except Ashley, who clearly does not appreciate Owen's play on her words. I am delighted. Then Owen says to Donald Howard, "Abby has great ideas for the Spring Fling, don't you, Abby?"

Okay, I say to myself, *he's lobbed this to you underhand. Knock it out of the park.* "Yes! We have several important projects coming up. I want to reinvigorate the spring event to showcase the museum and inspire folks to be involved."

"Like what?" asks Mrs. Howard.

"Well, like the Wilheimer exhibit, and the Cologne pieces, and—"

"No, dear, what kind of ideas do you have to reinvigorate the spring event?"

Oh. My mistake.

"Abby," says Mr. Howard with a hearty laugh, "my wife is all about the party. If you want feedback, she'll give you an earful. But I will say, those sound like great exhibits, and it's nice to see young people excited about the arts."

"It's my life," I say, breathless and flushed, partly because I know this is true. How could I not have known this before? "It's my passion."

"That's obvious," Mr. Howard says. "Now, let my wife help you give the patrons what they want. Her passion is parties."

I smile at them both, then at Owen.

"Abby, you must take down my phone number, and if I don't hear from you by the end of next week, I will be highly insulted," Mrs. Howard says.

I scrounge through my tiny purse for my mobile and add her name and number to my contacts. "Thank you so much, Mrs. Howard."

"Lydia, please."

"I look forward to working with you, Lydia."

"Oh, seriously," Donald Howard booms, "the pleasure is all Lydia's. She's not happy if she's not putting her time to good use." He gazes at his wife affectionately.

"Don," she says, patting his arm, "there are more important things than playing golf every day."

These people are rich and privileged, funny and generous, and I like them very much. Perhaps we were the prejudiced ones, Stella. Lesson 31,897. Check.

February

*S*tella My Rose, how do I tell you about the worry in my heart, the nagging static in my brain? It's not just piercings, tantrums, and sneakiness. Something sinister lurks.

But I don't need to tell you. For years you tried to explain this phenomenon to me. Rather than listen, I tried to allay your fears while secretly thinking to myself, *How paranoid can one woman be?*

Now I lie awake on Friday nights barely breathing so I don't miss the crunching of gravel under tires in the wee hours of the morning. I imagine her car in a ditch. Upside down. Water. A river, actually, swirling into the car. Olivia hangs suspended by her seat belt, suffocating in the folds of the airbag, water creeping higher and higher.

All the scenarios disappear the moment headlights diffuse the darkness. The familiar thrum of the Subaru's motor is as comforting as a baby's heartbeat.

I swear, Stella, something bad is going to happen.

I will never doubt the existence of mothers' intuition again.

February brings with it a foot of snow and perfect temperatures to enjoy it. I stare out the patio doors off the kitchen, transfixed by the twinkling white. I have to admit, with everything going on, I've had no chance to grouse about winter, let alone enjoy it.

~

Olivia drives me to the *Macbeth* auditions. Just because my hands are shaking uncontrollably doesn't mean I can't drive, but she insists. She keeps looking sideways at me and asking me if I am going to be sick. *Yes, I am going to be sick, so stop the car.*

Three miles and six Altoids later, we arrive at the Flynn and scurry across the snow-swirled parking lot into the tiny studio. The foyer is close and damp with heavy winter coats, boots piled everywhere, and the smell of nerves suspended like fog.

Olivia squeezes my hand, and I pull off a twitchy semblance of a smile. She looks mortified, and I wonder if she is not just a teensy bit sorry she got me into this.

But she was right to push me, and I don't want her to feel bad about it. I stand straighter, give her a real smile, lean over to her ear, and say, "I'll be fine."

She smiles uncertainly. "I'll be right here," she says, taking a seat near the door. I nod, and walk over to the other actors. Too soon, it's my turn.

Abby! I hear Stella's voice like a thunderclap and realize a light in the corner has fallen over. But when I close my eyes, Stella's voice is still there and I actually see her words etched in the crazy lines behind my lids: *This isn't about me or Olivia or anyone else. This is about you. Do you have the nerve?*

I open my eyes, and just before I speak, I hear one last line: *Don't you dare embarrass me!*

I giggle, and everyone turns to me. I take a deep breath and look at the script in my hands. Then I peer out into the audience that isn't there, that I could not see anyway. I recite the lines I know that I know, and it is all over in five minutes.

I hear a "Yes!" and wild clapping from the corner, which stops abruptly. I laugh as I walk off the stage and over to Olivia, my newest, biggest fan. She hugs me, tells me I was fantastic. Though I am shaking all over, I feel triumphant. I will not play Lady M, but I will be in this production, I know. Any part that allows me to play with these people five nights in a row, spouting Shakespeare at an audience that gets it, will be an honor. I glance over at Hector, but he is watching the next person intently, as he should be.

As soon as the reading is over, however, he finds me with his eyes and nods.

~

February 14 arrives with six more inches of fresh snow and sloppy roads. Midmorning, I receive a bouquet of flowers—more aptly described as an entire garden thrust into five pounds of molten crystal—with a card that says, *See you on Friday.* I toss the card and place the flowers in the tiny cafeteria, where everyone can enjoy them. I am teased about my secret admirer, and some guess it is Johnson, having seen our picture in the paper, but I keep mum.

At noon I am surprised to see Owen Montagne enter the museum, looking chilled, his glasses steamed. I walk over to him with my hand extended. "Owen? How nice to see you."

He grasps my hand, shakes it hard, and says, "Hi, Abigail. I was hoping you'd be here. I have only a moment, but I wanted to give you this." He removes a Phoenix Books bag from under his arm and hands it to me.

"What is it?" I ask, peeking into the bag.

"It's a journal." I look at Owen, and he suddenly seems uncomfortable. "I . . . I thought with everything going on with Olivia and all the changes in your life . . ."

"Well," I laugh, "it just so happens I seem to have lost mine in the move to Stella's." I pull the journal out of the bag. The tan cover is a buttery, bovine-friendly material; the pages are the color of parchment and faintly lined.

"Thank you, Owen."

He smiles, and a tugging starts in my chest. He gets me.

"Wait here," I say, heading down the hall to my office. I place the journal on my desk. Then, as I pass the cafeteria, I pull a single rose from the obscene arrangement.

I return to Owen, hold out the rose. "Happy Valentine's Day."

He looks flustered but pleased. He takes the rose, bows deeply. "Happy Valentine's Day to you, Ms. Abigail Solace St. Claire." Smiling, he takes his leave.

~

Over dinner I ask Olivia if she received a Valentine's Day gift from Ryan. She snorts, says that's not his style. "He said, 'VD is for losers, so don't expect anything.'"

I find this gauche, but guys weren't into Valentine's Day when I was in high school, either.

"Did you get anything?" Olivia asks casually, but my antennae are up.

"Why would I get anything?" I ask.

"Answering a question with a question is not an answer."

I smile at this Stella-ism. "I actually did receive a gift of sorts, though it wasn't a Valentine's Day gift. It's a journal."

"That's kind of romantic."

I hadn't thought of it in terms of romance, but in fact I was more moved by the journal than I was by the flowers I will not tell Olivia about.

"Who from?" Olivia asks.

"Actually, it was from O—Mr. Montagne."

Olivia's eyebrows shoot up. "I knew it! He has a crush on you. I think he had a crush on Mom, too." This gives me pause, as I recall Owen's admission that day I met him at the café. "Mom had that effect on guys."

"That's true," I say. "But she had this uncanny way of staying within boundaries."

Olivia snorts again, then recovers.

I glance at her. "What was that for?"

Olivia looks uncomfortable. "Most of the time," she says, looking at the remains of her oven-fried chicken.

"Owen Montagne?"

"God, no. She minded her p's and q's with him."

"So he's probably just transferring his crush on your mom to me."

"I'm not so sure," Olivia says, grinning at me. "He talks to me more now than he ever did when Mom was here, and he always manages to turn the conversation to you."

I reach over to swat Olivia's arm. "Well, it's not appropriate to hang out with your daughter's advisor." I suck in my breath as I catch Olivia's eye, and we both pause a moment, the phrase hanging between us. I look down. "You know what I mean."

"I think it's perfectly okay."

When I glance up, she is picking up her plate and heading to the sink. Okay to hang out with Owen, or okay that I just referred to her as my daughter?

∼

Our February boxes are swathed in hearts. Our charms are three intertwined, intricately wrought silver hearts. At the sight, we catch our breath and grab tissues.

Inside my box is a four-by-six-inch candid shot of Stella and Olivia, framed in delicate silver plaited in a scrolling pattern. Stella is smiling at Olivia, drinking her in; Olivia is smiling broadly at me, or so it seems. With Stella in near profile and Olivia staring straight on, I see a physical similarity I haven't noticed before and realize it is in their shared expression of happiness, humor, and love.

I tilt the picture toward Olivia. "Do you remember when this was taken?"

She smiles at the photo, but her sadness is palpable. "No, but it was before."

I glance back at the picture and realize she must be right. This was taken before leukemia entered the picture and removed joy this pure. I unfold the letter and begin.

> *Abby, my love!*
>
> *February is the month of love, providing the perfect excuse to talk about love in all its splendor. While I love you and Olivia to the moon and beyond, we all know that Valentine's Day is not about friendship or family. It's about romantic love, a notion we have spent hours eschewing. How did we get so jaded in our thirties?*
>
> *Rhetorical question. We've both been dragged through the knothole of love. But the bottom line is, we are wrong about love. That's right, Ms. Antirelationship has had a change of heart. It seems like all the other revelations I've come upon recently have been cancer-driven. This is the exception. This has been coming for a while, and cancer has only made me realize what a waste holding your breath can be.*
>
> *So exhale, Abby. Be yourself so he can find you, that man who loves all of who you are. You have always been good "at men." But you have always kept your heart to yourself. I'm sure I contributed to that, poisoning you against marriage, discouraging you from going too deep with a man in order to protect yourself. Part of it was genuine concern, but—I must admit this now—part of it was fear of losing you to a man. That part was selfish, Abby, and I'm sorry. While it seems incredibly self-serving to tell you this now that I am losing you to death, please know this: I was going to tell you anyway.*
>
> *Happy Valentine's Day, lovely Abigail Solace St. Claire. And when he finds you, tell this incredibly lucky man I approve.*
>
> *Love to you,*
> *Me*

I expect Olivia to be full of questions, but she remains silent. Slowly I fold the letter, deep in thought about Stella's words—potent yet harboring the secret of a man in London who changed her fundamental position on love.

I am roused by Olivia's slowly tearing the paper from her own package. Inside lies an identical silver frame, this one holding a photo of Stella and me, each proffering peace-sign gestures, our cheeks pressed together, our lips pursed in a kiss toward the camera. Olivia raises her eyebrows at me.

"That was taken on the Valentine's Day before I left for Greece, and before . . ." I say, my voice thick. "We were the only non-lesbian same-sex couple in the restaurant, according to the maître d', who took the picture. It was our standing date."

Olivia nods, smiling softly.

Dearest Olivia Rose,

How do I love thee? Ah, it is impossible to say in a letter, a dozen letters, a hundred letters. Words like "infinite," "endless," "bottomless," "limitless" all fail to convey the scope of my love for you. But this isn't about my love for you. It's about L-O-V-E.

In high school, for a dollar, kids could buy a carnation to give to a boyfriend or girlfriend, or a favorite teacher, or even a best friend, on Valentine's Day. For the most part, boys were too cool for public declarations of love. Most girls were the same, myself included. But deep down, I believed in Valentine's Day. I knew the world needed a day when it was okay—even required—to declare your love.

Then I stopped believing in Valentine's Day because I stopped believing in love. I felt it was superfluous, distracting, even, to the more noble pursuits in life, such as having a sound profession, a solid connection to one's higher power, being a good mom, a good friend, a generous human being.

Of course I still believe these are noble goals and pursuing them is integral to leading a full and rich life. But I no longer believe romantic love is superfluous or distracting. One can live a full life without a significant other. Sometimes love just doesn't come along, or it's lost and not replaced. But by fencing out the experience of being in love, I denied myself another of life's noble pursuits—that of navigating through the falling part, around the post-honeymoon part, and toward the forever part.

So once you have figured out who you are and what you want out of life and you are being your most authentic self, that forever person will come along. I trust your heart will open your eyes to your love's arrival. I wish for you the joy, challenges, and fulfillment of true love that become as integral to your existence as God and breathing.

And he (or she!) had better be good to you, or there will be hell to pay.

Love always to infinity . . .

Mom

"Wow," I say with a little laugh, "who wrote that?"

"That is *not* my mother," declares Olivia, her voice rising. "This is total crap!"

"Liv!" I say, startled at her outburst.

"All these years she's told me what a waste of time boys are, and love is overrated, and there's more to life than worrying about someone liking me. Now she's telling me to go off and find the man of my dreams! What the hell?"

"I think she meant—"

"You don't know what she meant," Olivia says, scrambling to her feet. "She was sick; she was confused." She grabs her wrapping paper and shoves it into the trash bag. "I have homework to do."

With that, Olivia descends the attic stairs. By the time I grab the teacups and make it down, Olivia is barricaded inside her bedroom, her world narrowed to what is coming at her from the computer screen and her earbuds.

～

On Monday at noon, Owen calls me from school. "So, Abigail, have you been able to reschedule that NYU visit?"

"Shit!" I say. "Oh, sorry, Owen. No, we haven't. I need to get on that."

"You have time. Hey, I heard Rothschild is retiring."

"Who hasn't heard? Jeez, it's like front-page news that never quite makes it to print. And no, he hasn't announced a successor."

"I was just thinking it must be unsettling."

"I'm sorry—I'm stressed these days. I'll get right on the school visits. Olivia did send out some scholarship applications," I say, hoping to score points.

"Excellent," Owen says, soothing as always. "How are rehearsals going?"

"Ugh," I say, "I feel like the old crone among all those young things. They need three times the makeup I do to become one of the witches!" Owen laughs, a river over rocks, and I smile. "I'm enjoying my little part, though. Have you bought tickets yet?"

"You bet," he says. "Do you have a rigorous rehearsal schedule?"

"Not as rigorous as the schedule for *Annie*," I say. Predictably, Olivia won the lead role and has been at rehearsals every day after school for three weeks. "I was thinking of swinging by this afternoon to watch."

"They don't have rehearsal on Mondays, just Tuesdays and Thursdays."

My mouth goes dry as I pace laps around my desk.

~

I text Olivia and tell her I'm thinking of going to watch her rehearsal. Twenty minutes later, she texts me back, saying today's rehearsal was canceled and that I should swing by tomorrow night. Clever girl. I call her.

"Liv, I need to know where you've been hanging out, and don't lie to me."

"Abby, this is crap. I'm seventeen years old."

I rise and shut the door to my office before hissing into the phone, "But you're not eighteen, and until you are, I have a right to know where you are and who you are with every second of every day."

"That could get tedious."

"That's fine. Let's start right now. Where are you going right this minute?"

Silence.

"Olivia?"

"Community service."

"What?"

"Seniors have to do forty hours of community service. I'm getting my hours in."

I say the first thing that comes to my head: "I don't believe you."

Before I can take it back, Olivia says, "That's your prerogative."

And I am listening to dead air.

∿

I call Owen. When he picks up, I spill out an abridged version of the conversation and request that he look into Olivia's community service records. He assures me he will, he does, and he gets right back to me.

"It appears she's been putting in her community service hours, and the times correspond to after school on Mondays, Wednesdays, and Fridays for the past few weeks. In fact, she has only a few hours to go."

Gulping audibly, I say, "Well, shit."

∿

Olivia walks through the door in an obvious huff and stomps up the stairs. I walk up after her and stand in the doorway as she settles at her computer.

"Why didn't you just tell me you were doing community service?"

"I thought you didn't believe me."

It's my turn to be silent.

Olivia swings around and looks me in the eye.

"Abby, can I ask one thing? I'd rather not say exactly what I do. I help people, I'm in a safe environment that's approved by the school, and I hope that's all you need to know right now."

"Why won't you tell me?"

"I know you don't trust me after I lied to you, but I need you to try. I will tell you soon, I promise. Right now I need to do this in my own way. Can you trust me on this?"

I look into those dark-honey eyes, pleading and hopeful, and I have no choice. "Okay, Liv. When you're ready, I'm here." I leave her alone with her homework and take my uneasiness with me.

～

On Wednesday I get the call I've been anticipating for weeks, ever since my dead-end conversation with Johnson about Stella's mystery man. When I see the London area code on my mobile screen, I quickly hop up to close the door to my office before hitting the ANSWER button. "Hello?"

"Hello, is this Ms. Abby St. Claire?" says a formal and familiar male voice.

"Yes, it is, Mr. Haversmith."

"Desmond, please."

"Desmond, thank you for calling me back. Did you enjoy your trip?"

"Indeed, Ms. St. Claire, we did."

"Abby, please."

Desmond chuckles. "Touché, Abby. Our holiday was extended unexpectedly when I managed to break my leg traversing rough terrain in the Alps. So much for a romantic getaway!"

"That is what Ms. Devonshire told me when I called last month. She said your wife grounded you until you were mobile. I trust you are healing well?"

"Of course. I was perfectly fit for travel, but my wife worries too much. Frankly, she loves French cuisine, and I suspect she was in no hurry. It had been too long since our last trip, and she doesn't trust the new me, who promises to travel more from now on."

I laugh. "Trusting in change is hard with people we know too well."

"Indeed," agrees Desmond. "Now, what can I do for you?"

After Johnson's defense of Stella's right to privacy, I worry that Haversmith may share the same concern. So I invoke my new acting skills. "I am putting together a photo album of Stella Rose's most memorable moments. But we have a major gap. We have no pictures of Stella's last trip to London. She became sick very shortly after returning from London, and things got . . . lost."

"Of course. I understand completely. How can I help?"

"Do you have a photo of Stella, preferably one with her partner? When we left your hotel, Ms. Devonshire insisted on taking our picture for the scrapbook, so I'm hoping you have one of Stella. I asked Ms. Devonshire, but she was unable to locate the pictures in your database."

Desmond laughs. "Yes, Ms. Devonshire has never quite adjusted to the computer age. Since we went digital, I've had to manage the scrapbook. Let me look for a picture, and I'll e-mail it to you."

"Desmond, you have no idea what that would mean to me," I say, nearly choking on each syllable.

"My pleasure, Abby. Ms. Rose was lucky to have such a friend as you."

As I hang up, I wonder, for the first time ever, if this is true. Does being Stella Rose's best friend give me permission to rummage around in an area of her life she kept hidden? Dammit, Stella. Why would you be dying to tell me something, then die before telling me?

~

Two days later, I have my answer. With shaking fingers I open the e-mail from Desmond, titled "Our Dear Stella Rose." In his e-mail, Desmond says, *Ms. Devonshire took this candid shot. It's the only one we have, but what a lovely photo, don't you agree? A woman is at her loveliest when in love.* I click on the attachment icon and watch as the picture fills my screen.

Confusion floods my head. Disbelief nearly stops my heart.

~

Stalking past Ashley, who is clearly taken aback by my indifference to her chirpy "Good afternoon, Abby!" I walk directly into Johnson's office. Empty. Ashley is behind me in a flash. "Johnson is in a partners' meeting right now. They won't be finished for at least forty-five minutes."

I wheel on her. "Then poke your pretty little head in there and haul his ass out this second, or I will go get him myself."

Ashley blinks, assessing my mental state, no doubt. By the third blink, she nods and, turning on her stiletto heel, heads down the corridor to the conference room. She is back in five minutes, a harried Johnson in tow.

"Abby, what's going on?" he asks, looking concerned.

"This," I say, thrusting a copy of the photograph at him. It's a simple black-and-white copy, but sufficient. One glimpse, and Johnson has me by the elbow, steering me into his office without so much as a glance in Ashley's direction.

Closing the door behind us, Johnson leads me to one of the overstuffed leather chairs next to the coffee table. He pulls its mate close so we are knee to knee. I am shaking so badly my teeth chatter, but it's not due to a chill, and Johnson doesn't offer me his jacket. Instead he stares at the picture now resting on the coffee table.

"Abby—"

I silence him with my hand. "I have only one question." Raising my eyes to his, I see pure anguish and am unmoved. "Did you love her?"

"Yes."

His answer, so swift and sure, shocks me into silence. Swallowing hard, I put my face in my hands, unable to look at him.

"Abby, I wanted to tell you so many times."

I let this sit as I gaze at the picture of my best friend and my lover—her lover. Desmond was right—Stella never looked more beautiful. She leans across a tiny, intimate table toward Johnson, laughing, apparently at something he said, her eyes on him, her smile the spontaneous one that lights her entire face—the entire room. Her tiny hand is holding a fork and poking it in his direction, clearly making a point that's been lost. Clasped around her hand is Johnson's, so large and familiar, and it's as though he is staying her hand, but the gesture is so intimate, the look in his eyes so soft and hungry at the same time, they could be lying in tangled bedsheets.

It was a stupid question to ask. Of course he loved her. As for Stella, she wears a look I have never seen before—not when she fell in love with Nate Charlebois in the eighth grade, or Seth Mayer in senior year, or Rob when we were twenty. How could this have happened without me?

Snatching up the photocopy, I stand to leave.

Johnson grabs my elbow. "Abby, let me explain."

"You've had months to explain," I say, straining against his grip. "Now it's clear. You loved her. She loved you. Case closed. Mystery solved." Yanking my arm out of his grasp, I head for the door.

"Abby, please."

My hand on the brass knob, I press my forehead to the heavy mahogany door.

"Abby, I tried to tell you."

"Bullshit."

"It's not bullshit, Abby. There were several times, but that day I asked you to lunch, that was supposed to be the day."

"But what?" I ask, my voice muffled against the door.

"We kept getting off track. It was like . . ."

"Like?" I ask, raising my head, still staring at the rich, marbled wood of the door.

"It was like you didn't want to know."

"That's the best you can do?" I start to turn toward him but don't.

"Not good enough." Turning the knob, I walk out without looking back. I feel Ashley's gaze on me, but I continue resolutely out the door of Keller, Keller, Beech, and Rose.

∿

The drive home is treacherous, and I welcome the all-engrossing challenge that prevents me from obsessing over these revelations. The usual twenty minutes stretch to forty-five, making the amount of time between my arrival at the house and bedtime that much shorter. Another good thing. I want to slip into oblivion, avoid the specter hiding on the periphery of my subconscious. A glass of chianti will help.

Once safely inside the warm house, I realize Olivia is not here yet. She must still be at community service. I walk through the house and I see reflections of Stella everywhere, hear echoes of her footsteps in each room. In the months since her death, I have felt comfortable here. Stella's presence, familiar and warm, kept utter desolation and grief at bay. But now, as I finger her possessions and survey her surroundings, I feel numb, and cold. I have slipped out of my mooring, am adrift, feeling the steel prick of anxiety between my shoulder blades.

Everything is on its head.

"There's this cute guy at work."

"Don't go there."

"Stella, just indulge me for a minute."

"Nope. Workplace romances are messy, and they fuck up your career."

"There are plenty of happy couples who met at work."

"First of all, I haven't met that many happy couples. Secondly, some couples do meet at work, but eventually one person has to leave, and that's usually the—"

"The woman. I get it, Stella; I just don't think it's an absolute."

"Maybe, but what makes you think you could possibly be that one in a million?"

"But he likes me."

"*Where does this guy come from?*"

"*Montreal.*"

"*Oh, well, thirdly—never trust metros from Montreal. Case closed.*"

Wandering into the kitchen, I put the teakettle on. Then I turn it off. On. Off. I go for the chianti.

At the kitchen table, the glass and its ruby contents in my grip, I stare out into the darkness littered with huge flakes of snow.

"*Stella, you don't understand. He and Stacey are separated.*"

"*Doesn't matter.*"

"*Can't you just be happy for me? Tony and I have been attracted to each other for years, and we never did anything about it.*"

"*I'm only saying this because—*"

"*You love me.*"

"*Because I love you, Abby. I don't know everything, but I do know you. One day you will obsess over his leaving Stacey for you, and it will destroy you.*"

"*You're not telling me this because you love me; it's because you're jealous!*"

"*Wow, I hadn't thought about that. But you could be right.*"

"*Well, that's a first.*"

"*Dammit, Abby, it's not a first. You're right all the time. You hear me only when I have a different point of view. So many times I've wished I were you. Don't you understand that?*"

A gust of wind throws snow, like a fistful of sand, against the French doors, jerking me back into the dark, quiet kitchen. Did Stella ever want to be me? Did I want to be her, deep down? How often I railed against her advice, and yet I didn't accept Jaime's advances and I never slept with Tony—though it was only by a thread, by an echo of Stella's voice in my head, a truth that resonated in my body that she was right, that Tony and I would regret it. Indeed, Tony and Stacey reconciled and had another child and, by all accounts, have managed to find happiness together. And when I run into them in the supermarket, I can look Stacey in the eye.

So was Stella's affair with Johnson her attempt to be me? I ponder this as I take another long sip of wine. That one relationship contained a critical mass of taboos I flirted with for years, the ones that drove Stella crazy with worry about me and likely kept me single and unsettled all that time. Then she changes the rules, alluding to it only in a deathbed letter to be opened months later?

The picture of Stella and Johnson fills my mind. I don't see taboos; I see love. Clear-eyed and uncluttered. After all these years, she found what had eluded us, what we eventually claimed we didn't need in the first place but both secretly continued to yearn for. She found it. And didn't tell me.

Part Four
Spring

If you came this way,
Taking any route, starting from anywhere,
At any time or at any season,
It would always be the same: you would have to put off
Sense and notion. You are not here to verify,
Instruct yourself, or inform curiosity
Or carry report. You are here to kneel
Where prayer has been valid. And prayer is more
Than an order of words, the conscious occupation
Of the praying mind, or the sound of the voice praying.
And what the dead had no speech for, when living,
They can tell you, being dead: the communication
Of the dead is tongued with fire beyond the language of the living.

"Little Gidding," Verse I
Four Quartets, by T. S. Eliot

March

I know what you were doing in London; I know who you were doing it with. I don't know what to say, what to think, or how to feel. I just can't talk to you right now.

March roars in like a lion pissed off at the foot of snow on his back. By the tenth, we set a snowfall record—no surprise to any of us who have been digging out for weeks. While I bitch about it along with everyone else, deep down I'm glad for the snow. If it's going to be this freaking cold, we might as well have lots of powder to play in. Not that I have ever actually played in the snow, but this year I have been snow-tubing twice, bought a pair of snowshoes I intend to use, and listened to Olivia say how goofy she is on her snowboard. After nearly forty years, perhaps I am finally thawing to winter.

But my heart is heavy with thoughts of Stella and Johnson and secrets.

Meanwhile, the rumor mill at work is in overdrive regarding Rothschild's replacement and the financial future of the Harmony. While I silently keep my money on the new chief financial officer, who showed up last month, several throw their support behind Jaime, who has ramped up the charm. I am amused and touched when my intern enters my office and declares, "You should take Dr. Rothschild's place."

"Thanks," I say, "but it doesn't work that way. I don't have the credentials."

"That's crap," Kristin says, reminding me just how young she is. "You've been practically running the place for years. Everyone says so."

"'Practically' and 'actually' are two different things. Mr. Rothschild has a much higher level of responsibility." I put down my pen and look Kristen in the eye. "You enjoy your master's program, right?"

"Yes," she says, standing straighter. "Especially working here."

I smile. "And when you are finished, you will have something I don't."

"Really?" she asks, clearly stunned.

"It never bothered me much, but I have to admit, at times like this it sure would be handy. Now, scoot. I've got work to do." I shoo her out of my office with a grin and try to dig into my paperwork before that familiar wave of regret washes over me.

$\sim$

Rehearsals for *Macbeth* become a welcome diversion, allowing me to sink into being someone else—even being a witch is preferable to my real life these days. Hector notices and nods approvingly. If only he knew where my motivation comes from.

Shrugging into my coat after Thursday's rehearsal, I grab my purse and head for the exit door. I'm surprised to see Owen Montagne there.

"Hi, Abigail," he says. "You looked great out there."

I'm a little embarrassed—and piqued. "I didn't know they let people watch."

"Guess security is lax." His smile dims. "I hope you don't mind. I wanted to follow up on a couple of things with Olivia, so I thought I'd catch you after rehearsal."

"You drove thirty miles to Burlington for that?" I ask tersely. I can see he is taken aback. "I'm sorry, Owen. It's been a rough couple of weeks."

"No, you're right. I should have called. I can call you tomorrow."

"Let's go to Kroger's for hot chocolate. We can catch up."

Though this cheers him, an awkward silence persists as we walk a block to the small coffee shop located on the intimate pedestrian mall, the heart of downtown. We order hot chocolate, find a small table at the slightly fogged window.

"So?" I ask, taking my first careful sip from the steaming mug.

"I wanted to follow up on the college trips with Olivia."

Knowing this was coming, I abandon my rehearsed excuses and say simply, "Not happening. I just can't get Olivia on the same page."

"Ah, I see."

"Do you? Because I don't." Defiance in my voice.

"Well, you've both been busy . . ."

"Busy, my ass, Owen. We've been avoiding this thing. It looms between us like a ghost." Bad choice of words. "Not a ghost, but a—a chasm."

"I'm sorry," Owen says, looking at me with soft hushpuppy eyes.

This annoys the shit out of me.

"Owen, you need to stop looking at me like that."

"Like what?" Owen asks, sitting back in his chair, clearly stung.

"Like . . . like you want to save me. Like you're rooting for the underdog. You want me to do what I just can't do."

"Abigail, it's not like that."

"No? It's not like you want me to get this right for Olivia, to not fuck it up? To fulfill Stella's wishes? Isn't that what this is about?"

Owen looks genuinely at a loss, and this spurs me on.

"Owen, you want me to be Stella! Everyone wants me to be Stella! No one gets that I'm just a lousy substitute. You had a crush on her;

you probably even loved her. Get in line—everyone did! Now you want me. But you don't want me. You all want Stella!" Tears stream down my face, and I'm fairly certain my nose is running, because Owen is thrusting napkins at me—déjà vu.

I blow my nose lustily as I stand. Wadding the napkins, I place them inside my half-empty cup of hot chocolate and grab my purse. Owen continues to stare at me, but I can't look him in the eye. I can't believe I just said what I said. I bolt, leaving him there alone, my diatribe ringing in both our ears.

Halfway across the square, Owen catches my elbow, locks me in place. Standing close behind, he wraps his arms around me, bends to my ear. "I don't know what that was all about, but it was not about me. For the record, you couldn't fuck it up if you tried. Stella was right about that." He releases me. As I turn, he is walking away and doesn't look back.

~

The next morning, I startle awake from another fitful night's sleep. I don't bother to cover a monstrous yawn as I push open the kitchen door and head for the Keurig, where a steaming cup of coffee awaits.

"Good morning, sunshine!" Olivia exclaims as I shamble over to the table.

"Well, this will certainly fortify me for another grueling day in the office," I grumble.

"It's Saturday."

"It is?"

"Yes," Olivia says, leaning across the table, looking me straight in the eye. "It's Saturday and you didn't even know it. What is going on?"

"I'm fine."

"Come on, Abby. I don't want to push, but whatever this is, it's getting worse. I heard you last night."

I look up. "What do you mean?"

"Talking in your sleep. Yelling, actually."

"Oh," I say, looking at my plate, suddenly full but scooping another forkful of eggs anyway. "What did I say?"

"I couldn't make out all of it, but clearly you were talking to Mom."

"I talk to your mom all the time," I say, though this has not been true for a while.

"Not like this."

My heart beats faster as I continue to avoid her eyes. "Like what?"

"You weren't happy. You were yelling that she kept something from you."

"Dreams never make any sense," I say, then take a long drink of orange juice.

"Abby, are you getting sick of being here with me?"

Choking on the juice, I grab my napkin and cough violently. Olivia is on her feet, but I wave her back into her chair. Once I have my breath back, I place my hands flat on the table and look directly at her. "First of all, no. *N-o.* No. Second, what in the world would make you think that?"

"Well," Olivia says, and this time she avoids my gaze, "you've been so distracted lately, as though . . . you might have second thoughts about doing this for Mom. Like maybe it's just too much trouble, or . . ."

"Or?" My gaze never leaves her face as she looks anywhere but at me.

"Or like something has made you change your mind about all this. You and I know you were drafted into service."

"Olivia!"

"It's true! I've thought a lot about this lately. You've had plenty of bad nights, and, well, you're not seeing Johnson anymore, and if it's because of me and Matt, I feel awful about that. If you want to be with Johnson, you should. I didn't mean to mess it up."

"Honey, my breakup with Johnson has nothing to do with you."

"What if it does?"

"It doesn't, Olivia. Trust me on this." *Teenagers. They do think they are the center of the universe.* "Johnson and I weren't meant to be."

"But it's more than Johnson, isn't it?"

I think carefully before speaking. "Yes," I say slowly, "but it has nothing to do with you. Olivia, look at me."

She drags her gaze to meet mine. And that's when I see her fear. I've caught glimpses over the past months, but this is full-on panic.

She thinks I'm going to leave her.

And why wouldn't she? My inability to commit is legendary; my inability to show up is all too familiar to Olivia. While I was busy managing details of Stella's waning life, Olivia was managing Stella's impending death.

My voice is barely a whisper. "Liv, we've been stumbling through these last months, and it hasn't always been pretty. In fact, it's been damned dark for us both. I have no idea what I'm doing half the time. But I know this: the brightest moments since June have been about you." I take Olivia's tiny hand—so much like Stella's—into mine. "Sweetheart, I love you, and I don't know what I'd do without you."

Olivia's face crumples. Getting to my feet, I round the table and crouch next to her chair. She flings her arms around my neck, and we both sob. After a moment, I pull back and stand. Placing a hand on each of her shoulders, I hold her gaze. "I'm not going anywhere, Olivia. I want to be here with you, as long as you need me. Got it?"

Olivia nods her head vigorously, her smile tremulous.

~

On St. Patrick's Day we meet in the attic to open our March boxes, festooned in green paper and ribbons. Our charms are, of course, silver four-leaf clovers. I wondered if recent revelations would cloud this monthly event, but I find myself as eager as always to see what Stella has to say—perhaps more so from this new vantage point.

Dear Abby My Solace,

March was always a tough month for me, with its teaser sunshine and sixty-degree temps one day, five inches of snow the next. Thinking of the next March arriving without me, I wish I had the chance to get it right, to be even more delighted by the mild days and gracious about the nasty ones, appreciating the contrast for the lesson it contains. The earth needs the snow and the rain to survive. So do we.

I miss you already, Abby. I write this not to inflict guilt, though I know you well enough to know the damage is done. When the pain subsides, I hope you take my words as intended. I miss you right now, but I meant what I said recently about not wanting you to sit around watching me die. True, I know you would have a difficult time doing that, and you fear you might even be incapable in the end. But I know something you don't: If I asked you to be here with me, you would come. And you would not leave my side.

Watching you watch me decline would only make this real. To see my pain and fear reflected in your eyes would be too much to bear. I am truly glad you are not here, Abby. It's more difficult with Olivia, because this is her home, but I've been limiting her time as well, feigning tiredness and actual sleep so she will leave me. When the time comes, I will call you both to me, and you will come.

So when I say I miss you already, I mean I miss our friendship already after my death. I trust this will make sense to you—it's so clear in my head, but I'm having trouble writing it. As much as I could not imagine life without you, I cannot imagine death without you. Who will I talk to about the dark—or the light? About what I now see, and what it all means? About what has been lost in translation between life and death?

For months I ignored the books on the afterlife you left for me, railing against your belief that, if not answers, at least peace could be found in the right book. But in the last two weeks I read every one of them and have wasted vast swaths of time on Internet research. You were right, Abby. Much as I thought I would go kicking and screaming, somewhere in all those written words, my soul absorbed peace. I can't even tell you which book or phrase held the key. I can say only that I am ready, which is good, since death is coming, ready or not. Thank you, Abby, for helping me get to this place. You are, as always, my Solace.

    Love and peace always,

    Your Stella Rose

"She meant it, you know," Olivia says quietly.

"Doesn't make it right."

"I think it does," Olivia says, expression thoughtful. "For a long time I was angry with you, Abby. Then that day, the day you came, I saw how you looked at Mom, and when she woke up how she looked at you . . . She told the truth."

Something in my heart clicks into place.

I exhale, releasing toxins of regret. For the first time in over a year, I believe I will find my way to forgiveness.

"Thank you," I say, sliding the heavy box closer to unwrap it. Lifting the cover, I find all the afterlife books I dropped off over those final months. I pick up the one on top, flip through the pages, finding several lines and paragraphs highlighted, words scrawled in the margins. Stella never even cracked the spines of her own books, preferring they remain pristine. Yet within these volumes, she spared few pages her death-inspired graffiti. If I have a heads-up on my demise, Stella will walk me through my own death.

Sighing, I look to Olivia. "Let's hear your letter."

She takes her letter in hand.

Dear, sweet Olivia,

    Like February offers a day to declare love, March has a day to reflect on the enigma of luck. I've known so many people who consider themselves unlucky, or chase luck recklessly, or—the worst fate—don't believe in luck at all.

    I believe in luck with all my heart. Luck is not an end. Winning the lottery is not luck; luck is not a prize. The only winners in Vegas are the casino owners. Luck is not to be coveted or feared. Luck is all around, like oxygen. Sometimes it is manifest in a beautiful sunrise or a wild garden. Sometimes it is hidden, such as in a pokey driver who slows you down just before the speed trap, or a missed flight on September 11. Most often it is latent in opportunities such as a chance encounter with a stranger, or an event that forces you to see someone in a totally different light, or, even better, to see yourself in a totally different light.

Some say you create your own luck. I think it's a matter of recognition and appreciation of luck. Once you accept that luck is there for you and you are willing to do your part in laying the groundwork for what you want, nothing can stop you.

My opportunity right now is knowing that I won't be here long, so I am laying the groundwork for a motherhood of one year that will last a lifetime. Who would not be able to recognize the luck in that? To appreciate the chance to say all the things too many parents never get the chance to say? I am blessed with good-luck genes.

So are you. Make the most of your luck, Olivia. Believe in it.
May love and luck shine on you always,
Mom

Olivia is quiet for a long time. I wait.

Finally she says, "That's a tough one."

"Um," I say, noncommittal.

"It will take me a long time to see Mom's death as lucky."

Olivia pulls her own small box toward her. Inside is a pocket-size, leather-bound book filled with affirmations. Olivia reads the inscription aloud. "For Olivia: I found this book among my mother's personal effects and read one each day for several years. I found comfort not only in the words but in sharing my mother's experience. These words must have comforted her, or she would not have kept the book all those years. I hope this book brings you comfort as well, Liv. Love and peace always, Mom."

"Maybe," I venture, "this book will help you find your way to being at peace."

"With Mom's death?" Olivia snorts as she gathers up the wrapping paper. "You *do* think all the answers are found in books, don't you?"

This hurts, but I don't respond. I get to my feet and help clean up the mess.

～

I awake Saturday with a sense of foreboding. Olivia is quiet at breakfast, and that only heightens my anxiety.

"Is everything okay?" I ask.

"Fine."

"Are you sure?"

Olivia visibly restrains herself from mouthing off.

Not wanting to go down that path, I backpedal. "Of course you're sure. I don't mean to be pushy; I just woke up this morning with one of those bad feelings."

"I get those sometimes."

"What are your plans today?"

"Going to the mall and then the movies with Cherie."

"Sounds like fun."

"Yeah," Olivia says with a shrug. "I'll probably spend the night at her house."

"Okay," I say, and we finish breakfast in silence.

～

I am out of sorts all day—snapping at the grocery cashier, honking obnoxiously at slow drivers, soaking myself with a wayward hose at the car wash. I force myself to go to bed after watching only one of the two DVDs I rented, ready to put the wretched day behind me.

At 2:00 a.m., the buzzing of my cell phone wakes me. Groping for it in the dark, I get it to my ear as I switch on the light. "Yes?" I say groggily.

"Abby. It's Trish." The tone of Trish's voice has me bolt upright and awake.

"What is it, Trish? Where's Olivia?"

"She's here at work, at the hospital."

"Hospital? Oh, dear Jesus, I'll be right there." I drop the phone and grab my robe, then run to the closet. I hear a noise and realize Trish is still trying to speak to me. I grab the phone again. "Trish!"

"Abby, listen to me—come to Emergency. I'll meet you there."

"Trish, is she okay?"

"She'll be okay."

"She'll *be* okay? She's not okay right now? Trish—"

"Abby, honey, get some clothes on and come down. Should someone drive you?"

"No, no, I'll be right there. Trish, tell Olivia I will be right there."

I am shaking so badly I cannot put my pants on. But I must get to Olivia. I look at the phone lying on the bed, and before I know it I am dialing Owen's number, asking him to come get me, take me to the hospital. I hang up, slightly calmer, get dressed. I run into Olivia's room and frantically look all around for the only thing I can think of that can help her right now. I am still tossing the place when the doorbell rings. I run down, open the door, sprint back upstairs into Olivia's room.

"Abigail, what are you doing?" Owen asks from the doorway. My head snaps toward him, and in that movement, I see the compass lying next to Olivia's computer.

I snatch it up and say hoarsely, "Let's go."

Owen has me at the ER in minutes, and I leap out of the car before it's completely stopped. Trish is at the door, as promised. The instant I see her in uniform, PATRICIA on the nameplate at her breast, I remember the first time I saw her. Trish is the Patricia without whom, Stella said, she could never have survived her death. She was the head nurse in charge of Stella's home care during those last long, lonely nights, including the last night, when Olivia and I sat vigil. How could I not have put this together before? And why did Trish never mention this?

Our gazes lock. "Where is she?"

"Come." Putting her arm around me, she leads me down a maze of hallways.

I glance behind and find Owen right there, his face a mirror of my own mask of worry. "What happened?" I ask Trish.

"It's not clear how it happened, but she's in pretty rough shape."

"How rough?"

"Her face, mostly, and some cracked ribs, a collapsed lung, possible head injury. She's in X-ray to check for other injuries. There could be internal bleeding."

"I'm going to be sick," I say, holding my arm out to the wall, bending over and heaving. Owen is there, taking my arm, helping Trish support me.

"You are going to be fine," Trish says sternly. "Olivia is going to be fine, too. We all need Olivia, and Olivia needs you, so you will be fine."

"Okay," I say, getting my legs under me. "Please, take me to her."

Trish keeps her arm around my shoulders, and Owen holds my right hand in his, warm and strong. I keep my eyes forward, but all I can see is Olivia's face: her beautiful, tiny, freckled nose; her exquisite cheekbones; her megawatt smile; and those eyes, the dark cinnamon version of Stella's eyes.

"Was it a car accident? A fall?" Owen asks.

"She was assaulted. Not sexually," Trish adds, anticipating my next question. "But seriously."

Trish seats us in a private waiting room. Looking meaningfully at Owen, she says she will be back with a progress report. I concentrate on a spot on the floor. Whenever I shift my gaze, I feel like I am going to faint.

"Abigail," Owen says softly.

"How do I do this?" I ask, my voice trembling. "I'm not strong like... like Stella."

Owen slides off his chair onto his knees so he can look up into my face.

"Stella was a wonderful woman." Owen reaches up and places a finger under my chin, guiding my face toward him. "But she wasn't perfect. She had weaknesses. Olivia was one of them. She was so afraid for Olivia. She worried constantly, struggled constantly to reach her. There is no perfect parent." He places his hands on my knees. "She talked about you a lot, how she couldn't have raised Olivia without you. She was right to trust you. Now you will do what it takes to make Olivia well again."

"Abby!" Both our heads snap up as Trish approaches. "You can see her now."

I am on my feet in an instant. "How is she?" I ask as we walk down the hallway.

"No internal injuries."

"Thank God," Owen and I say together.

"But she has brain swelling. The docs are figuring out the best way to manage that without—"

"Without?"

"Without permanent damage."

My knees give way, and Owen props me up.

Trish squeezes my shoulder. "She's in the best hands, Abby."

We pause outside room 225. "Now," Trish says, stern again, "she looks bad, so get any gushing out of the way while she's unconscious, okay?"

"Okay."

"Go on in."

I rush into the room and stop cold just over the threshold. The girl on the bed bears absolutely no resemblance to my Olivia Rose Weller. "Oh, dear Lord," I breathe. I look over my shoulder. Owen looks at me questioningly. I give him a slight nod. He enters and stands right behind me. I step slowly toward the bed.

A nurse hovers around Olivia's head, adjusting tubes inserted in Olivia's arms, which lie stiffly at her sides, strapped to what look like two-by-six boards. Her lovely, chiseled face is swollen beyond recognition, multicolored like a macabre rainbow. Her lips are swollen and cracked, dried blood still in the corners. Bandages are wound around her head and across the left side of her face, covering her left eye.

A few minutes later, Trish is at the door with two police officers. I grab her arms. "Trish, who did this to her?"

"Abby, these police officers—"

"Where's Cherie?" I ask, whipping my head back and forth, "She knows what happened."

"Ms. St. Claire," one of the officers says, trying his best to soothe.

"Abigail," Owen says in my ear. "Listen to what he has to say."

Folding myself into a chair, I place my hands in my lap and look up at the officer. I tremble so badly, I can barely keep his face in focus. "Okay," I say, taking a ragged breath. "Just tell me what happened to Olivia."

"I'll tell her." Cherie steps out from behind the officers. Trish tries to restrain her, but she says, "It's okay, Mom. I should be the one to tell her."

"Ms. St. Claire," Cherie says, her voice just above a whisper. "We were at a party. You and Mom thought we were at the mall to shop and then go to the movies, but we went to Jeff's house, two blocks away. Kids were drinking; things got kind of crazy. Cameron and I, we were in one of the bedrooms upstairs, fooling around." Cherie looks around, embarrassed but determined. "I knew Ryan had taken Olivia into the next room. Cam told me Ryan was getting tired of waiting around for Olivia to put out, so he was going to get it tonight one way or another."

My hands tighten in my lap, my lips a thin line.

"I asked Cam what he meant by that. He just laughed, said it was none of our business, that we had business of our own." She blushes but continues doggedly, as though reciting a story in English class. "We start fooling around again, then I hear shouting in the next room. I say, 'Shh. Listen,' but Cam is so not interested and keeps at me. Then I hear glass break and I roll off the bed and yell to Cam to go over there and see what the hell is going on. Then I hear something slam against the wall right next to me, so hard I can feel it shake." Cherie shivers, bringing her hands up to her arms. "I scream at Cam, 'Now!' and he gets this scared look on his face and says, 'Oh, shit' and heads out of the bedroom."

Cherie closes her eyes, inhales deeply. Behind Cherie, nurses collect at the end of the nurses' station, anxious as I, it seems, to know what happened next.

"But Ryan won't open the bedroom door and . . . and I scream at Cam, 'Kick it down! Kick the goddamn door down!' and he just looks at me. So I throw myself against the door, but it won't give, but I guess that makes Cam feel like he's got to step up, so he kicks at the door and it flies open."

Cherie's voice trembles as her eyes spill over and her nose begins to run. An officer hands her a tissue, which she ignores, dragging her sleeve across her nose instead, sniffling noisily. "And Ryan, he can't hear the door break because he's screaming at Olivia and he's—he's . . ." Cherie buries her face in her hands, muffling her voice so that we have to strain to make out her next words.

"He's got Olivia by the shoulders, and he is slamming her against the wall, slamming her and slamming her. She's just hanging there in his arms; her eyes are closed, and her head just keeps hitting the wall. It's like he's getting off on it. I yell at Cam to stop him. Cam yells at Ryan, grabs his arm. Ryan lets go of Olivia and takes a swing at Cam. I yell to the kids standing in the doorway to call 911. No one moves! No one moves!" Cherie's hands drop, and her eyes are far away. "So I tell Cam to go back in the bedroom and call 911, and he does. And finally the police and ambulance come."

Composed now, I say, "Your boyfriend knew. He knew all along— that's why he said, 'Oh, shit.'"

Cherie hangs her head.

"You all knew this kid was violent. Even Olivia knew."

Cherie cannot look at me.

Trish meets my gaze, her sorrow parallel with mine.

I look at the officer. "Where exactly is this piece of shit?"

"In custody. But you can't see him."

I look at him, shocked. "I have no interest in seeing him right now. I will stay with my daughter until she no longer needs me. Then I will see him. Make no mistake. I will see this piece of shit. You will not stop me."

I rise from my chair and head back into Olivia's room. I snap the curtain open between the beds and start to roll the second bed over toward Olivia's.

A nurse comes in. "Ma'am, you can't do that."

Before I can answer, I hear Trish say, "I'll take care of this."

I wheel toward Trish, ready to take her on.

Trish walks to the opposite side of the bed. "Pull your end, and we'll get it over there faster."

We place the bed next to Olivia's, close enough so that I can reach her. Owen stands in the doorway, unable to tear his gaze away from Olivia.

"Can I touch her?" I ask Trish.

"Of course," she says.

I take the compass from my pocket and place it in the crook of Olivia's elbow. I look at Trish and Owen, slightly embarrassed. "So she can find her way back."

They both nod.

Owen asks me if I need anything. I give him a list of items to get from the house.

The doctors arrive with an update: fractured cheekbone, four cracked ribs, collapsed lung, significant concussion. And possible loss of sight in the left eye—to be determined as swelling subsides, within a week or so.

Dr. Proctor, a short, round woman with a thick rope of onyx hair down her back, finishes the clinical assessment with the nonclinical observation "She is a lucky girl."

"That's a relative statement," I say.

"Indeed," she agrees solemnly.

I doze for a couple of hours and awake at 8:00 a.m. to voices outside the room.

"You can't go in. The patient is unconscious and in no condition for questions."

"I have a right to be here on behalf of my client and to know the extent of injury."

I slide off the bed and run a hand through my hair as I open the door wider and let myself out. "Johnson?"

He is obviously surprised to see me. "Abby, I-I'm so sorry about this."

"Yes, it's awful. Thank you for coming," I say, and Johnson and the officer stare at me. I think it is because I look like crap, but then it dawns on me very slowly that I have the situation all wrong. "Ohhhh," I say, laughing a bit hysterically. "You didn't come here to see Olivia or me. I mean, not to see if we were okay. I mean . . . This just isn't coming out right, is it? Your client is Ryan."

Johnson's face falls. "Abby," he says, stepping toward me. I hold up both hands.

"Abby," Johnson repeats, "I got a phone call at three o'clock this morning from Ryan's father saying his son got picked up for assault and battery. Didn't know the girl's name, just that his son had a fight with a girl and she ended up in the hospital. I asked at Registration if there were any teenagers brought in early this morning and found out it was Olivia."

"They aren't supposed to give out that kind of information," I say. He tilts his head at me and I smirk. "Oh, that's right, you have a way with the ladies."

Johnson ignores this. "So I came right up here to see how she is."

"Because you have a right to protect your client, right?" Johnson looks so remorseful, I almost feel sorry for him. "Get the hell out of here, Johnson."

"Abby, I said that to the officer so I could see if Olivia is all right. This has nothing to do with Anson or his son anymore. If Ryan laid a finger on her, I won't represent him."

"If?" I am roaring now. "Look at her!" I fling my arm toward the open door.

Johnson follows the direction of my arm, and I see shock register on his face. "Jesus," he whispers.

"You need to leave," I say, "and I will make sure these officers and the nurses allow no one from Ryan's defense league anywhere near Olivia. Got it?"

"Yes," Johnson replies, "and I will make sure the state pursues prosecution."

"Big of you to ensure the state does what it's supposed to do."

"Abby, Anson is a police officer. He will pull strings."

My heart sinks as I look at my broken little girl. I hear Johnson say, very quietly, "But I will cut every one of them."

I turn to see if I heard correctly, but he is already heading for the elevators.

$\sim$

By 9:00 a.m. Owen brings my things, including *Sense and Sensibility* from my nightstand. This touches me, but I cannot read a word. I watch Olivia sleep, watch her chest rise and fall, her fingers twitch. He offers to take over while I shower and change. I decline, but he says tactfully that I might scare the hell out of Olivia when she wakes up if she finds me so completely ungroomed.

Conceding a shower might do me good, I grab my stuff and head into the bathroom. I shower quickly and fix my hair with the door open. Owen has started reading my novel, and I smile at him lying back against the pillows, dutifully glancing toward Olivia every line or two.

At ten thirty, Olivia is wheeled down the hall for tests. Thirty minutes later, Dr. Proctor is part of the entourage that brings her back.

"The swelling in her brain has subsided. She is past the danger stage. I'm upgrading her condition to stable."

"Thank God. When will she wake up?"

"When she's ready," Proctor says quite seriously. "There should be no permanent damage, though I remain concerned about that left eye."

"Her eye?" I ask, nearly choking with fear of her response.

"We won't know until we remove the bandages, likely in a week or so."

$\sim$

We hear a slight moan. I rush to Olivia's side, take her hand in mine. Her eyes remain closed, but she begins to writhe.

"She's coming around!" Owen whispers, ecstatic.

"I think so!" I reply, hugging her hand to my chest.

"I'll get the nurse."

I look back at Olivia, and her unbandaged eye slowly opens. She looks side to side, fear spreading across her face. "Shh, Olivia, it's okay, I'm right here," I say, gripping her hand harder. Her eyes find mine and the fear disappears, replaced by relief, then confusion. She tries to speak, but it is painful for her to move her jaw.

"Olivia, you're in the hospital, but you are going to be okay. Do you hear me?" She moves her head imperceptibly. "Good girl. You are going to be just fine, hon. I'm right here, and I am going to make sure everything will be okay."

She nods and as she closes her eyes again, I feel a slight pressure from her hand in mine.

The doctor strides in, Owen on her heels. "So, young lady!" Olivia's eye struggles open again. "You've decided to join us just in time for lunch!"

Olivia's eye darts from the doctor's face to mine, and I smile encouragingly. What the hell must she be thinking?

"I'm Dr. Proctor," the diminutive angel in a crisp, snowy lab coat informs Olivia.

Olivia raises her right eyebrow ever so slightly.

"Yes, I get that a lot," Proctor says with a hearty guffaw. "I'm like a Dr. Seuss rhyme. Now, let's see how you're progressing."

Dr. Proctor takes Olivia's vitals and pokes her here and there, asking where it hurts. It hurts everywhere.

God, I want to kill Ryan with my bare hands.

The doctor instructs the nurse to increase the morphine, then leans over close to Olivia. "We are going to take very good care of you. Because if we don't, this person right here"—she gestures toward me—"will mow my ass like grass."

Olivia attempts a smile.

I lean close to Olivia and look into her unbandaged right eye. Her lips move. "Honey, don't try to talk." But she persists, her eye bright, imploring me to understand. I shake my head and say, "It's okay—you can tell me later."

She tries again, and I lean in very close. I think I hear her say, "I saw her."

"You saw her?" I say, and she nods very slightly, the effort bringing a grimace, but her eye brightens at my understanding. "Who did you see?"

She frowns slightly, then widens her right eye, as if to say, *You know who*.

I straighten and look around. We are alone. "Stella?"

Olivia smiles, closes her eyes. The morphine takes her under and away from me.

"Olivia?"

I turn and see Cherie in the doorway. "She's sleeping," I say curtly.

The girl looks stung but resolute. "I heard she was awake."

"For a few minutes."

"That's good, right?" She looks at me anxiously, and I give a little.

"Yes, it's good."

Cherie is visibly cheered. I notice she is in the same clothes she was wearing last night, and there is a large smear of blood across her chest. "Have you been home yet?"

Cherie looks down. "No, I couldn't go home, not while Olivia was here. Like this. Ms. St. Claire . . ." She takes a hesitant step toward me. "I just want you to know how sorry I am. I never meant for any of this to happen." Her lip quivers; a tear falls to the floor.

"Cherie, I know." I reach out and squeeze her left shoulder. Cherie winces under my touch. "Are you okay?"

Cherie nods vigorously and sniffs hard. "It's nothing."

"That doesn't answer my question. Let me see your arm."

"It's nothing."

"Cherie, I'm in no mood."

Stiffly, Cherie takes off her anorak, then her zipped hoodie. I help get her tunic off, and she stands before me in her bra. Large, ugly bruises in the shape of Ryan McCauley's handprints stain each arm, and her left shoulder droops inches lower than her right. "My God, Cherie, how did that happen?"

Cherie is crying now, her right hand gripping her left arm close. Gulping air every few words, she says, "I couldn't . . . let him . . . keep throwing her . . . against the wall. When Cam left to call 911, Ryan grabbed Olivia again. I got . . . between them . . . I lay on top of her . . . he kept trying to get me off. But I grabbed the leg . . . of the bed . . . and wouldn't let go." She looks up into my eyes. "I would not let go."

I fold Cherie carefully into my arms, rocking her. Then, slowly, I help her back into her hoodie. "Where's your mom?"

"Probably looking for me," Cherie says

"Does she have a pager?" Cherie gives me the number, and I call Trish and say I have her daughter. Two minutes later, Trish is barreling down the hallway and taking Cherie into her arms. Cherie winces. I alert Trish to the bruises and possibly broken or dislocated shoulder. She holds Cherie at arm's length and asks sternly if there are any other injuries. Cherie shakes her head, and Trish yells to the nursing station for someone to get Dr. Holmes here, stat.

Wishing to spare Cherie the strain of telling her story again, I say, "Trish, I'll tell you all about it once Cherie has been checked out. In the meantime, I want you to know your daughter saved Olivia's life." Cherie starts to protest. I raise my hand, adopting Trish's stern look. "I owe Cherie more than I can ever repay. You have raised an incredible daughter, and I am grateful." I squeeze Cherie's hand and usher them toward a gentleman coming down the hallway, presumably Dr. Holmes. Trish looks back at me quizzically and mouths, "Thank you."

~

Owen returns in the afternoon, and we sit quietly, waiting for Olivia to awaken. Though Rob was on the first flight out of LA, his flight from Chicago was delayed. When finally the door bursts open and he marches into the room, he is loaded for bear. He stops short at the sight of his damaged daughter.

I jump off my bed and stand next to him. "The doctors say she'll be okay."

"Except for her eye. They're not sure about her eye. I talked to the doctor between flights, and that's what she said. What she did not say was how the hell this happened." He turns his gaze to me, his eyes on fire. "What the hell, Abby?"

"Rob, sit with her for a few minutes; then I'll tell you everything outside. I don't want her to overhear us."

He opens and closes his mouth, wanting so badly to know, yet wanting to be with his daughter. Finally he says, "Yes, I want to be with my daughter. Alone."

I swallow his coldness. Though I loathe leaving Olivia, I honor his request.

After a few minutes, Rob joins Owen and me in the hall. He positions his chair so he can keep an eye on Olivia while I give him the essential details of the assault. His hands grip his knees, his jaw is set, his eyes blaze. "Where is this asshole?"

"They won't let you see him."

"The hell they won't. I'm the victim's father."

I decide not to challenge him on this. He can find out for himself.

Maybe he is right—maybe blood relation will move the police more than my guardianship status.

"So, you didn't see this coming?" Rob asks. I am taken aback by the question and its implication. "Could you not see this kid was trouble?"

"I—I never met him."

Rob collapses back in his chair. "What the fuck? She told me about him at Thanksgiving, for God's sake. And you've never met him?"

His words land like a slap across the face. But I take Rob's hand, hold his gaze. Tears course down my face. "Rob, don't think I don't blame myself for what has happened here. And don't for one second think my heart is not broken. I would trade places with Olivia in a heartbeat." I squeeze his hand for emphasis. "You know this."

Taking a deep breath, Rob says, "I believe you, Abby. I know how much Stella meant to you, and I know you love Olivia. But know this: I will be taking Olivia home with me to California as soon as she is fit for travel."

He drops my hand and heads back into Olivia's room.

～

After convincing Owen he has done enough, I send him home and I take a cab back to the house. En route, I make a mental list of things to do to prepare for Olivia's eventual release. And I need to contact Rothschild. He has been exceedingly understanding this past year, but a leave of absence now might be unacceptable. This scares me. Once this crisis passes, I will need my job more than ever.

Despite my best intentions, I walk in the front door and keep walking through the living room, through the swinging door into the bright, yellow kitchen, through the grilled French doors, through the sunlit glare of a brilliant and rare mild March afternoon that promises the worst of winter is behind us, to Stella's rose garden.

The Rose Whisperer was here, his handiwork evident in the uniform shape and size of hundreds of canes, long dormant, awakening with green shoots stretching into the thin, strengthening sunshine.

Piles of mulch have been dumped strategically around the garden, waiting to be spread in a few weeks. Though the sun teases the mulch into releasing its darkly sweet scent, the threat of frost remains.

The teak bench is warm under my thighs and the palms of my hands. Leaning back, I look up into the pale blue sky, strewn with wispy clouds teased into static waves by a breeze too high in the heavens to be felt on Earth.

"It's been a while, Stella. I haven't been ignoring you. Well, at first I was ignoring you, but then so much happened. But you know about that, don't you? You've been there all along. You've been watching Olivia and me, helplessly, as we've fucked up one thing after another, culminating in my nearly killing Olivia through my own—what's the phrase you would use?—gross negligence.

"But this is your fault, too. Not wanting Rob to have Olivia, using me to achieve that end. Overestimating my ability to do this, underestimating Olivia's spiral, discounting our grief and the lengths to which we would go to soothe the pain. Christ, Stella, what were you thinking?"

I lean forward, elbows on knees, feeling the sun burrow through my jacket, meeting the heat rising in my chest. "It's all so clear to me now, Stella. When Rob told me he was taking Olivia, I knew instantly how you felt at the thought of losing her. You would have wailed, 'No!' and beat him on the chest and screamed him into leaving her with you. In the end you didn't have the strength for that—and you didn't need it; you just needed a promise. You were always a step ahead, Stella."

Blinking into the robin's-egg sky, I hold the tears suspended like my thoughts as everything snaps into place across my fragmented mind. Can this be true? I yell into the empty garden, "Can it be, Stella Rose?" A stiff breeze tousles my hair, but no answer comes. "Is this why you didn't tell me about Johnson, too?" I'm fairly shrieking now. "Did you not want me to see how flawed you were? Afraid this would upset your grand plan? Is this why you shut him down, the love of your life? Could you be that controlled even as you were dying? If so, I'm glad I missed all that! I am!"

My throat feels shredded, bloody. I croak my final question. "Stella, did I ever know you at all?" The tears come hot and relentless. I curl onto the warm bench, my face against the soft slats, and let heavy, wet sobs take me over.

~

I hear Owen's voice calling my name. He sounds very far away. Slowly I open my eyes and glance around, getting my bearings.

"Abigail! Where are you? I know you're here!"

I rise stiffly onto one elbow, then swing my legs off the garden bench. "Over here," I say hoarsely, then clear my throat and repeat more loudly, "Over here!"

I hear the French doors sliding shut and soon his footsteps. "I'm here," I say again as he comes into view.

Owen sits next to me on the bench, elbows on his knees, his long fingers intertwined, staring through the screen of rose canes toward the house. "Are you okay?"

"No."

Nodding slowly, he says, "Not that there isn't enough going on right now to make you sleep on a bench in the garden in the afternoon. I get that. But from the puffy eyes and slat marks across your cheek, you've been at this for a while, and it's more complicated than Olivia's condition."

"You are an astute man," I say, placing my hand self-consciously to my cheek, feeling the ridges from the bench.

Owen takes my hand away and places his own to my cheek, rubbing gently. I feel the blood rushing to the spot.

"Thank you," I whisper.

He says nothing, just looks at me, his eyes soft, his hand salve on my heart.

"He's going to take her," I say.

"I was there."

"He should take her."

"Abigail . . ."

"It's the truth, Owen," I say, turning toward him, taking his hand from my face, holding it fast. "I can't do this anymore. This was a mistake. I'm okay with that. I need to get back to my old life, where my mistakes are my own, where I don't have to worry every second of every day. I'm so tired, Owen, so tired of the worry, so tired of being . . ."

He waits.

"Of being afraid."

Nodding, he squeezes my hand.

Then I am kissing him, pressing my mouth onto his, cupping his head in my hands, pulling him close. Feeling his hands on my hips, then on my hands, I kiss him harder until I realize he has my hands in his, he's pulling them away. He is, ever so gently, pushing me away. I let my mouth leave his, hang my head, tears heavy and threatening. "What is it?" I whisper.

"Now is not the time." He places his hand to my cheek again.

My insides throb. "I need you," I say, my voice breathless, my body leaning toward him with a mind of its own.

"I can't," he says, and something bursts inside me.

"You can't?" I am on my feet, whirling on him. "After all these months of . . . of . . . Look, I know you are attracted to me. If you care, you will help me get through this." My chest heaves as I stand before him. I have never felt so exposed.

Rising from the bench, Owen stands over me. I never noticed how tall he is, and I must tip my head all the way back to see his eyes, veiled now, looking down on me. "This is not a game, Abigail." His voice is hard, like a truck driving over packed gravel. "And for the record, I am not just *attracted* to you. I will help you through this, and when this is over, we will talk, you and I. Until then, you need to stay focused."

Shaking my head like a child in full tantrum, I shove him full force in the chest. "How dare you?"

He doesn't budge.

"How dare you?" I repeat, shoving him again. He is a mountain.

"How dare I?" he asks, his voice gaining momentum, a freight train cresting a steep grade, coming down the other side. I'm tied to the tracks. "How dare *you*?"

I blink at him, taking a step back.

"After all these months of . . . whatever this has been, how dare you try to seduce me now because you feel empty inside, because you think you've lost everything in your life—Olivia, Stella . . . Johnson."

I wince.

Owen grabs me by the arms, shaking me hard. "You want me to fill some hole inside you? Like a cliché? Like some consolation prize?"

A tear escapes my eye, and his grip slackens slightly. Dropping his voice, he leans in close. "If you want to fill a hole, I'm sure Johnson will oblige." I close my eyes against his words, and he shakes me again, more gently this time. His eyes are filled with anguish and bitterness. I bite my lip, letting him say what he must say.

"Maybe that makes him a better friend—the fact that he will do whatever you want, whenever you want. I didn't realize what a control freak you are. I thought you were different." Our eyes lock. "My mistake." He turns and leaves me standing alone in the middle of Stella's rose garden.

~

An hour later, dripping from a shower and toweling my hair, I hear the doorbell. I step into clean panties and sweatpants, throw on a faded Bon Jovi sweatshirt, and head down the stairs, winding my hair into the towel as I go. Pausing at the door, I peek through the sidelight to see who it is. Bracing myself, I open the door.

"I brought food. Fettucini carbonara," he says, holding up a delicious-smelling bag. "And Titanic."

"Why *Titanic*? Are we not depressed enough?"

"Because it's three hours long."

"Good thinking."

Owen sits next to me on the sofa, and soon I am curled in the crook of his arm. Nearly two hours in, I'm asleep. I jostle awake as Owen lifts me off the sofa.

"Bedtime?" I ask, snuggling into his neck.

"Yes," he says, reaching down to switch the television off, the strains of "My Heart Will Go On" lingering in my ears. *He sat through the whole thing?*

"I can make it up the stairs," I say, making no move to climb out of his arms.

"Yes, you can," Owen agrees, making no move to release me. He carries me up the stairs, to my room. "Are you wearing that to bed?"

"Yes," I say.

"Good idea," he says. Still holding me, he reaches down and pulls the covers back. Then he lays me gently on the bed, pulls the covers to my chin.

"Owen?"

"I'll be right here," he says, climbing over me, lying on top of the covers, fully clothed. Getting comfortable on his side, he stretches a heavy arm across me and closes his eyes.

Shifting onto my side, back to Owen, I, too, close my eyes. Exhaustion, sheer and complete, steals over me and I surrender to a deep, dreamless sleep.

~

I awake to sunlight streaming across my face and squeeze my eyes against the glare. Feeling weight against my back, I recall the events of last night and the preceding days.

"What time is it?" I ask.

"Nine o'clock."

"Nine o'clock!" I fling the covers back and swing out of bed.

"I called the hospital—no change," Owen says, stretching his long arms above his head. "I'll make some breakfast while you get ready." Before I can reply, he is up and out of the room, humming to himself.

Over cereal and toast, we plot the day. I call Rothschild and explain the situation. As ever, he speaks few words, yet conveys I can take the time I need to manage this latest crisis. "We'll be here when you return," he says, then adds, "I'll be thinking of you and Olivia. Take care." I think, *What will Harmony be like without Rothschild?*

~

As I approach the waiting area outside Olivia's room, I hear familiar voices and quicken my pace. Soon I am enveloped in the embraces of Paula and Cecile, cooing and shh-ing as one while I blubber on their respective shoulders. Paula holds me for a long time, with uncustomary gentleness. She is crying like I have never seen.

"Paula?"

"I know you must be kicking yourself all over hell," she says, holding me by the shoulders. "This"—she points toward room 225—"could happen to any of us, any parent."

"But—"

"But nothing, Abby. When we nearly lost Aaron last year in that motocross crash, the nurses wouldn't even speak to me. Bitches, all of them. High and mighty, saying I was unfit for letting him race in the first place. They nearly had me. They had no idea they were only repeating what was already in my head."

I recall Aaron's crash. By the time I heard about it, Aaron was out of the woods, having escaped with a broken leg and a couple of cracked ribs. How could I not have understood the enormity of Paula's ordeal? "God, Paula, I'm so sorry."

Paula waves my words away. "That's not why I'm telling you this. Listen up," she says, my Paula again. "Kids do what they're going to do. All we can do is sit by with a first-aid kit and pray." She pulls me into those arms that have held so many kids for so many years, and I feel the truth they carry.

April

*M*y world is upside down, and you're not here to right it for me. Maybe that is what I've been most angry about. Anger, kissing cousin of fear. I've been terrified, Stella. All is glass, shattering at the slightest touch. I've been walking on glittering fragments of all our lives, leaving bloody footprints everywhere for months.

And yet, irrationally, I awoke this morning and smelled spring before I even looked outside to see the grass greening and tiny purple petals of our crocuses nested in variegated leaves. It's like spring is inside me, Stell. After months of darkness and deep freeze, of emotional hibernation, something new is pushing up from inside, something green and unfolding, something like . . . hope.

So, while I should be telling you everything is dire—that Olivia remains in pain, that the bastard Ryan McCauley may actually make bail if they reduce the charges from attempted murder to aggravated assault, that the thought of Rob taking Olivia to California leaves me gasping for air—I find myself telling you about hope.

April is balmy, snow only in shady spots. Three days of sixty-degree weather, and I buy the illusion of winter's end. Ruffled tulips bob at me from their beds by the front steps, optimistic in their pink and cranberry petals. The sap has dried as maples push out thousands of tight red buds—leaves in waiting. Daffodil trumpets are fading, but I smile when I see them, remembering six-year-old Olivia calling them *dill-daffols*.

Despite all these sure signs of spring, the Vermonter in me keeps the snow tires on, just in case. You never know when the last snowstorm has come.

As Johnson predicted, Anson McCauley will stop at nothing to clear his son and his own name. He speaks to anyone with a microphone about his family's values, their strong Christian faith, and how alcohol is the devil, especially when ingested by someone as uninitiated in the ways of teenage partying as his son.

Rumors emerge around the McCauleys' recent arrival from Arkansas and Ryan's behavior at his former high school, how he was expelled, diagnosed as bipolar, and prescribed serious medication to keep mood swings in check. How he dispensed with his meds shortly after arriving in Fairleigh.

Johnson has kept his word, refusing to represent Ryan McCauley and forbidding anyone in KKB&R to represent him. He officially cited conflict of interest, due to the firm's relationship with the victim's deceased mother, but word spread quickly that he has launched his own campaign to nail Ryan to the wall. An apt metaphor. In the meantime, the McCauleys have retained Paul Dwyer, a piranha in pinstripes, to represent Ryan.

Ryan's arraignment proved difficult. Though Rob and I loathed leaving Olivia for any stretch, we were committed to seeing Ryan McCauley face the judge. Owen volunteered to stay with Olivia while we went to court. Rob drove, and we were silent, united in our hatred of this young man.

In the packed courtroom, Anson McCauley sat directly behind Dwyer, like a backseat driver. His mouth moved constantly, his large, beefy hand on Dwyer's shoulder, a deep chuckle escaping now and then. Rob gripped the bench in front of us, knuckles white. I had a flash of him standing before a judge, pleading not guilty, by reason of temporary parental insanity, to the murder of Anson McCauley.

Next to McCauley sat a tiny, gray-haired woman in a smart, if dated, suit, rosary beads pressed to her lips. When the doors opened at the side of the courtroom, the woman looked to her left and I was able to see her face. She was younger than I first thought. Her eyes met mine for an instant; I saw despair and fear. Ryan's mother.

"Bastard," Rob growled.

I turned my gaze to the door as Ryan entered the room. His eyes found his parents and he smiled at them, waving his hands at his waist, shackled as they were, handcuffs to leg irons. Glancing at Anson McCauley, I was appalled to see him smile, even wink, at his son, and give him two thumbs up. His mother kept her gaze fastened on her rosary.

Rob gathered his legs under him, preparing to rise. I placed my hand on his arm. "You don't want a contempt charge."

"It would be worth it."

"You can't be with Olivia if you're in jail."

Rob sat back in the bench. Together we watched the judge read the charges: attempted murder. He noted the charges could change depending on the alleged victim's condition. Rob and I shuddered in unison.

Predictably, Dwyer entered a not-guilty plea on Ryan's behalf. State's attorney Bill Morgan argued for no bail. Dwyer argued for release of Ryan to his parents' custody, noting Anson McCauley's law enforcement background. Snorting derisively, Morgan said, "Exactly what I was going to say. Please, Your Honor, this kid is a serious flight risk, and his father has all the tools at his disposal to facilitate that flight and impede his fellow law enforcement officers' ability to locate the perpetrator."

It was at this point I noticed Johnson sitting quietly right behind the state's attorney. He leaned forward, whispered in Morgan's ear. "It must be noted as well, Your Honor," Morgan said, standing again, "that

McCauley requires medication for a psychiatric condition. This medication should be delivered and monitored closely by Corrections."

Dwyer leaped to his feet, then seemed to forget what he'd intended to say. I glanced over at Johnson sitting back in his seat, arms crossed, satisfied.

In the end, the judge denied bail, pending a thorough psychiatric evaluation. Rob and I sighed with relief. I asked Rob to wait while I sought out Johnson to thank him for his support. But by the time I fought through the throng, Johnson was gone.

~

It has been two weeks since the attack, and Olivia is awake more than asleep and healing rapidly. The doctors are pleased. Today we will learn about the sight in her left eye. Rob has allowed me as much time as I want with her, but we have not mentioned California, as we don't want to upset her right now.

Olivia's room is awash in flowers; a steady stream of well-wishers flows through daily. Many are classmates, including Jason and Liza, but there are also many hospital staffers, which I put down to Trish's influence. For the next half hour, however, Olivia's room is off-limits to all but Rob and me.

We flank the bed in the darkened room as Dr. Proctor unwinds the bandage from Olivia's head, then the patch. We wince at the sight of Olivia's bruised and bloodshot eye. She squints painfully. Dr. Proctor's soothing voice instructs Olivia to blink several times; then she applies drops. Olivia blinks rapidly again, and Dr. Proctor places a paddle over Olivia's right eye. "Take your time. You may not see anything for a moment or two."

Rob and I hold our breath, watching Olivia. I can feel the tension in her body, feel her straining, willing herself to see. Then she smiles slowly. "Why does every hospital room and hotel room have Monets?"

I hug Olivia tightly. Rob squeezes her shoulder, a tear trickling down his face.

"An astute observation, Olivia," says Dr. Proctor, smiling. "Let's walk through the rest of the test." Our initial euphoria is tempered as we learn Olivia's vision is impaired: she has lost approximately 20 percent of sight in her left eye. However, Dr. Proctor is pleased, and optimistic that her vision could improve over time. Glasses or contacts should correct any long-term deficiencies. "You would be surprised at what can be fixed these days. Considering the potential damage, I am pleased with the outcome so far."

"Me, too," Olivia says quickly, smiling at all of us.

"Me, too," Rob and I chime in together.

"Can I go home now?" Olivia asks, echoing the question in my head.

"Soon, Ms. Weller," the doctor says, patting her shoulder. "Very soon."

~

The police interview Olivia several times, but she says she remembers nothing of the incident. Neither Rob nor I dare push Olivia directly for details, but we have asked her to consider seeing a therapist. Predictably, she's refused, but we are convinced there is only so much a seventeen-year-old girl can take in one year.

Then, the day before her discharge, Olivia says, "I want to explain why I can't see a shrink."

I stop folding Olivia's clothes into a duffel. I pull a chair close to her bed, place my hands in my lap, and look at her attentively.

Olivia takes a deep breath, then says, "What happened was my fault."

I sit up to protest.

Olivia holds her hand up with a severe shake of her head. "Hear me out, Abby. I'm not saying Ryan should have done this to me."

"I certainly hope not."

Olivia smiles a little, then sobers. "Before Mom died, I was all tied up inside. I could feel each day slipping away. I wanted to be with her every minute. Jason was wonderful, but I just didn't have room for him." She looks up at the sterile ceiling, then back at me. "Then he got the flu, remember?"

"I remember he was very sick."

"He ended up with pneumonia. He said he felt so sick he wanted to die. I went off. He didn't mean it; it was just a figure of speech, and he was so sorry for using those words. But it wasn't just his words," she says, speaking more rapidly. "I was scared. What if he did die? I couldn't take it. I couldn't nurse him while I was nursing my mother, and I couldn't lose her and lose him, too. I was . . . drowning."

I nod, place my hand on her arm.

"When he started feeling better, I told him we should take a break. He said, 'Fine, we can break up, but I will still be your friend and help you through this.' But he couldn't be just my friend. Every time he looked at me, I felt guilty." She bites her lip.

I say quietly, "You were losing someone you loved, the most important person in your world, Olivia. People react in all kinds of ways."

"My way gets worse. I couldn't get Jason to leave me alone. He was being too nice and I was losing my mind. So I started pushing him to have sex, which totally freaked him out, like I knew it would. He said we should wait. I said he was a loser. He was hurt but wouldn't leave. So finally I told him I was seeing someone else."

"Matt."

"Yes, and he didn't believe me."

"Why not?"

Olivia smiles. "Because he knows me, and I wasn't really seeing Matt."

I frown, trying hard to follow.

"I met Matt a couple of times at functions Mom dragged me to. He went to another school, so how would anyone know? I called and asked if he was seeing anyone. He said no, so I asked if he'd play along. I thought he agreed because he felt bad about my situation, but now I think he knew it would make a great story. Anyway, Jason still knew I was lying."

"He knows you well."

"I had to take it up a notch, convince Jason I was seeing Matt and that it was serious so he would be convinced I didn't need him. So I . . ." Olivia looks down at her hands clasped in her lap. "I asked Matt if he would say he was sleeping with me."

I groan involuntarily, pressing my eyes shut. Then squeeze her arm.

"It gets worse. Not only were Matt and I sleeping together, I was quite the lay, according to his stories. I was into all sorts of kinky stuff."

"Oh, Jesus."

"When I told Matt he went too far, he threatened to expose the whole thing. I had succeeded in losing Jason—he was pretty disgusted—so I kept my mouth shut. Matt and I 'broke up.' Then Mom died, and I just . . . lost track of all that."

"Then Ryan came along."

"He was so sweet, and understanding about Mom and all. We had fun; he was respectful. For a while. Then he got . . . aggressive. He would grab me hard, sometimes leave marks. At first I let it go. Abby, there was part of me that felt this was right, like I . . ."

"Deserved it?"

"Yeah, as crazy as that sounds. Everyone was being so nice to me, especially you, but you didn't know how dark and ugly I was feeling inside. I felt like I didn't deserve your treatment, or Liza's, or Jason's. When I was with Ryan, it felt . . . appropriate."

"Liv, I had no idea."

"How could you? But you helped, Abby. And Mom, with the letters. You both kept telling me what I needed to hear." Olivia squeezes my hand, letting her gaze wander around the room, filled with tokens of love from her extended family.

She takes a deep breath. "When things started getting out of hand, I said I wanted to slow down. He asked if I liked him more than Matt. I said yes—and that was true! He asked why I wouldn't go as far as I did with Matt. I said my experience with Matt was awful and I wanted it to be different with him. But he only heard rejection, and he . . ."

"Hit you."

"Yes," Olivia whispers.

"Liv, do you remember what happened that night?"

"Every detail until he knocked me out."

Oh, my poor baby. I stroke her hair as she continues.

"When we were alone in that bedroom, he started coming on strong. I pushed him away, and he came back harder. I started to cry, and he started making fun of me. Then I told him the truth, that I hadn't slept with Matt."

Olivia squeezes her eyes shut, then winces from the pain lingering in her left eye. "Then," she says, inhaling, "he called me a liar and slapped me. I got mad and said I would never let him hit me again and I was leaving. When I got off the bed, he—" She stops, her breathing labored.

I take her hand in both of mine.

She gazes out the window. "He grabbed me around the waist and threw me back on the bed. My head hit the headboard. I heard something fall off the bed stand and shatter. He laughed. He said, 'How did that feel, bitch?' I rolled off the bed and ran for the door. He grabbed me again, and I screamed. He slammed me up against the wall. My head felt like it had cracked open. A bolt of lightning zigzagged across total blackness. I couldn't see his face anymore."

We are both quiet for a few minutes. Then Olivia speaks again. "Then I saw her."

"Cherie?"

"No." She brings her gaze back to me. "Mom."

I swallow hard.

"I heard her voice first, far-off-like. Then her body was there, all fuzzy, then clearer. She spoke, but her lips weren't moving. She was smiling that big smile, and her eyes were full of, I don't know . . . emotion? It's hard to explain. They were full of . . . me. I was seeing myself in her eyes. I could feel her love—warm, real, safe."

I hold my breath in the quiet of the room. The hospital bustle outside seems miles away from Olivia, me, and Stella.

Olivia continues. "I couldn't speak, but it was like I didn't have to, because I thought, *Mom, thank God you're here. Take me with you.*

And she said to me with her eyes, *Olivia, I can't take you with me. But you can take me with you. I am so proud of you and Abby and your dad. You are strong, and you will figure all this out.*

"I started to panic and said, *Mom, I'm scared!* and she said, real stern, *Olivia, that's enough. You have a life to live. Now pull yourself together and fight for it. Don't let this bastard take that from you—do you hear me?*"

Olivia pauses and I'm dumbstruck, tears streaming down my face.

"And so," Olivia says, "I stared into her eyes, and she into mine. We had this complete understanding, and I knew this was the way it's supposed to be: Mom over there, me here, and one day, when it's right, we will be on the same side. And so I came back."

I realize she is finished, and I exhale. "Olivia, that's . . ."

Olivia looks at me, eyes wide. "Crazy! Abby, that's why I can't talk to a shrink! They'll lock me up. Dad will think I'm nuts."

"Slide over, Liv," I say, climbing in next to her, pulling her close. "Listen. I was going to say that is the most incredible experience I've ever heard, and that's saying something, considering all the conversations I've had with your mom the past few months." Olivia blinks at me. "Remember, we talked about this way back: conversations with Stella Rose. They haven't stopped for me, and obviously they haven't for you. So I say we keep this to ourselves for right now, or they'll have us in bunk beds at the loony bin. Deal?"

Olivia smiles up at me, then nestles into the crook of my arm. "Okay," she says.

"But there are plenty of other things to talk to a therapist about, if you're ready."

Pause. Then, "I'm ready."

"That's my girl."

Olivia yawns and snuggles deeper into my arms. "I love you, Abby."

A lump the size of Texas has surfaced where my voice should be. I squeeze Olivia tighter, kiss the top of her head. Glancing up at the ceiling, I mouth to my best friend, who talked our little girl back that night, "Thank you."

~

Small-town life has its advantages. Sure, everyone knows your business. But everyone knows your business. So you don't have to fill anyone in or return phone calls or make excuses for failure to show up for appointments or acting classes or rehearsals. Instead, you get heartfelt voice mails exhorting you to take all the time you need, reassuring you that the Spring Fling is in the manicured hands of Lydia Howard's Party Platoon, and saying that a part as one of the three witches in *Macbeth* is a smaller role that can be replaced, if necessary. Then the doorbell rings and you can't even see the poor delivery boy behind the profusion of daisies and roses and birds of paradise exploding from a porcelain vase. The card reads: *To my loveliest ladies: you will improvise your way through this madness, and I will be in your audience, cheering and applauding, always. Bravo, bravo—Hector.*

"*Macbeth* is in two weeks," Olivia says after reading the card. "Are you ready?"

Laughing, I say, "There are plenty of witches in the sea."

"But you've been looking forward to this! What will they do?"

"Actually," I say, placing my elbows on her bed, chin in hands, "I called Frank, the director, and he assured me he could fill my spot."

"That's a relief," Olivia says, then takes a sip of tap water. "I'm pulling out of *Annie*. I just can't do it justice. Do you think Mom would be disappointed? She paid all that money . . ."

I look down at her still-swollen face. "Liv, your mother never dreamed we would get so much out of those lessons. I'm glad you forced me into it. I learned things about myself I never would have known."

~

Rob has moved into the guest bedroom across from mine. With him in the house, Cherie practically living with us, and Paula and Cecile cycling through each weeknight, I am able to resume normal hours at the Harmony.

Everyone seems genuinely glad to see me and sincere in their appreciation for what I've been through. I throw myself into my job with gusto.

The Spring Fling is only three weeks away, and Lydia has everything well in hand. Inspired by Stella's March letter to Olivia about luck, our theme is Vegas in Vermont: What happens in Vegas stays in Vermont. We will have a strip complete with a mini Bellagio-style fountain, a mini Eiffel Tower, neon lights everywhere, and lots of fake gambling to raise real cash. With potential to be the Harmony's most successful fundraiser ever, it's coming just in time. Rumor has it the tough economy has decimated the museum's budget. The new CFO put the board of directors on notice: without a massive infusion of cash, the Harmony is history.

～

Johnson calls with devastating news: Ryan is out of jail. The conditions are several: twenty-four-hour supervision, ankle bracelet tracker, expulsion from school, forbidden from coming within one thousand feet of Olivia, and monitored drug testing—to rule out illicit substances and rule in court-ordered psychiatric drugs to address the bipolar disorder.

I summarize my thoughts on these conditions to Johnson: "Insufficient bullshit."

"I agree," he says. "I've arranged for twenty-four-hour security at your home."

"What?"

"There will be a guard outside your house day and night."

"You don't think that's extreme?"

"Do you?"

"Hell no, but it's not your problem."

"It's done," he says, and clicks off.

Suddenly California seems like a good idea, even to my bereft heart.

~

Four weeks after the attack, Olivia is on her feet, albeit slow and with a grimace she tries to hide. Rob is ecstatic. Friday night he announces he is going to make dinner. We will eat at the kitchen table like normal people. And, I know, he will talk California.

As much as secrets have wrecked my world, ironically it was my idea to keep Ryan's release a secret from Olivia. I do not want to slow her recovery with anxiety. This has been easy because she hasn't been out of the house since she came home from the hospital. As Olivia becomes more ambulatory, she will ask questions we can no longer evade, but our goal is to get her as strong as possible before that point, and ready to fly to California.

I am slowly realizing sometimes there are good reasons to keep secrets.

~

We make small talk through salads, and then Rob presents our entrées with a flourish.

"Pigs in a blanket!" Olivia exclaims, clapping her hands.

"Nothing's too good for my little girl."

Ten minutes in, Rob notes casually that Olivia has crossed a key milestone in her recovery: "You'll be fit to fly in a couple of weeks," he says.

Olivia nods as she dips a dog in a huge pile of ketchup and lifts it to her mouth.

"So, how about flying to California?" he asks.

I can no longer eat, so I play with my fries.

"Sure," Olivia says. "I can visit right after graduation."

"I was thinking before then."

Olivia looks up. "What exactly do you mean, Dad?" she asks, resting her chin on her hands.

"Well, after everything that's happened, I'd like you to come live with me. You will be far away from"—he sweeps his hand to take in the room and the entire state of Vermont—"all these bad memories."

"Really?" Olivia asks, but Rob misses the ominous tone carried in that one word.

"Yes. I've begun enrollment proceedings at the local private high school. There are plenty of terrific colleges nearby, so this would be a long-term arrangement. Savannah and your brother are quite excited."

"Quite."

"Indeed," Rob says, rushing forward. "I know you'll miss your friends—"

"Not so much."

This gives Rob pause, but he still doesn't get it. "Okay, I know you'll miss the house, but Abby will stay on and it will be here for you, as you know, from the will."

"That's not a problem," Olivia says pleasantly. "I have just one question."

"Shoot," Rob says.

"Not for you," says Olivia, turning to me. "For you, Abby."

"Me?" I croak, caught completely off guard.

"Do you think this is for the best?"

I look from Olivia to Rob, back to Olivia. "It's not my decision."

"Of course it is. You are my . . . guardian."

"And Rob is your father, Olivia. This is between you and him."

"Why?"

"Because . . . you're family," I say, my eyes filling instantly.

"Is that how you feel?" Olivia asks, her own eyes shiny.

I look down at my plate, then back at Stella's daughter, who has become the center of my world, and I whisper, "No."

"I didn't think so," she says with a confidence in her voice I have not heard in months. "See, Dad, the issue is Abby. She has been with me through the worst year of my life, and I haven't made it easy for

her. She's grown fond of me in the process, though I've done nothing to deserve it. I can't just leave her here. So, you see, it's Abby
and school *and* friends *and* the house. And it's Mom and what she
wanted."

Rob is quiet for a moment, then asks, "What about what I want?"

Without missing a beat, Olivia says, "What *do* you want, Dad?
Why are you asking me to come to California?"

Rob thinks a moment, then says, "Because I want to protect you."

Olivia's eyes fill again. "Dad, that means so much to me. What
else?"

Rob thinks longer this time. "I failed you. I've been a lousy dad."

Olivia nods, clearly expecting this answer. "I know that's how you
feel. But you've managed to be a great dad through Wife #2 and another
kid. You've been great since Mom died." She reaches across the table
and places her hand over his. "Dad, you couldn't have stopped what
happened to me."

Rob looks from his daughter to me and back to his daughter. Then
his gaze settles on me. I can read his eyes as clearly as if he were typing
out the words in the air: *The animal that tried to kill my daughter is
roaming free. I can keep her safe in California. Are you with me on this?*

I am.

Clearing my throat, I say, "Olivia, Rob is right. He can provide the
best place for you. You love it there; you've said how much you love
the surf and the art scene and—"

"Abby, what the hell are you saying?"

"You should go to California."

"You're kidding."

"No, I'm serious, Olivia." I look her straight in the eye. "It's what's
best for you."

"Bullshit."

"Olivia!" Rob and I say together.

"I'm not hungry," she says, pushing back from the table. She gets to
her feet and slowly but determinedly marches out the door.

~

When I awake the next morning to the first rays of dawn seeping under the curtains, Olivia is gone. I shake Rob awake, and he is wild-eyed, grabbing his cell phone, calling the security guard sitting right outside. He didn't see anyone leave. I check the garage. The Subaru is there.

"She can't be far, Rob. I'll head for the lake; you head down the road. We'll call each other as soon as we find her."

He jumps in his rented Explorer and peels out of the driveway, down Route 36, no doubt punching 911 into his cell phone. Perhaps I should share his sense of panic, but I have a strong suspicion about where she is. I head down the familiar path to the lake.

My knees buckle with relief at the sight of her at the end of the dock, silhouetted against a brilliant sunrise. Stepping back into the woods, I text Rob to let him know I've found her. Immediately he texts back: *Bring her home so I can wring her neck. Thanks.*

Olivia feels me step onto the dock before she can hear me, and she glances apprehensively over her shoulder. I give a small wave. She turns back to the glassy lake, which mirrors the ring of budded maples and birch circling the tiny bay.

"Gorgeous," I say, plunking down next to her.

Silence.

"I love this place," I say.

"Well, now it's all yours."

Ouch. "Liv, I want to explain."

She shifts away from me.

"Fine, I'll address your back." Nothing. "I shouldn't have let Stella talk me into this."

Olivia mumbles something.

"I can't hear you with your back to me."

Turning to me, she yells, "Sorry to be such a burden to you!"

"This isn't about you!" I yell back. Taking a deep breath, I collect myself. "I mean, it's become about you. But back then, it was about me and your mom and about how I let her control me." Getting to my feet, I begin to pace along the dock, my voice rising again. "This was too much to ask. Everyone knew that. Your dad knew it. Johnson, who didn't even know me then, knew it. Then he got to know me and was even more convinced. Strangers on the street knew it. 'My, what a shock this must be for you, raising a teenager!' What they wanted to say was, 'What the hell was that woman thinking?' And now look what's happened, Olivia! I let someone almost kill you!" I lean over and shout into her shocked face. "I never even met this guy; then he almost killed you! What kind of mother—guardian—does that make me? Huh? Tell me, Stella, how can I do this when I am clearly not qualified?"

"Olivia," she says quietly.

I look at her quizzically, losing my train of thought completely.

"You called me Stella."

Standing akimbo, I look out over the expanse of lake, which is growing bluer-gray with each passing moment. "Damn you, Stella!" I scream across the water, my words skidding across its choppy surface. "And damn you, Olivia, for putting me in this position. For being so . . . so stubborn and bullheaded and making me so af-afraid and being so sw-sweet on my birthday and making me coffee when I was sad and making me love you more than I ever wanted to." My knees give way and I sink onto the dock, pulling myself cross-legged, head in my hands, shielding my eyes from everything.

"Abby, you did the best you could."

"Not good enough."

"Okay. I won't argue. Seems pretty pointless. But, for the record, Mom knew what she was doing. I need to understand why you are breaking your promise."

"Promise?"

"The morning I was sweet and made you coffee," she says, smiling gently. "You promised you would be there for me for as long as I needed you."

I remember. "Liv, I can't keep that promise."

"Then you can tell me the real reason. All this 'it's best for you' is just BS. So quit stalling and tell me what's going on."

And so I tell her.

I explain what led to Ryan's release, the conditions attached thereto, as well as the precautions we have taken to keep her safe. Though she pales considerably, she nods and appears to take it all in.

"Are you okay?" I ask.

"I am now," she says, managing a smile. "Seriously, how drugged up do you think I've been? People crawling around the house, a local parked in the bushes at the end of the road, a jazzy new keypad by the door. Was I supposed to think that was a garage-door opener? An intercom system for a two-story house? At least I don't have to believe that Dad is completely paranoid. Or that you don't want me here with you."

"Sweetheart. You have to go to California."

"I know," she says.

For the first time in nearly a year, the three of us are in sync.

∼

Olivia assures Rob it is fine to return to California to be with Wife #2 and Keene for Easter. He will return on Monday, and they will prepare for the big move the following weekend.

We take advantage of Rob's absence and the holiday to open our April boxes first thing Easter morning. The boxes are covered with pastel Easter eggs, and our charms are tiny, ornate eggs.

Dearest AbbySol,

The Easter season—a time of renewal, resurrection, a time of thaw, when the earth renews itself, prepares to expand, exhales. My favorite time of year. When winter was on the wane, my hands would start itching for the garden. Remember how impatient I was? Wishing away weeks of my life to get to the "better" weeks of spring and summer. Never appreciating the quiet weeks of winter, the respite they brought, the nest-ing, restoring, regathering for spring, and the frantic pace of summer. Now I think how I wasted so much time wishing for what was next instead of savoring what is.

In considering the theme of this letter, I keep going back to beginnings—ironic, as I near my life's end. I can see beginnings in what is next for you. No details, of course, just hand-puppet shadows against a wall. I can perceive the outline of your life, how you will struggle over the next several months adjusting to your new life without your old friend, with Olivia, with new responsibilities at work. (Your piece on your trip will not go unnoticed. Am I right?) You will be overwhelmed as your closely held world cracks wide open like the shell of an egg, the contents spilling out seemingly without direction or intention.

I suspect about this time, April, your new life will begin to settle into its changed form. You have figured out how to manage the household, manage my wild child, take charge of this new life. I am happy for you—in what I see coming for you, in how you will emerge from the confines of your journaled life into the messiness of a larger universe, how the world will benefit from your presence. The world will get to see the Abby Solace St. Claire I kept all to myself these many years.

Inside this box is an egg as lovely as you. May it represent your new life, with the beauty you kept inside now on full dis-play on the outside, for all the world to see.

Happy Easter, happy spring, my love!

Yours, always—

Stella Rose

Olivia watches as I gently unwrap the small box in my lap. Lifting the cover, we both exhale in delight at the lovely egg, snug in a satin pillow. It's exquisite, decorated in heavy baroque styling. I lift the egg, feeling its heft, knowing its solidity. Holding the egg tight to my chest, I feel its strength. There is nothing delicate about it.

Then I glance at Olivia and nod. She removes her letter.

Dear, sweet Olivia,

Happy Easter, sweetheart! Before we Christians co-opted the spring equinox to force our attention on the resurrection of one particular, amazing man, cultures around the world celebrated this sacred season of birth and rebirth, the new and renewal, the potential of life in all its forms.

This Easter has special meaning for you, as this marks your own renewal. Perhaps all you see are endings—our physical relationship first; then graduation will mark the end of school; friends will scatter and friendships will fade into acquaintances; of course, sex at some point will signify the end of an innocence. In all these endings lie the seeds of your new life: college, new friends, new places, new experiences, and, through all of it, love as you've never yet known.

The egg is an ancient symbol of birth, mystery, and power— all stemming from the most potent force on Earth: potential. When I see you, Olivia, this is what I see. Potential thrums inside you—can you feel it? When I touch you, I can feel its vibration, and it makes me so excited for you and what you are becoming.

Own your potential, Olivia. Don't keep it locked up inside. Mine it. Wield it. Thrive with it. Leverage it to live the most amazing life. As with luck, don't ever doubt its existence. Believe in it, and you will live happiness.

I'm bursting with anticipation for all that awaits you, and all who will be touched by you.

Love, and love, and love,
Mom

We each take a tissue break before Olivia unwraps her box. We suspect it is another egg, and we are correct. But what an egg. This one, gilded like mine, though not quite as heavy, is cleaved—held together with a tiny gold clasp. Olivia works the clasp and opens the egg. Inside lies a lovely onyx stone etched in white with one word: POTENTIAL.

~

The doorbell rings. I glance at the clock in the basement, where I'm taking wet clothes from the washer and hanging them on clothes bars. How can Owen be here already? He called from his cell, so maybe he was well on his way already. Reflexively I glance in the mirror to check my hair as I head for the stairs.

The doorbell rings again, and something trips in my mind.

Olivia yells, "I'll get it!"

"No!" I shout back. A chill ripples down my spine. "Don't open the door!"

I race up the basement stairs as Olivia is coming down the main stairs, and we meet at the door. I glance through the sidelight, but whoever it is stands tight against the door. I can make out only jeans and a soft-shell ski jacket with a tiny, barely legible logo at the bottom. It's definitely not Owen.

I whisper to Olivia, "Does Ryan wear a Burton jacket?"

Sucking in her breath, she backs away from the door. "He's not supposed to be here."

"I know."

"He's not supposed to be here," Olivia repeats, and I watch as she folds completely into herself and away from me.

"I'm calling the police," I say, wondering where in the hell the security guard is. I'm reaching for the CALL button on the keypad when there is a pounding on the door. Olivia and I both jump. She opens her mouth, but I put my finger to my lips. I push the CALL button.

Nothing happens. Wasn't someone supposed to come on and ask questions?

We crouch by the door as the pounding continues.

Then we hear his voice.

"Olivia! I need to see you. Please open the door. I know you're in there."

We don't breathe; we don't blink.

"Olivia, please, I just want to talk to you . . ." His voice is plaintive now, like any jilted teenage boy. She looks at me questioningly. I shake my head slowly. Then terror supplants everything else in her face as she looks past me. I look over my shoulder and gasp as we see Ryan's face looking in at us through the sidelight.

"Peekaboo!" he yells, then laughs. "Olivia, let me in. I want to say I'm sorry."

"We've called the police!" I yell back.

"I don't think so. Let me in—I just wanna talk."

I grab Olivia's hand, and we run for the kitchen, where my cell phone is. Behind us we hear the crash of wood splintering. We whirl around and there is Ryan, standing where the door used to be. The boy is huge, so powerfully built he blocks out all the sunlight.

Shoving Olivia toward the basement door, I hiss at her, "Get down-stairs, run out the back, and keep running!" Turning back toward the kitchen, I push through the swinging door.

Then Ryan is on me. He has both my arms locked at my sides; he lifts me as my feet kick empty air. I try to claw and bite, but he holds me out from his body, twisting and thrashing like a fish on a hook.

"Let me go, you bastard!"

"No way," he says, as he carries me back through the swing-ing door to where Olivia stands glued to her spot by the basement door. Her expression is a horrible blend of fear, anger, and dawning comprehension.

Ryan sees her and stops, but his grip on my arms remains fast.

"Run, Olivia!" I scream, kicking again at Ryan. "Run!"

"He'll kill you," she says quietly.

"He won't kill me! Run!"

Ryan gives me a shake so violent that my teeth rattle; then he tosses me like a bag of trash. I thud against the wall of the staircase. My head slams into the edge of a riser, and I see stars as wetness trickles down my cheek. Everything is going black when I see Ryan grab Olivia and pull her to him.

"Why?" he says, the word a moan. "Why did you tell them I tried to kill you?"

Olivia is limp in his arms. He shakes her as though to rouse her. I want to get to my feet; I want to reach out and strangle him, wring the life from his body. I can only watch as the forms of Ryan and Olivia swim unsteadily before my unfocused eyes.

"Olivia, I love you. All you had to do was love me back. Look at me!" His voice rises and he shakes her again. My blood quickens; my eyes focus. I read insanity in his eyes. Wildly, I look around for some kind of weapon, anything to kill this son of a bitch.

I see the giraffes, Jezebel and Lucy, standing statuesque and oh so heavy just outside Stella's office. Summoning my senses, I struggle to my feet. In one staggering motion I lunge for Jezebel, grab her bronze legs, and, grunting at the serious weight she packs, swing her around toward Ryan. I catch him from behind, hear the sickening crack of bone as Jezebel connects with several ribs, each giving under her momentum—*snap, snap, snap*—and knocks Ryan to the ground.

Olivia goes down with him.

I leap over Ryan, grab Olivia by the elbow, tug her to her feet. Her gaze is fixed on Ryan, who looks at her, dazed, pain criss-crossing his face as he gasps for air.

"Let's go," I say, pulling Olivia toward the door. She turns to me and nods.

"You're not going anywhere."

We both freeze. I look back at Ryan, who is on his knees, his breath labored and rattling. Nestled in his hands is a 9mm semi-automatic pistol trained on Olivia's heart.

I stand in front of Olivia.

"No, Abby!" Olivia grabs me from behind, tries to shove me out of the way.

I widen my stance.

"Abby, it's me he's after. He won't stop until he kills me. Then it will be over."

I don't move a muscle. I stare into Ryan's face, though his gaze never leaves Olivia. He adjusts the gun to fire into my heart. I think, *You cannot have my heart.*

I feel Olivia step to the side. I turn, hold her fast, whisper in her ear, "When he shoots, you run, do you hear me? He can shoot again in a split second."

"Abby," she wails, her jagged voice wrenching my heart.

"It'll be okay, Liv. I love you."

As I put my arms around her, I see her eyes widen and I know he is going to shoot. Terror grips me so hard I can't even scream. But Olivia does. I squeeze her close, the sounds reverberating in my aching head, and I hear the gun go off.

I squeeze Olivia harder until we are both on our knees and we are in the church again and Stella has died and I feel nothing but Olivia's arms around my neck and her emptiness merging with mine, bonding us in sorrow, but no longer empty, uniting us in pain, but we are no longer alone. I see Trish's face like an angel's and I think, with bottomless relief, *Trish will help Rob take care of Olivia.*

Then, with wonder, I think, *Is this how death feels? I feel no pain and I'm not afraid. Olivia is alive. Trish will take care of her. I can face Stella and tell her I did as she wanted. I loved her daughter as best I could.*

~

Olivia's voice comes to me from far away, then closer, and closer, until I can feel her breath on my face. "Run!" I say weakly. Doesn't this girl listen to anything I say?

"Abby, I'm not leaving. There's a huge gash on your head. You need to lie still."

I struggle to sit, but she holds me down. Her face shifts into focus, and she is smiling Stella's smile, her eyes streaming. "Your nose is running," I say, and she looks up and says to whoever is there, "She's going to be okay." Wiping her nose on the hem of her T-shirt, she looks at me seriously. "You were right—it's all going to be okay."

"How?"

"Her," she says. My eyes focus on her lovely, healing face. Then I follow the arc of her slender arm. I see Ryan slumped facedown on the floor. Standing over him is a woman I have never seen before but recognize immediately. She is in overalls, work boots caked with dried mud, long gray hair pulled back in a ponytail from a deeply lined, perpetually sunburned face. She still holds a shovel in her hand as she leans over Ryan's body, feeling for a pulse.

~

Owen arrives ten minutes after the police and the rescue squad. From my perch inside the ambulance, I watch him leap from his car, leaving it running, driver's-side door wide open. He sprints to where the front door used to be, where Olivia intercepts him. She winces as he grabs her arm. He steps back, but she smiles and gives him the *Reader's Digest* version. She points to the ambulance, and he is running toward the vehicle, toward me; then he's beside me, my hand in his firm grasp.

"Hello, Abigail."

"Hello, Owen."

"I should have been here sooner."

"There was nothing you could have done." I squeeze his hand. "This is how it was supposed to be."

~

Dr. Proctor diagnoses a concussion worthy of six hundred milligrams of ibuprofen every four hours. Olivia and Owen smile with relief. A nurse arrives to say the Vermont State Police are outside to take statements as soon as we are ready. I look at Olivia and she shrugs. "Ready whenever you are," she says.

To my surprise, it's Johnson who enters the room. He approaches Olivia first. "Olivia, how are you doing?"

"Fine, Mr. Keller."

He holds her by the arms, but gently. "I am sorry. No one should have to go through the last four weeks of your life. The last year and a half, for that matter."

"Thank you," Olivia says.

"You mother would be proud of you, incredibly proud."

Olivia bursts into tears, throws her arms around Johnson. "Mr. Keller," she says into his shoulder, "thanks for saying that. Thanks for all you've done these past weeks." She pulls back to look him in the face. "Mom would be proud of you, too."

And just like that, I realize: she has known about Stella and Johnson all along.

"That means the world to me," he says. After a long moment, Johnson turns to me. "You are welcome to representation of your choice, but I thought I'd be here just in case you hadn't thought about that."

We haven't.

"Why would they need representation?" Owen asks.

"A crime was committed in your house today," he says, sweeping his gaze across the three of us. "The son of a law enforcement officer was assaulted and remains in critical condition, in a coma. There will be a full investigation."

"It was justified!" Owen says.

"Of course. But there are steps that must be taken to sanction any conclusion," Johnson replies, turning back to me. "I told the staties we'll appear first thing in the morning. In the meantime, I'd like you to tell me exactly what happened."

~

I'm released within the hour, and Olivia insists on driving me home, repeating doctor's orders over and over. "And one more thing," she says quietly, looking at the familiar road unfolding ahead of us. "You should see a shrink. Today was the kind of day that will keep coming back to us."

"Is that what the past few weeks have been like for you?"

"Yes," she says. "I mean, Mom's death was unbelievably hard. But what Ryan did to me was . . . different. Violence like what we experienced today, it seeps in, you know? It gets in your bloodstream and taints everything."

"I'll see someone," I assure her. "How's your dad taking all this?"

"Totally freaking out."

"That's appropriate. When will he be here?"

"Tonight."

"That's good."

"Yeah," she says, glancing over at me. "It is. But . . ."

I know what she is thinking. Reaching for her hand on the wheel, I squeeze it. "You are not going anywhere."

Gaze forward, she nods vigorously. "Okay," she says.

~

Because it's an active crime scene, we cannot stay at the house, so we grab some essentials and head to Trish's. I told her we would rent a room with a kitchenette at the local motel, but she would hear none of it.

"You need to be with family," she said, with no hint of irony.

Rob arrives at nine o'clock, with an unexpected companion.

"We were on the same Chicago flight. Now Jesus Christ, Abby, come give your mom a hug!"

I stand rooted to the threshold of Trish's kitchen, staring at this wild-haired, four-foot-ten-inch beanpole of a woman. I have never been so glad to see anyone in my life.

"Mom," I say, my voice cracking, and she is there in an instant, folding me down to her, hugging me tightly to her tiny frame. "You're trembling, Mom!"

"Am not. You are."

"Am not."

"Okay, we both are," Mom says, finally letting me up for air but still holding my forearms in her bony hands. "What do you expect? You scared the living shit out of me."

I hug her again, just to rile her further, and she waits a full thirty seconds before beating me off again.

"Okay," she says, fluffing herself like a hen. "So what the hell happened?"

Trish feeds us scones and tea while Olivia and I take turns telling the story of how we were saved by a giraffe and a gardener.

~

Johnson meets us in the parking lot at 8 a.m., escorts us into the Vermont State Police barracks and to a private conference room. As we get settled, he cuts to the chase. "They are going after Suzanna Kane."

We all exchange glances; then I put it together. "TRW?"

Johnson raises one eyebrow, so Olivia elaborates. "The Rose Whisperer?"

Not helpful.

"I don't know her name," I admit. "She's the gardener."

Rob looks at me, incredulous. "This is the same gardener Stella had for years, she comes into the house and saves your lives, and you don't know her name?"

Keeping my gaze on Johnson, I say, "It's complicated. You know Stella." *What would Rob think if I told him I didn't even know TRW was a woman until yesterday?*

"Well," Johnson says slowly, and my heart skips a beat. "Things with the gardener are complicated."

My heart sinks.

"Complicated?" asks Rob. "The woman is a hero. She saved my daughter."

"It's a government matter," Johnson says vaguely.

"So she's undocumented," Rob says, guessing correctly. "This should get her automatic status!"

"It's not that easy," says Johnson. "Right now, we need to focus on Abby and Olivia. You must be very clear on the details, so we'll go over it again. If I hear anything of concern regarding culpability, I will tell them you have lawyered up and there will be no interview today." Johnson explains that the bruises on Olivia's arms and the lump on my head should be enough to substantiate our stories, but there is no room for inconsistencies. "Remember," Johnson cautions, "McCauley is a state trooper. These guys are a tight team."

My mouth goes dry.

"It'll be okay, Abby." He places his large, sure hand over mine. "Trust me."

I do.

~

The door to the conference room bursts open, and two Vermont state troopers march in. They acknowledge Johnson with identical nods. The taller, a slim man with a grim expression and curly, dirty blond hair barely contained under a wide-brimmed hat, motions for us to take seats at the conference table. The shorter, dark-haired trooper— a burly, mustached bull of a man—stands sentry at the door, arms crossed, bulging biceps stretching taut the sleeves of his olive drab shirt.

The taller trooper removes his hat and places it on the table as he pulls out a chair. "We would prefer to interview these witnesses separately. I'm sure you understand," he says to the room in general.

"It's all of us together or not at all," Johnson says. "I'm sure you understand."

"It was worth a shot," the trooper says, then catches himself. "I'm sorry, ladies, that was in poor taste. I'm Trooper Simmons." His voice is surprisingly soft. The good cop. "My partner, Trooper Lucas," he says, indicating the officer by the door. "I know you've been through an ordeal, so we'll make this as brief as possible." He levels his gaze at me. "Ms. St. Claire, could you please tell me exactly what happened?"

After taking a deep breath, I tell the officer how the incident unfolded, up to the point where I fainted.

"So," Trooper Lucas offers from the doorway, "you didn't actually see the victim assaulted."

Victim? Turning to him, I spit out, "I didn't need to."

Johnson lays his hand on my shoulder lightly, but it's an anchor. "Ms. St. Claire is telling you what happened. If this gets the least bit confrontational, we will stop the questioning and you will have to get your information the hard way."

Simmons shrugs noncommittally, but Lucas's glare is menacing. Simmons turns to Olivia. "Did you witness the assault?"

"Yes," she says, her voice clear and even.

"Can you tell me exactly what happened?"

"Yes, I can. Abby was facing me, blocking me from Ryan, ready to take the bullet. I struggled to get her out of the way, because it was me he wanted to kill. Then I saw Ryan's eyes and I knew he was going to kill both of us."

"You can't see what someone is thinking. Please just stick to the facts," Simmons says smoothly.

"That is a fact," Olivia says, equally smooth. "Then," she says, before either officer can object, "Ms. Kane, our gardener, was in the doorway. She saw what was happening and she saved our lives."

Lucas snorts, but Simmons raises a hand to silence him. "Exactly how?"

"She yelled and hit Ryan with a shovel just as he fired, so the bullet missed us." Olivia rubs her arms, now covered in goose bumps. "And it was over."

Rob is on his feet. He wraps his arms around Olivia, rocking her and glaring at the officers. "That's enough," he says with that tone of finality I have come to appreciate.

"I agree," said Johnson, giving Olivia's arm a squeeze. "Officers, I believe you have what you need. The injuries sustained by these women corroborate their version of events, as do the condition of the home and Mr. Kane's statement."

Simmons nods slowly. "We're done for now. Where can we reach you if we need anything further?" he asks, looking from me to Olivia.

"You will call me at my office," Johnson says, placing a business card on the table and pushing it across to Simmons, who takes it and places it in his notebook.

We all rise, and the officers leave us. Rob has Olivia in a bear hug, tears rolling down his face. I stand next to Johnson, take his hand in mine. "Thank you."

"Abby," he says, his voice tight, "you never have to thank me. Is that clear?"

"Yes," I say, smiling up into his handsome, pained face.

∼

For days Owen has not answered my calls or text messages. Chagrined, I show up at the school and wind my way to his tiny office, where I perch myself on a mini–student desk chair for a good forty minutes until he finally walks in. I smile brightly at him, but he looks uncomfortable.

"Hi there!" I say, but I think, *What the hell is wrong with you?*

"Hi," he says brusquely, walking around his desk, seeming eager to put as much furniture between us as possible in this close space. "What can I do for you?"

I blink at him, amazement spreading over my face. "Owen. What's going on?"

"I'm sorry. I meant to ask how you're doing, and Olivia. Are you okay?"

"Well, yes, all things considered . . ."

"Have you considered seeing a professional to help you through this?"

"Owen, come on, I'm not here to talk about that. I'm taking care of myself, I have an appointment with a therapist—at Olivia's insistence—and I will be just fine."

Owen appears relieved. "Good," he says. "So what did you come to talk about?"

"Us!" I say, my frustration spilling over. "You and me and whatever this is."

Owen just sits there, blinking at me.

"Christ, am I talking to a wall here?"

"Abigail . . ."

"What?" I ask, my voice like thunder in the tiny room.

Owen flinches, looks down at his hands gripping the edge of his desk.

"Oh," I say, realization dawning. "I can't take a hint. I thought . . . but now my life is too fucked up to get involved in. I can't blame you. I'd keep away, too!"

Nothing.

Getting to my feet, I lean across the desk. "Owen," I say, inches from his face.

His face is inscrutable. "Listen," he says. "I can't do this. It's not you. It's me."

Stepping back, I stare at him, incredulous. "How can it be you? After all you have done for me? After being so patient, and kind, and kicking me in the ass when I needed it, and being there for me even when I was not there at all? How can it be you, Owen?"

For a split second I see pain in his eyes, so sharp it takes my breath away; then resolve replaces it. "Abby. I just . . . can't. I have to go," he says, rising and grabbing a folder off his desk.

Standing awkwardly, I open and close my mouth, a fish out of water. I back out of his office and make my way blindly down the corridor, out to my car. All the way to Trish's I scream "Fuck you!" and pound my fists on the steering wheel until my head throbs.

Sitting in the driveway, I gulp fresh air from my open window. Dizzily I make my way up the cement steps. Just as I reach for the knob, the door swings open and Olivia scoops me into her arms. She doesn't ask, just hugs.

"Johnson is on his way," she says, pulling me into Trish's cozy living room.

Trish enters bearing a tray of teacups and a plate of Nilla Wafers.

"Trish, you are a saint," I say, "with ESP. This is just what I need."

Trish smiles her now-familiar, lovely smile. "Along with a shot of bourbon?"

Laughing, I pat the sofa cushion next to me. She removes her latest craft project, tucking it into a large wicker basket with yellow satin ribbon spilling out of it, then sits by my side. Olivia heads down the hall to Cherie's room, and we hear music briefly as the door opens, then closes again.

"Rob is working in Justin's room," Trish says. "I'll let him know when Johnson gets here. How was your day?"

I look at Trish for a moment. "Men."

"Owen?"

"Yes, he would be the particular man in question."

"What's wrong?"

"He hates me."

"He loves you," Trish says, smiling.

"Well, that's what I thought, too. But you and I were mistaken."

Trish laughs, a light tinkling sound. "That man loves you. Not the 'I've got the hots for you, baby' kind of love. The 'I could stare at your face forever' kind."

I sit back into my soft sofa cushion, staring at my new friend in awe. "Really?"

"Duh. So what happened?"

I spill the entire story and mop up some sympathy before Johnson arrives at noon.

～

When Trish leads Johnson into the living room, we all settle around the coffee table to hear his news.

"First of all, you two have been cleared of any charges," Johnson says, smiling at Olivia and me.

We all exhale.

"As for Ms. Kane," Johnson says, pausing as though trying to decide exactly how to proceed, "she will go before a grand jury within a week to ten days."

"What?" we all exclaim, a chorus.

Johnson holds his hand up, and we fall silent, though we are impatient for details.

"Ms. Kane assaulted a minor. And with her status . . . she's in a tough spot."

"I'll pay for her representation," Rob says.

"Me, too," Olivia says, then adds, "I'll borrow against my trust fund."

"I want to help, too," I say.

Johnson smiles that toothpaste-model smile. "What a woman," he says, shaking his head. "'Cause I found someone to do this pro bono."

I see Rob bristle. Men. Everything is a competition.

"Listen," I say, "does she have family?"

"In a village outside of Mexico City."

"Tell your friend to keep track of the hours. We'll pool our resources and send that amount to her family. It's the least we can do since she's no longer working, and who knows what will happen?"

Rob regards me admiringly. "Brilliant."

"Told you, Dad!" Olivia laughs, throwing her arms around me.

May

*S*tella, I am working hard to assimilate all I have learned about you over the past few months into the person I knew for thirty years. Your affair with Johnson was huge, but this situation with the Rose Whisperer—knowingly employing an undocumented worker? I can't believe you didn't tell me.

Scratch that. I can believe it now. And I understand this wasn't your secret to tell. So while I am learning that I don't need to know everything, I still fervently hope there are no more secrets, Stella Rose. No more secrets.

It's May Day, soft and glowing, with maple, oak, and birch in their late-spring chartreuse, and grass lush and dotted with rogue-dandelion sunshine. Standing at my window, sash raised, I breathe in the morning and exhale months of angst. Robins, blue jays, and chickadees call to one another, an avian Tower of Babel in my backyard.

Slowly I retreat from the window and head into the bathroom to shower and get ready for another big day. Today we testify before the grand jury.

Shivering, I crank the temperature to scalding, then rinse conditioner out of my hair. Turning my thoughts to Olivia, I am smiling again. Olivia will stay here with me, with Rob's blessing. "Olivia belongs here with you," he said simply.

I turn off the water, step out of the shower. Smiling at myself in the steamy mirror, I feel something I haven't in months—not since that dark day two Septembers ago.

I've never felt this way ever, actually.

Maybe you need to go to hell and back to feel this way.

I feel strong. And light.

Maybe everything is light because I am strong.

I can live this life and not simply be carried along by it. I have Olivia, I have my home, I have my sense of self, my own mind, my heart. And I can take care of my heart.

Wrapping myself in a towel as I march into my room, I grab my cell phone out of my purse. Punching in his number, I let the towel drop and stand naked before my window, relishing the slight breeze. After only two rings, it goes to voice. *You little shit! You're screening me!* I wait for the beep. "Owen, it's Abigail. I know you sent me to voice mail hoping I'd hang up again. But those days are over. Brace yourself. I'm coming for you. I. Am coming. For you." I hit END, lean my head against the window casing, and gaze into the greening rose garden. Through the canes of the barely budding rosebushes, I see the bench Stella and I spent too little time on, see the pile of rocks under which half of her ashes lie. "I'll let you know how it all turns out, Stella."

∼

Two hours later, Rob, Olivia, and I meet Johnson at the Chittenden County Courthouse. Ashley is by his side, like a burr. We exchange frosty glares before I turn my attention to Johnson. He ushers us into a tiny, windowless room. We seat ourselves in plastic chairs in a semicircle around a small table.

"Ryan remains in a coma; his prognosis is poor," Johnson says quietly. "Prosecution is going for attempted murder. If Ryan dies, the charge will be murder."

"We can't let it get that far," I say. Everyone nods.

Unlike the dark-paneled, stuffy old courtrooms on television, this grand jury room has smooth walls of pastel green with yellow trim, and light floods every inch, streaming in through the floor-to-ceiling windows lining the southern wall. Johnson leads us to seats right behind his desk.

Judge Cushman, a homely man with owlish features exaggerated by wireless glasses perched on a beak of a nose, calls Olivia to the stand. She looks like a tiny bird in the large leather nest that is the witness chair, but she holds herself erect and speaks clearly as the state asks her question after question about what happened on that day.

Then it is my turn. Familiar, guttural stage fright claws at my belly as I approach the stand. But I am not the same woman I was a year ago—hell, six months ago. I couldn't stand up for my best friend at her funeral, but I will stand up for her friend today. Clearing my throat, I inhale deep from my diaphragm, as Hector taught me so well. Placing my still hand on the Bible, I state clearly for the record my full name and that I will indeed tell the whole truth and nothing but the truth, so help me, God.

And I do.

Halfway through my testimony, I see four familiar shapes sitting at the back of the courtroom. Paula has taken a day away from her crazy life. Cecile probably talked Phil into driving her disabled clients all over town to get their groceries and meds so she could be here. I know Trish worked a double shift yesterday, but here she is, riveted to my story despite the fact that she's heard it already a dozen times.

Just a bit apart sits my mother, her hair tamed by hot rollers, her diminutive frame swimming in a smart suit. She has her hands pressed to her mouth, her gaze is fixed on me. Then I see her fingers slowly curl into a fist, which she shakes ever so slightly. She is saying to me, in mother-speak, *You go, girl.*

When I finish, Judge Cushman clears the courtroom for Suzanna Maria Kane.

~

As we leave the courthouse, Ashley tap-tap-taps up to me, practically on tiptoe in fine leather stilettos. "We need to talk," she hisses in my ear.

"Johnson said we could leave," I say, turning my back to her.

She tugs on my elbow, and I wheel on her. "What do you want?"

"I need to talk to you privately. Now."

Her tone compels me to comply. I signal to Rob and Olivia that I'll catch up.

Ashley steers me to a wooden bench in a secluded alcove overlooking Quarry Street, quiet at this hour, its neat row houses with identical lawns and front porches—some screened, some open, all with rockers of some kind, some occupied, most not.

"What's this about?" I ask.

"Owen. There's something you need to know."

Oh, dear Jesus. There is always something I need to know. There is an infinity pool filled with all the things I don't know—some I need to know; some I don't need to know but want to know. It's endless and it's exhausting.

"Tell me," I say. "Lord knows he won't. I don't know what I did! I'm trying to cope with all this . . . this *stuff*; then I reach out to him, and—"

"This is not about you!" Ashley shouts, shedding her demure demeanor. She is on her feet, bending over me, cheeks flaming, eyes blazing. "I know you've had a tough year. Man, everyone knows you've had a tough year! We're all sorry for you!"

"I never asked for your sympathy!" I yell back, getting to my feet. We stand akimbo, in each other's face.

"You never had to! The totality of the circumstances speaks for itself!" She flings the words at me like a gauntlet. "That's not my point. Owen has a soft spot for wounded birds. He's addicted to feeling needed—that's why he's a guidance counselor. He loves helping people figure out their lives."

"And . . . ?"

"And things were going along fine until . . ."

It hits me. "Until things started falling into place."

Ashley looks at me, confused.

I work it out as I go. "When things start coming together—Ryan out of the picture, everyone is safe, I'm getting back on my feet—he doesn't want me anymore."

I look up at Ashley, and she is staring at me, open-mouthed. "What the hell are you talking about?" she asks.

Now it's my turn to be confused. "But you said he likes to help people, he's addicted to it, so now that I don't need help—"

"Jesus, Abby, you are way off. First of all, let's pretend you don't need help anymore." She rolls her eyes, indicating what a stretch this would be. "That is not what I am getting at. He started out helping you, like he's helped hundreds of others like you. But they weren't like you, or so he says, and he fell in love with you."

Did she just say that?

Ashley plows on, "And I'm thinking, *Great, poor Owen doesn't stand a chance against Johnson.*"

Internal cringe.

"But then that fizzles and it looks like just maybe you can appreciate Owen."

"Appreciate Owen?" I ask, indignant. "I more than appreciate Owen."

"Sure, sure," she says, raising her palm to silence me. "Anyway, I'm thinking maybe I was wrong, maybe this could work out. I knew you weren't right for Johnson, but maybe what made you not right for Johnson made you right for Owen."

I am having trouble following her but don't dare interrupt.

"But then you nearly got yourself and Olivia killed."

"Like I did that intentionally?" I am officially pissed off now.

"No, of course not," she says, waving her hand impatiently. "I'm just saying that when that happened, it set Owen back five years."

"What does that mean?"

"Five years ago, Owen got involved with a mother and a student."

I stare at Ashley, something niggling in the back of my mind.

"It started out innocently enough. The student was struggling, Owen shared his concerns with the mother during a parent-teacher conference, they all became very close."

I nod slowly. "Then she died."

Ashley looks at me, surprised. "How did you know?"

Now I'm surprised. "It wasn't Stella?"

"Who wasn't Stella?"

"The mother he fell for."

"No, it wasn't Stella. He liked Stella. Who didn't? But not that way. Second, he didn't fall for this woman. He was always careful about that—he used to be, anyway. But he was very invested in their situation."

"So what happened?"

"She found her son hanging in the closet."

"Oh, dear God."

"Then she hung herself next to him."

Oh my fucking word. I collapse onto the bench, putting my head between my knees. "Oh my God. Poor Owen." I look up at Ashley, tears coursing down my face.

Ashley's posture softens. She sits by me, places a hand tentatively on my back.

"He never told me."

"He doesn't talk about it."

"I never asked him, Ashley." I look sideways at her. "I never asked him anything about himself, about his history, his hobbies, his favorite color . . ." I sob into my hands.

Ashley fumbles in her purse and hands me a tissue.

As I blow my nose, I think, *How many people have handed me tissues in the past year?* "Thanks," I say, taking a deep breath.

"Sunrise," she says.

"What?" I ask.

"His favorite color."

"That's not a color."

"That's what I say, but he insists it is, and that it's his favorite color."

"How do you know, Ashley? How do you know Owen so well?" I ask, ready for any answer she gives.

"Because," she says simply, "we're best friends."

~

After dinner, Rob, Olivia, and I return to the house, which has slowly been restored to our home. Rob insisted on replacing the door himself—it's a heavy, dark cherry door with a peephole. He replaced the sidelights with cedar shakes to match the rest of the house. I'll miss the light, but right now, and all we have is right now, I value the privacy—the safety—that solid wood provides. I was touched when Olivia, onto my residual fear, replaced all of Stella's lacy, too-transparent curtains with heavy drapes, held open by antique brass pullbacks but providing instant coverage if ever I need to feel shielded.

Rob disappears into the guest room to call Wife #2. My pre-divorce fondness for him has returned, and I know, like I knew twenty years ago, that he is a good man doing his best. He always was, but I had to choose sides. Now I don't.

"Abby?" Olivia asks, standing by the new door. "Do you want to go for a walk?"

Olivia has never asked me to go for a walk with her, so of course I say yes and slip my shoes on before she realizes she has better things to do. I think, *All mothers of seventeen-year-olds must feel this way. We—they—will take any crumb of attention from these young women slipping out of their grasp with each passing day. How do mothers endure eighteen years of this when I'm nearly buckling under a few months?*

Though I know where we are going, I let Olivia lead me out back and down the path through the woods to the familiar dock that stretches out onto our beloved bay. Taking off our shoes, we let our feet skim the water, still winter cool.

"I want to tell you something," Olivia says, her eyes focused on the budding maples straining across the water toward us from the opposite bank. "It's about college."

My heart skips a beat, but I keep my face passive. Even if she says she's taking that dreaded year off to backpack across New Zealand, which is the new Europe, I will simply nod and say, "That's fine, Olivia. I support you."

So she stuns me when she says, "I've been accepted to three great schools."

"You've . . . what? When? Where? I mean . . ."

Olivia laughs again, taking my hand in hers. "I'm sorry I shut you out of this, Abby, but I had to see if this was really what I wanted. And it is. I'm sure of it." She squeezes my hand. "It was so hard to admit I was not going to NYU to study theater. I think if Mom was still here, that's exactly what I would be doing."

This pains me, and Olivia is quick to continue. "Mom never understood my love for theater. But at the same time, she loved that I loved it, and it was exotic to her."

"I know exactly what you mean."

"I knew you would. Mom would always say, 'Abby was like an angel up there on that stage.' I could hear in her voice that she loved that about you." Olivia turns her gaze back to me. "That's what got me into theater in the first place: her fascination with your passion for the stage. Dancing wasn't my thing, but acting was magic to me. I could be someone else, but also who I wanted that person to be, you know?"

"I get it now," I say, smiling.

"I would try to explain it to Mom, and she would say, 'I don't understand,' but I knew she loved that she didn't understand, you know?"

I nod.

"Well, when Mom got sick . . ." Olivia pauses, and I glance over to see her pensive gaze straight ahead. "I thought, *Acting is the perfect escape*. I threw myself into it deeper. Then I couldn't escape anymore. Mom's illness was too big. When I was onstage I felt like I was missing Mom's life, my own life. I wasn't in real time anymore . . .

"And when I was with Mom in the hospital and with all those

people dealing with death every day, I thought, *This is so real—real time, real life.* I watched my mom dying, and people around her in the cancer ward were dying. I saw all this death, and I had never felt more alive." She takes a deep breath and looks at me, apprehensive. "That's why I've decided to go into nurse counseling, specializing in HIV/ AIDS care."

I am rocked. Why would this vivacious young woman consign herself to a career filled with sadness and death?

"I know what you're thinking," Olivia says.

Busted. "I'm just surprised, that's all," I say, unable to meet her eyes.

"You think I'm nuts. My therapist does, too. But Mr. Montagne thinks it's great."

"Owen?" I ask, my voice rising.

"Don't get pissed at him," she says quickly. "He's just doing his job, advising me. He begged me weeks ago to tell you, because it was killing him not to. But then . . . well, everything happened and he told me I could tell you when I was ready."

"Of course," I say, my mind spinning. "Liv, are you sure?"

"Yes, and I'll tell you why: I've been volunteering at the hospital."

"Oh," I say slowly, as another fact clicks into place. Community service. Trish wasn't the only reason Olivia had so many nurses visiting her at the hospital. They knew her, had worked with her, loved her as one of their own.

"I volunteered in various departments, wherever they needed me, but Trish—"

"Trish knew?"

"Yes, but I told her you already knew and that it was a sensitive subject, so she shouldn't bring it up. Abby, I put these people in a very tough spot. If you're pissed, you should be pissed at me, not them."

I laugh. "I'm not pissed, Liv. I'm just integrating this latest web of deceit into the evolution of my thinking about secrets. It's been an enlightening year on the topic. At first I was hurt that your mom kept things from me, since I thought best friends simply share everything. Then I was angry—how could she leave me here to sort all this out, to look foolish? That was a pride thing—I see that now. I also see the dif-ference between secrets and privacy, that some things are meant to be private, that best friends—real best friends, and guardians—respect that. You needed to work this out on your own. I am proud of you."

Olivia smiles. "Just because I didn't come running to you doesn't mean I did it on my own. You helped me lots, often by mistake, but still."

I swat at her arm. "And it's not like I didn't have secrets of my own."

"Like your second fling with Mr. Keller?" she asks, her head cocked, smiling broadly. "And did you tell him you spent Thanksgiving with Mr. Montagne?"

"How did you know about that?"

"I have my sources. Anyway, we all keep secrets, Abby."

I am quiet for a moment, then say, "You know, Liv, I have spent this past year in a spin over Stella's secrets, and then Johnson's, and yours, and not once did I acknowledge my own or question my own motives. None of us meant to hurt anyone. My primary motivation was to protect, and now I see that this was true for all of us."

Olivia is all seriousness. "We're all human, Abby. Please remember that, okay?"

I look at her closely. "Why do you say that?"

Avoiding my eyes, Olivia says, "Please just remember, okay?"

"Okay," I say, a tiny knot forming in my stomach, but I sense now is not the time. "So, where were we? Trish was in on this little scheme?"

Olivia smiles a little, then gets back into her story. "I told Trish I wanted to be in oncology, so she put me there at first. It was terrible, of course. It didn't take long to realize the oncology ward was definitely masochism. Then a woman in the ICU died of pneumonia after years of battling HIV."

I wait.

"She had two kids, teenagers, and they were torn apart. They had been expecting this for years but never thought it would happen. I talked with them for hours, listening to their stories, helping them voice their feelings, holding their hands. And that's when I knew what

I wanted to do. I want to help people through the death of their parents. I have experience—mostly in what *not* to do—and I want to do this. I want to help people move on the way their loved ones pray they will."

"Liv, that's amazing."

"Yes, it is. So I applied at three medical schools in New England—the University of Vermont, Dartmouth, and Johns Hopkins. I was accepted at all three."

"And?"

"And I want you to help me choose."

Turning to Olivia, I take her chin in my hands and say, "I would be honored.

~

Dawn is barely a whisper when my feet hit the cool wood floor next to my bed. Quietly I pad to the bathroom, take a quick shower, brush my teeth, smooth my wet hair into a ponytail, and tiptoe down the stairs and out the door. The darkness is just starting to soften around the edges when I pull into Owen's driveway. Ashley gave me directions earlier this week, and she wasn't kidding when she said his place was tiny and out of the way. I walk around the back and stop in my tracks, whistling low. What. A. View. How can he sleep through this every morning?

Trotting around to the front, I find the spare key under the brightly colored gnome peeking through weeds in the forgotten garden near the front stoop. I allow myself only six inches of open door through which to squeeze myself into the tiny foyer, take a moment to eyeball the premises.

Neat and tidy. No surprise.

Entering the galley kitchen, I see the coffee is set to brew at 7:00 a.m., when Owen was going to get up. Not today. I flip the switch and watch with satisfaction as deep-caramel liquid runs into the carafe.

Glancing out the window, I see the horizon lighten faintly. Gotta hurry.

Coffee mugs in hand, I head down the short hallway to the second door on the right, which stands slightly ajar. I nudge it open with my butt, backing into the room, flicking on the light with my elbow.

A form stirs in the bed, and I shout, "Rise and shine!"

"What the . . . ?" Owen cries, shielding his eyes from the glare of the overhead light.

"Chop chop!" I say, kicking his foot. "Here's a cup of joe for you," I say, setting his mug on the nightstand. "Grab some pants and join me on your deck, pronto!"

I leave him and make my way out to the tiny back deck. I'm sitting in one of two Adirondack chairs, blowing on my coffee, when he appears at the door, hair extra spiky.

"Abigail, what is going on?"

"I am here to watch the sunrise with you."

"Why?"

"Because it's your favorite color."

"What? How did you know that? Nobody knows that."

"Best friends know these things."

"Ashley. What else did she tell you?"

"Lots of things. Come sit with me and drink your coffee," I say. "And for heaven's sake, be quiet. I'm trying to enjoy this amazing view."

"I—"

"Shh," I say, admonishing him with a wave of my hand. "Just watch with me."

And we watch. Ashley and I checked the weather channel and agreed that today, given the predictions of rain later, would offer the most auspicious sunrise.

We were correct.

"Wow," he says.

"Yeah," I say.

~

Olivia and I sit in the front row of Fairleigh High's intimate theater to watch the opening-night production of *Annie Get Your Gun*. The understudy does a fine job. Olivia is generous in her applause, honored as the cast asks her to join them for the curtain call. My clapping falters as, for an instant, I see Stella clearly where Olivia is standing.

When we get home, we head upstairs and into the attic, pull out our May boxes. The master cartons, once chock-full, are now nearly empty, each containing only an envelope adorned with the word June. These contain letters we will read next month, on the anniversary of Stella's death, as she surely intended.

For now, we hold our May boxes close, savoring them, anxious to open them yet reluctant to put these behind us. Our charms are intricate yin/yang symbols.

My darling AbbySol,

I enjoyed spending time with you this week—before the sadness and helplessness crept into your eyes and I had to banish you again. I see a quiet strength emerging—or perhaps I'm only now seeing what was there all along. You have an assuredness, a competence, an "I've got this" going on. Not only does this make me even more confident in having you watch over Olivia, it assures me you will be fine without me. In fact, you will thrive out there in the sunlight. I realize what a wide arc of shade I created for you. Your yin to my yang—we've made an amazing team. Now I see your own yang evolving.

And I see my yin evolving as well. Shocked? So am I! There is nothing like terminal cancer to bring out your yin. I could never understand how you spent hours so quietly, thinking, processing, weighing options. I was so busy racing against someone's clock, making decisions, growing to-do lists for the thrill of crossing stuff off.

Now, though time is short, the days are long. Writing exhausts me. Talking takes away my breath. I cannot take care of another living soul at this point. At first I resisted; then I accepted. I asked myself, What would Abby do?

Now I cherish. I am . . . quiet. Thinking. Processing. Breathing in. Breathing out. Finding wonder in the act of discovery. Did you know my favorite color is a subtle red-orange? Or that I held a grudge against Shelley Reynolds not because she slept with Corey at summer camp but because she didn't invite me to her thirteenth-birthday sleepover three years earlier?

Fate has brought out the you in me, and vice versa. In yin-and-yang fashion, we segue into each other, cycling through aggression and passivity, through light and dark, through life and death. I have always been your biggest fan. Now I know why. What drove me crazy about you is what I loved about you, and now, finally, I understand it.

This time of quiet is a gift. I can't imagine charging into what's next without fully examining what is. With you as my role model, I have made peace with my life and found comfort in my soul.

So, as crazy as living in my house with my daughter may get, I trust in that wellspring of yin that runs deep inside you to keep you grounded, and to preserve the AbbySol I love so very, very much.

With quiet affection, infinite respect, and undying love,
Your Stella

"Told you," Olivia says, her voice thick.

I shoulder-bump her, since I cannot speak. Then I point to her letter and she reads.

Darling Livvy,

Motherhood didn't come easily to me, so I worked very hard at doing it right. I worked hard at doing everything right. And soon the doing became more important than the right part. I strove to instill this "doing" ethic in you, rewarding achievement and productivity, revering medals, playbills, and other tokens of success.

In all this doing, I did you a disservice, my sweet girl. I never encouraged you to slow down, look around, breathe, stretch, go inside, stay there. Think, process, meditate.

It is clear to me now this is a big reason I want you to spend this next year of your life with Abby, who is the queen of quiet, of thoughtfulness in the sense of contemplation, of observation without commentary and rash judgment, of appreciation.

There are those who seek to create perfection and those who seek perfection in what is created. I never understood the latter, but I do understand this: the world could not survive without both. Art needs artists and patrons, vintners need sommeliers, musicians need listeners, writers need readers. If a tree falls in a forest and no one is around to hear it, does it make a sound? Exactly.

So while there are creators and appreciators, we all benefit from practicing the other side, rounding our own experience of the world. This time with Abby will afford you a look into another way of doing things and may tap into heretofore-unrealized propensities in your own soul. I suspect you are a doer, like me. However, I hope you endeavor to cultivate your quiet side, learn to exhale fully, to pause, observe, appreciate.

Loving you deeply, quietly, and completely,
Mom

Olivia sighs and looks toward me. "It's so hard, figuring out how to be."

Laughing, I lay a hand on her arm. "When you figure it out, let me know. Your mom's trying to squeeze decades of parenting into a dozen letters, covering her bases."

"She wants me to be like you."

"She wants you to be you, not to box yourself in. Over the years we pushed each other outside our comfort zones. I pushed her to do yoga; she pushed me to take more responsibility at work. I dragged her to meditation; she tossed me on a plane to Greece. Though we each stayed true to our nature, we were richer for stepping into each other's shoes."

Olivia nods slowly and turns her attention to the box in her lap, the last gift she will ever receive from her mother.

Carefully she removes the shiny paper and lifts the top off the small jewelry box. Her features crumple ever so slightly; then she pulls herself together as she extracts an antique oval locket on a thin golden chain from its velvet pillow. Working the tiny latch, she opens the locket, stares intently at its contents, then hugs it to her chest, her eyes shining. Then she turns to me, opening her palm so I can see the tiny picture of Stella Rose and Olivia, taken just before illness stole the vitality and vigor so present in Stella's eyes, or the innocence and joy radiating from Olivia.

"It's lovely," I breathe.

"She's lovely."

"Yes, she is. And so is her daughter."

We sit for a moment; then Olivia says, "It's your turn; you didn't open yours yet."

I was so caught up in the letter, I didn't open my own box. I suspect it is a locket, and I'm right, and I open it slowly to reveal the picture within. To my surprise, the picture is not of Stella, or of Stella and me. It is Olivia and me. And not just any picture—the exact picture Olivia gave me for Christmas. When I show it to her, she grins at me crookedly and we both laugh in that familiar, jagged, sobby way of ours.

⁓

On Friday I arrive at work in a terrific mood. I relish the simple acts of getting up in the morning, twenty minutes of yoga, a cup of coffee for the ride in, and another engaging day at the office. I enjoy these loony people I work with, enjoy what we do. I love this place and am glad I didn't end up a wildly successful ballerina. No regrets.

At 8:45 a.m., Rothschild appears at my door to announce we are having an off-site lunch meeting a Marylene's Diner.

I know this is when he will tell me who is taking over curatorship of the museum, and about my role in the transition. Glancing around my tiny office, I sigh. *Change is good*, I remind myself. Why should it be confined to my personal life?

Promptly at noon, I walk into Marylene's and canvass the room for Rothschild. I spot him in a booth near the back, engrossed in the menu card. As I sit across from him, I am suddenly unconcerned. It simply doesn't matter who my new boss is. If I don't like him, I have options. I smile at this very Stella thought of my own.

"You're smiling," Rothschild observes, looking amused himself.

My smile broadens because it is rare to see him like this. "Mr. Rothschild, it's been a crazy year, hasn't it?"

He looks surprised at my impetuous statement, but not put off. "Yes, I know you have had much to deal with this past year, Abby."

Sobering, I nod.

"I lost a dear friend of mine twenty-five years ago. He was my college roommate—accomplished, brilliant, and salt of the earth."

I nod again, surprised and pleased to hear Rothschild's story.

"We had a complicated relationship—or so I thought at the time. Now, frankly, it all seems quite simple. I could call him anytime, under any pretext. He would pick up the phone no matter what and talk to me." Rothschild smiles somewhat shyly. "He was my touchstone. I didn't realize how much so until he died. A week later, I picked up the phone to tell him I had two tickets to the Red Sox game and would he like to come? When his wife answered, I was just about to ask for Barry when I realized he wasn't there."

I stare at Rothschild, transfixed.

"Barbara, his widow, said, 'Hello? Is anyone there?' I simply couldn't speak, so finally she hung up. That was in the days before caller ID, so she never knew it was me, and I never told her about it. In fact"—he glances away—"I've never told anyone."

"I did the same thing!" I exclaim. "I was sitting in Stella's own house! I called her from my cell and heard her voice on the answering machine. I just sat there and cried."

"Maybe it's a dead-best-friend phenomenon," Rothschild says, smiling a little.

I laugh out loud, and he joins me.

"So, Mr. Rothschild, let's talk about your retirement and what is to become of our museum. I assume you and the board have chosen your successor."

"I have, and it's been conditionally approved," Rothschild says.

"I want you to know," I say, looking him in the eye, "that it has been an honor working with you for the past ten years. While I'm sure the new curator will be great, and I promise to give him a chance, I also know he can't hold a candle to you."

"She."

This throws me. So it's not the CFO heir apparent. Or Jaime—poor Jaime! "She has very big shoes to fill."

"That's kind of you to say."

"Not at all. You view managing the museum as more than a job. I know it's hard for you to leave. But rest assured I won't let the new curator fail, and I won't let the museum go downhill. You have my word."

"That's a relief," Rothschild says, grinning broadly, "Madam Curator."

I blink at him. He nods encouragingly, letting it sink in.

"Me?" I finally manage.

"Of course, Abby. Who else?"

"But . . . me?"

"Are you questioning my judgment?"

"No, sir," I say. "I'm simply aware there are candidates out there with MBAs and other credentials . . ."

"That's true, Abby. As noted, your nomination is conditional."

I swallow hard. "How so?"

"If you accept, in September you must enroll in the eighteen-month MBA program at Champlain College. Once you successfully complete the program, I will advise the board and your transition to the post of curator will be official."

"But who will run the museum in the meantime?"

Rothschild stares blankly at me, then says, "Me, of course."

"But you're retiring."

He waves a gnarled hand dismissively. "It will be a long good-bye."

I stare back at him. "When did you decide on me?"

Rothschild holds my gaze. "When I heard you put yourself between Olivia and that lunatic with the gun."

I look down into my cup, not sure how to take this.

"You've been my first choice for two years. You love the museum as much as I ever did, and you have a quiet, assured manner that people respond to. You bring calm to our chaotic environment. Some think you are too quiet, but I strongly disagree. Perhaps you don't grab the nearest megaphone to broadcast your accomplishments, but I know what you are capable of. That's why I sent you to Greece, to prove to folks what you could do. And you knocked it out of the park! But, frankly, your lack of an MBA proved a persistent hurdle for the board." He takes a long sip of coffee, then removes his spectacles and cleans them with the hem of his perpetually untucked oxford shirt.

As he puts his glasses back on, he resumes. "When I heard what you did that day—and I heard it over and over—I stopped caring about the board's reservations, stopped thinking about what you lacked and thought only about what you bring. You keep your promises. You take care of what you love."

"Thank you. That means so much to me," I say. "But this means you have to stay on nearly two more years. That's a huge sacrifice."

"Abby St. Claire, you have taught me about real sacrifice. You set aside this year of your life to care for your best friend's daughter, a young woman who has put you through more than many parents ever endure, and you have done so with your whole heart. I think I can swing eighteen months at a job I consider my second home, and will do so gladly if it means I can help you become the best curator Harmony has ever had."

Smiling, I place my palms flat on the table and lean toward my mentor. "Then I accept your conditions. I will enroll in the MBA program; I will attach myself to your hip over the next two years and learn all I can to fill your enormous shoes."

"That's what I'm talking about," Rothschild says, raising his coffee in salute.

~

The next morning I stand in Olivia's doorway, watching her sleep. Her hair is loose, her charm bracelet glinting in the morning sun. My heart throbs at the sight of her, and I wonder, not for the first time over the past several days, how I will ever manage when she's away at Dartmouth. Despite her promises to come home every other weekend, I know enough moms and dads who've been down this road to know that won't last. And I truly hope it doesn't, because it will mean her life is expanding, but that will be cold comfort come September.

I spend the morning puttering in the garden, missing TRW with each weed, mourning the loss of someone I never formally met and never will. Suzanna Maria Kane was not indicted by the grand jury, but she was deported. Johnson assures me she took the news well, that she looked forward to reuniting with family and living life out of the shadows. Our clandestine contribution to her family should help her transition.

~

By noon it is eighty degrees, unseasonably hot for the middle of May. I come back in, sweaty and filthy. Olivia sits at the kitchen table, hands clasped around a mug, looking amused. "You're quite the gardener," she says, grinning at me.

"That's me," I say, giving a thumbs-up. "The Garden Guru. I'm going to the dock for a swim. Want to join me?"

"The water is freezing!" Olivia says, shivering in her chair.

"Yes, but it will feel good right now," I say, pulling granola bars out of the cupboard. "I'll be back in a bit."

I jog down the path through the woods to keep my body temperature up. If I cool down too much, I'll lose my nerve. Shoving granola wrappers in my pocket, I run the last hundred yards to the dock, shuck off my clothes, and jump in before I can think twice.

The cold shocks me into screaming before I reach the surface. I splutter and choke as I breach, but the sun is warm on my head and shoulders. Soon I am back-floating out toward the center of the tiny bay. Cirrus clouds combed into loose curls blend into a soft blue sky, at the center of which sits the yolk-yellow sun.

Kicking my way back toward the dock, I find the soft bottom with my feet and wash all my body parts clean of garden grime, dunking under a couple of times for good measure before hauling myself onto the dock. I spread a bath towel on the warm wood, lie down on my back, and place my shirt loosely over my chest, my shorts loosely over my bottom, leaving my underwear in a tight wad near my feet. I'm in the middle of nowhere, but one never knows. Closing my eyes, I let the sun dry my skin and warm my bones until I drift off.

Drip. Drip. Drip. Damn, it's raining! Eyes wide open, I sit, clutching my shirt to my chest. Looking up, I realize even the cirrus clouds are gone. It's definitely not raining.

More drops of water land on my back. I whirl around. Nothing. What the . . .

Just then, a head of shiny, wet hair emerges from the water just off the dock; then Owen's face and hands appear and he flicks his fingers, sending droplets of water my way, onto my exposed thigh. Pulling my shirt closer and readjusting my shorts across my lap, I yell, "What the hell are you doing?"

"Swimming!" Owen says, diving under again.

My eyes bounce from spot to spot, trying to determine where he will surface. I spy my underwear by my toes and reach over gingerly to grab them. I have my bra on in two seconds and am pulling my T-shirt over my head when Owen surfaces, now to my right. "Don't splash me!" I warn, holding my hand out.

"You're no fun," he gripes, running his hand across the surface of the water and sending a huge wave up over the dock and across my legs.

"No, I'm not!" I say indignantly, pulling my legs carefully to the left so as not to disturb my perilously perched shorts.

"Come in—the water is nice," he says.

"I've been in already."

"I can see that," he says, smiling wickedly.

I gulp. What else did he see? How long has he been here? How long have I been here? I glance at the sun, but I've never been any good at telling time that way.

Some things I'll never know.

Some things I don't need to know.

Besides, the Owen in the water is my old Owen. I smile at him, happy just to watch him bobbing in the cold water, smiling back at me.

"How did you find me?" I ask.

He swims to the dock, resting his arms on the edge, his chin on his hands. "Your daughter told me you were down here."

"Owen, you called her my daughter."

"Did I?" he asks, genuinely surprised. "It wasn't intentional. I hope that's okay."

Smiling at him, I say, "It is very okay. I'm glad it wasn't intentional. It's like I've spent the last year trying to make it very clear to every-one—to Olivia, to Rob, mostly to Stella, I guess—that I'm not Olivia's mother. I'm just the guardian."

"But it's more than that."

"Yes! It is more than that. It's always been more than that. I've loved her since she was born, and—this is going to sound so selfish—having her all to myself this past year, well, it's been magical. Like some meta-physical transformation. She is my daughter, too. I think she can be more than one mother's daughter . . . can't she?"

"Of course," Owen says, his voice reassuringly matter-of-fact.

I wag my finger. "You didn't come down here to talk about me and Olivia."

"No," he agrees. "I didn't." He pulls himself up onto the dock, water sluicing down his surprisingly tanned, deeply freckled back. His body is lithe, muscles taut like marine rope, naked as the proverbial jaybird. As my face goes scarlet, I wonder what generation I was born in, anyway. It's not like I haven't seen naked men, or swum with them. My mind flashes on Greece.

There are some things no one else needs to know.

"May I share your towel?" he asks. I move to get up so that he can wrap the towel around himself, but I misunderstood. "No, stay there; just scoot over so I don't get a splinter in my ass from the dock."

Has he ever said "ass" before?

I swivel my butt so he has room next to me. He sits so close I can feel the coolness of his skin, goose-fleshed in the slight breeze. He smells like fresh lake water.

"Abigail," he says quietly, and just the sound of him saying my name wraps my heart in a vise. I realize then and there that no matter what he says now, or what he says ever, whatever he does or doesn't ever do, I love him and will love him forever. He may never know this—maybe he never needs to know this—and it doesn't matter. I'm the only one who needs to know. Because this, how I'm feeling right now, is mine.

"Yes," I say, looking across the lake at the familiar maples, their green coats darkening every day, leaning toward us, listening in on our conversation.

"I'm sorry about shutting you out. I was afraid."

I nod.

"You know about Andrea and Miles. I cared about them very much. When they died, I knew in my gut I should have done more. So when Ryan attacked you and Olivia, right under my nose, well, it was horrific déjà vu. I just couldn't handle it."

"I know." I feel Owen look at me. "When Ashley told me, it all made sense. I've thought about it a lot since that conversation, and more pieces have fallen into place."

"So now you know I'm damaged goods."

Sighing, I pull my gaze from the serenity of the lake and look directly at Owen, his inner struggle playing out across his handsome face. "Sweetheart." I place my hand on his cheek. "We're all damaged. I'm relieved that I'm not shattered china you need to put back together. Me being broken, you being the fixer—that wouldn't work for long. I want a partner who's struggling like I am to move forward and make a happy life."

Owen closes his eyes and places his hand over mine, still resting on his cheek. Then he takes my hand and presses my palm to his lips, sending a shock down the entire length of my body. I shudder involuntarily.

Owen opens his eyes. "Cold?" he asks.

"Not exactly." I lean toward him, into him, settling my lips on his, and it is the softest kiss I have ever known.

∼

Olivia and I make our way down the hospital corridor toward room 703. Johnson helped ensure Anson McCauley would not be in the building, but I suspect Linda McCauley will be there.

I'm right.

Ryan's mother is on her feet the moment we enter. I hold her gaze, extend my hand.

"I'm Abby St. Claire."

"I know. Call me Linda." She takes my hand in hers, warm and dry. Then she turns to Olivia. "I'm sorry for everything that's happened," she says.

"It's not your fault."

"Ah, fault is a slippery thing," Linda says, her face impassive, no doubt from days and weeks—maybe years—of bracing herself for this moment.

We approach Ryan's bed. He appears to be resting peacefully, half his head still wrapped in bandages, a little swelling and discoloration on the left side of his face. I reach for Olivia's hand, which is stone cold.

Linda McCauley's even voice saws through my tangled emotions. "He will never hurt you again."

My insides boil as I turn to face her, to shout, "How do you know that?" But the suffering on her face extinguishes the fire in my chest.

"I've signed the papers. If—when—he wakes up, he will be admitted to West Addison, and he will never be released." Linda reaches down, traces the side of her son's face. "His injuries may be so severe he won't even know he's there, which may be for the best. But even if he is aware, he will never, ever be outside, where he can harm another human being. Never again."

Stunned, I stammer, "B-but . . . his father—"

"Cannot stop me." She laughs, a short, barking sound. "Oh, he is trying, but he won't succeed. It stops here." She looks up at me, then at Olivia. "You have my word."

~

The drive home is silent, but when I glance over at Olivia, see her profile against the darkening evening, I see her jawline is softer, her shoulders more relaxed. I reach over, squeeze her hand. She squeezes back, her grip strong, sure. Her nod, nearly imperceptible, assures me she's okay.

We have been set free.

~

It's the Harmony's big night, and all the last-minute details have me late for my own party. I nearly lose a heel as I fly downstairs, applying lipstick as I go.

"You look amazing!" Olivia says, clapping enthusiastically.

"I do?" I check myself one more time in the mirror in the foyer.

Indeed, the extra pounds have helped me fill this new sequined, plunging-neckline number quite nicely.

"Very curator-like, Madamoiselle St. Claire," Olivia says, winking. "Good thing what happens in Vegas stays in Vermont." Then she adds, "You deserve this night, Abby."

Spontaneously I throw my arms around her. "My life is so full, Liv!"

She hugs me close. "Does Mr. Montagne have anything to do with this?"

"And you, and things with Suzanna Kane, and Trish, and the girls, and Harmony—but most of all, you. I'm so blessed, Liv."

Though Olivia continues smiling, a shadow crosses her face.

"What's wrong?" I ask.

"Nothing," she says, shaking her head. "Why?"

"You look troubled."

"You know me too well. Go off and join the party. It's nothing to worry about—I'm not in any danger or trouble," she says, shooing me out the door. "Cherie's waiting for me upstairs. This is your night. We'll catch up tomorrow."

~

The neon lights are visible from four blocks away, and I smile as I weave through traffic to my reserved spot behind the museum. Through the alley, I pass three Elvis impersonators, four men with blue faces, and two men carrying a huge white papier-mâché tiger. As I reach the parking lot, I am delighted to see slot machines lining the sidewalk in the semicircular drive, each with a swarm of quarter-thrusters vying for their chance to play.

Above the normally sedate entrance of the museum flashes a retro neon lightbulb–festooned sign that reads HARMONY IN VEGAS. Posted at each side of the entrance are sixteen-foot-tall women in period garb—one blonde, one redhead, both with their curly hair piled impossibly high, both playing violins violently in an effort to compete with the ambient carnival-esque noise, yet both smiling broadly at my arrival, graciously bowing me inside. Upon closer inspection, I see they are in fact beautiful men in pancake makeup, perched upon ten-foot stilts under amazing, velvet-draped hoop skirts.

Stepping inside, I blink several times to get my bearings. The foyer has been transformed into a casino, sophisticated and at the same time raunchy enough to rival any on the Strip. The adjustable walls have been removed to enlarge the space, and the room is teeming with gamblers queuing for black jack, roulette, craps—you name it.

Making some quick calculations based on head count and pace of transactions on the floor, I know this event will shatter all previous fundraising records for the museum. I close my eyes and savor the moment.

"We are going to make zee kill."

"Killing. We're going to make a killing," I say, eyes still closed, still savoring.

"*Oui*, this is true. Look at all these people, all of them spending the entire evening donating money. Whose bright idea was this, anyway?"

"Mine," I say, finally opening my eyes to see Jaime standing there.

"Damn. This is also true. Congratulations, Abby."

I'm not sure if he is talking just about the event, until he clarifies: "You totally deserve to run this place. It will be an honor to work for you."

~

At eight fifteen, Johnson enters with his usual entourage. I catch his eye and he smiles, waving me over. I excuse myself from Owen and meet him in a quieter corner.

"How are you, Abby?" Johnson asks, eyeing me closely.

"Great."

"You sure look it," he says appreciatively.

"I'm sure there will be emotional fallout from all this at some point, but right now I am in a very good place."

"I'm glad. By the way, Ashley says I can't hit on you anymore, says you hooked up with Owen Montagne, the Clark Kent of guidance counselors."

"You sound jealous."

"Absolutely."

"That's nice, Johnson. By the way, I've grown kind of fond of your secretary."

"Yeah, me, too," he says with a significant smile.

"Johnson," I say in my warning voice, "don't break that girl's heart."

He bends over, kisses me on the cheek. "I'm happy for you," he whispers.

~

The next morning I awaken late to find a note by the coffeemaker: *Grab a coffee and join me in the garden.* I pour myself a cup, then pull on a sweater and head out into a cool, late-spring morning.

Olivia is waiting on the garden bench, tiny in an oversize sweatshirt and running pants, her face pinched with cold and whatever it is she needs to tell me.

"There once was a girl with a secret," she begins.

Dutifully, I continue, "And she didn't know how to tell her . . ." I'm stuck.

"Her mom's best friend," she supplies. So this has to do with Stella. "Because the reason she kept the secret at first turned into another reason to keep the secret and another and another, until it was too late to tell."

Oh, man. "So then," I say, "she thought maybe it didn't need to be told at all. Maybe some things are better left as secrets."

"But she knows her mom's best friend deserves to know the truth."

"And yet something holds her back."

"She's afraid."

"Just like everyone else, because telling the truth can change everything."

"And she doesn't want things to change."

"But deep down, she knows she can't stop life changing, whether she tells or not."

"Mom told you about Johnson."

I turn to Olivia, caught off guard by the sudden end to our improv. "What?"

"She told you, but I intercepted it."

My brain comes to a screeching halt. "What in the world are you talking about?"

"Near the end, she sent you an e-mail, a long e-mail telling you about Johnson."

"I never got an e-mail about Johnson."

"I made sure you didn't get it." Olivia leans forward, elbows on knees, her gaze fixed on the koi flashing around the tiny pond. "Mom was so drugged up most of the time, and she obsessed over telling you this secret. I didn't know what it was, she wouldn't tell me, but she would get agitated about it, so much that it scared me. She wanted to tell you so badly, but you . . ."

"Never showed up."

Olivia looks at me for the first time. "Yeah, you never came. You were busy taking care of all those details, and taking care of the museum, and . . ."

"I was avoiding Stella," I say, the truth finding its voice.

"I knew that. So part of me was pissed. But I see things differently now."

"It doesn't change what I did—or didn't do."

"Abby," Olivia says, looking me straight in the eye, "we all did the best we could, and we all made mistakes. Even Mom. Anyway, I was pissed at you, but also I couldn't stand the thought of Mom holding this secret inside. It was hurting her so bad. So I created a special e-mail account and sent Mom an e-mail, pretending I was you."

I stare at Olivia in amazement.

"I told her you set up this non-work e-mail account so you could have private conversations, since you couldn't be with her as much as you wanted. You would continue to use your work account for general topics related to taking care of her business but would save the Gmail account for personal stuff. I figured if she said anything you really needed to know, I could forward it to you and no one would know."

"And she bought it?"

"She was desperate. She thought she had manifested it! She immediately went online and spilled the beans."

"But what if I had shown up? Wouldn't it have been obvious I didn't know?"

"You didn't show up."

"But what if I had?"

"I was willing to take the chance." She holds my gaze.

There was no real risk. I didn't show up until the very end, and by then Stella was in no shape to discern anything beyond the fact that I was finally there.

We sit in silence as the enormity of Olivia's confession sinks in. Months of emotional upheaval over this secret, only to find out there was no secret after all.

I glance over at Olivia and find her staring at me, eyes streaming. "Please say something," she begs, her shoulders heaving.

"Baby, come here," I say, wrapping my arms around her. She sobs into my lap.

"I'm so sorry, Abby."

"Liv, you said it yourself. We were all doing our best. You figured out an ingenious way to relieve Stella's suffering. You were pissed at me. If I got hurt in the process . . ."

"I only wanted to hurt you in the beginning. Then, when she told me—you—all this stuff, it just seemed so unlike her. When you came just in time and helped Mom leave us, I was so grateful. I wanted to tell you then. But you started telling these stories about her, and it was clear you loved her the way she was. I didn't want to . . ."

"Taint her memory? How ironic."

"Yeah, right? Now I realize how complicated your relationship was, that this information would probably have impressed you! Then you started dating Johnson . . ."

"That must have been surreal."

"Totally. Things spiraled. There was the drama with Ryan, the attack, me moving to California. I thought if I told you then, you'd pack my bags for me."

"I wouldn't have done that."

"I know that now," Olivia wails, throwing her hands up. "I totally underestimated you and me, you and Mom, you in general, I suppose."

"Happens all the time," I say, grinning at her.

"It's not funny!"

"And it's not the end of the world, either," I say, brushing her hair out of her eyes. "I have learned so much this past year. About you, Stella, myself. If you had told me at any other time, so many incredible events might not have happened."

"But you were so sad, thinking Mom kept this from you."

"I was," I agree. "And I got over it. I learned a bigger lesson about friendship, and it's not about sharing every little secret. It's about trusting on a larger scale, about taking care of each other, and about love. Stella trusted me to take care of you. She took care of me by giving me this year with you. And she loved me, Liv. This I know."

"She did. Her biggest wish for me was to have my own Abby Solace St. Claire."

We sit with this for a few minutes. Then I ask, because I am dying to know: "Why did she wait so long to tell me?"

"I'll let her tell you herself."

Sitting up straight, I say, "You saved the e-mails?"

"Of course," Olivia says softly. "I tried to delete them, destroy the evidence. But these were Mom's words. Her feelings. The last part of her I could keep forever."

~

As we walk toward the house, Olivia says, "One more thing."

"There always is."

"There's a diary."

I stop. "Stella thought diaries were a colossal waste of time and pretty paper."

"She kept a diary of her time with Johnson. For you. And I haven't read it."

"Why the hell not? Are you the queen of restraint?"

Olivia laughs. "No, she password protected it. Only you know what it is."

"How would I know?"

"The password is her favorite word in the whole world, which she told you when you were both eight years old."

Part Five
Anniversary

We shall not cease from exploration
And the end of all our exploring
Will be to arrive where we started
And know the place for the first time.

Through the unknown, remembered gate
When the last of earth left to discover
Is that which was the beginning:
At the source of the longest river
The voice of the hidden waterfall
And the children in the apple-tree
Not known, because not looked for
But heard, half-heard, in the stillness
Between two waves of the sea.
Quick now, here, now, always—
A condition of complete simplicity
(Costing not less than everything)
And all shall be well and
All manner of thing shall be well
When the tongues of flame are in-folded
Into the crowned knot of fire
And the fire and the rose are one.

"Little Gidding," Verse V
Four Quartets, by T. S. Eliot

June

June has returned without you, Stella Rose. Life as we knew it ended on June 21: the first day of summer, the last day of your life, the first day of a new life for Olivia and me—without you. This past year should be a blur. Yet I see it all so clearly, in fragments held together by an evolution of thought and discovery. The most amazing transformation, though, is the one least expected: my relationship with you.

While the pain of losing you eases and the hole in my life fills slowly with Olivia and new friends and new adventures, I carry you in my heart every day. It's strange how I've learned so much about you in the past year—what would have happened had cancer not taken you away? Would I have known you this well?

Know this: I would trade all I've learned and all that is newly mine for one more year with you in it.

With the flip of a calendar page, we are in a new month, one filled with reminders that tug our hearts back in time. This June could not be more different from its predecessor. The sun, omnipresent and intense, lures boaters onto the lake and into our tiny back bay, which is dotted with bass fishermen trolling the shallows within feet of the sun-scorched dock. My skin is pinking and my scalp prickles under the heat even as my submerged feet cool, bringing my body temperature down.

I wonder: Was last June really so cold? Or was it me?

The grass, already a green deep and lush, beckons, and I obligingly hop down the hot planks and onto the soft, shady bank, sit and sink my feet into feathery coolness. Squinting upward through spindly branches of a young beech, I smile at the sparse clouds stalled in a breezeless azure sky.

I reach into my cargo shorts, pull out the dog-eared e-mail. I have committed it to memory but read the words as hungrily as the first time Olivia pulled it up for me:

Dear AbbySol,

I've tried many times to share this with you, but now I don't know where to begin! Goddamned cancer fucked everything up. I can't explain how all this could slip away from my mind. I can tell you only that for months it was as though it never even happened. Cancer blotted out everything, Abby. Every. Thing.

Tears blur the words. I breathe in the scent of the clover. Then I read on.

It wasn't just the cancer, though. Whenever I thought of this event, the awful beauty of it all, I was that much closer to what I was about to lose. Losing you and Olivia was too much. But to lose this, too?

And there is this: you know me better than anyone, ever, yet I worry about how you will react. Once you know this, you will never see me the same way. Before the diagnosis, I was okay with that. We would have a lifetime to see how our relationship evolved with this folded inside it. I actually looked forward to it—to you seeing me as mortally flawed, to forcing you to see me as I am, so I could see me, too. All of me.

But then . . . without that lifetime to explore all this with you, I panicked. I thought, I don't want Abby's last impression of me to be this deeply flawed event. All that had seemed exotic mere months earlier became contemptible. And just wrong.

So I pretended it never happened—which was surprisingly easy in the beginning. Like I said, it was a scary place to go for so many reasons. And then it got harder, because it did happen, and it changed me, and I wanted you, my best friend, to know. But how to tell you after all this time, with everything else going on? It was much easier to let the days slide by, to lose myself in the minutiae of dying.

But truth finds a way. Over these months of preparation, I have, by some miracle, come to a place of calmness. From here I can reflect on what happened a year ago, appreciate it, and share it with you in a manner closer to where I was last September. So you and I must be on the same wavelength, because when you suggested we communicate by e-mail, I knew it was the perfect venue to share this with you.

I place a hand to my chest and massage the tender ache there. If Stella only knew her words would be like a salve, however misinformed she was at the time.

To do this in person would be too exhausting, but to be able to take my time and pull this together for you, it's ideal. So, here goes:

Shortly after you left for Greece, I fell in love.

It's true! It came out of nowhere, leaving me dazed and wondering, How the hell did this happen? To me? Stuff like this happens to Abby, not me!

It was wonderful—but full of complications. I shattered all the rules I threw in your face over the years. For example:

He works at the firm (think: Jaime).

He is married (think: David).

He is too handsome (think: Jaime and David, and your guy in Greece?).

He is arrogant.

He is a mover and shaker.

He is a serial womanizer.

Why didn't I tell you while you were in Greece? There are a couple of reasons, which wouldn't make sense to most, but you'll get it. First, I was excited for you—traveling overseas for the first time, immersing yourself in an exotic place. Then you met Luca on, what, day three? I didn't want to overshadow that. Besides, following up your romantic tale with "I'm having an affair with a married man at the firm" seemed lame!

But mostly I wanted to tell you in person, especially the part where I say what a self-righteous, know-it-all bitch I've been all these years. How could you stand me? Here you were, faced with real life, while I holed myself up in my control bubble, pontificating virtues meaningless in the wilderness of the heart . . .

I digress.

This was uncharted territory I needed to process with you. So I started a diary.

That's right. Me, Stella Rose, who burned all her childhood diaries in a bonfire in the backyard years ago, who never understood your compulsion to write your thoughts and dreams in a book where anyone could stumble over them and see into your soul.

I started a diary to share this fantastic, scary, awesome odyssey with you—and me. It forced me to slow down, maybe figure out what the hell I was doing.

Last September I was going to give you this intro, then hand you a thumb drive and have you read it all, right there, on the spot. I would have watched you, with anticipation and anxiety, looking for signs of delight and/or disgust. In the end, I believe you would have turned to me and said, "For Christ's sake,

Stella, what were you worried about? Welcome to the human race!" You would have hugged me, we would have laughed. You would help me see being a messy human being was my destiny.

Or you could have been pissed, turned to me and said, "For Christ's sake, Stella, it's okay for you to do all this, but never for me? All those times I held myself back because of your self-righteous attitude, and you go and do this?"

This thought freezes my heart. But this is not about me. It's about us. You deserve to know about this, about who this makes me, about how this shapes our relationship. We don't have a lifetime to set this right, but in my heart, I know we need only a moment.

The attachment is password protected, and the password is my favorite word in the whole world, as shared with you near the chin-up bars when we were eight.

I love you, Abby.

Always,

Your Stella Rose

Crushing the paper to my chest, I press my forehead into the cool grass. Pretending to be me, Olivia's response to Stella was simple and perfect:

To my Stella Rose:

For Christ's sake, Stella, what were you worried about? Welcome to the human race!

Thank you for telling me this, thank you for the diary, and thank you for letting me see you in all your messy glory. I will treasure this always. Let's leave this here, our secret held in cyberspace, but I want you to know one thing: I am so glad this happened to you, Stell. I am so glad you knew this kind of joy.

I love you, Stell.

Forever,

Your AbbySol

~

I pull myself to my feet on the bank and gaze into the shallow water. A thousand startled minnows dart toward the middle of the bay, where half of Stella's ashes have long since assimilated.

The password, of course, is Solace.

I blow a kiss across the lake, turn, and make my way back home.

Rather than head inside the cool house, I find myself in the garden, collapsing on the warm wooden bench. The scent of burgeoning rose-buds overpowers me. I close my eyes, surrendering myself to their magic, still clutching the printed e-mail in my hand.

Olivia is convinced this e-mail exchange was Stella's act of letting go. In those final days, Olivia told a fading Stella that I was downstairs, that I had just left, that I would be right back. The truth is, I showed up only one day before Stella died. For the three preceding days I had heard Stella's voice in the strangest places—in the car, in my kitchen, in the shower. She was calling me, her voice growing more urgent, until the morning of the twentieth, when I awoke screaming, "Stella, I'm coming!"

I threw on a pair of jeans and a sweatshirt, called in to work from my car and told Penelope I was taking a personal day. Olivia met me at the door, and, after the briefest hug, I rushed past her, up the stairs, into Stella's room, where she lay impossibly thin, impossibly sunken, her hair limp and damp. The antiseptic smell, once familiar, now alien after weeks of absence, slapped me in the face; the taste of metal was on my tongue.

Stella's eyes were closed, eyelids soft, crepey and thin as faded pink rose petals. Her hands were like twigs, yet expressive, even in repose.

My legs shook uncontrollably as I sank to my knees, gripping the cold hospital-bed rail. I heard a soft scraping noise, felt a hand on my shoulder lifting me to my feet, then easing me gently into a wooden chair. A soft voice, unknown to me then and now so dear, said, "She's glad you're here, Abby." I looked over my shoulder but saw only Trish's back as she left me alone with Stella. And a mountain of guilt. And fear—oh, my God, Stella was leaving me. Alone. With Olivia.

Don't go, Stella, don't go.

Olivia ran in, her eyes wide, casting from my face to her mom's and back. I realized I had spoken aloud, that Olivia thought it was over. Her face registered an avalanche of relief as she realized Stella was still with us.

Unable to look her in the eye, I stammered, "Olivia, I-I . . ."

"I know" was all she said. She pulled a chair up to the opposite side of Stella's bed. We spoke quietly, telling Stella stories, as the afternoon blurred into night. Then I felt the tiniest squeeze on my hand. My eyes widened and Olivia smiled at me.

"She's awake," she said, looking at Stella.

"Stell?" I gripped her hand tightly. "Open your eyes, pretty girl. I want to talk."

Stella's mouth twitched slightly, the smallest of smiles, more than I deserved. Slowly her eyes opened. She blinked twice, then smiled in earnest. Olivia reached for a container on the nightstand and drew out a dab of petroleum jelly. Gently applying a thin layer to Stella's parched lips, she said, "Hello, Mommy" and kissed her forehead.

"Hi," Stella said, her voice a hoarse whisper. "How are my two favorite girls?"

"We're great, Mom," Olivia said, smiling brightly at me.

Then Stella's eyes were on me, and they held none of the reproach or anger or disappointment they could have. Instead, they were filled with sorrow and love. And pain. So much pain. Couldn't someone stop the pain?

"Stell . . ."

"I knew you'd be here, Abby."

And with that, she absolved me.

~

And now, one year later, I absolve myself. I recount the last words we shared—how we laughed a little, cried a lot, made promises, said what mattered. I see Stella so clearly, the beauty in her rawness, her gestures strained and kind and generous.

How she shooed Olivia out of the room on the pretense of getting some fresh water, then looked me in the eye: "I don't want to go, AbbySol."

"Good to know, Stell, 'cause all this grace under fire is freaking me out."

"You know me better."

"I know you are the bravest woman I've ever known."

"And you're mine."

"Each other's biggest fans."

"To the end."

I pulled my chair closer still, laid my head next to hers, my arm across her chest to shield her from what was coming, though we both knew I couldn't. A few minutes later, Olivia joined us, retaking her seat. We talked quietly, punctuating every sentence with "I love yous" until Stella drifted off. Olivia and I fell asleep as well, lying across Stella on opposite sides of the bed.

And this I've shared with no one: in the middle of the night, like a dream, a fourth presence joined us—an angel, quiet and efficient, exchanging hushed words with Stella.

"It's time," whispered Stella.

"If you're sure."

"I am."

"Then it's time."

"Thank you."

When I finally opened my eyes, the angel was gone. And so was Stella.

~

Owen and I sit close to the front of the packed and stuffy recreation center, fanning ourselves with our paper programs.

Stella would have been so proud of Olivia today: she's graduating in the top ten of her class, despite everything.

When will I approach a milestone in Olivia's life not from the perspective of what Stella is missing, but as a parent in my own right? Maybe, I think, after the twenty-first.

The principal and the superintendent give short speeches, followed by a prominent local businessman and one of our state senators. Liza, as class president, delivers a moving speech about how to face what's ahead. Robust applause greets her remarks. Then she leans once more into the microphone. "And now," she says, smiling over to her left, "Olivia Rose Weller, please come to the mic." Applause erupts, whistling and foot stomping. I glance at Owen. He shrugs, smiling.

Olivia joins Liza at the podium. They hug each other as the crowd slowly quiets.

"Friendship." Olivia says, letting the word linger. "This is what I want to talk about. But first, a huge shout-out to my father. Thanks for your love and support this year. You are the best dad ever." Olivia blows him a kiss, and he grins.

"Of all the things I learned from my mom, the most important, the most meaningful, is friendship. We all have them—friends from day care, grade school, high school, summer camp. We learn not all friends are created equal. Some are fun to hang with, some give great advice, some keep your secrets.

"Losing my mom hurt so bad, I didn't want to feel the pain." Olivia pauses, swallowing hard. "To protect myself, I stayed away from my friends—Liza, Jason, and others. They tried to help me, but I pushed them away in creative, bizarre ways. Soon I was alone and numb, making the pain bearable. Or so I thought.

"I was wrong. I underestimated friendship, especially Mom's friendship with Abby. See, Abby did the craziest thing. She promised Mom she'd take care of me. Even if she had known how difficult this year would be, how intent I was on making it hell for us, she still would have made that promise. Because that's what best friends do."

Cheers from the audience erupt around us.

"Friendship is persistent. Despite my best efforts, I found myself making new friends. Some were false friends who hurt me, but my true friend saved my life. Because that's what friends do."

More applause. More cheering.

Olivia's gaze locks on mine. "If I let myself believe I could have only one best friend, I never would have met Cherie or recognized that Liza was still my best friend, too. Now I have two best friends, and who knows who's waiting down life's road? A lifetime of best friends—how amazing is that? So, Abby, I know Mom's death has left a big hole in your life. Fill it with best friends."

I feel the entire auditorium shift toward me. I nod vigorously.

Olivia continues, "I learned that Mom was so not my best friend. She was my mom. We were tight. We were . . . close." Olivia's voice is a whisper now. "But she had a mom agenda; I had a teenager agenda. We had our dance going on—and then the music stopped. I told myself I missed my best friend . . ." She pauses again, closing her eyes. When she opens them, she looks directly at me. "But what I wanted was my mom."

Full-on sobs erupt two rows over. I feel Owen's arm slip around my shoulders. But I am no longer crying. I'm in the grip of Olivia's story, our story.

"Abby tried like hell to be my friend. Tried to be cool, tried not to hover, not step on Mom's toes. She assured me she couldn't replace Mom, would never try to.

"But she totally sucked at the 'Olivia's BFF' thing. See, while losing Mom eventually taught me about having more than one best friend, having Abby taught me about having more than one mom. Because, though she failed miserably at being my friend, Abby was wildly, passionately successful at being my mom."

Stunned, I blink. Owen hugs me while Rob pats my back and says, "You deserve every word, Abby." Thunderous applause shakes the walls. I see a forest of legs around me in a standing ovation. I should be on my feet, but I can't send a message from my brain to . . . anywhere.

I feel myself lifted, and I realize Owen and Rob each have an elbow, urging me into the aisle. Olivia is running toward me. She crushes me to her chest, her strong arms wrapped tightly around my neck. Inhaling the scent of her ponytailed hair, I wrap my arms around her waist, rock her back and forth. Looking up, I expect to see the arched wooden beams of St. Mary's Nativity Church. Instead I see rows of fluorescent lighting against a gray, riveted-steel ceiling, and it is lovelier than the inside of any church.

It's been a year, and what a year it has been.

~

My back begins to stiffen against the casing of the window seat in Stella's room, but my commitment to greeting the sun on this day, the anniversary of Stella's death, finally pays off. Watching a sunrise from a house in the woods with no discernible horizon teaches appreciation of subtlety. *Watch, watch, watch,* I say to myself as the blackness of night imperceptibly cedes to navy, then yields ever so slowly to woolly gray, which invites the palest pink to enter at the place where earth meets sky, somewhere through the thicket of shadowy trees emerging on the periphery. The first chickadee's chirp elicits a sleepy response from the maple just outside the window.

Despite Stella's continuing efforts to slow down her life, I know she not once allowed herself the privilege of sitting here to greet a new day. Neither have I.

But I will.

Because what has more potential than a new day?

Stretching my hands high above my head, I slip from the window seat and perform the first in a series of sun salutes. Halfway into my routine, I catch a whiff of coffee brewing and smile. I'm not the only one ready to celebrate this day. Easing into each pose, I breathe deeply and fully, truly, for the first time in a year.

~

As I head down the stairs, my phone dings with a text message. I trot back to my room to check. It's Owen: *Thinking of you today. Call me if you need anything. I'm here.*

I love this man.

By the time I swing open the kitchen door, Olivia is lifting bacon out of a pan and onto a plate covered with a paper towel. She expertly spatulas scrambled eggs into a serving bowl. I take the eggs and bacon to the kitchen table, already set for two. An early rose, still sparkling with dew, rests in a crystal bud vase.

Clasping my hands, I telegraph my delight with a huge grin. Olivia smiles back. We make small talk over breakfast, slowly sinking into the depth of this day .

∽

When Johnson arrives at nine o'clock sharp, I lead him to Stella's office, where a brown paper–wrapped package waits. I lift the package, extend it to him. "Stella's diary."

Johnson's brow furrows, and he looks wary.

"It's about your relationship," I add helpfully.

"Our relationship?" Johnson asks, clearly unnerved. "A diary?"

"Today is about Stella and endings and beginnings. And love. This"—I tap the package—"is love. You should know how much you meant to her, that what you shared was real, far more real than what came after."

He looks at the package, then back at me, still perplexed.

"See, she felt she couldn't tell me about this while I was in Greece, and she knew when she did tell me in person, I would want all the details, so she kept a journal."

"You make that sound like a normal thing."

"It's a Stella thing."

"And you're giving it to me? Is that what Stella would have wanted?"

"It's not what she had in mind, of course. This was for my eyes only. But if she knew how much you've missed her, she would want you to know these things."

"So," he says, sitting with the package on his knees, "you know every detail."

"Does that bother you?"

"Should it?" he asks.

"No."

Johnson is quiet for a long time, before whispering, "I'm afraid to read it."

"Don't be," I say.

~

By late morning, Olivia and I are winding our way down the path through the cool woods to the dock, warm and graying under our flip-flopped feet. Sitting at the end, we swing our legs, breathing in summertime.

"Are you ready?" I ask.

"Yes," says Olivia, not taking her eyes off a bank of ballooning cumulous clouds that appear snagged among the tops of the trees ringing the opposite bank.

I reach into the canvas bag and remove the two *June* letters. After all these months, the master cartons are now empty, broken down, sitting in the recycle bin for Thursday's pickup. These are the last letters from Stella Rose.

"Here is yours," I say.

Olivia wrests her gaze from the sky, looks down at the letter, takes it from me. Gently she lifts the flap of the envelope, releasing the faded scent of gardenia. The letter, closed for over a year, opens crisply. Olivia's voice is wobbly but determined:

> *My Dearest Olivia,*
>
> *It's been a year since I had to leave you, and I can only imagine what has transpired since. I picture friends and dates, movies, rehearsals, homework, exams, college visits, prom, graduation, a trip to an exciting place. I hope all this happened.*

I also picture tears, anger, fear, angst, disappointments, hormonal upheaval—all the things that make being seventeen legendary, and all shot through with grief that has surely compounded things. I am so sad it has to be this way.

One thing I know: you are stronger, wiser, braver, and even more beautiful than you were a year ago. Knowing this gets me through the days, and will allow me to let go of this life and let you move on with yours.

Being your mother has been the privilege of my lifetime. Even if I had lived one hundred years, I could not have loved you more or been more filled with your love. Thank you for your generosity, Liv. Too many moms are denied demonstrations of love from their children through benign neglect. Kids are busy with their own activities and dramas, and we parents often are left with only the crumbs scraped off the table. But you were not like that. You were quick with hugs and kisses well beyond middle school. Your desire to link arms at the mall—even at parent-teacher conference night at your high school!—warmed my heart. I never told you, for fear of jinxing it all, but these gestures are priceless and I am keenly aware of how lucky I've been.

I wish for you someone who will warm your heart as you have warmed mine. You have given me a wonderful life, my darling daughter. For that, I will be grateful always.

While these may be my last written words to you (and how I wish they could be more eloquent and inspiring!), know that I will be with you always and forever. Keep these words with you, and all those whispered between the lines of these pages and between the lines of this world and the next.

I love you, Olivia. Now and forever, always.

Mom

I palm away my own tears, then reach over and brush away the lone tear trickling down Olivia's cheek. She grasps my hand, squeezes it.

It's my turn. My hands tremble slightly as I take my envelope, extract the letter.

My Dearest AbbySol,

How I wish I could sit with you on the dock or the garden bench in early-summer sun and hash out this entire year. What happened, why, and what does it all mean?

I must be honest, because there is no time to be anything else. There is a big part of me that is jealous of you, Abby. With each letter I imagine more and more of the year ahead without me. I am just now understanding—duh—that there will be so many years without me! How can this be, Abby? Writing these letters somehow contained my death to one year—what was I thinking? That I would just pop back in afterward and resume my post? Now it is all too clear, as it must surely be to you, that this is a permanent situation.

In the beginning, all these letters seemed like too many— how would I ever finish them all? Would I finish them all? Or would leukemia finish me first? It became a footrace—leukemia in the lead, Stella making up ground—and here I am! I've won!

And now I want to write more letters, because there is so much more to say. I have not done an adequate job of telling you about Olivia, telling you about me, telling you about you and how much I admire you, adore you, envy you almost to hatred, and love you all to pieces. I've already thanked you a hundred times for taking care of my beloved Olivia, but a million times wouldn't be enough.

If I'm honest, though, there isn't any more to say. I'm stalling. You know I'm a procrastinator—always starting, never finishing. It's time to bring this project home.

It's time.

The next time I see you will be the last, this I know, and I will bring the memory of your lovely face with me to comfort

me, keep me from being alone. Please find someone to comfort
you. Don't be alone. You have my permission to find another
best friend. I won't be jealous. Well, maybe a little, but I'll work
on that. Pinky promise.

I love you always, Abigail St. Claire.
You are my Solace. Always.
Love,
Me

Olivia says, "Well, then."

"Uh-huh" is all I can muster. She hands me a wad of tissue. We sit for several minutes in silence. Then we head back to prepare ourselves for the next phase.

I go upstairs to lie quietly in bed, perhaps to read for a bit, before Olivia and I venture to the garden. Slowing, as usual, outside Stella's door, I catch a glimpse of something on the bed: a dozen yellow roses bound by a familiar yellow satin ribbon. No note. I know who left the flowers, and suddenly I know why.

~

She opens the door at my first knock, unsurprised. I enter, walk straight to the large dining table taking up three-quarters of the space in the kitchen, and seat myself at one end. She puts on the teakettle, pulls two mugs from a cupboard, places a Lipton tea bag in each. She turns to face me, her back against the counter, as the kettle starts to rock gently over the blue flame.

"You were there that night."

"I was there every night," Trish says, "for four months."

I swallow this as the kettle begins to gurgle and hiss. "I heard you."

"I thought you might."

"Why take the risk?"

The hiss heightens to a scream. Trish turns back to the kettle, whisking it off the burner and filling the mugs. She places one in front of me, takes the other to the chair at the opposite end of the table, a mile of solid oak between us.

"It's what she wanted," Trish says quietly.

"She never told me. She would have told me something like that."

"No," Trish says, "she wouldn't have told you something like that."

"Why not?" I ask, my voice rising.

"Because that's one thing best friends do not do."

"Bullshit."

"What would you have done if she had told you?"

I open my mouth, but nothing comes out. I blow across the top of my mug, take a tentative sip. Looking up at Trish, I say, "I would have done what she wanted."

"Is that true?" Trish asks gently.

It's not true. Trish knows it, I know it, and Stella sure as hell knew it.

I take another sip of tea. "So," I say, "what was the plan?"

"A few months before she died, she began exploring. Many terminal patients do. I helped her explore." She fixes me with large, sad eyes. "I listened, explained the medical implications of various options, as well as ethical and legal implications, of course."

I nod slowly, skin tingling.

"Stella circled for a long time," Trish continues, glancing out her ruffle-curtained window, "before making her final choice. She was growing weaker, had several projects going. She wanted me to help keep her strong enough to finish them; then . . ."

I bite my lip, waiting.

Trish turns to me, eyes shimmering. "She would let me know when it was time."

We both sip our tea, digesting what amounts to a murder confession.

"So," I say, trying to piece it together, "when the pain got to be too much and she was ready to die, you would up her meds, and that would be that."

"Essentially."

The questions materialize the moment they are answered. How did Stella know she would die in June? What if she didn't die until

July? What would have happened to the letters, which fit so neatly into sequence? For months, in the back of my mind, I have wondered how upset she would have been to put all that work into those gifts and letters, only to live into July and screw it all up.

She would never let that happen. She was truly Stella Rose until the end, pulling that very last string. "Those damned letters," I say, finally looking back at Trish.

Composed again, Trish nods solemnly.

"Stella wanted to make sure she died in June, before her birthday, preferably, to kick off the Year of Grief."

"Yes." Trish gazes out the window, her bottom lip quivering slightly.

"So what was the signal?"

Trish turns back. "You."

I start, sitting back in my seat. "Me?"

"It all hinged on when you showed up."

I recall the days preceding Stella's death, all the times I heard her voice in my head, beckoning me with increasing urgency. "What if I hadn't come until July?"

"She was getting a bit nervous," Trish admitted, "but she had a backup plan. She'd have me call, say things were going downhill. She knew that would get you there."

"Thank God it didn't come to that."

"That's what I thought the day you showed up," Trish says, smiling for the first time since I walked in. "I thought, *Thank goodness she's here of her own accord. Stella will be so pleased.* Then—"

"Then you thought, *Today is the day.*"

"I knew it was possible. I called the hospital to say I would be staying the night again. I arranged for Cherie to be at her dad's. Then I waited."

"You are a patient woman," I say.

"I needed the time. I needed to hear your voices, hear you and Olivia laughing, imagine Stella laughing with you, quietly, between those tiny coughs. I needed to hear you telling each other you loved each other a thousand different ways. I needed—"

"You needed to know you were doing the right thing."

Trish shrugs. "I'll never know if it was the right thing. I take responsibility for what I did, but I can't say whether it was right or wrong. I guess I needed to know Stella got everything she needed before she said good-bye, that she got to leave on her own terms, when there was nothing more, nothing lingering for her."

I nod as a sensation of relief mixed with peace washes over me, from knowing Stella's life—and death—were in the hands of this generous, gracious woman.

"When the room quieted," Trish continues, "I slipped in to check Stella's vitals. As I was poking around, she opened her eyes and she said—"

"'It's time,'" I say, finishing the story. "You said, 'If you're sure.' She said, 'I am.'"

Trish nods.

We are quiet, staring into mugs of cold tea. Then I stand and take mine to the sink.

"Abby," Trish says, "you can file a complaint with the medical board."

"Must I?"

"It's protocol."

"Following protocol and doing the right thing are not always the same." I walk over to Trish, kneel next to her chair. "You said it yourself: you don't know if it was right or wrong, I don't know, a medical board sure as hell won't know—or care—if it was right or wrong. That's not what this is about." Taking Trish's hands in mine, I say, "Filing a complaint against you for preserving Stella's wishes? That's something best friends do not do." With that, I squeeze her hands, kiss her soft cheek, and take my leave.

~

As I pull into the driveway, I see my mother's little silver Toyota sitting in the yard. *Great timing, Mom,* I think. *I don't have time or patience for mama drama today.*

I open the door to laughter, find my mother and Olivia on the couch, leaning over what appears to be a large book open on the coffee table. "What are you looking at?" I ask as I hang my coat, kick off my shoes.

"You!" Olivia says, gesturing toward the graying photos under clingy plastic in what I now recognize as one of my mother's old photo albums.

Sure enough, there I am at six with the shiner I got the day our neighbor's St. Bernard knocked me down on the ice. Seeing the picture brings back the pain, and my hand instinctively goes to my eye.

"Everyone gets a black eye one way or another," my mother says. "We all heal."

"She was just about to tell me why your middle name is Solace," Olivia says.

I glance at my mother, eyebrow raised. I realize I have never thought to ask.

"Well," Mom says, hands in her lap, "near the end of my pregnancy, my mother told me she was dying, and I was pretty devastated."

Olivia and I exchange glances. I shrug to let her know this is all news to me. I knew my grandmother died shortly after I was born, but Mom never editorialized.

"Having Abby inside me was such a comfort, and the day she was born, I knew I was going to be okay. I couldn't give her a middle name like Comfort, so I asked her dad to get me a thesaurus. He looked at me like I had three heads, but after the labor I'd just been through, he didn't argue. I looked up 'comfort' and found 'solace,' and I thought, *That is the loveliest word I've ever heard.* Robert wouldn't let me name her Solace outright, but he could live with Abigail Solace St. Claire."

We all sit with this a moment, and then my mother says, "I won't stay, Abby. I know this is a busy day for you and Olivia. I just wanted to stop by and pay my respects."

This is an odd choice of words, but this is my mother, after all. "Thanks, Mom."

"Olivia, do you mind if I speak to Abby alone for a minute?"

"Of course not," Olivia says, rising from the couch and heading up to her room.

"What's up, Mom?" I say, settling next to her.

"This," Mom says, tugging at the ring finger of her right hand. Taking my hand in hers, she slips onto my finger her antique platinum ring, in which are nestled three tiny, perfect pearls. Whenever I've asked about this ring in the past, my mother has always said, "When the time is right, I will tell you, Abby."

Now is the time.

"My mother gave me this ring the day you were born. Her mother gave it to her on the day she had me."

I stare at the ring in amazement.

"I should have given it to you a year ago today. But honestly, I just didn't know how it would all turn out. A few weeks in, though, I knew you were going to be okay."

"Not months?"

"Nah, I knew when you were obsessing over what to get Olivia for her birthday that you were going to figure out this mom thing. Nobody obsesses over someone else's happiness like a mother over her child's."

I look at my mother and see someone I've just met inside someone I've known my whole life. "Since we're being honest, I have to say it's hard to imagine you obsessing over my happiness, Mom. You always seemed so . . . busy."

She doesn't even blink. "Some mothers are flamboyant with their obsession. I'm subtle."

Snorting, I slap my mother's arm. "I would *never* describe you as subtle, Mom."

Pain appears in her eyes. "Honey, your happiness is the most important thing in the world to me."

I bite my lip, unable to speak.

"I took raising you seriously. The most important lesson I could teach you was to lead a full life of your own. I realized early on I would never accomplish that if I was leading your life for you, and if I wasn't setting an example. Practice what you preach—that's my motto. If that came off as me not caring about you, let me set the record straight. I've cried rivers of tears over you, lost countless nights of sleep I will never get back, and bitten my tongue till it bled to keep from giving all kinds of advice you could have used but never asked for. Jesus Christ, Abigail Solace, I am your mother!"

Throwing my arms around her, I mumble into her Aqua Net hair, "You are the best, Mom. I love you so much."

"I love you, too, honey," she says, patting me on the back.

I pull back and say, "For the record, Mom, I was scared shitless, especially in those early days. The only time I felt better was after talking to you. I can see so clearly now how you were there for me, watching over me. Thank you so much."

"You can't do that." She winks at me. "This is supposed to be a thankless job."

~

The sun relinquishes its intensity by late afternoon, so Olivia and I trade our gardening clothes for jeans and sweaters before heading back out. We each carry our parting gifts, which we have been working on for a couple of weeks, ever since Olivia got the brilliant idea of giving back to Stella on this day.

Now we sit on the cozy bench in the garden that we've spent the last three hours tidying. While working, we talked about the Rose Whisperer, hoping she has found another Eden. We talked about how we can keep the garden going this summer, but that we should think about hiring another gardener for next summer, when Olivia will be interning at Fletcher Allen Health Care and I will be running the museum. We also agree to lower our standards, but even as we spoke, we knew we would knock ourselves out before we let Stella's garden go.

"You first?" I ask Olivia, and she nods.

Unfolding her letter, delicately penned on gardenia-scented stationery, she clears her throat and reads her letter.

When she's finished, I say, "That's lovely."

"Do you think so?" she asks, her voice anxious. "It seems . . . not enough."

"Liv," I say, tilting her chin with my forefinger. "It's perfect."

I unfold my letter, handwritten on soft mauve stationery, and read aloud.

When I'm done, I close my eyes. I feel Olivia's hand on mine, then her head on my shoulder. We sit for several minutes as daylight slowly dissipates.

"Abby," Olivia whispers, "are you crying?"

"No," I say, opening my eyes and glancing down at her in surprise.

She lifts her head off my shoulder and looks at me, dry-eyed. "Neither am I."

"Doesn't mean we're not going to cry like babies tomorrow," I warn.

"True. But this must be a milestone."

"Indeed. One worth celebrating."

"Chocolate?"

"Of course. I picked up some B and J's New York Super Fudge Chunk."

Olivia groans with anticipation.

"Are you ready?" I ask.

"Let's dig," Olivia says as she leaps from the bench and grabs the landscape shovel. I take mine, and we gingerly turn up the earth on either side of the piled stones beneath which Stella rests. We place our respective containers in our respective holes and backfill, gently stepping the soil into place. We rest a moment, paying silent tribute.

"C'mon," Olivia says, standing now, extending her hand to me.

"Okay," I say, reaching for her hand. "Help me up."

"I'm right here," she says, grasping my hand and pulling.

Looking up, I catch my breath. The sun, low in the sky, hanging just behind Olivia, blurs her features, and her voice echoes softly in my head. *I'm right here.*

"I'm glad," I say, dusting off my hands, then linking my arm through hers.

Together we walk out of the rose garden and toward the soft lights of home.

Epilogue

Dearest darling Mom,

God, how I miss you. Every day, I miss you more, but this is not a bad thing. It's good to know that rather than fading from my life, you grow in my memory every day. I know you must be watching me, because I hear you and feel you all the time.

Your letters this year have been amazing. You always said the right thing at the right time—though it didn't always feel that way! But mostly you told me how much you love me, and this is all that matters.

So I want to return the gesture. Every year I will write you a letter to sum up the year, to fill you in on what you might have missed, and to keep you posted on who I am becoming. Every year we will dig up this Tupperware container and add our letters, and we can all see how we've grown and changed and stayed the same.

I'm a little afraid of this coming year, a year without letters and tokens and rituals that you are participating in. But with all your letters in my heart, and your best friend in my corner, I know I can face anything.

Thank you, Mom, for taking such good care of me this year. I love you always and forever and forever.

XOXOXOXO to infinity . . .

Love, your daughter,

Olivia

To my most darling Stella Rose:

Where to begin? At the end? How much fun could we have dissecting these looping questions until we throw up our hands and break out the chocolate? Alas, those days are over. But you and I, we are not over. We are . . . suspended, connecting over time and space in memory, in flashes of insight, in the inexplicable.

This past year I've learned so much about so much, but nothing more fascinating than what I learned about you, my best friend with so many secrets. I learned about who you are— and are not—and in so doing learned about who I was, who I am not, and who I want to be.

You knew me better than I knew myself. You knew I would come to your house that day so you could die, and your house would become my home. You knew I could take care of a teen-ager—even one as wild as you were back in the day—and that I would grow to love Olivia with a fierceness only you could comprehend. You knew how much I would miss you and how lonely I would be if you didn't do your damnedest to toss me back into the game.

The girls and I are meeting at McAdams later to toast your empty chair on this most auspicious occasion. We will be joined by our newest member of The Girls, Trish. Nice work there, Stell. Two birds with one stone. So, while no one can fill your chair, no one needs to. There are plenty of chairs. So don't fret, my love—there are friends, a daughter, and a lover to fill the hole in my heart.

But there will never be another Stella Rose. This is as it should be, and this comforts me, truly. Having known you, and carrying all our memories into the future, makes the world a very large place to explore. We'll be back in a year to share what we've seen and experienced. Until then—

I love you, Stell.

Forever,

Your AbbySol

Acknowledgments

*T*hank you, Paula Banyea, my first storytelling partner—together we tag-teamed original stories for hours, days, and weeks at a time. Thanks also to Amy Magnus, my high school English teacher and so much more, for stopping me at my locker that day to say, "You're a writer."

Thank you, Sarah Ward, my writing sister who wrote by my side countless afternoons at Phoenix Books and elsewhere. To the Tuesday Night Writers Who Meet on Wednesdays for years of prompts, read-backs, commiseration, and camaraderie, and to Sarah Bartlett and Women Writing For (a) Change for bringing the women of TNWWM(on)W together, thank you. Special thanks to member Lucy Bogue, whose personal experience with leukemia inspired the plot for this novel.

Thank you, Leslie Payne, the editor who made me ask myself all the right questions, then answer them one by one, thus making me a better writer and Stella Rose a better novel.

Thanks to Stephen Payne, who, as we both lamented the arduous journey of novel writing over milkshakes, asked this question: "How do you want your readers to feel?" To which I replied: "The way Oprah feels when she talks about Gayle." He was unfamiliar with the Barbara

Walters interview I referenced, but no matter. The question—and the answer—crystalized for me why I was writing Stella Rose.

For bringing this project home, I thank my "Launching Stella Rose" team: Amy Magyar, the first to say my passion for friendship was bigger than the book; Cara Mezitt, who said the exact same thing a week later, then read my manuscript, got it, and manifested Stella Rose in living color—designing the perfect book cover, my author website, and friendship blog; Dave Buckland, who suggested I answer some basic questions about what I wanted before stumbling headlong in the wrong direction; She Writes Press, for being what they are—a welcoming press run by generous women for women, specifically, Brooke Warner for being a task-master, Cait Levin for gently and firmly holding me accountable to Brooke's tasks, Annie Tucker for slashing the exactly right 20k words, and all the SWP authors helping each other cross the finish line.

It takes a village to write and publish a book. To all my friends who have cheered me on for years—you know who you are—I love you for your unflagging encouragement, your genuine enthusiasm for this book. Thank you! To The Girls, who taught me that friendship judges not, loves always, and endures despite life's distractions, you have my undying love. To my coach and friend, Lea Belair, who keeps my feet to the fire and my motivations clear, my deepest appreciation and affection.

To Angela, for holding the mirror steady, you have my eternal love, gratitude and devotion.

To my parents, I thank you for teaching me that "lazy" is a four-letter word, and for teaching me never to be afraid to break a sweat because that's what it takes to get anything worth having.

Finally, I thank Wally for supporting my habit. For years you have listened to clacking laptop keys and held down the fort while I holed myself up at writing retreats or spent weekends writing with Sarah or attended writing conferences. You made my writing life possible.

And to my kids, Aaron and Ariel: You inspire me. Every. Single. Day.

About the Author

© Jessica Anderson Photography

Tammy Flanders Hetrick has been telling stories all her life: refining her skills at age ten through marathon tag-team storytelling with her best friend, honing her craft through decades of business writing, and ultimately finding joy in extracurricular creative writing. She has published short stories in *Your Teen Magazine*, *Blue Ocean Institute's Sea Stories*, and *Route 7 Literary Journal*.

Hetrick lives in Vermont with her husband of thirty years, their two cats, and a beagle/bull-terrier mix. She loves her two grown children more than anything, and she appreciates the amenities of an empty nest. And every year she looks forward to the Annual Girls Weekend with The Girls.

You can contact Tammy Flanders Hetrick at tfhetrick@gmail.com, join the conversation at TammyFlandersHetrick.com, and you can follow her on Facebook, Twitter (@tigerslily), and Instagram (tfhetrick).

SELECTED TITLES FROM SHE WRITES PRESS

She Writes Press is an independent publishing company
founded to serve women writers everywhere.
Visit us at www.shewritespress.com.

The Rooms Are Filled by Jessica Null Vealitzek
$16.95, 978-1-938314-58-2
The coming-of-age story of two outcasts—a nine-year-old boy who
just lost his father, and a closeted young woman—brought together by
circumstance.

Play for Me by Céline Keating
$16.95, 978-1-63152-972-6
Middle-aged Lily impulsively joins a touring folk-rock band, leaving her
job and marriage behind in an attempt to find a second chance at life,
passion, and art.

Shelter Us by Laura Diamond
$16.95, 978-1-63152-970-2
Lawyer-turned-stay-at-home-mom Sarah Shaw is still struggling to find
a steady happiness after the death of her infant daughter when she meets
a young homeless mother and toddler she can't get out of her mind—and
becomes determined to rescue them.

Warming Up by Mary Hutchings Reed
$16.95, 978-1-938314-05-6
Unemployed and depressed former musical actress Cecilia Morrison
decides to start therapy, hoping it will get her out of her slump—but ultimately it's a teen who cons her out of sixty bucks, not her analyst, who
changes her life.

A Cup of Redemption by Carole Bumpus
$16.95, 978-1-938314-90-2
Three women, each with their own secrets and shames, seek to make
peace with their pasts and carve out new identities for themselves.

Fire & Water by Betsy Graziani Fasbinder
$16.95, 978-1-938314-14-8
Kate Murphy has always played by the rules—but when she meets charis-
matic artist Jake Bloom, she's forced to navigate the treacherous territory
of passionate love, friendship, and family devotion.